THE CROSS ON THE DRUM

THE CROSS

Doubleday & Company, Inc.

ON

Garden City, New York

THE DRUM

BY HUGH B. CAVE

All of the characters
in this book
are fictitious,
and any resemblance
to actual persons,
living or dead,
is purely coincidental.

AUTHOR'S NOTE

Some readers of an earlier book of mine called HAITI: HIGHROAD TO ADVENTURE may decide that the island of "St. Joseph" in the present story is also Haiti. It is not. THE CROSS ON THE DRUM is a work of fiction against a composite Caribbean background, and its people, all of them, are wholly products of the mind.

Certain *vodun* scenes in the present book, however, are similar to material in the earlier volume. This was unavoidable. HAITI: HIGHROAD TO ADVENTURE contains a study of *vodun* written after a long residence in Haiti, and were I to shun the facts simply because they have been set down before, I should have to invent a *vodun* that does not exist.

I might add that HAITI: HIGHROAD TO ADVENTURE has been used as a reference book by other novelists as well—not always with permission.

THE CROSS ON THE DRUM

1

O N MAPS OF THE CARIBBEAN the road along the north coast of
the island of St. Joseph has no name or number. It is not paved.
In the rainy season it is frequently not even passable. The
Reverend Arthur Barry Clinton had never been over it before, though
he had served for three years at a mission only thirty-odd miles to
the south.

He drove without haste, expertly guiding the mission jeep around
holes and boulders, not wanting to shake up too much the white-
haired man seated beside him or the dark-skinned youth perched on
the mound of cartons in back. He should be desolate this morning,
he supposed. In assigning him to Ile du Vent, the Bishop had certainly
intended this road to be his private highway to oblivion. But he felt
no desolation. He was intensely eager to see his island.

"This is the place, Barry," the white-haired man said. "Pull off here."

They had reached the outskirts of a village. Barry steered the dust-
coated vehicle to the side of the road and shut off the engine. He
looked about him. He had no sensation of being an outcast. He felt
like a small boy about to unwrap a Christmas gift.

On his right the mountains of the St. Joseph "mainland" tumbled
like storm waves to the sea, massive and black, leaving only a three-
hundred-yard strip of level land between their splayed ridge toes and
the beach: room enough for the road, a bit of wind-bent sugar cane,
and the village. The village—it was called Anse Ange—walked part
way into the sea on stilts, its cluster of rusty roofs gleaming redly in
the morning sunlight. Scrawny pigs that resembled dogs foraged on
the black-sand shore.

On his left lay the Channel of the Wind, a calm-looking strip of
water seemingly coated with blue and green enamels awaiting a breeze
to blend them. It separated the mainland from Ile du Vent, two
miles offshore. The Isle of the Wind itself rose seventeen hundred
feet out of the sea in a mist of plateaus and ridges, an excitingly
mysterious wilderness six miles long, two miles wide at its widest point,

and notoriously a hotbed of the native religion called *vodun* or voodoo.

Mine, Barry Clinton exulted. A place of my own at last.

The dark young man in the rear of the jeep dropped to the road and went around to the front, limping. He always limped. Barry wondered if he had to. He wore a clean white shirt and well-pressed khaki trousers, or at any rate the shirt had been clean and the trousers pressed at the start of the journey. Now, like Barry and the Reverend Peter Ambrose, he was layered with limestone dust.

"I'll go and see about a boat, sir," he said importantly. "You'll want one that won't be too crowded. Monday is the big market day here."

He hurried down to the beach where a dozen sailboats lay at anchor in the shallow water.

They were sizeable boats, most of them, but crudely made and cantankerous-looking. They were owned by the men who built them: enterprising islanders who earned a living transporting passengers and goods across the channel. Sometimes their owners overloaded them or attempted a crossing when the channel was living up to its name. Then on Ile du Vent the drums throbbed and there was wailing.

Barry eyed the boats with misgivings and turned to the man beside him. "It doesn't look two miles off, Peter."

Peter Ambrose shrugged. He was forty years older than Barry and had been a missionary in St. Joseph for twelve years. Only his bright blue eyes looked young enough to cope with the endless perplexities confronting a man of God in this land of peasant superstitions.

"It's far enough. You'll know by the time you get there."

"It's more rugged than I expected."

"You won't have to climb the whole distance. The mission is about half way up."

"I can't wait to get there."

Peter glanced curiously at his companion and saw a well-built man of twenty-eight with an attractively homely face, close-cropped hair that looked a bit like coconut fiber, and unusually large hands and feet. He frowned. He had been Barry Clinton's superior at Fond Marie for the past three years. It was possible to learn a good deal about a man in three years.

Banished to Siberia was the thought that had been running through Peter's mind as he gazed at the island offshore. But the eagerness in Barry's face did not wholly surprise him.

A strange young man, Barry Clinton. Unlike most young missionaries, who came to the islands hoping to save souls, this one had come with a belligerent skepticism of accepted missionary methods and a driving determination to battle sickness and starvation. Being master of his own island, a king with four thousand barefoot subjects, undoubtedly appealed to him, even if the island was the last knot at the end of the rope.

The answer lay in Barry's background, Peter was sure. He was from Massachusetts originally but had grown up in the islands, moving from one to another as his father was shuffled about on various State Department appointments. He had become infected with an obsession to do something about the poverty in these troubled countries. Quite deliberately he had chosen the church as his instrument, but what the church stood for was incidental, really. If his teachers at theological school had insisted he memorize the Bible backward to qualify for the mission field, Barry would have done so.

He had read a good deal. He knew something of medicine, agriculture, history, philosophy. Perhaps he had read too much. Peter recalled, with a mental grimace, a conversation on the rectory veranda a few evenings back.

"It's in the Bible, my boy, if you'll look for it," he had said carelessly in reply to some question.

Barry had turned on him with a gesture of impatience. "Of course it's in the Bible. Everything we're taught to believe is in the Bible, isn't it? That's our rule book. But must we believe it's infallible, or that everything in it means what the learned interpreters say it means? Must we try to befuddle the primitive mind as we do our own, when we ought to be teaching what was and is a simple religion of love?"

Peter had been more amused than annoyed. "We teach as we've been trained to. At least I do."

"I can't believe it's the best way. The faith we teach should be *easy* to understand, as it was when Christ taught it. And even before that, or at least along with it, these people need desperately to be told how to farm their worn-out land properly and avoid the tropical sicknesses that make them so miserable!"

"My boy, I try to keep them well with my clinic. I've allowed you to improve their farming."

"You, yes. But you're the exception, Peter. Most of the others——"

"We were sent here, after all, to teach Christianity."

Barry had subsided at that. He seldom continued his rebellions beyond the point of friendly discussion. Actually it was difficult to be annoyed with him, for despite his theological shortcomings, if one should call them that, he did the work of three ordinary men at the mission.

I'm going to be lost without him, Peter thought. Why the devil did he have to write those articles?

The articles in question had appeared in Stateside church publications, and, of course, the publications had found their way back to St. Joseph, and the Bishop had not been pleased. Recalling the Bishop's visit to Fond Marie, Peter made a face.

"The Episcopal Church has been here in St. Joseph nearly thirty years, Mr. Clinton. Isn't it possible that we old-timers might know a bit more about the nature of our problem than you who have been here only three?"

You didn't argue with a Bishop, of course. Not even with a hidebound one who in thirty years had accomplished so pathetically little. It didn't matter, either, that some of the points Barry had brought out in his writings were undoubtedly worth consideration. The Bishop was an angry man.

Ile du Vent was to be Barry's punishment. And Barry was delighted.

"Look at it, Peter," the young man was saying now. "It's like something straight out of an adventure novel. The most attractive——"

"Everything in this country seems attractive from a distance," Peter said with a wry smile. "You should know that. It's only when you get close to things that you notice the muck and sickness—how the dog is alive with fleas and the donkey dying from festered sores." He looked at Barry with affection. He was really *very* fond of this difficult young man. "But cheer up. Ile du Vent *is* an interesting place. And cool too, especially up there at the top. I'll envy you that in a month or two when I'm gasping for air back at Fond Marie."

The boy from the jeep had come up the beach with half a dozen barefoot followers. "It is all arranged, sir," he said to Barry. "These men will carry your things to the boat. I said you would pay them fifty *centimes* each."

Barry hesitated. Pradon Beliard had been born on Ile du Vent and undoubtedly knew the ropes, but was a little too sure of himself for Barry's taste. He worked at the Plantation Couronne near the Fond Marie mission, a sisal company that owned land on Ile du Vent too and maintained a launch for its man in residence there; but the launch was being repaired just now and Warner Lemke was at Fond Marie with his wife. This efficient young man with the limp had been sent along to help Barry get settled, an arrangement Barry had accepted with reluctance. He didn't want the boy. But he wanted less to hurt the feelings of Jeff Barnett, the Couronne manager.

Fifty *centimes* was a fair enough fee, however. "What time does the boat leave, Pradon?"

"Within an hour. Of course, if you wish to pay extra——"

"No, thanks. I can wait."

When the men had lifted the cardboard cartons and single mildewed suitcase from the jeep and carried them to the water's edge, Barry strolled down the black-sand slope with Peter to watch them put the stuff aboard. They did so by lifting it to their heads and striding into the sea with it. By the time they reached the side of the boat only their shoulders and heads were dry. Barry was glad he had sealed his medical supplies in plastic.

Almost everyone on the beach was watching him. He turned to his superior, saw an unexpected sadness on Peter Ambrose's face, and was sentimentally touched by it. "Do you know who'll be coming to take my place?" he asked gently.

"No, but it will be someone green as grass, you can be sure. Just as you were three years ago."

"I'm going to miss you, Peter."

"You'll miss having someone to talk to when you're certain the next word in Creole will start you screaming. I know. I was five years at Fond Marie before they sent me my first assistant."

"I'll miss our evening discussions." And that was no lie, Barry told himself. Not that he had ever won Peter over to his way of thinking or ever could, but at least Peter had listened without being indignant. A more hidebound superior might have crucified him. "Well, Peter" —he put out his hand—"I'd better go aboard, so you can start back. I won't say good-by. As the crow flies, we won't be thirty miles apart."

"The crow has a good many advantages over jeeps and native sailboats," Peter said. "Hadn't you better empty your pockets? That is, unless you plan to go aboard on someone's shoulders, the way old Mitchell does."

"Thanks. I prefer my feet." Barry put the contents of his pockets into his hat and replaced the hat on his head. "Well——"

They shook hands. Then with the whole beach watching, the new missionary strode into the sea to show them he could do it as well as they could. When he reached the boat, husky black hands promptly reached down and swung him aboard, amid a chorus of cheers.

He waved to Peter. The white-haired man waved back, turned, and trudged slowly up to the road.

How would it end? Peter wondered. Would Barry Clinton do well on his island or would he, like old Leander Mitchell, wind up sick and disillusioned? Would he find something to believe in or go on doubting and questioning? What about his private war with the Bishop? And what about the girl at Plantation Couronne, Jeff Barnett's daughter Edith, who had been waiting so long for him to propose marriage?

Would Ile du Vent answer some of Barry's problems or simply be another one, more formidable than all the rest put together?

2

THERE WAS SCARCELY AN INCH OF SPACE left on the boat when its captain decided he had a full load, an hour and a half later. Barry sat on the stern deck with his back against the low wooden rail, wedged between two barelegged women. One was old and fat and sucked noisily on a mango seed. The other was young and pretty, with dark eyes that kept questing over his face, and a taut young body whose firmness he felt through his clothes. His clothes were still damp from his walk in the sea.

Another woman leaned on one of his outthrust legs, numbing it, and beyond her were other passengers, men and women, overlapped and intertwined, covering every inch of the deck fore and aft.

In the yawning waist-well it was worse. There the massed humanity had to contend for space with overflowing market baskets, sharp-pointed garden tools, an ugly roll of barbed wire, and his own collection of cartons. His fragile suitcase, already weakened by three years of tropic damp, was being used as a seat by a young woman with a baby at breast, but he soon became so amused at the infant's voracious appetite that he gave the suitcase no further thought.

These were his people. He studied them while the crew tugged on frayed ropes, and the clumsy sail, patched with feed bags that still bore the most interesting inscriptions, creaked slowly to the top of the single mast. The mast had been axed from a tree trunk and was not very straight. Nothing in St. Joseph was ever very straight. Even the houses leaned. These people just couldn't see the sense in fussing over things that seemed unimportant to them. Pradon Beliard, he noticed, had found a place in the bow, at the base of the mast, beside an islander who was evidently a friend of his. The two were chatting with their heads together.

Barry remembered suddenly that he was not a good sailor, and hoped the passage would not be rough.

It was rough enough. Once the clumsy craft had crept away from the mainland shore and caught the full sweep of the channel breeze in its sail, it began to pitch and sway alarmingly. He found himself lurching first against the woman with the mango seed, then against the girl with the hard young body. He pressed the palms of his hands against the rough deck to steady himself.

The girl glanced at him and smiled. She was only a child, eighteen or so, but extremely attractive. Her dress was clean too: made of a gay multicolored print featuring butterflies in flight, whereas most of the other female passengers wore feed bags or faded blue denim. He looked away from her but was aware that she continued to study him.

The girl saw nothing rude in staring. He was the new missionary, come to take the place of the old one who drank too much; therefore he was a legitimate object of curiosity. A good-looking man, she decided. A man who appeared to have honest blood in his veins, not the ice water that passed for blood in the shriveled body of old Father Mitchell. She thought of all missionaries as "Father." Everyone did in St. Joseph. Now and then one of them might protest, patiently explaining the difference between Protestant and Catholic, but it made no difference. Men of the church were *mon Père*. How else could they be addressed with the proper respect?

This new Father, now, was young. He had big hands that looked strong and capable. He had a large, strong mouth and good dark eyes that seemed friendly. It might be exciting, having him on Ile du Vent. The only other white man on the island was M'sieu Lemke at the plantation, a blustering bully who thought he did girls a favor by inviting them to sleep with him.

The new Father glanced at her and she smiled again, not a childish smile now but a bold one. "Hello, Father," she said. "*Comment sa va?*"

"Not too well, thank you. Is it always this tipsy?"

"Only for a little while." She was amused by his discomfort and glanced about to see if others had noticed it. No one at the moment was much interested, however, and she focused her gaze on his face again. "You're the new missionary, aren't you?"

"I am."

"I believe I'll come to your church."

"I hope you will," Barry said with a smile. "You haven't told me your name."

"It's Micheline."

"Is that all? Just Micheline?"

"Laroche."

"Thank you. I'm happy to know you."

The blunt bow of the boat crashed into a sea at that moment, and the shattered wave flew the full length of the deck. Some of the women voiced shrieks of laughter or dismay, and all over the wallowing craft was a flurry of movement as the passengers sought to make themselves smaller targets for the next bombardment. Barry was as wet again as when he had walked in the sea. The girl named Micheline Laroche huddled against him, giggling.

He thought it best to ignore her, lest he encourage a boldness that might become embarrassing. They were devils for making a white man feel foolish, these young peasant girls. It was a game they loved playing. For something to do he looked for Pradon Beliard again. The plantation boy and his friend were still talking.

It was then that Barry noticed the resemblance between the girl at his side and Pradon's companion. No doubt it was only a racial resemblance. They were descended from many different African tribes, these people. Their ancestors had been brought to St. Joseph packed like living logs in the holds of slave ships. A certain tribal purity still existed in some country districts, and it was often possible to look at a person and say with some degree of accuracy, "This one is a Mandingue" or "That one is an Arada."

He found he could not identify the strain common to Pradon's chum and the girl, but it certainly existed. Both had high foreheads and sharp, slender noses. Both had attractive mouths, full but not thick. The pupils of their eyes were bright, the whites clear.

A handsome pair, he decided, and wondered whether they might be brother and sister. There was nothing distinctive about the man's dress. Except for faded khaki trousers he was naked. But he sported an enormous ring on the middle finger of his left hand, a ring with a square green stone; and on a slender gold chain about the girl's throat hung a similar stone, winking prettily against her smooth blue-black skin. Fortunately she hadn't a missing front tooth to flaw the picture, as he had. Her teeth were beautifully small and even, like a row of tiny white shells.

THE BOAT LURCHED ON, every little while plunging into a wave and drenching the passengers with spray. Barry felt ill. He tried shutting his eyes, certain he was about to be sick, but opened them again almost at once on becoming aware that he felt even worse with them closed. He tried taking deep breaths and then holding his breath for seconds at a time. Nothing helped much. He was going to make a spectacle of himself, he was sure.

"Just a minute more, Father," the girl said.

He nodded, unable to answer. Heaven help him if he had to do this often. He would never get used to it. But before the heaving in his stomach grew unbearable, the motion of the boat became less violent and the sound of the wind's rushing diminished. They had reached a point where the eastern tip of Ile du Vent broke the wind's back.

He waited a moment longer, then lifted his head and looked at the island. It was now close enough so that he could distinguish a dozen shades of green on its steep slopes, and a shimmer of sunlight on a sheet of metal that must be the roof of the church, halfway to the top. Thatch-roofed *cailles* snuggled among the trees. Coconut palms leaned gracefully over a score of tiny white-sand beaches, shaking their tops in the breeze.

A paradise. There was no other word. Only in St. Joseph could such an island exist in a still primitive state. Americans or Englishmen would have built a good road from the capital to the channel shore, provided motorboats to take tourists across, and established hotels to accomodate them.

Look, they'd have said. Here's a place that was once a rendezvous of pirates and buccaneers! Henry Morgan sailed his ships through this channel. The terrible L'Ollonois was here, and Montbars the Exterminator, and Pierre le Grand, Bartolomeo Portugues, John Davis, and dozens of others who made history in the West Indies. Here on Ile du Vent stood a town where rum flowed in the streets and women of loose morals strutted about in lace and jewels from plundered ships! This is history!

In St. Joseph no one cared. Tourists stayed in the capital, balked by lack of transportation, atrocious back-country roads, and the baffling Creole spoken by the peasants. But Barry was glad Ile du Vent had no roads or hotels and was all but impossible to get to. He wanted no intrusion.

He would not teach these people to hold out their hands and mumble "Gimme fi' cents" as the poor in the capital did. They were a proud, fine people. He would teach them farming and sanitation, something of their dramatic history, and, if they were receptive, something of Christianity.

He would learn from them. Perhaps, as Peter Ambrose and so many others insisted, there was nothing in their primitive religion

worth knowing. Perhaps it *was* a hopeless faith, to be condemned
for having kept them all these years in poverty and ignorance. That
remained to be seen. At least he would be free here to investigate, if
he could.

His companion smiled at him. "Was it so bad, Father?"

"Bad enough."

She laughed at his expression. "You should see Father Mitchell
when he makes the voyage. Someone always has to hold his head."

"Father Mitchell is an old man," he scolded, and wondered if it
were true, as Edith Barnett had said, that old Mitchell was a victim
of *vodun.*

He had talked to Edith last night at a farewell party given for him
at the Plantation Couronne. Everyone of importance had been there.
Most of them had seemed genuinely sorry that he was leaving. The
one exception had been Warner Lemke, the manager here on Ile
du Vent. But then, Lemke was a ruggedly athletic young man who
looked on all church people with contempt.

He had talked to Edith for some time on the bungalow veranda,
first about themselves and then about the job he was going to. "Barry,
haven't you been told *why* Mr. Mitchell asked to be relieved?" she
had asked.

"His health, according to Peter. He hasn't been well."

"He was poisoned."

Recovering from his shock, he had let a wry smile form at his mouth
corners. "Really, Edith."

"It's true. When he went over there just fourteen months ago to
establish a mission, he thought he knew everything. He'd lived in
St. Joseph for years. But he's been poisoned."

"People get queer notions about *vodun,* Edith."

"Queer notions! Oh, you churchmen are all alike. You don't know
anything."

"You forget I was a boy in these islands."

"Have you ever seen a real *vodun* service?"

"Well, no, I don't suppose I have. But——"

"You never have. You never will, now that you're in the church.
You're going to Ile du Vent without the faintest notion of what
you're up against!"

Barry had wondered if she knew what she was talking about. Of
course, *vodun* did exist on the Isle of the Wind. It existed in one
form or another everywhere in St. Joseph, even in the capital where
thrill-seeking tourists, escorted to ceremonies by the agency people,

came away complaining it was a fake, not knowing that the same "fakers" in the same *hounfors* communed with the *vodun* gods in deadly earnest on nights when the tourists were not welcome.

He wished he knew more about it. As a boy he'd seen very little, his parents, especially his mother, having flatly forbidden him to "get mixed up in it." And now, of course, as Edith had pointed out, he was looked upon as an enemy.

"Have you proof that Mr. Mitchell was poisoned?" he asked.

"Warner Lemke told me. He heard some of his workers discussing it." She stepped to the veranda rail and stood with her back toward him, gazing out into the darkness. "I asked Pradon Beliard about it afterward. His home is on Ile du Vent. His aunt is Mr. Mitchell's housekeeper." Suddenly she had turned, reaching for his hands. "Barry *must* you go?"

"You know I must."

"When am I going to see you again?"

"Soon, I'm sure. I'll be coming back here quite often. I'm bound to."

"Will you?"

"I'm leaving most of my clothes and books, for one thing. And I'll need advice. There'll be people on the island who will require medical help beyond my capabilities. I'll have to bring them here to Peter's clinic——" His voice ran down as he looked into her face. All this was difficult, so damnably difficult. "I'm sorry, Edith. What else can I say? I can't possibly take you with me."

It was true, of course; he couldn't take her. The Bishop would never permit it. A bigger truth nagged at his conscience, however. He did not want to take her. At least, he was not sure.

In the beginning he had been flattered by her show of affection; she was a most attractive girl and he a man who had had little time for romance. Then, slowly, he had come to realize that she sought his companionship only because there was no one else. She had been buried at Plantation Couronne for years. Her schooling had been managed through books and the mails, some system by which lessons were sent from the States to be completed and sent back for grading. Her sole recreation was a monthly visit to the capital, where for a few days she might enjoy the company of people her own age at the club maintained by the foreign colony.

She couldn't be in love with him, really. Nor, probably, did he love her. They were simply two people thrown together by circumstance.

"Edith, I'm sorry," he said again, moving to her side.

Her mouth quivered. She said with an effort, "I think we'd better go in now. Just—just be careful on your island, Barry. Please."

Had Mitchell been poisoned? By people like these on the boat? He didn't believe it. With a shake of his head he put the plantation scene from his thoughts and turned to watch the approaching shore.

A crowd had gathered on the island beach where the boats landed. Naked children noisily pursued one another over the sugar-white sand and into the shallow water, swooping and diving as gracefully as the white sea birds above their heads. Aboard the boat the passengers had begun to gather up their possessions.

Presently the water became beautifully transparent and, peering over the side, he saw formations of coral that resembled buildings in an undersea city, and patches of sand and shells that looked like streets and parks. It was like something seen in a dream.

Never had he seen anything more breathtakingly lovely. If there was a heaven, as he had been taught to believe, it must be like this. Here on Ile du Vent he would surely find answers to some of the questions that troubled him. Where there was so much beauty there must be truth.

WITH THE ANCHOR DOWN the people crowded to the bow and dropped overboard into knee-deep water, the handful of men going first and reaching up to help the women. There was a good deal of squealing and giggling from the latter, inspired, Barry suspected, by sly pinching and squeezing on the part of the gallants. When his own turn came, he found the girl named Micheline just ahead of him at the rail.

She glanced back at him, smiled, and nonchalantly hitched the butterfly-print dress up about her sleek thighs. It seemed a natural thing to do. She was, after all, about to leap into the sea. But some of the older women giggled, and Barry felt a flush spread over his face.

She *had* lifted the dress higher than she needed to, he realized. Had it been intentional, to embarrass him? He had no way of knowing. Having dropped into the water, she went straight ashore without a backward glance, and when he reached the beach himself, she had vanished.

Pradon Beliard was waiting. "It will take a little time to bring the cargo ashore," the boy said. "Why don't you go on up to the mission, sir?"

"You can arrange to have my things brought up?"

"Of course." He seemed almost offended. "Go straight past the little house there and follow the path. There is only the one path in that direction."

Barry saw that the people were busy with their own affairs and decided there was nothing to be gained by waiting. He preferred to walk alone in any case. At the back of the beach he circled the hut Pradon had pointed to and discovered the path. It began to climb almost at once. It could hardly do anything else.

Judging by what he had seen from the boat, his island possessed no level land other than the beach, and even that was more sharply tilted than most beaches. There might be something different beyond the ridge, however.

He looked back after climbing a short time, and the view increased the feeling within him that here on Ile du Vent he might find contentment. Green slopes fell abruptly, everywhere, to the trim thatched huts along the shore. He saw tiny fishing dugouts, each apparently fashioned from a single tree trunk, tucked away in a necklace of sheltered coves. There were other huts on the hills, among garden patches that transformed the slopes into fanciful checkerboards. He wondered why he saw no people.

His clothes dried as he climbed. When he stopped again he emptied his hat, returning his possessions to his pockets and strapping his watch back on his wrist. Soon the trail emerged from the cool shade of mango and breadfruit trees and became a ladder of boulders open to the sun.

He began to sweat and glanced up. The sun, almost overhead, was a naked flame that seemed determined to melt him among the stones. He took off his coat, understanding now why the gardens were deserted. No one in St. Joseph worked at this hour. With a longing glance at the next clump of trees impossibly far above, he sank onto a boulder to wait for new strength. His three years on the Fond Marie plain had softened him for this sort of thing. It would take some getting used to.

He took up a handful of earth and examined it. Was it good earth? The peasant farmers could judge by smelling and tasting it, or claimed they could, but he knew no such simple way to evaluate it. Color was not a reliable guide; most of the soil in St. Joseph was a rich-seeming dark red, yet much of it was worthless. The smell-and-taste test was probably worthless too. Just another native superstition, like their belief that a cool stone touching the head would kill you if you were perspiring, or their fancy that pineapples were fatal to pregnant women. They were children. Still, his own Massachusetts-born mother had firmly believed that cherries and milk taken together meant certain illness . . .

A sound of footsteps brought his head up. He saw a man in khaki trousers climbing toward him with complete lack of effort, long legs flowing and arms lazily swinging as though the ascent were nothing at all. It was Pradon Beliard's pal from the boat.

"*Bon jour, mon Père.*" Despite the missing front tooth, the voice was clear and pleasant.

"Good day to you. I wish I had your knack on these paths."

"It will come, Father." The polite smile became a frown almost at once. "But not if you sit like this too long, eh? This sun can eat a man!" In Creole the phrase sounded oddly like a threat. "*Soleil-sa kab mangé youn moun!*"

"You're right, of course." Barry struggled to his feet. "I'll move along." He leaned aside to let the man pass, wondering what there was about the fellow that made him seem familiar. The answer came quickly and almost made him laugh.

He was looking at himself, he realized. This islander with the blue-black skin was a dusky image of the Reverend Arthur Barry Clinton: the same 160-odd pounds, six feet of height, narrow hips, modest shoulders, longish arms and legs. He wore different clothes, of course —in face he wore practically nothing—and his hair looked like a skullcap of black periwinkles, but in every other respect the resemblance was startling. There was even a facial likeness.

"*Compère,*" Barry said curiously, "how old are you, if you don't mind the question?"

"Old, Father? Twenty-eight."

"That really wraps it up."

The fellow frowned. The white man's last remark had been in English, which he did not understand. He waited, not sure the conversation was over. Odd, his encountering Father Mitchell's successor like this, actually coming over on the boat with him. He had meant to avoid him until he could learn more about him, size him up as an adversary. The *loa* may have had a hand in this; it was entirely possible. He had gone over to Anse Ange this morning to buy candles for the *hounfor*. For no other reason. The business of the *loa*, pure and simple. On the beach below, he had made a point of talking to some of his people, so as to give the new Father time to reach the mission ahead of him. Now this.

Something else was strange. This man was young. My age, he

thought. My height. My weight. A remarkable thing. If our skin were the same color, we might be brothers. Is there some truth, perhaps, in the belief of my ancestors that every man has somewhere a twin, a *marassa*? Curious, this thing. Very curious. The *mystères* had a hand in it perhaps.

He waited. The white man said at last, with a gesture, "Well, friend, you'd better go first, or I'll delay you."

"Not at all, Father. After you."

Barry resumed the climb. All the way to the top of the slide, which turned out to be the plateau on which the mission stood, he heard the measured slap of the other's bare feet behind him. It was a most uncomfortable feeling, like being pursued by an unshakable shadow. He wondered who the fellow was.

3

"I T ISN'T MUCH OF A PLACE," Peter Ambrose had said in an attempt to prepare him.

It certainly wasn't.

There were two buildings: a miniature church cringing under a crooked wooden cross, and an L-shaped one-story house some forty yards distant. Both had corrugated-iron roofs dark with rust streaks but were otherwise constructed in the same fashion as the island huts. They leaned atrociously because the poles they were framed with had been hacked from tree trunks crookedly with machetes. They appeared to be disintegrating because the white limestone mortar on their walls of woven palm fronds had begun to crack and fall off.

The ground around them was red and bare. Only a few struggling tufts of grass poked through it. There was but one tree, a very old campêche or logwood, lightning-struck, thirty feet from the house.

Barry crossed the baked red earth to the house and halted by its door, which stood open. With a cheerfulness he did not feel, he called out in English, "Hello! Is anyone at home?"

He heard a muffled grumbling, followed by the sounds a man might make on waking and groping about in a dark room. "Who is it?"

"Barry Clinton, from Fond Marie."

"Good heavens! At this hour?" The sounds of groping became louder and the grumbling was lost in a spasm of wheezing and throat clearing. Then, "Come in, come in!" the voice croaked. "Just let me find my trousers."

Barry stepped inside, glad to get out of the sun. This wing of the house consisted of two rooms. The one he stood in was a reception room, apparently. It contained a number of peasant-made chairs and a rude desk. The other was Mr. Mitchell's bedroom.

Just now the old missionary was evidently struggling into his clothes after getting out of bed. Or, more properly, getting off the bed. In this climate it was the custom to stretch out on top of the bed in one's underwear, or one's shorts at least, for the noon siesta.

A strip of once-white cloth with green holly leaves and faded poinsettias on it hung in the connecting doorway. It must have been a Christmas tablecloth once. The floor was of pine planks and not very clean, showing the prints of dusty bare feet.

The tablecloth rustled aside and Leander Mitchell, once of Baltimore, shuffled into view with two limp hands outthrust. His appearance to Barry was a shock. He was a hunched-up little man with fever-bright eyes, dressed in wrinkled dark trousers and an unbuttoned shirt that badly needed laundering. The native-made sisal slippers on his small feet were coming apart.

"Welcome, welcome! I didn't dream you'd climb from the beach in this heat!"

"It was a climb," Barry admitted.

"Sit, sit!" The old man thrust him toward a chair and went past him to the doorway. "I'll get us something to drink. Hot today. Been like an oven since Friday. Lucille!" he shouted, his voice disintegrating with the effort. "Lucy!"

He turned and hobbled to a chair, mopping the back of his stringy neck with a soiled handkerchief. He looked hard at Barry's face. Young, he thought. Much too young.

"How old are you, Mr. Clinton?"

"Twenty-eight."

"Even worse than I thought. You're too young for this place. You'll be lonely, lonely. Can you stand being alone?"

Barry smiled. All his life he'd been alone. As a boy with no brothers or sisters, only an eternally preoccupied father and a mother always busy with social affairs, he'd been alone. At college and theological school, among young men who were uninterested in the things he thought important, he'd been alone. What was so terrible about it?

"It must be difficult," he said. "Especially at night when the work's done."

"At night? No, no, not at night. You've time to read then, write letters, listen to the radio if it works." The older man shook his head, looked at the moist handkerchief in his fingers, and thrust it back into his pocket. "It's being among *them*, among people who don't understand you, can't understand you, never will and never want to; that's what gives you the feeling." He sighed. "I've a nice little place here, don't you think?"

Barry had seen a number of mission rectories in his three years in St. Joseph, even some of the more remote ones back in the mainland hills. This was by all odds the most primitive. "Very nice indeed," he lied.

"Should have a concrete floor, of course. The dampness, when it rains. But you can't have everything. How's my good friend Peter Ambrose?"

"Fine. He's looking forward to seeing you tomorrow. He'll be there with the jeep when you get off the boat."

"The boat. Oh, my Lord." Mr. Mitchell seemed almost to turn green for a second, but shook himself like a large, bony terrier and raised his head again. "I'm always sick, even when the channel's smooth as glass," he said with a sad smile. "Always have been. And since the trouble with my stomach, it's worse."

Barry was about to say "What trouble?" when a woman appeared in the doorway. He looked at her with a start. She was the least attractive woman he had seen all day. Her face was long and gaunt. She was thin as a stick. She wore a blue denim dress that appeared to be no more than a mass of patches held together with grime.

"Lucille, this is Mr. Clinton. He has come to take my place."

The woman looked Barry over from the dusty shoes on his feet to his coconut-fiber hair. "I am pleased to know you, Father."

"Thank you, Lucille. I'm pleased to know you too."

"We'd like something to drink," Mr. Mitchell said.

"Rum, you mean?"

The old man glanced at Barry, who smiled wryly and said with a shake of his head, "Not for me, thanks. I'm still climbing that trail."

"Some coconut for Mr. Clinton, I think, Lucy," the old man decided.

His housekeeper went out without a reply.

"I don't think she likes me very much," Mr. Mitchell sighed. "I imagine she's disappointed in me."

"In what way?"

"Well, you know, she lived for a time in Anse Ange, and our man there has accomplished a good deal. He has a handsome stone church and a school, all quite impressive. He isn't at the end of the trolley track as I am, you see, and doesn't have to contend with *vodun*. At least, not the same sort."

"I wanted to ask you about that."

The island cleric sighed again. "Ask me how to fight it, you mean? If I'd discovered that, I wouldn't be turning my job over to you, would I?"

"I was told you've been poisoned."

"Who told you?"

"Miss Barnett, at Couronne. She heard it from Warner Lemke and a boy named Pradon Beliard. Beliard is a nephew of your Lucille, I believe."

"It doesn't matter. I suppose I have been poisoned. I really don't know."

"But surely——"

"Oh, they don't always use the famous 'three deadly drops.'" The old man waved a limp hand in protest. "When they just want to discourage you, they have milder methods. You wake up one morning with a headache and blame it on the heat. Take aspirin. Headache seems to go away but next morning you have it again, worse, with an upset stomach to boot. You're not really sick, understand. Nothing like dengue, malaria, tick bite, that sort of thing. You just don't feel right. You never quite feel right. Day by day it gets you down a little more——"

Lucille came in, bearing a rusty metal tray on which were balanced a half-full bottle of St. Joseph rum, an empty glass, and a second glass filled with cloudy coconut water. Reaching for his drink, Barry welcomed the moment of silence.

The trouble here was age, obviously. The Bishop had blundered in sending a man as old as Leander Mitchell to such a place. Old men did well enough in established missions, but Mr. Mitchell had had to move mountains with no one to help him. He'd had to build the church and this house. Probably he'd lived in a native hut while doing so. He'd had to wrestle with *vodun* for a congregation. All this when he was tired, discouraged, half sick from the heat, and lonely. He couldn't be blamed for failure.

Leander Mitchell poured himself a generous measure of rum and drank half of it down at once, leaned back on his chair, and frowned at his successor. It would never work, he told himself. They might have made it work by sending a man of fifty or so, with solid years of experience behind him, but this one was too green, too innocent. Ile du Vent was no place for a man so young. The *vodun* was only part of the problem. He'd be faced with temptation constantly. Every time he walked about the island there would be girls bathing. Nude girls, in the streams and on the beaches. A man would have to be blind not to see them, and a hundred years old not to notice how attractive they were. He knew what it was like, and he was seventy-two. You thought about it too much. Why, only last week a girl as lovely as Eve, a girl he knew well, had stepped out of a stream as he passed and tried to drag him off the path. "I want a white baby, Father," she had begged. "Give me a white baby!" And when he had been indignant and lectured her, she had spat at him. And he an old man!

No, young Clinton would never last. V*odun*, loneliness, temptation—the odds were too great. He was too young, too good-looking. There'd be no peace for him.

The old man poured a second rum and sipped it. "Stomach," he muttered apologetically. He waited a moment for his housekeeper to depart, then went on, "It began about five weeks ago. I'm not really sick, you can see that, but I'm not well either. I have to lie down every two or three hours or——"

A commotion in the yard interrupted him. Finishing his drink, he struggled from his chair.

Barry Clinton thought him a very sick man indeed.

AT THE DOOR Mr. Mitchell said, "This is your gear, I imagine. We'll just stow it here in the office for tonight, and after I'm gone tomorrow you can put it where you like."

Pradon Beliard had come into the yard with five men from the beach, all but Pradon burdened with Barry's belongings. The men looked hot and tired. Motioning them to put down their loads, the boy said to Barry, "I told them you would pay them a *gourde* apiece."

"Take the stuff back," Mr. Mitchell rumbled.

"What?"

"You know the going rate as well as I do. They get fifty *cob*. If you promised them more, you'll pay the rest out of your pocket."

Barry felt uncomfortable. "I really don't mind——"

"Don't be a fool," the old cleric cut him off in English. "The lad's just trying you on for size."

"But is it wise to make an enemy of him?"

"Wiser than getting off on the wrong foot before the lot of them. Give them fifty *cob* each. Pay them yourself. Don't let him do it."

It was not the way Barry would have handled the situation, but he followed instructions. The old man's sudden spurt of efficiency surprised him. It was a mistake to judge a man too quickly. He paid the men from the beach and they departed without comment. He turned to Pradon Beliard and was startled by the malevolence in the boy's eyes, then doubly startled by its abrupt disappearance.

"Good for you, sir." Pradon was grinning now. "They told *me* they wouldn't come up here for less than a *gourde*. No, no," he protested as Barry began to count out money for his own services. "Mr. Barnett instructed me to help you get settled."

Barry hesitated. He was not sure he wanted help in getting settled, or clear about how he could be helped. He neither liked nor wholly trusted this fellow. But I could be wrong, he thought. Surely Jeff Barnett knows the lad better than I do.

"Well, there's nothing to be done today," he said.

"I will be here tomorrow then. A *demain, mon Père*." Without a glance at old Mr. Mitchell, Pradon swung on his heel and limped away.

LEANDER MITCHELL LED THE WAY back to the house, pausing only to peer at the word *médicaments* on the topmost carton of the pile by the door. Inside he took up his empty glass, frowned at it, and put it down with a sigh. "He's a sharp one, that boy," he said. "I'd be careful of him if I were you."

"But he's your housekeeper's nephew."

"I know. And a more honest woman than Lucille you won't find on the whole island. But that doesn't make *him* honest. Lucy herself has precious little use for him."

"I see."

The old man smiled. "It's hard, isn't it? They all look so much alike, you're tempted to think they *are* alike."

No, Barry thought, recalling the faces on the boat. They're not all alike, even in looks. They're big and little, thin and fat, short and tall, ugly and beautiful. A common blackness of skin doesn't make them similar. It would be as foolish to say that all whites are alike.

"You asked about the *vodun*," Leander Mitchell said.

Barry emptied his mind and leaned forward.

"It's hard to know what to tell you. I almost think you'd be better off if I went without saying anything at all, let you discover things for yourself and put your own value on them. I've been wrong so many times."

"Anything you can tell me would be a great help, I'm sure."

The island missionary looked longingly again at his empty glass, half shoved himself from his chair, then fell back and fumbled for his handkerchief. He drank too much. He knew he drank too much. Before coming to Ile du Vent he had scarcely touched the stuff—only a bottle of cold beer now and then on a hot day—but here it was like medicine; it helped a man to keep going. "There are four thousand people here." His voice had become thick. "They know what the church is, most of 'em—they've been over to Anse Ange—but here on the island, before I came, they worshipped their gods of *vodun*. They still do, I'm afraid." He shook his head in sadness. "I can count on one hand the few I've really won over. But that's beside the point, isn't it? What you want to know is who'll be fighting you."

Barry nodded, trying to be patient.

"Number One is a man named Catus Laroche. He's the big fellow here."

Barry's mind, though an empty bowl extended for filling, nevertheless was active on the perimeter. "I met a girl named Micheline Laroche on the boat. Very pretty girl. Very friendly."

"His sister."

"Then I know your Catus, or think I do. There was a fellow on the boat who looked ever so much like her. Fellow about my age and build, with thin lips and a sharp nose. Had a front tooth missing."

"And wore a ring with a square green stone?"

"That's right, he did."

"His wedding ring," Mr. Mitchell said dryly. "He's married to one of the *loa*."

"I don't think I understand."

"Who does, really? It's a queer business. There was a girl in the capital some years back, a popular dancer, married to one of the gods, or at least they said she was. One day every week she disappeared; spent the day communing with him, I suppose. She tired of it finally and became the wife of a young fellow in the dance troupe. Within a month he was dead, laid low by some devilish sickness that wasted him away. The girl went back to the hills where she came from." Mr. Mitchell shrugged. There was so much he could tell this young Clinton about *vodun* if he got started. He had no intention of getting started. Tell the truth and you were thought queer or accused of drinking too much. But he knew what he knew.

"The only thing you've got to understand," he said, "and thoroughly, is that Catus Laroche is a devil. I mean that. He'll fight you every step of the way, every move you make, every breath you draw. You'll begin to think after a time that he was put here by *the* devil for the express purpose of tormenting you."

"Isn't he young to be so important?" Barry asked. If there was one character in the scriptures he considered a creature of pure superstition, it was the devil. But this was no time to say so.

"Young but smart. What he knows he learned from old Salmador, who died here about four years ago. I've been told, by people who ought to know, that Salmador was the most powerful *houngan* in all St. Joseph. You know what a *houngan* is, don't you?"

"Yes, of course. A high priest."

"Catus Laroche was this one's protégé. Catus is a big *houngan* himself now."

Barry recalled his brief conversation with Laroche on the trail up the mountain, and his shock on discovering how much he and the fellow resembled each other. "He seemed decent enough," he protested mildly.

"Heaven help you."

"Oh, I don't mean that I intend to take your advice lightly. It's just that when I talked to him——"

He fell silent, aware that the island missionary was no longer listening but was gazing past him at the doorway. Barry turned on his chair and rose slowly to his feet. The man they had been talking about stood framed in the entrance.

"YOU CAME HERE from Fond Marie, did you not, Father?"

"Yes."

"You worked at the clinic there?"

"I did."

"Does this mean you are a doctor?"

Barry returned the gaze and felt himself stiffen against its challenge. He did not answer at once. With the words of Leander Mitchell fresh in his mind, he felt this was the time to size up his adversary and make at least a tentative mental list of his apparent faults and virtues. He should, he supposed, classify the fellow as evil without any qualifications. It was against his nature to do that. He appraised his foe in silence.

He saw only a little more than he had seen before. The same graceful body garbed only in khaki trousers. The almost handsome face with its intelligent, alert eyes. The gap where a front tooth ought to be. The massive ring with its distinctive green stone on the third finger.

The one added feature he noticed was not a feature at all, really. Perhaps it was no more than a product of his imagination. He thought he detected a hint of mockery in Catus Laroche's level gaze.

"I'm not a doctor," he said at last. "But I do know something about medicine. Why do you ask?"

"A child of my sister is dying."

"Dying!"

"She cut her foot on a machete some days ago. The wound would not heal. Now the sickness has traveled all through her."

"Where is she?"

"At my sister's *caille*. I could not bring her here; she is too sick."

"And you want me to go there with you? Is that what you're asking?"

It was the *houngan's* turn to initiate a silence, and this time Barry was certain of the mockery. But still it was only a phantom turn of the lips, nothing so obvious as a sneer or a shrugged shoulder.

Laroche did not know his lips had moved. He was embarrassed, uncomfortable. It was a terrible thing, his having had to come here to ask the Father's help. It would lower him in the esteem of every living soul on Ile du Vent. He was a *houngan*. A *houngan* held the secrets of life and death. To admit that he could not save the life of his own sister's child was to confess that he was out of touch with the *loa*.

He had thought all this over before coming. For a long time, or what seemed a long time, he had knelt beside the mat on which the child lay moaning. With all the force of his mind he willed the *mystères* to help him; the effort had caused sweat to stream down his face and drip on his knees. What else could he do, short of holding a service? A service would take too long. The child must have help at once.

He had to say something now; the Father was waiting. He took in a deep breath, hating the man for forcing him to beg. But he did not beg. Not even to save his own life could he have made himself do that. "You are a priest," he said, "and you say you know something of medicine. I ask you nothing. It is a priest's duty to help the sick, is it not?"

Barry Clinton sighed and lowered his gaze in defeat. So endeth the first battle, he thought. He turned to old Mr. Mitchell. "I don't suppose I'll be long. Why don't you go back to your nap? We can talk again when I return."

"This is a strange thing," the old man said in English.

"Why is it?"

"In all the time I have been here, this man has never asked a favor of me. Yet before you are here an hour he is forced to ask one of you. It must be an omen. It could be an act of God." He pushed himself to his feet. "While you're unpacking your medicines, I'll get you some water in a thermos. If they offer you anything to eat or drink, don't take it."

4

A S HE STEPPED OUT OF THE HOUSE with his medical bag and the thermos bottle of water, Barry felt the full impact of the sun and wondered what madness had caused little Mr. Mitchell to build the church and rectory in such an unlikely spot. He resolved to do something about it quickly. Then he had other things to think about.

He had to walk fast, for the long legs of Catus Laroche devoured the ground in gulps. It apparently made no difference to Catus that the path began to climb as soon as it left the red-earth clearing. A lifetime on Ile du Vent had hardened him to climbing. It mattered to Barry, though.

Struggling to keep pace, he found it next to impossible to see anything of the terrain he trudged through. Only scattered impressions. On both sides of the path were gardens and thatch-roofed *cailles* behind crooked fences. A man mending a fence stopped work to look at him. Children playing in the yards fell silent. A woman sorting coffee beans in a hut doorway looked up to watch him pass.

He spoke to them, just as he had always spoken to his parishioners at Fond Marie. Here, though, a nod was the friendliest answer he received. No one waved, smiled, or spoke. The children actually seemed frightened, as though afraid to be caught showing any interest in him.

In the village in which he presently found himself it was the same. The place was called Terre Rouge. It was small, no more than a widening of the footpath between rows of close-packed houses, but there were people. Quite a few people for this time of day. They certainly were aware of him as he hurried past in Laroche's wake. But none gave him an honest greeting.

He tried not to let it upset him. One thing at a time, he told himself, forcing his thoughts to focus on the injured child and what he could do for her.

At the end of the village street Laroche halted, eyeing him without compassion as he caught up. "You are tired, Father?"

"Don't ask silly questions. Of course I'm tired."

"Perhaps I walk too fast for you."

"You'll see the day when I can keep up with you. Get along now."

Catus shrugged as he turned away, but did shorten his prodigious
stride a bit and looked back more often. Beyond the village he paused
again to let Barry catch him. This time he glanced at the thermos
bottle. "You must be thirsty."

Barry unscrewed the top, poured water into it, and held it out to
him. Catus seemed not to understand.

"Go on, drink it."

The *houngan* scowled at him. "After you, *mon Père.*"

"As you wish, then." Barry emptied the cup and refilled it. This
time Catus drank.

Now why did he do that, the *houngan* wondered. Is he trying to
make me believe that color means nothing to him, that whites and
blacks are all the same? *Does* he feel that way? Or was it a trick to
make me *sympathique?*

THE JOURNEY ENDED just beyond the village when Laroche turned
from the path and passed through a gap in a cactus hedge. A neat
wooden gate hung in the gap and the hedge was five feet high, a
solid mass of thorns. Catus didn't like intruders, Barry told himself.
They entered a small swept-earth yard, prettily shaded by a large
mapou with great spreading roots.

The hut was the usual thing but larger than most and a good deal
cleaner. There were two rooms with a curtain between, just as in
Mr. Mitchell's house, but the curtain here was of woven sisal, not
an old Christmas tablecloth. The little girl lay naked on a sleeping
mat in the front room. A number of adults, at whom Barry scarcely
glanced before kneeling to make his examination, stood about in
the semigloom.

"A light, please." Why in heaven's name did they always build their
huts with such miserably small windows, shutting out both air and
light as if those God-given elements were poisonous? Why didn't
they dispense with walls altogether in this climate, at least up here
on the mountain where mosquitoes were not a problem?

Someone handed him a kerosene lamp made of a condensed-milk
can. He placed it on the mat where the child could not accidentally

knock it over. His examination finished, he allowed himself a sigh of relief.

He had been terribly afraid that he would not know what to do for the child. At Fond Marie there had always been Peter to turn to for advice. But the child was not dying. Catus had exaggerated.

They always did exaggerate, these people. Having no doctors, they lived in constant terror of sickness, for when it struck them down their only hope lay in their so-called leaf doctors, or in *vodun*. He remembered that Catus was a *vodun* priest. Good. This should be proof to them, then, that the powers of a *houngan* were mostly in his imagination. Or in theirs.

He glanced up, caught the *houngan's* eye and motioned him to come closer. Now that he was certain he could help the girl, it would be criminally foolish not to make the most of the situation.

"What have you done for the child?" The implied accusation in his tone was deliberate.

Catus met his gaze without flinching. With, in fact, unmistakable defiance. "Everything I knew how to. No one could have done more without medicine."

"I see." All that Barry really saw was that it was going to be difficult to get the best of the fellow. "Well, you were right about the wound. It's badly infected. The poison has spread and she has a high fever." He took his penicillin supplies from the bag on the floor beside him. "I don't promise to cure her. I can only do my best."

Catus said nothing. The others moved closer, watching him as he assembled the hypodermic. When he plunged the point into the little girl's round black bottom and she voiced a bleat of surprise and pain, there was a noisy sucking of breath behind him, then a murmuring.

He dressed the foot, then looked at his patient more closely in the light of the lamp. She had a cherub's face with enormous, shining eyes that gazed back at him in terror. Her snub nose looked for all the world like a tiny twitching mouse. Her skin was smooth and soft, her hair like a cloud of smoke. He could not help noticing how clean she was. They weren't, most of them. Yet the people on the boat had been clean enough. Perhaps they bathed more often here on Ile du Vent, where they had the sea all around them and a number of handy fresh-water streams.

"What's your name, *ti-fi?*" he asked her with a smile.

She turned away from him like a playful seal.

"Her name is Fifine, Father. For Josephine." The voice was

familiar. He stood up and found himself gazing into the face of the girl from the boat, Catus Laroche's sister.

"We thank you for coming," she said, holding her gaze on his face. "I speak for all of us. This is my sister Dauré César, the child's mother, and her husband Louis César." She motioned the others forward with the barest movement of her hand, as though she were used to giving orders in that house. Only then did she stop looking at Barry and step aside.

Barry felt strange. More than strange. He felt as though she had embraced him. He felt that she had flung her golden arms around his neck and pressed her body hard against his own. It was a very real feeling, more real than his certainty that nothing of the sort had really happened. Her arms *were* golden in the lamplight. Her face, too. She still wore the butterfly dress, and the green stone gleamed in the cleavage between her bold young breasts.

He scarcely heard the expressions of thanks murmured by the child's mother. Scarcely looked at her, except to notice that she was attractive, as indeed all these Laroches seemed to be, and was also well along in pregnancy. He felt dizzy. There was an odd prickling sensation on the backs of his hands. Not until the husband stepped forward was he in full control of himself again.

He shook the man's hand, receiving a second shock. The hand was enormous. It wrapped itself about his own as though he were a mere child. He had to look up into the man's face, and he, Barry Clinton, was six feet tall. The average native of St. Joseph would think that very tall indeed. Louis César was the largest individual he had seen since coming to St. Joseph three years before: six feet five or six and easily weighing two-hundred-fifty pounds. A giant. The man's mouth was working. His whole great ugly face was working. Barry strained to catch what he was saying.

Impossible. There was something amiss with the fellow's speech, just as there was something wrong with his right ear, the upper half of which was only a knob of gristle or hard flesh. Probably the result of an old fight or accident. Chopped with a machete, more than likely. Lord, he was ugly. A mountain of ugliness. Skin dead black, not a glimmer of life in it; features splashed on as though flung from a bucket. Or had they been squashed into that grotesque shape by the same accident that mangled the ear? Awful. Yet the struggling voice was surprisingly soft and pleasant, almost a crooning.

Barry murmured, "Yes, yes, it's quite all right," and extracted his hand from the other's grip before it could be crushed. "Well, I'd better be going." He glanced at the child again. "Let her rest. I'll give you some pills for her, to stop the pain, but let her sleep all she can. Don't move her. Give her food if she wants it, but don't force it on her. I'll come tomorrow."

Micheline stood before him again. "Will you not stay for coffee, Father?"

"Coffee? No. No, thank you——"

Perhaps his expression gave him away. After old Mitchell's warning, the offer had put him immediately on the defensive. At any rate her brother, Catus, was smiling at him.

"You're not afraid, Father?"

"Afraid of what?"

"That you might be poisoned."

"No, no. It's just that——"

"*Père* Mitchell was not poisoned, Father. He thinks he was, but it isn't so. His sickness is his own fault."

"How do you mean, his own fault?"

"He drinks too much. He has been drinking too much for weeks. Rum is all right in small amounts, but not as a substitute for water. There is no danger of your being poisoned, Father. If you think so, you do me a dishonor. I am a *houngan*, a respected member of my community, not a *bocor*, a witch doctor. It is the *bocor* who poisons people."

Barry returned the man's gaze. Strange. He had been on Ile du Vent only a few hours, yet already he felt more inclined to believe Laroche, supposedly his worst enemy, than the man whose place he was taking. Was he being naive? Was this knack of winning a stranger's confidence a secret weapon that Laroche planned to use against him?

"I believe I *would* like some coffee," he said. The fact was, he was not at all eager to return to the rectory and listen to more of old Mitchell's rambling talk. He preferred to sit here, getting to know these people better. There was so much they could tell him if they would. As he spoke, he glanced at Micheline and smiled.

Micheline made the coffee outside somewhere and brought it into the *caille* on a mahogany tray with tiny cups and saucers. She poured it from a blue enameled pot that must have come from one of the houseware shops in the capital. Barry waited in vain for a sugar-bowl to be produced, then sipped.

He frowned at the girl. "This has an odd taste."

"You find it different?" She seemed concerned as she leaned toward him. "Perhaps this is the first time you have tasted coffee made with cane juice instead of water."

He sipped again. It was really very good. No need for sugar. Very good indeed. He smiled at her and let her refill his cup, and when she bent toward him her thigh touched his knee and he felt her give a little start. He, too, had reacted involuntarily to the contact by almost dropping his cup and saucer. To cover his embarrassment he asked how many persons lived in the cactus-enclosed clearing.

Seven, they told him. There were three *cailles*. Louis and Dauré César lived in this one with their baby. Dauré's father and mother, who of course were the parents of Catus and Micheline also, lived in the second hut with Micheline. The third and largest was occupied by Catus himself.

"You live alone?" Barry asked, surprised.

"I am a *houngan*, *mon Père*. A *houngan* must have a *hounfor*, the place where the altar is kept. Also a *tonnelle* for the drumming and ceremonial dancing."

"You aren't married?"

"I am—no, I have never taken a wife."

Except the *loa* or whatever you call her whose ring you wear, Barry thought, recalling old Mitchell's explanation of the ring and the tale of the dancing girl in the capital. He did not press the subject.

They discussed the island and its problems. There were many problems, they told him. Sickness, for example. Catus, who knew much about herbs, leaves, and roots, as all *houngans* did, was able to cure some maladies. But if a man chopped himself with a machete or came down with a serious illness, the nearest medical help was hours away on the mainland. "But for you, Father, we should have been planning a funeral here in this very house tomorrow."

"Perhaps not. I certainly hope not."

There was a shortage of land suitable for raising food, they complained. "Our hillsides are steep and difficult. We do the best we can, but not all the soil is productive, and when the fishing is bad many of us go hungry. Yet the government has allowed the Plantation Couronne to come here and plant hundreds of *carreaux* of the best land to sisal, making our problems even more acute. Why? Everybody knows why. Because some politician saw a chance to fill his pockets with money. They care nothing for us, the politicians. Were every soul on this island to perish of starvation or disease tomorrow, the newspapers in the capital would probably not mention it."

Barry nodded. They exaggerated, of course. People with grievances always exaggerated; peasants especially. He recognized a core of truth, though, in what they said and encouraged them to tell him more. By the time he stood up to go, he had learned a great deal.

"Thank you for telling me these things."

"I will walk back with you, Father." The big fellow, Louis César, touched his arm. So that misshapen mouth *could* make words, after all. He was relieved to know it. Evidently it was only a matter of getting used to the sound of them, just as one had to become accustomed to the fluid slurrings of Creole itself.

"That's kind of you, Louis. If you don't mind, though, I'd like to have Catus walk back with me." He turned to the *houngan*, smiling. "That's only fair, isn't it, Catus? You came and got me."

"Certainly, Father."

"Come along then. And this time I'll set the pace, if you don't mind."

THE PACE BARRY SET was deliberately slow. There were some things he wanted to discuss with his "enemy."

When they were clear of the house, he said, "You haven't got along well with Mr. Mitchell, have you, Catus?"

"It was impossible."

"Why?"

"For several reasons. He came here to teach us a new faith. Very well. I am a *vodun houngan*. I didn't ask him to come here. But if a man has something to say, I am willing to listen, provided we can meet and talk as friends. Your *Père* Mitchell would not be friends. He went up and down the island calling us superstitious savages for believing in *vodun*. We were all fools, he said, believing in nonsense. But did he try to find out *what* we believe? Did he ever ask us, or let us show him? He did not."

"You make a hard case against him."

"That isn't all. We *need* help on this island. We are too often sick and hungry. But *Père* Mitchell could not see what we needed. He had nothing to offer but sermons full of angry attacks on the faith of our ancestors. We don't need sermons. Certainly not that kind."

"Therefore you fought him."

"Did he expect us not to fight him?"

Probably not, Barry thought, if Mitchell's own teachings were a declaration of war. Why, why did so many of the older missionaries feel it was necessary to destroy everything before they could build? Why couldn't they see that a faith of any sort, no matter how primitive, was better than none at all and could be used for a foundation? But Catus was waiting for an answer.

"He hoped you might be reasonable, I'm sure."

"He doesn't know much about us, then." The odd stone on the *houngan's* finger bounced a beam of green light into Barry's eyes as Catus lifted a hand to rub the side of his nose. "If you expect us to be reasonable on the same terms, you must be as big a fool as he is. Why should we be?"

"I suppose you mean," Barry said, "that your people have always had to fight to preserve your *vodun*. That it's been outlawed down through the years by everyone from plantation owners in slave days to recent heads of the republic. And that I'd be silly to expect to drive it out of existence with words. Is that what you mean?"

"I mean that if you try to destroy *vodun* on this island, I will do my best to destroy you."

"But Mr. Mitchell wasn't simply trying to take something away from you, Catus. He wanted to give you something better in return."

"Your faith, you mean? Who says it is better?"

"I do, for one."

"It would be interesting to hear your evidence."

They had reached the village, and Barry fell silent as they passed through it. He welcomed the silence, paying no attention now to the villagers who stared without offering a greeting. He had not been prepared for this sort of argument and had the feeling that to get in much deeper without adequate preparation might be unwise. Whatever else Catus Laroche might be, he was not a fool.

He fumbled at a shoelace to let Catus go ahead of him, then straightened and studied the man as he followed. A devil, had Mr. Mitchell said? It was far too soon, of course, to attempt any analysis of what went on inside that well-shaped head, but he felt the stirring of a powerful urge to be friends with the fellow. Not simply to avoid having him for an enemy, either.

He caught up as the village fell behind. "Let me ask you a question, Catus. Will you give me a chance to tell you what I believe in? I may be able to show you some good in it, you know."

"Have you asked me what I believe?"

"I intend to."

"In that case I will listen to you. But you won't find it easy to outtalk my ancestors, I warn you."

"I can try."

Catus looked at him strangely. "If you fail, will you go away from here and leave us alone?"

Barry wished he had foreseen the trap, but having blundered into it, knew it would only hold him more tightly if he squirmed. "I can't promise that. I was sent here to do a job. I'm bound to stay and keep trying."

"Even if you are destroyed?"

"I suppose so, if that's the way it has to be. But I may be able to convince you, you know."

"I am not easy to convince."

No, Barry thought, I'll bet you're not.

They trudged on, past the fences and gardens and houses. At the edge of the red-earth-mission clearing Barry halted and held out his hand. He managed a smile. He didn't feel like smiling.

"Well, Catus, at least we know where we stand with each other."

The *houngan* accepted the proferred hand, then folded his arms on his chest. "You will come to see the child tomorrow?"

"I said I would."

"I thank you for saving her life."

"And I thank you for being honest with me. I can find much to admire in an honest man, even when he's an enemy."

Catus, his arms still folded, watched the new missionary walk across the clearing. There was a man he would have to think about, long and hard. A good man in many ways, dangerous in others. It would be wise to learn as much about him as possible, where he came from and what kind of people his ancestors were. There was that old Guinea belief, too, about every man's having a twin. He wished old Salmador were alive, so that he might consult him on that point.

At any rate, go slow, be careful. And keep an eye on Micheline, who had given the new Father many a strange look back there at the house and might, if not restrained, make matters extremely difficult and complicated.

THE FRONT ROOM was empty when Barry entered the rectory. He drew the Christmas tablecloth a little way back and saw Mr. Mitchell asleep on the bed.

He went out again. He wanted to see the church and preferred to look at it by himself. Hurrying across the clearing, he went inside.

The heat under the iron roof struck him like a blast from an open furnace door. He winced. The impact of the ugliness was almost as great.

He walked down the aisle between the two rows of rude wooden benches, shaking his head at the dust stirred up by his shoes. The whole place smelled of dust. He halted and held a finger under his nose to stop a sneeze, shook his head at the untidy dirt floor, the greasy rail, the soiled hangings at the altar. There wasn't a window in the place and it was dark and gloomy, even with the sunlight blazing in the doorway behind him. Not a breath of breeze entered to dispell the heat.

What must it be like on Sunday when crowded with people?

He knelt for a moment, then hurried outside, sweating more from his few minutes in the church than from his walk with Catus. In the front room of the rectory he sank onto a chair and closed his eyes.

WHEN CATUS REACHED HOME after leaving Barry at the mission clearing, he found his sister waiting for him at the gate in the cactus hedge. She took him by the arm and drew him toward the big mapou. Under the tree she had placed two chairs.

"Sit down. I want to talk to you."

He was willing enough to sit after his walk.

"What are your plans for the new Father?" she asked him.

Catus tipped his chair against the bole of the tree and scowled at her. The question did not surprise him.

How old was his sister? Eighteen now. Not a child any more. Not a long-legged tomboy who ran naked out of the house whenever her mother's back was turned, and danced like one possessed about the yard, shouting and singing at the top of her lungs. She was old enough to be thinking about men. She must have been thinking about them for quite a while now.

She was attractive. She had a good face, a bosom any man would find interesting, strong straight legs, and a hard little bottom. Even her feet were well formed. Oh, yes, she was good-looking. She was also determined and hard to manage. Long ago she had learned that what she wanted she could usually have, if she used her smile or her temper to obtain it.

"I have not made up my mind yet about the new Father. Why?"

"You will drive him away?"

"Possibly, if I think it necessary."

"*Can* you drive him away? He is no *Père* Mitchell. He is young and intelligent and—and——"

"And good-looking," Catus said, scowling. "And therefore you are interested in him. I warn you, leave him alone!"

She rose from her chair and came over to him. Her hand stroked his hair. "Why should I?"

"If I find you playing around with a white man, I'll kill you. Stop pawing me." He jerked his head away from her hand. "I'll kill both of you. I told you that the day M'sieu Lemke came here to the island."

"What's wrong with my liking a white man?" she demanded, pouting.

"You are black."

"Old Père Mitchell once said we were all alike, no matter what the color of our skin. It was one of the things his faith would teach us, he said. The new Father has the same faith, hasn't he?"

Catus remembered the Father's offer of a drink of water from the thermos. It had startled him. If he had accepted the drink, would Père Clinton have drunk from the same thermos top afterward? Or would he have drunk from the thermos itself?

"What the new Father believes, I don't know. But I know this: in St. Joseph when a white man looks at a native girl he wants only one thing, and after he gets it he is through with her. Our family is a good one. We are respected. If you do anything to endanger that respect, even the loa will punish you, not to mention what I'll do to you myself."

Micheline turned her back on him and went toward the house, laughing. He was always the same, her brother. So serious. So certain the world would come to an end if one didn't follow the rules exactly as they were laid down. Well, he didn't know everything, even if people thought he did. There were many things he didn't know.

The new Father had a nice smile. He had looked up at her when she brushed against him, serving the coffee. Tomorrow he would be coming here again.

5

THE REVEREND LEANDER MITCHELL departed from Ile du Vent the following morning at eight o'clock. "There's no sense in your coming down to the beach with me," he told Barry. "No sense at all. You'd only have to drag yourself back up again, and for what? Just to stand there and wave good-by when I'll be too seasick to look at you." But despite the old man's protests, Barry accompanied him to the boat, helping him over the rough spots on the path. Four boys trailed behind, carrying Mr. Mitchell's belongings on their heads.

When the boat sailed, Barry stood on the beach watching it. What would become of the old man, he wondered. What was left?

He returned to the mission, had breakfast, and went straight to the village to keep his promise to Catus. Little Fifine's fever had all but disappeared. He gave her a second injection of penicillin. This time, instead of turning from him in terror, she flung both arms around his neck and put her cheek against his. He dressed her foot again and kissed her. She was an adorable child.

He accepted coffee without hesitation. While he was drinking it, Micheline came into the *caille* and sat down. She thought up things to say, mostly the very things they had all discussed yesterday. Barry in vain sought a chance to depart.

Big Louis supplied it in the end. "How can we pay you, Father?" he asked when the girl gave him an opening.

"You don't have to."

"We wish to."

Barry frowned for a moment. He could use a man as husky as this one. "Would you like to work for me, Louis?"

"Work, *mon Père?*"

"I want to set out a garden. There isn't one at the mission. Mr. Mitchell never thought of having one, I suppose."

"Nothing will grow in that soil."

"On the ridge, then. The church owns some property up there,

I'm told. At any rate, I can use you and two or three others if you're willing to work. I'll pay the standard wage."

Louis' homely face became a question mark. His wife, squatting beside the child on the mat, looked up quickly and said, "He will help you, Father."

"Good." Barry glanced at Micheline. She had seated herself and was gazing at him with curious intensity. He guessed why she had come over from her own house. She had forgotten to button her dress, he noticed. It was all she had on and was too small for her. He tried not to look at her half-revealed breasts.

"Can we start this morning, Louis?" he asked. "I think it's important not to waste time."

"I will meet you on the ridge," Louis said.

BACK AT THE RECTORY, Barry went into Leander Mitchell's bedroom. It was his now and he was glad to have it after sleeping on a cot in the office last night. He opened his suitcase, selecting khaki trousers and a short-sleeved sport shirt. He was in charge here now; he could wear what he liked. The clerical outfit would be saved for Sundays. The peasants would understand, even if the Bishop raised an eyebrow. What must the peasants have thought of poor old Mitchell, staggering about under a tropic sun in clothes suitable for New Hampshire in winter?

He went in search of Lucille and found her in the kitchen, in the other wing of the L. This wing was larger. It contained, in addition to the kitchen and Lucille's tiny bedroom, a small dining room and a kind of storeroom. The woman sat on a stool, slicing string beans lengthwise with a sharp knife. She wore the same ragged dress. He leaned against the table, watching her.

"There are some things I ought to know, Lucy, that Mr. Mitchell didn't have time to tell me."

She looked up, her hands still.

"Are you the only person he employed?"

"*Oui, mon Père.*"

"Do you mind telling me what he paid you?"

"Forty *gourdes* a month."

Eight dollars. Not a bad salary for St. Joseph. It was two dollars less than Peter Ambrose paid his housekeeper at Fond Marie, but Peter employed a cook and a yard boy as well.

"I'd better plan on paying you the same, for the time being. That is, if you're staying on. You will be staying, won't you?"

She let a moment of silence pass, then looked straight at him, her long slack face pulling itself together so that it was almost attractive. "I will stay until *Père* Mitchell sends for me. Then I must go."

He was startled. Until *Père* Mitchell sent for her? What kind of talk was this? Mitchell was never going to send for her.

Barry looked closer. The woman had been crying, by heaven! She had been fond of the old man. She actually believed he would want her to look after him at his next post.

"Well—all right, Lucille. You'll stay until he sends for you. By the way, is that your only dress?"

She looked at herself. "No. I have another."

"I mean do you have another work dress." She had a white one for Sundays, of course, and shoes and a hat to go with it. They all did.

"No, *mon Père*."

He took two five-*gourde* notes from his billfold and pressed them into her hand. "Please buy one then. Throw that one away. I'm going up to the ridge now. I've work to do." He smiled at her and stepped outside to go to the office for the strongbox in which old Mitchell had left the mission's records, including the deed to the property at the top of the island.

Before the office doorway an old man in rags leaned on a *coco-macaque* stick. Around his jaw was tied a strip of filthy blue cloth. He slouched forward.

"*Mon Père*, I have a tooth that is killing me," he mumbled. "You helped the little César girl, they say. Can you find time to do the same for me, please?"

IT WAS AFTER ELEVEN when Barry started for the ridge.

The old fellow with the abscessed molar had been only the first patient. After him had come a young woman with a sick baby, a lad of fifteen with a nasty coral cut on one hand, and an old grandmother with a grandson crippled by polio.

He had welcomed them all, not only with his smile but with an inner exultation that must have made him seem a little strange to them. This was what he had come to Ile du Vent for, to help these people who so sorely needed help.

He pulled the tooth, calling Lucille from the kitchen to hold the old fellow's head. He treated the young woman's baby for a bad cold that could easily have turned into pneumonia. He washed and dressed the coral cut and told the boy to come back. He patiently showed the grandmother how, with the proper massage and exercise, her grandson's useless arm might be made useful again.

What a miracle it was, his having treated the César child so soon after his arrival! The word had got around. He was accepted already as a man to be turned to in time of trouble.

I'll have to make the office over into a clinic, he thought. Even that won't do if they keep coming. I'll have to build a clinic. I must ask Peter to send me more supplies . . .

The path to the ridge went up and up, becoming steeper at every turn, yet most of the land was planted. On Ile du Vent a farmer could kill himself by falling out of a garden patch. At times he stopped to examine the corn, millet, and sweet potatoes growing near the trail. The soil looked rich enough and certainly supported some healthy-seeming weeds, but the vegetables were poor.

He reached the top in twenty minutes and stopped to take in the view. Almost the entire island was in sight. Far below on one side lay the multicolored waters of the channel, the pretty beaches lined with coco palms, the two channel-shore villages. On the other side the land dropped steeply to a broad bed of boulders. He saw a number of dugouts among the boulders but no sign of life, no houses. Evidently the natives fished there occasionally but no one lived there. He could hear the sea pounding on the rocks.

He looked along the ridge. A lively breeze fluttered the legs of his trousers. The air was salty-sweet and untainted. The grass at his feet was ankle-high and green, and the glossy dark-green leaves of countless pomme-rose trees danced in the wind. He felt again an almost spiritual reaction to the island's beauty.

A hundred yards distant big Louis César and two other men rose from an outcrop of limestone at sight of him. Barry waved.

"We have been waiting," Louis said when he reached them. "We did not know what to do."

Barry shook hands with all three and showed them a paper he had taken from the strongbox. It was a sketch-map of the island showing the location of the church property. Leander Mitchell had purchased two *carreaux*, about six acres, on the ridge. The eastern boundary was the outcrop of limestone on which the three men had been sitting. It was marked with an iron pipe driven into the ground.

"I wonder why Mr. Mitchell bought this land," Barry said.

"He intended to build the church and house up here. But after obtaining the property, he discovered there was no water."

That old St. Joseph bugaboo, water. Barry wistfully looked about him. What a place for the mission! The rectory leaped full-blown into his mind, two stories tall to take full advantage of the breeze, a veranda running completely around the second story. The upstairs rooms would be the bedrooms, open at each end so the air could sweep through them no matter which side of the island it came from. Downstairs would be the clinic, with beds for patients who required hospitalization. He sighed. At least he could have a garden here.

There were other stakes. When Louis had pointed them out to him, he sat on the outcrop and with pencil and paper showed the big man what he wanted. It would not be a large garden at first. The important thing was to get started.

"Did you bring any tools, Louis?"

"We have our hoes, *mon Père*."

"How soon can you have the ground ready for planting?"

"If we start work at once, by tomorrow evening, perhaps. Certainly the day after."

"Good. I've got some seeds at the house, and I'll get more. Let me have your hoe for a minute."

It was a primitive tool, wickedly heavy, the massive iron head fitted to a handle hewn from a small tree trunk. The first experimental stroke told him that if he attempted any real work with it he would be staggering in a few minutes. Nevertheless he would not have forgone the exquisite pleasure of turning up the first few clods of earth for anything in the world.

Big Louis and the others watched him. Presently the great ugly-gentle face blossomed in a grin.

Barry worked until the sweat streamed down his face, and the monstrous hoe handle had burned his palms crimson. Grinning himself, he handed the tool to its owner. "I'll leave it to you now. I've got to clean the church today for Sunday's service. If I finish in time, I'll come back——"

There was a movement among the pomme-rose trees. A slender shape in khaki trousers and a white sport shirt, the very attire Barry wore himself, came limping toward them. It was Pradon Beliard, the boy from Couronne. His sharp eyes took in Louis and the other two with a quick glance. He halted before Barry with an expression of one deeply offended.

"You should have waited for me, sir. I told you I would come today to look after you."

"So you did." And I haven't missed you a bit, Barry thought. "But you weren't around."

"I came as soon as I could. I live in Petit Trou."

Barry frowned. If he dismissed the lad, Jeff Barnett might be offended. "Well," he said, "now that you're here, you can help if you like. I was just going down to the mission to clean the church."

Pradon seemed to hesitate. "Sir, don't you think you should call on M'sieu Dufour first? He was asking me about you."

"Dufour? Who's he?"

Felix Dufour, Pradon explained, was the magistrate on Ile du Vent and a most important person, perhaps *the* most important person on the island. Ile du Vent had no government as such; it was only a sadly neglected stepchild of the Department du Nord. Dufour ruled it with a small police force in charge of one Jean Marie Edma, who was a sergeant in the army of St. Joseph. "It would be wise, sir, to call on both men," Pradon advised. "It will not take long. They live in my village."

Barry shrugged. "I guess I'd better, if it seems to you worth a speech as long as that. All right, let's go."

FELIX DUFOUR turned out to be a white-haired, pockmarked little rooster outlandishly attired in white trousers, pink shirt, black tie, and two-toned shoes. His teeth were bad and he talked with a lisp. He was certainly important, though. He occupied the largest house in the channel-shore village of Petit Trou, a much too attractive community to deserve the name of "Little Hole," and obviously thought himself king of the island.

They talked on Dufour's pleasantly cool veranda, over sips of sugared rum. "You ought to have a mule, Father," the little man said. "It isn't good to be walking in this heat."

"I could use one. I can't understand why Mr. Mitchell didn't have one."

"He was too old, he said."

"Well, I'm not too old and I did plenty of riding at Fond Marie. I'll have to get one."

"They are expensive."

"Are they? How expensive?"

"In Anse Ange, seventy-five dollars." Dufour rubbed his nose. "But I could sell you one for less."

Barry managed to conceal his surprise. "You have mules here, you mean?"

"Two. They are the only ones on the island, except those at the plantation."

"I'd like to look at them."

The little magistrate had a boy bring his animals around from the back yard, and Barry was examining them when the police chief came up the road. Sergeant Edma was not much bigger than Dufour but was younger. About thirty, Barry guessed. In a much-washed khaki uniform he was entirely presentable. He murmured "*Mon Père*" and shook hands as though the meeting were an event.

The mules appeared to be in excellent condition. Barry inquired the price.

"The gray one I can let you have for sixty dollars," Dufour said after turning the problem over in his mind. "The other I do not like to sell."

Barry glanced at Pradon Beliard, saw approval on the latter's face and said, "Have you also a saddle I can buy?"

Dufour's boy brought one, plus a bridle and blanket. The equipment was far from new but would serve. "How much?"

Dufour shrugged. "Thirty dollars?"

"That's a bit steep, don't you think? Make it twenty." In St. Joseph one always bargained. It was almost an insult to accept a man's first price.

"Twenty-five."

"I'll tell you what. I'll give you seventy-five for everything if you'll come to church on Sunday and put a dollar in the plate. Is it a deal?"

It was the sort of offer that could not fail to delight a St. Joseph politician. The magistrate showed all his decaying teeth in a laugh like a duck's quack. He slapped his thighs. "It's a deal."

"Bring the animal up to the house this evening and I'll pay you. Don't forget a bill of sale, please." Barry shook hands with both men and excused himself, then thought of something else. "By the way, Sergeant, I'm hoping to see you in church too."

"If I am not busy with police work, *mon Père*."

As he walked with Pradon through the village, Barry had to smile. His second day here and he owned a mule. That was progress.

Petit Trou sprawled prettily along the shore under wind-bent coconut palms. There was little activity, but where he found people to talk to, he stopped. He used the same formula on them all. "I'd like to see you in church on Sunday." They probably wouldn't come, but it could do no harm to invite them.

Tête Cabrit, the other shore village, was a disappointment, scarcely more than a cluster of fishermen's shacks. But, Pradon explained, few of the island's four thousand inhabitants lived in the three villages. Stupid people, they preferred to isolate themselves on their little garden plots or, if fishing was their means of earning a living, in clusters of shacks along the shore.

"What we need here on Ile du Vent is organization," Pradon said loftily, "with, of course, an intelligent leader to do the organizing."

Barry glanced at him in surprise. *Meaning you?* he wondered.

As they climbed to the plateau at three o'clock he summed up the results of his day. He had laid the groundwork for a clinic, started a model farm, asked quite a few islanders to come to church, and established relationships with two important men. Not forgetting the mule.

A fair start. He hadn't cleaned the church, of course. He would do that tomorrow. At the edge of the mission clearing he dismissed Pradon with a word of thanks.

DRIVEN BY CONSCIENCE, he spent the rest of the afternoon scrubbing and sweeping the church after all, then slept and had to be waked by Lucy to eat the supper of chicken stew she had prepared for him. It was a very good supper.

An hour later little Felix Dufour delivered the gray mule.

Dufour came into the clearing on foot, followed by his boy. The boy was leading the mule, Barry noticed, not riding it. Barry had half a mind to try the beast before handing over the money, but was too tired. The mule was sound enough, he was sure. If it had a mean disposition or a few cute tricks, as many did, he was experienced enough to deal with the situation.

He did make certain the bill of sale was in order, and, to be doubly safe, had Lucy make her mark on it as a witness. Then, after tethering the animal at the clearing's edge, he retired to his office and wrote two letters.

The first was to Peter Ambrose, but when he read over what he had written he tore it up, realizing he had said things about old Leander Mitchell that might be unfair. His revision was much shorter, stating simply that he was unpacked and already at work, he thought the island a beauty spot, and as an amateur doctor he had already attended his first patients. He hoped Peter would be able to spare some medicines.

The second letter was addressed to Edith Barnett at the plantation, and he found himself thinking about her with surprising sentimentality as he put the words down. It was even something of a struggle to avoid being sentimental in what he wrote.

She would like Ile du Vent, he told her, and went on to describe the island in rather flowery prose, becoming almost lyrical when he wrote of the wonderfully cool green garden spot at the top, with its breathtaking view of the sea and the channel. He liked the people, most of them at any rate, and had no fear of being poisoned in the pursuit of his work, despite her warnings. He was quite sure Mitchell had not been poisoned, except possibly with rum. (He could say this to Edith, knowing she would be discreet.) But there were some problems.

"With one of these you could help me," he wrote. "I've started a model garden. These people haven't the faintest notion of what good vegetables look like and will think I've come straight from heaven if I can turn out corn, spinach, turnips, leeks, carrots, beets, etc., etc., of the sort we grew at Fond Marie. It's the same old story: they plant each season's crops with seeds from the last one, quite unaware of the need for a fresh start. I'll wager there hasn't been a packet of seeds on this island, or in Anse Ange either, within the memory of the oldest inhabitant. Would it be possible for you to send me some quickly, or, even better, bring them in person? I didn't bring nearly enough."

The letters finished, he went to bed, resolving to replace the Christmas tablecloth between the two rooms as soon as he could obtain a piece of plain cotton or denim for the purpose. What day was market day in Terre Rouge? It didn't matter. Each of the three villages had a different day, probably. He could send Lucy. No sense fretting over it now. Better go to sleep. Tomorrow he must finish cleaning the church.

But he could not sleep. His mind was too active.

Strange, that he of all people should have been entrusted with the task of saving souls in a place like this. He was hardly the man for it. Or was he? They certainly weren't ready, these people, for any infusion of abstract religion; old Mitchell had found that out to his sorrow. But it might be possible to implant the Christian idea by example. After all, that was the way Christ had taught, wasn't it? By helping them with their more pressing problems, he might slowly win their friendship and confidence. Then they might accept spiritual help as well. It would take time, of course. A lot of time. But he himself needed time. He wasn't ready.

To be inspiring, a man had to be inspired himself. To lift up, he had to have his feet planted on something solid. That would come, perhaps. Meanwhile, it couldn't be forced. He had tried to force it in theological school and only floundered deeper into doubt. He had plagued Peter Ambrose with questions, hoping some of Peter's remarkable faith would rub off on him, and it hadn't. Perhaps his work with the people of Ile du Vent would provide some answers.

But they had to be real answers. They had to be something more substantial than Peter's "It's in the Bible if you'll look for it, my boy." Otherwise he preferred to go on doubting. He was like his father in that respect. His father's determination to weigh all sides of a question had been a byword in diplomatic circles. His mother, on the other hand, had been like Peter, accepting any opinion, any belief, provided she could fortify her acceptance with the findings of "greater minds than mine." His mother had been a very placid woman, his father restless and unhappy.

He sat up to pour a drink of water from the pitcher Lucy had left on the washstand. Yes, perhaps Ile du Vent would answer his problems. At any rate it would keep him busy, and out of honest toil might come some of the answers he sought. Thinking had produced none. He sighed, remembering the windswept ridge at the top of the island. If only he could build a clinic there . . .

He almost dropped the pitcher. By heaven, he *could* build on the ridge! Why not? The lack of water was no real problem—no problem at all. It rained there often. You could tell by the way the pomme-rose grew. The right sort of roof, with gutters to direct the runoff into metal or concrete tanks—it would be simple!

But—would the Bishop give his consent?

6

BARRY HAD COME TO ILE DU VENT on a Monday. On Thursday of that week Warner Lemke and his wife Alma returned to the island from Fond Marie.

Theirs was a strange homecoming. They had kept up a pretense of compatability on the ride from Fond Marie to the channel, but only because Jeff Barnett and not one of his men was at the wheel of the jeep. (A necessary gesture, Jeff had felt, since his daughter Edith would be visiting the island soon and would have to be a guest of theirs.) On the launch, all pretense had been dropped completely. There was no need for it. The boy in charge of the boat did not matter.

Now they were riding through the sloping fields of young sisal to the plantation house, on horses that had been sent down to the island beach for them. They were dismounting under the mango tree that shaded the front of the bungalow from the sun. They were climbing the veranda steps. They had absolutely nothing to say to each other.

On the veranda Warner Lemke glanced angrily at his wife. She was attractive this morning. She was always attractive, of course—he never would have married her otherwise—but this morning she had taken special pains, it seemed, to accent her best points. She wore silver-gray slacks and a filmy white blouse that let her bra show through. She was the only woman in St. Joseph who ever wore slacks. She only laughed when the peasant women gawked at her in astonishment and the men smiled secret smiles.

Why had she dressed so alluringly today? Why had she fussed with her hair and spent so much time with make-up? Was it to torment him, the way she had tormented him by deliberately paying attention to other men at the farewell party for dear Mr. Clinton, after discovering his secret? He turned away and went inside, to avoid looking at her.

The house was a square bungalow with a large front room that was used for an office and sitting room and, behind that, off a short hall,

two bedrooms and a bathroom. It ought to be larger, but the plantation on the island had been in existence less than two years. It had
returned nothing yet on the investment. No sisal had been cut. His
job was to watch the stuff grow and see that the natives allowed it to
grow. He was a watchman, nothing more; no matter how he tried to
be more, he was simply a watchman. Anybody could do the job as
well.

Two bedrooms, he thought, and from now on both of them would
be used. Alma had made that clear at Couronne last night.

He recalled their conversation. She had left him on the veranda
having a nightcap with Jeff and Marian after a session of bridge, and
when he entered their room half an hour later she was in bed, looking
at a magazine. She had watched him undress. When his clothes were
off and he was groping in the wardrobe for his pajamas, she had said,
"There's something you ought to know. When we return to the island
I'm going to use the guest room."

It was the first time she had brought up the subject of his infidelity
since the night of the farewell party. He was startled, because after
throwing it up to him that night—"bombarding" him with it was the
word—she had gone into a long sulk. She was probably bringing
it up again now because they would be on their way back to Ile du
Vent in the morning.

He had put his pajamas on before turning to face her, then said in
a voice perfectly under control, "Are you going to tell me who told
you?"

"No, I'm not."

"It isn't hard for me to guess, you know."

"Guess, then."

"I already have. I already know."

"Do you?" she said. "Good. We won't have to discuss it then."

He took a step toward her. Damn her, didn't she know what
happened inside him when he saw her in a nightgown? She knew,
all right. When they were first married she'd made good use of the
knowledge, too. He'd always known when she wanted new clothes
or a trip to New Orleans or new furniture for the house. She didn't
come out with it as most women would. She made sure first he was
in the right mood, meaning a mood to give her anything she desired
in return for her love-making.

She'd had a thousand little tricks. She would call him into the
bedroom and let him surprise her with no clothes on, or almost none,
and then say, "Darling, I didn't mean you to jump right up. I meant

when you'd finished reading your paper." She'd ask for the loan of his razor after her bath and then call out, "I'm making a mess of this, dear. I wish you'd show me how to use it."

A thousand tricks. But when she didn't want him in that mood, it was a different story. He was oversexed. He was unnatural. He was a beast. What he needed was a machine, not a wife. That was how it had been in the beginning, when they had lived in Louisiana and he had worked for the sugar company there. That was still how it was when they had first come to St. Joseph after three years of marriage.

On Ile du Vent she had changed. There was nothing on the island she wanted. No shops with pretty clothes in them. No furniture stores. No neighbors' homes with bright new gadgets that she just had to duplicate. So there'd been no reason for her to play up to him. He was a beast *all* the time. He was someone to avoid.

But he always wanted her. Damn it, even then as she lay in bed with the magazine, her eyes mocking him, he had wanted her.

"This needn't be the end of the world, you know," he had said.

"Needn't it?"

"Other men make mistakes."

"Perhaps they do. But they're a little less casual about it, I hope. *And* a little more selective."

"Oh, for God's sake, Alma. Men and women are different. You ought to know that. You'd been giving me a hard time and this girl was there waiting and——"

"Oh, go to bed," she said, turning her back on him.

He stood for a moment undecided. If he got into bed with her, what would she do? No, he couldn't do that. It was too soon, much too soon. He'd have to wait. He retreated to his own bed, still gazing at her. He got into bed and put out the lamp on the table between them. He lay there in the dark looking up at the ceiling.

He could win her back. As time passed, this unpleasantness would recede in her mind and become less important. He shook his head, blowing a long breath out between tight lips. He was still dazed by what had happened.

It had happened because the girl in question, an island girl named Anita Something-or-other—he didn't even know her last name—had left Ile du Vent and gone to the mainland; and he hadn't known about it because he hadn't been seeing her lately. He certainly hadn't expected to find her working at the Fond Marie mission when he went there to have Peter Ambrose look at an infected finger.

And now Alma knew. She knew and would never forgive him, or

said she wouldn't. But of course she would, eventually. She was no saint herself, if there was any truth to the tales he'd heard when he first began dating her. There'd been other men before him. Any girl who worked in a textile mill and shared an apartment with another girl instead of living at home with her folks . . .

He looked across at her. "Alma, are you awake?"

"I don't want to talk."

"What I have to say won't take long."

"It won't take any time at all, because there's no point in your saying it." Her voice was deliberate, each syllable distinctly enunciated. "So you listen to me instead. If you have any ideas of a reconciliation, forget them. There isn't going to be one—not this time. Touch me and I'll scream until every soul in this house comes running to find out what's wrong, and when I've got an audience I'll tell them. Do I make myself clear?"

Very clear, he thought, feeling his lips flatten against his teeth. He didn't answer her. She was capable of doing exactly what she said.

But they wouldn't be here after tonight. Tomorrow they would be returning to the island.

HE WALKED THROUGH THE HOUSE to make sure nothing had been disturbed during their absence. He spoke to Alberse, the houseboy, about putting his things away when the beach boys brought them up. It was not up to him to go out to the cook house and tell Renée, the cook, what to prepare for lunch; that was Alma's job. He waited for her to do it. Then he went out.

He walked toward the western tip of the island, through the plantation. It was only just after eleven o'clock—they had left Couronne early—but the day was already hot. Every day was hot in this miserable place. He followed a footpath through a sea of young sisal plants that stretched from just above the shore to halfway up the ridge. Small green lizards sat on the rubbery leaves and cocked their heads to watch him pass.

He looked about, admiring his handiwork. The sisal was well planted and well looked after; he was proud of it. It was a bloody shame, of course, to use the best soil on the island for a crop that would do nearly as well in poor stuff. Especially when the islanders were half starved. But that was Couronne's business, not his. Some big-shot politician in the capital had heard that Couronne wanted to expand, and had offered them the place here at a price they couldn't afford to turn down. That was how it went in St. Joseph. No matter how desperately the peasants needed something, there was always a big shot in a position to put his own needs above theirs. A month after the deal had gone through, this one had been riding around the capital in a new Cadillac with gold-plated horns mounted on its fenders. It was a good thing there were no roads on Ile du Vent to tempt him to bring it here. The people would probably throw every loose stone on the island at it.

He looked back. He had reached the end of the planted area, where the ruler-straight rows of sisal gave way to peasant plantings of plantains. The house was out of sight. He followed a path through the plantains to a native *caille*. A woman sat on a chair beside the doorway, tipped back so that the wall of the hut supported her shoulders. Her eyes were closed, but they opened as he halted before her.

"*Comment sa, commère?* I'd like to speak to Tina."

"Tina, *m'sieu?* She is not here."

Damn, Lemke thought. All this walk for nothing. "Why isn't she here? I told her I'd be back today!"

"*M'sieu*, it is not her fault. She had to visit her sister beyond Terre Rouge, who is expecting a baby."

"When will she return?"

"Who knows? Who can tell when a baby will arrive or how long the mother will need help afterward? Of course, if it is important I can send someone for her."

"Never mind," Lemke grumbled. He looked about him. Since he had come this far and would get nothing out of it but exercise, he might as well walk back along the shore. He might find a shell or two. Alma could say what she liked about him, call him a beast, accuse him of having a mind that was always in the gutter, but he had a damned fine collection of shells. She had to admit that.

He took his time. The coast here was a succession of short strips of sand separated by clumps of mangroves. The path turned inland at each mangrove cluster. The bushes grew close together in a solid bright-green mass, and the tangles of twisted roots were impossible to get through. He found a tiny, almost perfect conch and dropped it into his pocket. Two beaches farther on he picked up a pink shell the size of a half dollar, that he could not identify. He must get a book some day.

He stopped. He had come round a tangle of mangroves to still another small beach. He had been thinking about Tina, how he would have to be more careful or Alma would find out about that one, too.

The word "divorce" might rear its ugly head if she did, and Jeff Barnett might not be pleased. He'd have to go slow. As a matter of fact, a man was crazy to play around with these peasant girls. He ought to cut it out altogether. Maybe he would. Sooner or later, if he didn't, there'd be the devil to pay in the form of some wild-eyed boy friend with a machete.

He'd cut it out, that's what he would do. Never again. That was a promise to himself, a solemn promise. Never again. Never.

On the beach before him were three women. One was on the beach, at any rate; the others were in the water. Those in the water had a thing like a laundry tray: a piece of wood three feet long, hollowed out like a flat-bottom boat. They were walking into the sea with it, pulling it between them. It didn't contain laundry. He could see a bottle of kola, a glass, a plate with a knife, fork, spoon, and napkin on it. He could make out a circular slab of cassava bread and some fruit.

He remembered witnessing once a service to Agué, the god of the sea, in which a similar wooden tray—a *barque*, they called it—had been set adrift by the people of Petit Trou to insure the safety of the fishermen. This must be something of the same sort, though smaller.

He watched the two women walk the laden tray into the sea. They were crones, both of them. One was at least seventy. They wore dresses made of feed bags. The water climbed to their hips, their breasts. One of them reached for the kola bottle and the other, with an angry outburst, slapped at her hand.

An argument ensued, the two crones standing in the sea screaming at each other with the tray between them. Suddenly Lemke's attention was drawn to the one on shore. He had not been watching her. He took in a breath.

She had silenced the two crones with an angry shout of her own. Now she was stripping off her dress. He noticed the dress for the first time. It was an attractive cotton print. Birds. No, not birds; butterflies. She dropped the garment on the sand and strode into the sea, naked as Eve. Handsome as Eve, too. By God, she was handsome. Her breasts didn't bounce as she forced her way through the water; they rippled. She swung her hips from side to side. Her thighs rippled. She was young. It was something to watch.

Lemke's mouth had gone dry. He wet his lips with his tongue but never took his gaze off the girl. She strode into the sea as if it were her home and she were returning to it. He fully expected her to arch that gorgeous body in a graceful dive and disappear. But she didn't dive. She halted between the two crones and spoke to them sharply. She took the wooden boat from their hands. The crones fell back, silently watching her.

She dipped a handful of sea-water and tossed it in four directions, intoning some chant or prayer that Lemke could not hear well enough to interpret. She poured kola into her palm and repeated the gesture. Replacing the kola bottle, she gave the boat a little push, watched it glide out of reach, then crossed herself, spoke angrily again to the two crones, and strode back to the beach. She snatched up her dress and pulled it over her head.

Without waiting for the crones, she turned and marched up the beach. A clump of *malfini* bushes swallowed her from sight, the almond-shaped fruit trembling in a phantom dance to mark the way she had gone.

Lemke wet his lips again. My God, he thought. My God. He waited for the two crones to come out of the water and then strolled down to greet them. He was very polite. He was so polite that they giggled.

"What have you been doing?"

"Nothing, *m'sieu*. Only a little offering to Agué for the protection of the children. One was attacked by a shark two days ago."

"The child was hurt?"

"Only a little, *m'sieu*. But badly frightened."

"That's something to be thankful for," Lemke said. "Tell me, who was the girl who just left?"

"She came from Terre Rouge to help us."

"Oh? What's her name?"

"Micheline Laroche, *m'sieu*. She is a sister of Catus Laroche, the *houngan*."

Micheline Laroche, Lemke repeated to himself as he resumed his walk. I'll remember that.

ALMA LEMKE finished her instructions to the cook and returned to the house, stopping at the refrigerator in the hall to fill a glass with ice. It was a kerosene refrigerator. There would be no generator at the Ile du Vent plantation until a processing plant was built. In the sitting room she added rum and soda to the ice. Then she sat on the veranda and let herself relax.

Home again, such as it was. Where had Warner gone?

There would be a divorce eventually, she supposed. She was in no particular hurry, provided Warner left her alone. She didn't hate Ile du Vent as he did; it was as good as any other place. Anyway, if the price of sisal kept slumping, they probably would be recalled to Fond Marie. There was no sense trying to foresee problems and solve them in advance. People drove themselves crazy that way. Live from day to day, that was the thing to do. Make the best of a bad situation. As Warner Lemke's wife she had no future.

Her drink was finished. She always drank the first one fast. She thought about getting up for another but felt lazy and called the houseboy instead.

"Fix me a drink, Alberse, will you? Rum-soda."

"*Oui, madame.*"

"Alberse."

He swung back to face her.

"Do you know where *M'sieu* Lemke went?"

"No, *madame.*"

"All right. Fix me a drink."

Why had she married Warner in the first place? She shrugged, knowing the answer well enough. She had been too young to see past his good looks and know what he really was like. She had been bored with her job in the mill, desperate for a change, and Warner was a good-looking boy with an expensive car and a good salary. He'd been a football hero in college and had a scrapbook full of pictures and clippings. That was enough at the start to put him head and shoulders above anyone else she was likely to land.

Later, when he had taken her to Ohio to meet his folks, she had been thrilled. That was the word, *thrilled.* His folks were wonderful. They really were. His mother was a sweet, white-haired woman right out of one of those small-town movies where people talked for hours and nothing ever happened. His father sold insurance and thought "darn" was a swear word. They had a big white house that must have been a hundred years old but still looked expensive and had called her "daughter" before they knew her name well enough to remember it. Some contrast to her own folks and her own home. Brother.

But it hadn't worked out. Whatever it was Warner wanted, it was something she couldn't give him, something no one woman could give him. He was the kind of man who had to keep on proving himself with one conquest after another. There had been other women in the States when he worked for the sugar company there before coming to the islands. He thought she didn't know. She knew, all right. There had always been other women, beginning with that red-haired trollop in his office less than a month after they were married. There always would be other women.

"Okay, Alberse. Thanks."

She drank half the second rum-soda and went to the end of the veranda to see if she could see him. He wasn't in sight.

"Oh, Alberse."

"*Oui, madame?*"

"I'm going to move my things into the guest room. I'll need some help."

"Now, *madame?*" The boy's face was a study in lack of expression, as blank as the plywood ceiling.

"Now."

They worked for twenty minutes, carrying her possessions across the hall. When the job was done, she went to the veranda again. Still no sign of Warner. Sisal, that was all she could see: long, straight rows of sisal plants. Pretty, sort of, if you didn't mind the monotony of it. Turn your head slowly and the lines seemed to turn with it, like spokes on a revolving wheel. She turned to get the effect. A boy in a white shirt and khaki trousers was standing at the foot of the steps.

"*Bon jour, madame.*" He raised a hand as if to tip his hat, though he wore none.

She said "Good morning" and frowned at him. "I've seen you before. Who are you?"

"Pradon Beliard, *madame*. I work for Mr. Barnett at Fond Marie."

"That must be it. I've seen you there. What do you want?"

"Is Mr. Lemke here, *madame?*"

"No."

Pradon seemed disappointed. "Will he return soon, perhaps?"

"I suppose so. I don't know."

"If I may wait——"

She only shrugged, and Pradon went to the mango tree and sat in its deep green shade, looping his arms about his knees. She watched him for a moment, then shrugged again and returned to her chair.

Five minutes later Warner Lemke came along the path from the beach. The boy rose to greet him.

They talked for some time by the tree. The woman on the veranda could not hear much of what was said; only an unconnected word or two. Pradon used the word *bête* several times. He used the word *diable*. He mentioned a sum of money, so many *gourdes*. Whatever it was about, it was apparently funny. Pradon grinned and her husband laughed aloud.

Toward the end, Warner did all the talking. She could not hear him, his voice was too deep to reach the veranda, but she saw his lips moving and could tell that Pradon, his back to her, was intently listening. Warner took money from a billfold and gave it to the boy. He laid a hand on the boy's shoulder in dismissal. Pradon went down the path and Warner came to the house.

"Why the secrecy?" Alma asked as he climbed the steps.

He leered at her. "Wouldn't you like to know?"

"Of course I'd like to know. I live here, don't I? What was he saying about a beast and a devil?"

He halted in the doorway on his way into the house. "I don't seem to remember. Maybe he was telling me that all women are beasts and devils. Present company excepted, of course."

"Of course." She finished her drink and stood up. "Are you ready for lunch?"

"When I've had a drink and washed."

She thought she knew where he had been. "Do wash," she said. "Thoroughly."

"Don't be a bitch."

She went to tell Renée they were ready. Warner poured himself a rum and downed it, then strolled down the hall to the bathroom. A glance into the bedroom, as he passed, told him his wife had made good her threat to move across the hall. He shut the bathroom door behind him with force enough to rattle the bottles of medicine on the shelf.

His face in the mirror above the wash basin glowered back at him; then his scowl changed to a grin. It had been quite a morning. First that girl on the beach, Micheline Laroche, and now the good word from Pradon Beliard. Quite a morning. He had an idea he would be a very busy man from now on. Much too busy to care a damn whether his dear wife approved of him or not.

7

O N SUNDAY MORNING the Reverend Arthur Barry Clinton counted
seventeen persons in church and was delighted. Not bad for
his first week on the island, he told himself.

More than half of them were people he had treated at the clinic—he
now thought of his office as such—during the past five days. He had
treated more than these, of course. Many more. About half of them
had only thought they were sick, and some of the others had been
very sick indeed. Yaws, mostly. It was a lucky thing that yaws could
be arrested with a good jolt of penicillin; otherwise he would have had
his hands full. He wondered what he would do about the armless
little girl who had so pitifully begged him to make her like other
people. Perhaps that school for handicapped children in the capital . . .

He surveyed his congregation again. Lucille, of course, was present.
So were big Louis César and his wife Dauré, the little magistrate
from Petit Trou, Micheline Laroche, and Alma Lemke. The latter
two puzzled him. He certainly hadn't expected the *houngan's* sister,
and as for the Lemke woman, she was the last person in the world
he would have thought interested in things spiritual. He had met her
at Couronne affairs and always felt slightly uncomfortable in her
presence. She seemed to think every man she talked to or danced with
was secretly longing to be her lover. And what would her husband
think of her being here? Warner despised clerics, or said he did. To
the great football hero, men of the church were odd ducks, not
entirely masculine. Well, he was glad Alma had come, even though
her presence in church was a real surprise. As a matter of fact, he
hadn't been aware that she and her husband were back from Fond
Marie.

He tried to hide his pleasure under a mask of sternness. "Many
others should be here," he said, wondering vaguely what old Leander
Mitchell had done with his time during his months on the island.
"Apparently some were afraid to incur the displeasure of"—he was

going to say "a certain individual whom they fear" but changed his mind in midsentence; why beat about the bush, after all?—"of Catus Laroche. This puzzles me. I have talked with Catus. We have a gentlemen's agreement. I feel sure that if he had forbidden anyone to come here this morning, he would have been forthright enough to tell me so."

There was, of course, no answer.

"I welcome those of you who are here," he went on, taking pains to include them all in his gaze. "Especially the two sisters of the man mentioned. Their presence would seem to prove my belief that Catus issued no orders."

That was enough of that, he decided. He hoped they would notice he had cleaned the church.

He had, in fact, spent hours cleaning it and was proud of the results. With Louis' help, after the garden on the ridge was planted, he had even knocked some rectangular openings in the walls to let in light. The only real remedy, of course, would be a new church in a location where there was a breeze to be let in too, but he knew what the Bishop would say to that. Still, this was better than it had been. The windows lent a feeling of airiness, even though the atmosphere was still a mass of hot cotton. The floor and benches were clean, the altar and rail had been scrubbed, and the church had lost its look of neglect.

He led his little congregation in some of the hymns from the Creole hymnbook, selected after a talk with Lucy. If he ever did get a new church, he would have to find an organ for it, he told himself; hymns without an organ lacked something. One of those little ones with the pedals would do. Peter Ambrose managed nicely with one at Fond Marie, and they were not expensive. He'd have to play it himself, he supposed. The sour notes would certainly fly. But the peasants did love music . . .

He talked to them about the conversion of Paul. Paul, he pointed out, had been a good deal like someone they well knew, misunderstanding the church and stubbornly setting himself against those who carried on its work. Yet God had found a way to reach into his heart and win him over. He hoped they understood what he was driving at, and watched them for a clue.

Their faces told him nothing. Lucy, on the bench directly in front of him, sat with her long hands clasped in her lap and her back straight as a stick; she was the new Father's housekeeper and let there be no doubting it. She wasn't wearing her Sunday dress but the new one she had bought with the money he had given her: a hideous pink thing that came halfway to her ankles. She wore new shoes as well, and had had her hair done. He had watched the hair operation yesterday afternoon, from his office. For two solid hours she had sat statue-still on a kitchen chair under the campêche tree while some girl from the village, hardly more than a child, had fussed over her. The result was a beehive sort of thing that made the old girl look like an African jungle queen.

The others were only slightly less expressionless. His gaze traveled over them and he catalogued Louis César as hot and bored, Dauré as bewildered, the little magistrate as faintly amused, the islanders only curious.

Of Catus Laroche's sister he could make nothing. It was folly to guess at what went on behind those remarkable eyes. She never once looked directly at him as he spoke. Yet she was never still. He sensed that she was aware of his every word and gesture, even aware that she held his attention a good part of the time. Little things she did, like taking a slow deep breath that caused her white dress to tighten over her breasts; letting a shoulder droop; languidly reaching down to rub an ankle . . . all of it was deliberate, he was certain.

And Alma Lemke—what was on *her* mind? Leander Mitchell hadn't mentioned the Lemkes, but if they were in the habit of attending services now and then, it would be a great boost for the church. A plantation manager was a man of influence, a lot bigger in the social scheme than a new minister.

Her costume struck him as odd for church. Trousers, of all things. Her blouse was modest enough, a long-sleeved affair with a sort of collar—but trousers! He was puzzled, even a bit shocked, until he realized suddenly that she must have come on horseback; the plantation was a journey of several miles. He smiled at his stupidity. She saw him and smiled back.

When it came time for the offering, he asked Felix Dufour, whose white trousers gleamed this morning, to pass the plate, and led a hymn while the little man did so. The plate when returned to him contained five small coins and two single dollar bills. Alma had dropped one of the bills in, he guessed. The other had come from Dufour himself. He nodded solemnly at the magistrate before turning to the altar. At least there was one honest man on Ile du Vent.

"Praise God from whom all blessings flow," he sang, and was pleased to hear them singing with him. Then, as the service drew to a close, he heard the drums.

He stood motionless before the altar, aware that his little congregation was watching him and waiting to see what he would do. They must have known, of course. All of them but Alma Lemke, at any rate. Sunday morning was no usual time for a *vodun* service. Most unusual, in fact. To hold one at such a time, Catus would have had to announce his intentions beforehand. He let his gaze travel from one face to another. On Lucy's he saw indignation. Louis César and his wife seemed embarrassed. Dufour gazed innocently at the underside of the iron roof.

He frowned at Micheline. She was adjusting the neckline of her dress.

He was very angry. "The grace of Our Lord Jesus Christ, and the love of God, and the fellowship of the Holy Ghost, be with us all evermore. Amen." He knelt for a moment, trembling in his anger, rose from his knees, and strode down the aisle in silence. Without looking back he crossed the clearing to the rectory at a fast walk. His hands still shook as he removed his vestments and hung them up.

When he had drunk a glass of water he went out again, carrying the saddle and bridle he had bought from Dufour and striding a straight line to the edge of the clearing where the gray mule was tethered. His congregation stood outside the church, watching him.

He saddled the mule quickly and swung his leg over. It was a bit like a scene from a Western movie, he thought: the crowd standing tense and silent, watching the young sheriff mount his trusty horse to ride out and hurl his challenge at the forces of evil. He gave the animal his heels and it reared under him, pawing the air with its forefeet, then answered his knees and took off at a run. It was a good mule, a bit hard to manage but strong and sound. Perhaps they were waiting to see if it would give him a bad time. Only Lucy knew that he had been on its back before, putting it through its paces around the clearing.

HE HAD NO TROUBLE locating the ceremony. The sound of the drums would have led him to it even if he had not known where the *hounfor* was. Dismounting at the gate in the cactus hedge, he tied the mule to a gatepost and hurried into the yard.

From a chair in the doorway of the Césars' house an old woman looked up at him in surprise. She was watching the child, he supposed, while the parents were at church. She said nothing and he went past with a nod.

Directly in front of him was a packed crowd of people.

He halted. A propulsive mixture of anger and curiosity had carried him this far. He had not thought of danger. Now he hesitated. The crowd filled an enclosure a hundred feet long and thirty or forty wide under a roof of thatch supported by poles, and swelled out toward him into the yard. To see what was going on in the center he would have to force his way through.

He could leave if he wished. He had not been seen yet. Every back was toward him.

He hesitated only a second, then stepped forward and used his hands. "Let me through, please." It was rather comical. They turned in anger to see who was pushing them, saw who it was, and made way for him. He had only to keep reaching and saying "Let me through, please." Then he saw a ring of white-robed women moving with quick, jerky steps about a painted central post, and geometric designs faintly outlined in white on the dark earth, and drummers bent over their instruments. He was aware of having propelled himself into a whirlpool of sound that deafened him. The women were chanting. The drumbeats bounced off him like blows. He came to a dead stop, confused and out of breath, not knowing which way to turn.

Catus Laroche in a bright red shirt moved leisurely toward him. The drummers and dancers went on without missing a step or a beat but watched to see what would happen. The crowd through which he had forced his way closed in behind him, shutting off any possibility of retreat.

Catus said, "Good morning, Father. This is unexpected."

Barry wished the drums would be still for a moment. What a religion! How could they know what they were doing in such a din? How could they think? He turned his back to the drummers and looked at the *houngan*'s outthrust hand. He accepted it. You had to shake hands.

"What do you mean, holding a *vodun* service on Sunday morning?" he demanded. But his challenge had no force. It conveyed nothing of his indignation. To have spoken in anger above the thunder of the drums he would have had to scream and make himself ridiculous. The drums effectively reduced his words to a simple question.

Catus shrugged. "This is a special kind of service, Father."

"What special kind?"

"Yesterday my sister's child walked on her injured foot. This is our way of thanking the *loa* for saving her."

"Thanking the *loa?*" Blast the drums, Barry thought. How could you make a tone of voice mean anything?

Catus smiled at his discomfiture and lifted a hand. The tumult diminished. The drummers still bent over their instruments, their hands were still a swift blur, but the sound dropped to a murmur. It was as though, by raising his hand, Catus had turned the dial on an overloud record player.

"You were saying, Father?"

Barry looked about him. They were all watching. The circle of faces had come closer. The dancers were barely moving their feet. He and Catus might have been actors on a stage before an audience hanging on every word.

"You know very well what saved your sister's child," he said sharply.

"Certainly. You did, Father."

"Then why a demonstration such as this? Why couldn't you have come to church this morning and said your thanks properly?"

"Because, Father, we are not sure who guided you in your efforts. Perhaps it was the God you believe in; perhaps it was one of ours. Try to understand, please. If it was one of the *loa* who told you what to do, and we neglected to show our gratitude, there could be trouble not only for the child but for all of us. Perhaps even for you."

Barry looked into the *houngan's* face and saw no mockery. "You can't believe that."

"We do believe it. We have no wish to offend you. All we do here is offer thanks."

Barry shut his eyes for a moment and sighed. Would he ever understand these people? Ever reach them? They were still children; one could not reason with children. He looked again at the silent crowd. He could not be angry. He fashioned a wry smile.

"How? How do you offer thanks?"

Catus spoke to someone behind him. A chair was brought and the *houngan* invited Barry to sit. "I can't promise you the *loa* will come," he said. "In this case we don't know which one we owe thanks to, and may not have drawn the correct *vevé* or performed the proper invocation. There are many *loa*. But if we have done what is necessary, and the *loa* does come, you will see how we offer thanks. Unless, of course, you prefer to denounce us as superstitious savages, as *Père* Mitchell did. In that case I would not advise you to stay. The *loa* would surely be angry."

Barry sat. The chair had been placed some distance from the circle of dancing women, but he could see well enough. Catus, standing at his side, signaled the drummers and the sound was turned up full again. It became an uninterrupted thunder that crept through the hard-packed earth of the *tonnelle* floor to the soles of Barry's shoes and worked its way through the leather to his feet.

He would have heard it even if he were deaf, he told himself. He would have felt the rhythm of it in the air that pressed against his chest, in the wobbly arms of the chair he sat on, in his blood. He remembered having read somewhere that the secret of *vodun* "possessions"—the strange business of a participant's thinking himself "mounted" by a god—lay in the hypnotic effect of the drumming. It could easily be true. In so many of these primitive religions drumming played a major role. The sound did something to one's mind. There was no question of it.

He watched the three men at the drums and thought of the few times he had attended folklore performances in the capital. The drums there had been eloquent too, but not like this; there was a difference. At the folklore he had admired the drummers' technique, their showmanship. Here he sensed in them a fanatical devotion to the assigned task.

There were three drums. The man at the largest made thunder with a hammer-shaped stick and his empty left hand. The one at the smaller central drum used a bow-shaped length of wood and a straight one. The smallest instrument was played with two slender sticks, rat-a-tat, rat-a-tat, in a nervous, rapid rhythm that never varied. The blended tones were overwhelming: an awesome thunder, a rhythm that forced one to respond to it, a relentless chattering staccato that set the nerves on edge. He wanted to scream at the players to stop. He wanted them never to stop.

Catus had joined the dancers. It was not hard to follow his movements; the red shirt among the white robes was a blaze of color, a flag. Barry was lost in admiration watching it. At the folklore performances the dancers played to the audience, seeking applause, but Catus cared nothing for this audience. His dancing obsessed him. He had begun to spin and weave the moment he stepped through the ring of women. Now he whirled about the central post like a blur of scarlet paint spun in a bowl. He was a whirling flame. Without the red shirt to mark his passing he would have been only a spinning cone of shadow. It was incredible.

The ring of women had widened to give him room. A girl stumbled over Barry's foot, caught herself and glanced at him with a foolish grin. The dance carried her away from him and he watched her, wondering. Had she been drinking? Perhaps that was the answer. He had read somewhere that there was little or no drinking at genuine *vodun* services, but it was hard to know what to believe. So much nonsense was written about *vodun*. And rum or *clairin* would explain so much of this . . .

The women had come full circle again, with Catus a scarlet streak in the center and the sound of the drums growing louder with every beat. Suddenly one of the dancers threw her arms wide and became rigid, her body balanced on wide-spread legs and head flung back as though her back would break. She was directly in front of him. He pushed himself sideways to get out of her way. His chair tipped. He would have fallen to the ground had not a hand caught the back of his chair and held it. He turned his head. Micheline stood behind him.

She paid him no attention beyond holding the chair until she was sure he had recovered his balance. Her gaze was fixed on the stricken dancer. It was the same girl, Barry saw then, who had stumbled over his foot.

Therein lay the miracle. She had drawn his attention to herself before—unwittingly, he was certain—by stumbling against him. He had looked into her face and thought her drunk. If not a drunken face, it had been a stupid one. Now before his eyes she changed.

Her rigidity vanished and she stood poised, swaying, her whole body undulating in rhythmic motion. She grew taller. It was no illusion; it had nothing to do with the drumming or the effect on his senses of Catus' incredible dancing; the girl grew taller. Inches taller. Her face lost its youthful stupidity and coarseness and became more mature, more serene, a thing of strange beauty. It was like a movie trick happening before his eyes, close enough for him to touch. Everyone in the place was aware of it. The drummers let their frantic hands flutter to a halt as they watched. Catus Laroche stopped whirling. A stillness flowed over the spectators.

The girl turned to Catus and extended her hands. He looked into her eyes, frowning at her. She gestured impatiently. He took her hands and held them.

She spoke softly, and Barry strained to catch what she said. He heard her but did not understand. It was a puzzling thing. She spoke Creole, or what sounded like Creole, but he could not translate it. She continued to speak. The *tonnelle* was a place of statues and held breath. Somewhere outside a dog barked. Another answered, farther off. Barry felt a shiver begin at his knees and travel to his shoulders, down his arms to the tips of his fingers. The girl turned to look at him.

Step by step, still murmuring the Creole-sounding words that were not Creole, the girl led Catus Laroche to the chair on which Barry sat. Step by step Catus permitted it, his own face shining with sweat and his bare feet dragging themselves over the ground. The girl looked at Barry and spoke again. Barry understood nothing. Catus fell to his knees in front of her, violently trembling.

For a moment the *houngan* knelt there, gazing up at her. His eyes rolled. Flecks of foam ran from the corners of his mouth. Suddenly his shoulders moved spasmodically and he dropped his head, pressing his lips to the ground at Barry's feet. Barry recoiled from him. The girl in the white dress stepped back.

Behind him Micheline whispered fiercely, "Stand up! Greet her!"

He rose. It was impossible not to. "I—*moi dit bon jour*," he stammered.

The girl exhaled a long, shuddering sigh and Catus Laroche rose from his knees to peer into her face. Her features lost their strange beauty. She was dull-witted again. Catus took her by an arm and led her away. At once the drummers recommenced their infernal pounding.

Micheline said quietly, "You may sit down again, *mon Père*. It is all right now. Aïda Ouedo has gone."

He obeyed. He fumbled a handkerchief from his pocket and wiped his face, and the handkerchief came away soaked. Dazed, he watched the women in white bustling about at some sort of ritual involving the preparation and cooking of food, but in his mind all he could see was Catus Laroche kissing the ground between his dusty shoes. The rest, whatever it signified, was anticlimax. He supposed it was the actual thank-you offering to the god for saving the child, or for helping him to save her.

The atmosphere of the ceremony had changed. There was laughter now. Catus returned, followed by the girl. She at once dropped onto a chair and sprawled there, grotesquely limp and seemingly asleep. No one seemed interested in her any more. Men and women faced each other, hands on hips, shuffling their feet in time to the drumming. Catus came toward him, scowling.

"Well, Father?"

An hour ago I was in church, Barry thought with a touch of panic. I was saying the benediction . . .

"Is it finished? May I go now?"

"You may go now. Perhaps you would like some coffee? Micheline would be glad to make you some."

"No. No, thank you." He wanted to leave. It seemed important to get away from here, to go home. Yet something held him. Something kept him standing there, staring into the *houngan's* face.

"I don't understand this, Catus."

"If I may call on you this afternoon," Catus said, "I will try to explain."

He nodded. That was it: a long talk in the peace and quiet of the rectory. Questions and answers. He felt immensely relieved.

When he left, some of them spoke to him. The service was finished; the dancing now was a social affair and people had drifted into the yard. They stood around in groups. Some of those who spoke were people he had greeted on his walks to the village to see the sick child, people who had ignored him. Something had altered their attitude. Was it his work at the clinic or the the thing that had happened just now at the service? Or was it simply that he had come *to* the service? He would never understand these people.

At the gate he paused to wipe his face again with his handkerchief. He would be glad to get home. A shower, a chance to sit and think . . . He felt as though he had been drugged. Outside the gate a crowd of children had gathered, filling the path. The gate itself was a montage of round eyes peering at him. Go away, he thought. Go away, please. Leave me alone.

They fell back as he opened the barrier and stepped through. Kids of all ages, from toddlers up. He made pushing motions at them with his hands, said "Scat!" and turned his back on them to untie the mule. He turned the mule and put a foot in the stirrup.

He had no premonition of disaster. He had shooed the children back and was concentrating on getting into the saddle, an awkward task with the mule stepping sideways, forcing him against the cactus hedge with its inch-long thorns. He saw a boy dart from the group on the outside of the path but was putting a leg over the saddle and trying to turn the mule's head.

He felt the beast lunge under him. He heard a noise, the sound a heavy fruit might make on falling to the ground from a tree. The children screamed and pointed to something behind him.

He threw himself out of the saddle and saw the boy lying there in the path, at the base of the hedge. He saw blood. The mule had swung its rump against the hedge and he had to push it aside to get through. As he did so the beast kicked out again, missing him by a scant inch.

He ducked past and pulled the fallen child out of range, yelling at the others to keep away. Only then did he see the handkerchief. It must have fallen from his pocket in his struggle to mount. The boy had run behind the mule to pick it up for him.

He used the handkerchief to wipe away some of the blood, and felt a tightening in his throat. Good Lord, this was serious. The boy's chest looked as though a boulder had fallen on it. There were broken ribs, surely; perhaps worse. The lad was unconscious.

He stood up with him and turned toward the gate. The mule had gone down the path a little way. The children were silent now, watching him. The grown-ups were hurrying from the *vodun* service.

Dauré César reached him first. "What is it, *mon Père?* What happened?" She looked at the boy in his arms and her eyes widened. "God in heaven!"

"My mule kicked him. I need help." He must have instruments and medicines. He must make a complete examination.

Her husband, big Louis, pushed through to her side. Barry laid the boy in his arms. "Carry him to the rectory for me, Louis. Be gentle. He has broken ribs. But hurry." He could do nothing here. There were fifty people crowding around now, all trying to see, all talking at once. He plucked at Louis' sleeve and hurried down the path.

The mule blocked the path, tearing up mouthfuls of the tough grass at its edge. He caught the bridle and jerked its head up and could have sworn he saw triumph in the mean eyes that returned his gaze. He led it from the path so Louis could pass without danger, then handed the animal off to a sturdy peasant who looked capable.

"Take care of him for me, please."

The fellow said morosely, "There is only one way to take care of this *bête diable*. With a machete!"

Pretending he had not heard, Barry hurried after big Louis.

8

ALMA LEMKE WAS WAITING in his office, sitting on the cot he had placed there for his patients. He nodded but went past her quickly to draw aside the curtain, so that Louis might carry the injured boy into the bedroom. As he scrubbed his hands at the washstand, Alma watched him from the doorway.

"What happened?"

He told her briefly. When he turned from the washstand she had entered the room and was bending over the bed. "It looks bad," she said. "Is it as bad as it looks?"

"I hope not."

Lucille came in. Someone must have told her the story, for with scarcely a glance at the boy she said crisply, "Dufour is to blame for this. He knew that mule was a devil when he sold you the beast." When Barry failed to answer, she went on in a bitter tone, "It's partly my fault, too. I should have warned you. But you seemed able to handle the animal."

"Heat some water, please, Lucy," he said.

He worked over the boy for half an hour, with Alma and big Louis silently watching him and Lucy trotting back and forth between bedroom and kitchen. So far as he could determine, there were three ribs fractured. It was not too disastrous then, provided there were no other injuries. The boy's breathing made him anxious. But for the moment, at least, he could do no more.

He rose from the edge of the bed and moved to a chair, momentarily exhausted. "Who is he, Louis? What is his name?"

"Toto Anestor, *mon Père*. He lives in the village with a no-good aunt who never takes care of him. His parents were drowned three or four years ago when a boat turned over in the channel."

"How old is he?"

"I think about nine or ten."

"He is badly hurt," Barry said gravely. "I'm not sure how badly, but even if there are no injuries that I can't see, he will have to stay here for some time. If there are internal injuries I may have to take him to Fond Marie. Can you stay for a little while, Louis? I may need you."

Louis said, "I will wait outside, *mon Père*," and left the room. When Lucy followed him, Barry turned to Alma Lemke. It seemed a long time ago that he had discovered her in church and been surprised to see her there. Had all this really happened in only an hour or so?

He drew a breath. He had wanted a shower, he remembered. He had wanted to sit and think. Half an hour ago he had thought that if he could not sit and think, he would explode.

"I'm glad you're here," he said. "You don't know what it means to have someone"—he groped for the word—"someone from one's own world on hand at such a time."

She frowned. "I stayed to find out what was happening. The drums. The way you dashed off. If there's anything I can do——"

"There's nothing to be done. Not now, anyway. We wait and watch."

She sat down. There were just the two of them in the room now. "I suppose you're wondering why I came to church this morning," she said. Why *had* she come, she asked herself. To satisfy a woman's curiosity? To get away from Warner for a time? She certainly hadn't come for the service. Even as a child she had never gone to church.

"I did wonder. You hadn't mentioned being a member of old Mitchell's congregation."

"I wasn't."

"Why did you come, then?"

"For something to do, I suppose. And to see how you'd get along at your first service. Were you nervous?"

"I might have been, if there'd been more people."

She looked idly about the room. How could a man live in such a cell, she wondered. It wasn't big enough to turn around in. How could he stand it? For that matter, how could he endure his job? What possessed a man to make him give up everything worth while in the world and devote his life to preaching sermons to a lot of stupid people who didn't want to listen?

Of course, he wasn't just a preacher. He didn't just sit around all week as old Mitchell had done, waiting for Sundays to come so he could lecture on sin and salvation. This one was a worker. But even so, what satisfaction could he possibly find in it? The clinic, for instance? Did he actually enjoy looking after a lot of dirty black-skinned peasants? Didn't it bother him that they *were* black? It certainly would bother her. She mightn't hate her husband so fiercely if the girl hadn't been black.

She looked at Barry. What kind of man was he, anyway? His face held no answer. She couldn't picture it as the face of a saint, all radiant with dedication and noble sacrifice. Those rough, homely features belonged on a farmer. He looked more masculine than Warner, who considered himself very masculine indeed. Not a single thing about Barry Clinton fitted the mental picture she had of a sanctimonious cleric. Even in church he hadn't seemed especially religious.

The picture of him in church induced another one. "Who was the very attractive girl in the white dress this morning?" she asked. "The one who kept rearranging herself."

Barry had to smile at her description. "Her name is Laroche. Her brother is the big *houngan* here."

"It was her brother who interrupted the service, then? Those *were vodun* drums, weren't they?"

He nodded.

"Is that where you went when you dashed off on your mule?"

"I was angry with him."

"What happened when you confronted him?"

"Nothing, really." He was not anxious to discuss what had happened at the *tonnelle*. Not until he had talked it over with Catus, at least. He turned to the boy on the bed and listened to the lad's breathing for a moment. There seemed to be no change. "Am I to expect you in church every Sunday?" he asked then.

"Perhaps."

"With Warner?"

"Don't be silly." Her laughter was short, with a note of bitterness in it.

"You might try to persuade him. It would set a wonderful example for the people."

"My husband sets a different sort of example for the people," she said. "Let's skip him, shall we? He's my problem and I didn't come here to have you solve it for me. You've a few of your own just now."

He thought wryly, You don't know how right you are, and was aware that even while talking to her he had been thinking of other things. Of Catus Laroche. Of the hypocritical little politician in Petit Trou who had criminally sold him the mule. He certainly had no desire to be drawn into any marital squabble between Alma and her husband, if that was what it was.

The boy on the bed moved and made a moaning sound. Barry was over him instantly. The lad's mouth opened to exhale a noisy, bubbling sigh, and the bubbles were crimson.

He turned quickly to Alma. "Can I go across to the mainland on your launch?"

"Of course. You mean he's got to be taken over?"

Answering her with a nod, he hurried through the front room to the yard. Louis César was talking to Lucy in the kitchen doorway. "Louis!"

How on earth would he manage it? Big Louis would have to carry the child to the plantation; any attempt to ride him there on Alma's horse might cause irreparable damage. But what about transportation from the mainland landing place to Fond Marie, after he crossed the channel in the launch?

Alma answered the question for him. "I'll ride ahead and use the short wave," she said. She was looking at her watch. "We keep a schedule with Couronne at noon every day. I'll have them meet you on the mainland with a jeep."

"Can you ask them to pick up Peter? The sooner he sees the boy, the better." Dear God, whatever had made him think he was a doctor? At the moment he was utterly helpless, terrified. If young Toto's life depended on him, it would be the end of the boy.

He folded the bed sheet about his patient and fastened it with safety pins, lifted the lad gingerly, and placed him in big Louis' arms. "We're going to the plantation, Louis, and across to the mainland in the launch."

"Go straight to the plantation beach," Alma said from the doorway. "I'll meet you there."

CATUS LAROCHE was talking to his sister at the edge of the black shadow cast by the *tonnelle* roof. His hands were clenched.

"You were late for the service this morning because you went to the Father's church. Why did you go there?"

Micheline stood with her feet wide apart and her fists resting on her hips, a posture that only served to increase his anger because it made her look like a peasant woman arguing in the market place. That was how the *marchandes* always stood when shouting insults at one another.

"Why shouldn't I go there?"

"You are my sister!"

"Dauré is your sister too, isn't she? You're not angry with her for going."

"She went with Louis because the Father helped their child." Catus snatched her hands away from her hips and held her by the wrists. "You had no reason for going, except to defy me."

"I went because I wanted to."

"Why should you want to?"

She tossed her head. "I'm eighteen years old and have a mind of my own. I don't have to explain myself. If you want to fight him, that's your business, but you won't get me to fight him for you, no." A look of shrewdness came into her dark eyes. "Besides, how can *you* fight him after what happened at the service?"

"I'll fight any white man who looks at you!"

"Well, you needn't worry; he doesn't look at me. If you must know the truth, he doesn't know the difference between me and a donkey."

A husky peasant came into the yard, walking with a wary eye on a mule he was leading. It was a powerful beast, the color of dirty limestone mud, with a curled and twitching upper lip. His left hand gripped the bridle and his right held a stout *cocomacaque* stick. He looked nervous. Catus knew him. His name was Monestimé and he came from Petit Trou. He had been at the *vodun* service.

"The Father told me to take care of this animal," he said to Catus. "What am I supposed to do with it?"

Catus walked around the mule, frowning at it. "Isn't this the beast Felix Dufour bought in Anse Ange a couple of months ago?"

"It is."

"The one he never could ride? The one that broke the leg of that market woman?"

"The same."

"He said last week he was going to destroy it."

Monestimé showed his teeth in a crooked grin. "He found a better way to get rid of it. He sold it to the Father."

Catus stopped pacing and stood lost in thought for a moment. "Dufour should not have done that, no. To palm off a sick animal on an unsuspecting stranger might be considered smart, but to sell a beast that might kill someone—for a trick like that a man ought to be ashamed of himself."

"The day Dufour feels shame for anything he has done, I want to be around to see it," Monestimé said. "Only yesterday he doubled the tax in the market and threatened to triple it when the women protested. He thinks he owns Ile du Vent, Dufour does. Do you want the job of punishing him?"

"Tie the beast to the hedge over there, out of the way," Catus instructed. He did not discuss his thoughts with everyone who passed by. Let the others do the talking. He preferred to listen.

ALMA LEMKE was trying to establish contact with Jeff Barnett on the short wave when her husband came into the room. Warner sent a suspicious glance in her direction as he went to the little sitting-room bar for a drink.

"What the hell are you doing?" he demanded. "It isn't time for the schedule yet."

"I hoped Jeff might come on a few minutes early." She turned on her chair and told him about the injured boy.

His reaction surprised her. He had no particular love for the peasants, so far as she knew; yet when she described how the lad had received the injury—only repeating, of course, what Barry Clinton had told her—Warner stopped what he was doing at the bar and looked at her strangely, his face actually pale.

He finished pouring his drink and swallowed half of it at one gulp. "Who is this boy?" he asked. "Anyone important?"

"An orphan, I believe someone said."

"Oh." Her husband seemed relieved as he finished his drink and put the empty glass on the bar. "Well, tell Jeff about it and we'll get down to the beach. We may be able to lend a hand."

They had to wait ten minutes on the shore for Louis César and Barry to arrive. Alma watched her husband, puzzled by his behavior. He spent the time walking back and forth at the water's edge, frowning at the sand as though searching for shells. He glanced up at her only when some distance away. When he saw Barry coming along the beach, followed by Louis, he went to meet them and scowled at the big man's burden.

Alma hurried forward too. Only the boy's face could be seen. The rest of him was wrapped in the sheet. The sheet was wet with blood, the boy asleep or unconscious.

"How is he?" Warner asked.

"He needs attention quickly. Is the boat ready?"

"Is he in pain?"

"No. He's had morphine." Barry motioned Louis toward the pier where the plantation launch, a stubby, broad-beamed work craft with the word COURONNE on its stern, waited with its engine softly coughing. "Is Peter meeting us, do you know?" He put the question to Alma.

"Jeff promised to bring him," she said.

"Thank God." The relief was like a long drink of cold water after the forced march over the island trails from the rectory. Once, halting to examine the boy, he had thought him dead and been seized with panic.

He followed Louis out onto the pier, stepped into the boat, and reached up to take the youngster from the big man's arms. The boat boy watched, awaiting a signal to cast off. Louis hesitated on the pier.

"Come with me," Barry urged. "You can return when the launch does."

Louis stepped in and the craft rumbled out into the channel, Barry carefully holding the boy, Louis wide-legged beside him, the boat boy braced on bare feet at the wheel. Alma and Warner Lemke watched from the pier in silence.

It was some time before Lemke spoke. He said then, turning with a frown to his wife, "How did you get mixed up in this, anyway?"

"I was at church."

"Church, for Christ's sake!"

She looked at him without expression and turned away. "Perhaps for my sake. Who knows?"

ON HIS WAY THROUGH TERRE ROUGE to make himself useful at the Father's house, Pradon Beliard saw the gray mule in the yard of Catus Laroche and stopped. If the mule was there, the Father must be there too. He passed through the gate in the cactus hedge and made inquiries.

"No, the Father is not here," Dauré's mother, sitting in the doorway of the César house, told him. "There was an accident. He has gone to Fond Marie on the mainland."

Pradon questioned her. As she told him what had happened, he began to sweat. This was a bad thing, a very bad thing. There was going to be talk about it. People were going to blame Felix Dufour for selling *Père* Clinton a dangerous animal.

Pradon felt himself shaking. If people did blame Dufour, what was to prevent the magistrate from squirming out of it by revealing that Pradon Beliard had put him up to it? Something would have to be done about this, quickly.

There was only one thing that could be done. He knew that. The way to stop people from thinking about something was to give them something else, something more sensational, to think about. He murmured his farewells to the old woman and went on down the path to the village. By the time he reached the village proper he had stopped sweating and was nodding his head.

It was a Sunday. On a Sunday no one worked. The occupants of the houses sat about in the shade of the trees in their yards, bored with having nothing to do and hoping something would come along to relieve their boredom. Pradon stopped to talk. They were always glad when a passer-by did that. This business of the mule was something to talk about, too: a refreshing change from the usual discussion of bad crops and the weather. Pradon was glad he had put on a clean white shirt this morning and persuaded *maman* to run an iron over his trousers. A man well dressed was one to be looked up to and listened to with respect, even if he *had* been born with one leg shorter than the other.

He talked by asking questions of his own. Oh, such innocent questions. Wasn't it a terrible thing, what had happened to young Toto? Such a good boy, too. An accident, of course. But what could the Father have been thinking of, to leave a notoriously dangerous animal on a main path where it was almost certain to hurt someone? Of course, he may not have known the beast was ill-tempered, but he had owned that mule for several days, hadn't he? How could he not have known? He had been riding mules for years, no? A man shouldn't be so thoughtless of others. Really he shouldn't.

He spoke gravely with just the right amount of head-shaking. It wasn't necessary to be insistent or indignant. Just plant a thought or two and pass on to the next yard. He knew these people. The peasant mind was an amusing instrument. Drop an idea into it, and in a short time its owner would forget where the idea came from and be absolutely certain he had thought it up himself. Then, puffed with pride for his mental offspring, he would hasten to show it off to his neighbors.

Pick the right people, say the right things, and you could start a rumor on Ile du Vent in no time. And once it was set in motion, nothing short of a bigger and better story could stop it. So, of course, you made your story big in the first place. You stuffed it with mysterious hints and innuendoes. The peasant mind loved to build mysterious maybes into monstrous facts.

What a turn of luck, this accident! Pradon was grinning now. He had foreseen nothing like this. He had hoped simply that the Father might be thrown from Dufour's *bête diable* in front of witnesses—a mere incident for the people to laugh at.

This was really something, this was. By the time *Père* Clinton got back from the mainland, his name on the island would be a word to frighten babies with.

9

J EFF BARNETT AND PETER AMBROSE arrived in the plantation jeep
soon after the launch reached the mainland. Peter examined the
injured boy and shook his head.

"My guess is that a broken rib has punctured a lung. It's more than
I dare tackle. I think we'd better take him straight to the capital."

They dropped Jeff off at the plantation. Arriving at the hospital
just at dark, Peter and Barry remained there while the lad was oper-
ated on. It was a bad night for Barry. He could not forget that young
Toto had been hurt trying to do him a favor. When the lad recovers,
he told himself, I'm going to make it up to him.

When the youngster was brought from the operating room, Barry
sat beside the bed, waiting. It was four in the morning when the
anaesthetic wore off.

He held the lad's hand. "When you're well again, you'll be taken
to Fond Marie, Toto. *Père* Ambrose will send word to me and I'll
come over from the island to get you. Would you like to live with me
at the mission?"

The boy looked at him as though he had promised heaven. "*Oui,
mon Père! Mais oui!*"

"Good. I need someone like you around the place to liven things
up. I'll arrange it with your aunt, and the day you arrive we'll have a
celebration." He wanted to say more but knew he mustn't; even at
this much the lad had begun to tremble. "You rest now. Sleep. You
need lots of sleep. I'll see you at Fond Marie."

The youngster's gaze was still on him when he turned in the doorway to wave good-by.

On the way to Fond Marie, Barry did the driving. He did not feel
like talking and Peter did not press him. They were more than halfway
to the mission before he was able to shake off the effects of what had
happened. Then under his companion's gentle prodding he told of
his success on the island, the clinic, the garden, the size of his first

congregation. He didn't mention the *vodun* service or his conversations with Catus Laroche.

"I'm going to have to enlarge the rectory, I can see that," he said. "It's hopeless the way it is now. I need much more room."

"For your clinic, you mean?"

"Yes. As it is now, if two parents come with a child, one has to wait outside while I make an examination. That confounded office is nothing but a box. I'm thinking of another wing with one big room or possibly two, one of them a waiting room. I can pay for it without going to the Bishop. My folks left me several thousand dollars that I've never touched." He gazed wistfully through the dusty windshield. "What I'd really like to build is a combination clinic and rectory on the ridge."

"Where old Leander Mitchell first thought of putting the mission? There's no water."

"Gutters and tanks would solve the water problem. There's plenty of rain."

"It would cost something."

"Hang the cost. But for a project like that I'd *have* to have the Bishop's approval."

Peter Ambrose sent a curious glance at him. "You really do want a clinic, don't you?" he murmured. What a strange young man Barry was, really. So intense, so impatient to get things done. The ordinary young fellow in his situation would be groping along with the greatest care, wary of every forward step lest he blunder into some unseen pitfall and come a cropper. Poor old Mitchell, it seemed, had stumbled at the very start and accomplished nothing. But Barry was no Leander Mitchell. He was a young man who knew where he was going. If ever he acquired a faith to match his eagerness, there would be no stopping him.

"Suppose I talk to the Bishop for you," Peter said mildly.

Barry stiffened at the wheel. "You mean he might listen?"

"It's not impossible. He visited the island last year and must know what you're up against. I'll be seeing him in Raphael tomorrow. He's stopping there for lunch. Suppose I feel him out."

Barry wanted to shout.

HE WENT TO THE PLANTATION that evening, saw Edith, and told Jeff Barnett his plans. Jeff seemed interested. Perhaps it was a relief to discuss something other than the slumping price of sisal.

"I'd forget about a wooden building if I were you and think in terms of stone," the plantation manager advised. "It would be expensive to truck lumber from the capital to Anse Ange and get it across the channel. There's good limestone on Ile du Vent. I can lend you Clement St. Juste. He's a smart man with stone."

Barry could scarcely control his eagerness. He felt he would burst out of his skin.

"I don't see that you have much of a problem, really," Jeff went on. "We'll draw up a simple set of plans and St. Juste can show your island workmen what to do. We've some sheets of corrugated iron left over from the warehouse we built last year. You can have those for your roof. I believe we've even got some plastic pipe."

If only the Bishop consents, Barry thought.

He drew a sketch of the rectory as he wanted it, and they sat about a table discussing it, Edith leaning over Barry's arm to make suggestions. She was in one of her happy moods this evening. She seemed almost childishly gay. He would have to include a guest room, she joked; she was planning to visit him, no matter how much scandal it caused. Her father and mother smiled at her happy chatter.

Her father filled sheets of paper with figures, redrew Barry's rough sketches, and worked out a system of gutters for catching the water. Marian Barnett suggested ways to improve the kitchen. It was after midnight before the talk turned to plantation affairs.

"We're having a rough time," Jeff said. "We may have to tighten our belt and let some of our people go. I don't know what's going to happen here if the market keeps falling."

Barry was startled by the man's tone. Something happen to Couronne? It didn't seem possible. The company's holdings extended along the coast for miles and crept back inland to the very base of the blue-black mountains that made a moonscape of St. Joseph's inhospitable interior. Couronne was one of the biggest things *in* St. Joseph. Annually the plantation shipped thousands of tons of sisal to the States to be made into twine.

Jeff probably exaggerated. He was by nature a dour sort of fellow anyway, an odd contrast to his wife who was always determinedly cheerful. Still, he should know what he was talking about. He had worked in the tropics for years. He'd met his wife in the islands— she'd been an embassy secretary in the Dominican Republic—and Edith had been born on a Caribbean coffee plantation. If anyone could see into Couronne's future, Jeff should be able to.

On the way back to the mission Barry thought about it. But the prospect of a new clinic for Ile du Vent was too joyful a thing to be darkened by Jeff's gloom. If only the Bishop would say yes!

AT FOUR THE FOLLOWING AFTERNOON Peter returned from Raphael. "The Bishop approves," he announced triumphantly, "with one reservation."

Barry's heart sank. "Reservation?"

"That you build a new church first. The one Mitchell put up is a disgrace, he says."

"I'll build ten new churches!"

"One will do for a start." Peter smiled. "You should be able to do both jobs for five thousand dollars in a place like that, he says. He's allotting you that amount. If you go over, you're on your own."

BARRY WENT TO THE PLANTATION for dinner, and Jeff presented him with a set of finished drawings for the rectory. "They wouldn't do for a house building job in Massachusetts, I imagine, but they're all you'll need here. Just be sure you get your markers in the ground properly, so the house will be where you want it, and leave the rest to St. Juste. You'll have no trouble getting workers. Be sure they understand the pay scale, of course. And if you're wise you'll hire a boss boy to referee the minor disputes that are bound to keep cropping up. Pradon Beliard should be a good one for that."

Barry hesitated. "Pradon's been away from Ile du Vent rather a long time, don't you think? I might do better with someone they know more intimately."

"That's true. But at least you know he's to be trusted."

Do I, Barry wondered. Beliard would have cheated me that first day if old Mitchell hadn't stopped him. Well, he would solve that problem when he came to it. He told Jeff about the church.

"No trouble there," Jeff said, promptly reaching for pencil and paper again. "I helped Peter build his."

Clement St. Juste stopped in later for a chat. He was one of the dark-skinned plantation men who had attended the farewell party: a tall, thin young man with a firm handshake. He looked forward to being of help, he said, and was ready to leave for Ile du Vent at once. He seemed delighted with the prospect of spending some time on the island, as though it would be a kind of vacation for him.

After dinner Barry and Edith went for a walk, at Barry's suggestion. He wanted to talk to her about his work, he said. They strolled down the road a quarter mile and took a path through the fields of sisal that led to the shore. There was a strip of beach there where the plantation people went for picnics and swimming. He had used it occasionally when he was at Fond Marie. *Raisin-la-mer* bushes formed a barrier between the beach and the sisal, and there was one large *figuier* tree with broad round leaves under which, in the daytime, bathers could escape from the sun.

He found it pleasant sitting under the tree with Edith, on a carpet of fallen leaves. They had the beach all to themselves at this hour; no one came here after dark. The incoming waves broke with a soft rushing sound on a small reef near shore, and there was a constant rustling of little crabs at the water's edge. A breeze stirred the leaves overhead. He talked to Edith about his garden project.

"I have the seeds you asked for in your letter," she said. "Freddy had to go to the capital last week and I gave him a list." She smiled at him. "But you weren't serious when you said the peasants had never seen seeds in a packet."

"I was. A real garden will be a revelation to them."

"And an inspiration to go and do likewise?"

"I certainly hope so. That's the whole point of it."

"I wish I could help you set it out," she said.

"I wish you could too. You've always had green thumbs."

She was silent a moment, then took his hand and looked at him. "Have you been lonely, Barry?"

"In less than a week? Many a time when I was here at the mission I went longer than that without seeing you."

"I thought it might have been different, your being alone there on the island."

"It was different." He put an arm about her and drew her closer. "I've thought about you more than I should have."

It was the truth. He had thought about her a great deal there on the island, especially at night when he lay on his cot, in his cubbyhole of a room, going over the day's events. Here in Fond Marie she had been someone to pass the time with, an available escape from the routine at the mission. There it was different. He had wanted to talk to her about his plans and problems. Not just anyone, but her. She would understand, he had felt. He had really been lonely for her.

She put her head on his shoulder and moved his hand so that it lay over her breast. "Is it true what you wrote me about old Mr. Mitchell, that he drank too much?"

"He was certainly drinking more than a man ought to, living alone like that."

"And he wasn't poisoned?"

"I doubt it very much."

"But there is *vodun* on the island, isn't there?"

He told her of his talks with Catus. "As things stand at the moment I don't regard him as an enemy, at least not an active one. He may be later on, of course."

"When you take a stand against his *vodun*, you mean?"

"Yes. But I don't see that I'm even close to the point of conflict yet. I've a church and rectory to build, the clinic to look after, the garden to work at."

"But you do hold services?"

"I hold services." He smiled, enjoying the warmth and softness of her body against his own, and the sounds of sea and breeze and the cool fresh smell of the air about them. "But look at it this way. My job is to make them better people. There are two ways of doing it, as I see it. I can stand up Sunday after Sunday expounding and explaining church doctrine, or I can offer them the simple story of Christ the humble teacher, persuading people like themselves to love one another for their own good. Which approach would you choose?"

She frowned. "*Only* Christ the teacher?"

"If I insist on more, I shall have to spend all my time trying to explain a mystic birth they could never understand. I'll be hopelessly floundering in the maze of the trinity and atonement. These are *simple* people, Edith."

"I'm not sure the Bishop would approve," she said, shaking her head.

"He doesn't have to be practical. On Ile du Vent I'm back in the same sort of world Christ himself was in. The same people, same problems. *He* didn't complicate his teaching with dogma."

"Well, I suppose there's no harm——"

"Catus Laroche and his people aren't going to discard their *vodun* beliefs just because I recommend it. They've got to be convinced that I've something better to offer them. Not just a better doctrine, Edith. A better way of life."

"Won't it take a long time?"

"Very long, I'm afraid."

She lay back on the carpet of leaves and Barry turned sideways to look down at her. Her face seemed strangely pale in the darkness.

Her eyes were wide, gazing up at him. "You'll be going back tomorrow?" she asked.

He thought of young Toto in the hospital with a punctured lung, of the church and rectory he had to build, of the people on the island even now waiting for him to return so that they might line up at the clinic for the help they needed.

"Yes, I'll be going back tomorrow."

"Then you'd better take me home now, don't you think?"

"Yes, I suppose I'd better."

He stood up, brushing the sand from his clothing. He waited for her to get up and after a while, a long while, heard her doing so. He took her hand. They walked back to the plantation house in silence.

BARRY LEFT FOND MARIE the next morning in a plantation pick-up, with Clement St. Juste and a driver. In the truck were his books and the rest of his clothes, a supply of medicines given him by Peter, and some tools donated by Edith's father. They arrived in Anse Ange at ten.

He and St. Juste walked about the town, doing the shops. It was not much of a place. Still, it was the largest town for miles and the shops contained a surprising assortment of merchandise. He bought bags of cement and some tools that Jeff had not been able to provide, saw a wheelbarrow and bought that, acquired buckets, nails, nuts and bolts, hinges, shutter-hooks, and such an assortment of other small items that the size of the load, when he saw it all together in the truck, gave him a moment of panic. How in the world was he to get it all up the trail to the rectory?

He counted the money in his wallet. He had spent more than seventy dollars and had less than two hundred left. "We'd better call on the rector here," he said wryly to St. Juste.

The Anse Ange rector was a round, jovial man who didn't hesitate a moment to accept a check on Barry's personal account and deal out a stack of ragged *gourde* notes in exchange. "Small stuff is what you want," he chirped, "and the dirtier the better. They're always suspicious of clean money, these people." He produced a sisal *halford* and stuffed the paper notes into it, thrusting some at Barry with the advice to keep them in his pocket where he could get at them. Then he insisted on making rum cocktails "to settle your stomachs for the channel crossing."

It took half an hour, with more than a dozen husky natives making a noisy game of it, to transfer the load from the truck to the boat. After the crossing, the boat crew were an hour unloading it. Barry stood on the beach beside his small mountain of property and breathed a sigh of relief. The way to do this job was to move forward a step at a time, he told himself. Face up to a problem, solve it, then face the next.

Instructing St. Juste to keep an eye on the pile, he climbed the beach. There were always men on hand when the boats came in. Some were fishermen who lived in the huts along the shore; others came to meet relatives returning from the mainland, or were simply curious. He halted with a cheerful *"Bon jour, compères"* before a group of five or six.

At once, by their lack of expression and reluctance to return the greeting, he knew something was wrong.

"I've a lot of stuff to be carried to the rectory," he said, apprehensive. "I can use a dozen men, at least."

They looked past him and shrugged their shoulders. Sorry, they said; they had things to do. But they were not sorry. They were sullen. The group broke up, its members slouching off in several directions. Puzzled, he tried a smaller group near by.

It was the same. They were busy. They could not help.

"Something's wrong here," he said to St. Juste. "Do you mind guarding the stuff while I go up to the mission?"

St. Juste said he would wait.

Climbing the trail, Barry recalled his first conversation with Catus Laroche at the place where the path became a ladder of boulders. Was Catus behind the islanders' refusal to help? It was certainly possible. If Catus thought a new church would threaten his role as high priest of *vodun*, he would do everything possible to stop it.

But I haven't told anyone here that I'm building a church, Barry thought.

The mission clearing looked as though it had stood unused for years; as though old Mr. Mitchell had walked out with never a backward glance and Barry Clinton had never existed. He went past his office to the kitchen. Lucille sat there at the table, her head on her folded arms. When he spoke her name she raised her head to look at him and seemed bewildered for a moment, then quickly stood up.

"Mon Père!"

"Is everything all right, Lucy?"

"Oui, mon Père." Everything is all right. But you did not say when you would return."

There was no time for that now. He leaned toward her, his hands flat on the table. "I have some things on the beach that must be brought up here, Lucy, and the men won't carry them. Why won't they? What's happened?"

A look of anger came into her homely face. "They are saying it is your fault, what happened to the boy, *mon Père*. You are to blame for his death."

"His death! What are you talking about?"

"They say he was dead when you took him to the mainland. You took him there so they wouldn't know."

Barry groped for a chair and sat down. "But Louis César knows that isn't so! He carried the boy!"

"They don't believe Louis. You gave him money."

"Of course I gave him money! He carried the boy all the way to the plantation for me."

"They say you paid him to lie for you. Everyone says so."

He was shaken. This was the sort of thing old Mitchell had warned him about. Drops of sweat formed on his forehead. He stood up. Who had spread the story? Who was his enemy?

It could be only one man. This was no personal attack, but an assault on what he stood for. This was war.

He forced himself to control his anger.

"It's a misunderstanding, Lucy. The boy isn't dead and isn't going to die. In a little while he'll be back here. Get on with your work now and expect a guest for lunch. I'm going to the village."

CATUS LAROCHE came to the door of his *caille* and said with a slight lift of his heavy eyebrows, "*Bon jour, mon Père*. Come in. I didn't know you had returned." He waited for Barry to be seated and turned to take glasses and a rum bottle from a mahogany sideboard. While pouring the rum he said over his shoulder, "What brings you to see me?"

"The lie that is being told about young Toto," Barry replied, scowling. "Who told the people he was dead, Catus? I can't believe you would do such a thing. Not after my efforts to help your sister's child."

Catus turned quickly to stare at him. "I?"

"Have I other enemies?"

Catus placed a glass of rum in his caller's hand and sat facing him. "I am not your enemy, Father. At least, not yet. I thought that was understood between us."

"Then who started this story?"

"I don't know. It puzzles me."

Barry wondered if it did. Sipping his drink, he sought to read the truth in the *houngan's* face but knew he was wasting his time. The dark eyes returning his gaze were level and steady. What was Catus thinking? That I don't believe him, probably, Barry mused.

He said with a sigh, "I'm in a spot, Catus. I've a lot of stuff on the beach that must be carried up to the rectory, and no one will carry it."

"What kind of stuff?"

Barry told him.

"Louis is in his house," Catus said. "Let me speak to him." He went out, and Barry watched him stride, a handsome, erect figure, across the yard.

Louis, when told of the problem, stood for a moment with his great ugly face twisted into a scowl. "I will see what can be done," he said, "though if you want the truth of the matter, I would rather beat their lying heads together than ask their help." He was very angry, Barry saw. His usually soft voice was a snarl. He passed through the gate in the cactus hedge and disappeared down the path to the village.

Barry turned again to the priest of *vodun.* "Can you find out for me who started this story, Catus?"

"I have already tried."

"I shouldn't think it would be difficult for a man in your position."

"It is very difficult. Such tales spread through the island with great speed. The *télédiol,* we call it: the word-of-mouth wireless. I am not even sure this lie began in Terre Rouge, though I suspect it did because the boy was hurt here."

"Have I offended anyone?"

"You should know that better than I."

Barry was silent. There seemed to be nothing more to say.

LOUIS RETURNED IN HALF AN HOUR with four reluctant villagers, two of them the fathers of children Barry had treated at the clinic. They were the best he could do, he grumbled.

He himself led the march to the beach, setting a pace that had Barry struggling for breath. There the men sorted the supplies into loads they could handle, Louis swinging such a weight to his massive shoulders that he staggered under it.

St. Juste, with a glance at Barry's damp face, gathered up a load of his own. "You've walked up there once," he said. "It's my turn now while you stay here on guard duty."

On the next trip Barry took a load, and on the fourth and last trip he wearily gathered up another. If anyone had told me a week ago that I'd be toiling up this trail three times in an afternoon, he thought, I would have called him crazy. It was a fearful job. Halting on the path to look back at the people on the beach—men and women who for hours had simply stood about watching, without offering to help—he felt his hands clench in bitterness.

Build your church and rectory of stone, Jeff Barnett had advised; there's plenty of it on the island. But how was he going to get the stone to the ridge if no one would carry it? How, with an insidious enemy spreading lies about him, was he to win back the confidence of the people?

Was he to wind up like old Mitchell, after all, nursing a rum bottle and staring into space?

10

I
T WAS SUNDAY AGAIN, two weeks from the day of the accident. Warner Lemke had just finished talking to Jeff Barnett on the short wave when Alma returned from church. He swung about on his chair to scowl at her, yet was scarcely aware of her presence. His lips lay flat against his teeth. He had not been so angry since the night of the party at Fond Marie.

He could still hear the words of his superior droning over the radio, instructing him to call on Clinton and offer to "lend a hand" with the church project. "I'm afraid Barry hasn't had much experience at this sort of thing," Jeff had said, "nor is he likely to anticipate the inevitable difficulties. It will be a relief to him to have someone he can turn to for advice and help."

Advice and help, Lemke thought bitterly. By God, I'll give him advice and help. He saw that his wife had halted by the table and was curiously gazing at him. It showed on his face then, his anger. He didn't wonder.

He walked past her to the liquor cabinet and poured himself a glass of rum and drank it down, silently cursing the heat. Lord, it was hot this morning. There wasn't a breath of air in the house. Last night had been the same. He had risen at two, unable to sleep, and paced the living-room floor for an hour and then sat on the veranda, trying to drink himself drowsy. Probably he had drunk too much, but what was a man to do?

His wife spoke at last. "You're still at it, I see."

He mopped his face and neck with a handkerchief, glaring at her. Damn it, how did she manage to look so cool and fresh? She had ridden all the way to church and back, easily twelve miles, yet looked as though she had just stepped out of a cold shower and put on fresh clothes. She was wearing slacks, as she always did when riding, and a long-sleeved blouse that looked sedate enough for a nun until you gave it a second glance; then you saw how damned little it left to the imagination. What a bitch she was.

"I take it you've had a lovely time singing hymns," he said.

"I enjoyed myself."

"You and dear Mr. Clinton, of course. Does anyone else show up at his services?"

She said with a frown, "Not many have been there since the accident. This stupid story that's going around about the boy's being dead—they believe anything they're told, these islanders."

Lemke grinned. "The *vodun* is at work, hey? Your dear Barry won't last long."

"It isn't *vodun*. Laroche, the *houngan*, was in church."

Laroche, he thought. His mind pulled at the name for a moment and then it came to him: the girl on the beach. It was time he did something about getting to know her. By God it *was* time, after last night.

He poured another drink. Alma glanced at him in disgust and went to her room.

He smiled crookedly as the door clicked shut behind her. Go ahead and close it, he thought. You needn't be afraid I'll make a fool of myself again.

He had made a rare fool of himself last night, he knew that. It must have been the rum. Still, he hadn't had a whole lot of rum, not then. More likely it was that damned story in the magazine. They shouldn't print stories like that. You read them and they seemed too bloody real, and the first thing you knew you were thinking, Now maybe that's how *she* really feels but she's too proud to show it, and if I came right out and begged her forgiveness . . .

He remembered looking across the room at her and thinking how attractive she was. It had been a warm evening. The current of air from the fan in the window kept lifting her hair and she kept raising a hand to brush a strand from her forehead. She was wearing a sleeveless dress with a loose front, and reading one of the historical romances she was so fond of. A book like that ought to put her in the right mood, he had thought, watching her. Damn it, she must know how he felt, she always knew how he felt. And she couldn't be too sore with him, or why had she put on that particular dress?

He must have watched her for half an hour before making up his mind to approach her. Then he wanted a drink badly but was afraid to go to the cabinet for one lest he break the spell. She was waiting for him to go to her, he was certain. He could feel it in the atmosphere of the room, an invisible cord stretched taut between them: a cord she kept twitching by lifting her hand to push her hair back. He was trembling when he rose from his chair.

He went straight to her and stood beside her chair, afraid to touch her, just standing there waiting for her to look up from her book. When she did, he spoke in a mumble. "Al, listen. I want to talk to you. I want you to know——" The words would not come.

"You want me to know what?"

"I'm sorry, Al. I was a damned fool. I really was a damned stupid fool."

She rose from her chair and looked at him, just looked for a moment; then her lips curled downward at the corners and she said, "You still are a fool if you think there'll ever be anything between us again. There won't be." She tossed her book onto the couch and walked toward her room.

"Al, wait!" he had mumbled, reaching for her in his misery. "I said I was wrong!"

She halted. She looked at his face and shook her head slowly at what she saw there. "You know, it's a funny thing," she said. "I don't really hate you. I don't feel much of anything at all, really. If it had been some girl who meant something to you—if you'd been looking for something more than just a bedmate—I probably wouldn't have thought very much about it. I never did before. But a *black* girl——" She shook her head again. "A *black* girl. My God. Even *I* have *some* pride."

"It was a mistake," he had said in desperation. "I said it was a mistake, Al."

"I couldn't care less," she retorted, and went into her room.

All right, Lemke thought, you couldn't care less. Neither could I. Go ahead and soak up religion as a substitute. Or is it the man himself you're after?

What was that girl's name again? Laroche. Micheline Laroche. She lived in Terre Rouge, close by Clinton's place. Well, Jeff Barnett had ordered him to look Clinton up and offer assistance, hadn't he? And it was Sunday, when the peasants hung around the house hoping to God something would happen to relieve their boredom.

He looked at his watch. He would shave and put on a clean shirt, and after lunch he would obey orders. Let his darling wife spend the afternoon with her book.

BARRY AND CLEMENT ST. JUSTE finished their lunch and strolled together in the rectory yard. The supplies brought up from the beach still lay there near the kitchen door, under a canopy of thatch erected by big Louis and his workers. There was nowhere else to put them.

St. Juste said, "We ought to have a shed for this stuff, Mr. Clinton. The thatch keeps it dry, but if we don't get it under lock and key some of it's going to be stolen."

Barry absently nodded. There was so much to be done, and all of it was so difficult with the islanders treating him as though he were a criminal. They actually believed young Toto was dead and that he had tried to conceal the fact from them by spiriting the boy's body off to the mainland. Who had started the fantastic story he didn't know, nor had Catus been able to find out for him. But the whole island accepted it as the truth, and he was right back where he had been on that first day. People ignored his greetings and glared in silence when he walked past.

He hadn't enough workers to begin the new church. It would be impossible to obtain help until Toto returned to the island, big Louis said. But when would that be? There'd been no report from the hospital, no word at all. Meanwhile the island watched him, waiting to see what he would do, and there was nothing he *could* do. The two weeks since the accident were a total loss.

He had other problems. Lucy was complaining of the high price of vegetables in the market, blaming the increase on some sort of illegal tax imposed by the magistrate. He must do something about it, she insisted. He must slap Dufour down. Even St. Juste was a problem. To put the man up he had been forced to clean out the storeroom, but the storeroom with its one tiny window was no better than a prison cell.

Problems.

There was one ray of light, however. The peasants, thank God, were still coming for treatment. They might regard him as some weird sort of monster and refuse to attend church, but when a tooth ached or a child ran a fever, they turned to him for help. He might have to build a wing on the house after all, if it continued. The office had become a full-fledged clinic.

Another thing. Catus Laroche had come to church this morning. True, he had stood just inside the door through the entire service, but at least he had come.

And I shall keep my part of the bargain and attend the next *vodun* ceremony, Barry told himself.

St. Juste said, "I think I'll walk up to the ridge, Mr. Clinton. Want to come along?"

"I'd like to, but I'll have patients."

"I'll go along, then. We've got to locate some building stone."

When he had gone, Barry went across the clearing to move the gray mule to a different location. Catus had brought it back to the mission the day after his return from the mainland. He wondered what he would do with it. Just yesterday Louis had offered to make the animal useful, hinting that the instrument of persuasion would be a club, but he had put off giving an answer. There must be some better solution to that problem.

He frowned. This morning in the midst of the service an odd thought had come to him. He had been looking over his pathetically small congregation and his gaze had fallen on Pradon Beliard, dressed like a capital dandy at a political gathering. He had not seen much of the lad with the limp since the accident, yet Pradon was supposed to be helping him, wasn't he? Those had been Jeff Barnett's instructions, and Jeff was still paying him a salary.

He had remembered suddenly that it was Pradon who suggested he visit Felix Dufour, and Pradon had been present, voiceless, when he bought the mule. Was it possible the boy and Dufour had conspired to cheat him?

But of course Pradon may not have known the mule was dangerous. Except for brief trips to the island to visit his mother, he had worked at Couronne for the past two years.

It was something to think about, though.

MICHELINE LAROCHE sulkily ironed a shirt for her brother and wished she were doing something else. She was angry with Catus for having refused her permission to go to church that morning. Why shouldn't she go to church if she wanted to? Was she a child, to be told what she might and might not do? Dauré and Louis had attended the service. So had Catus himself. Who did he think he was?

He was afraid she might lure the Father into an affair, she supposed. But why shouldn't she, if she were able to? The Father was young and handsome, every bit as handsome as her conceited brother. If she could make him look at her, so much the better for Catus. The church would never let him go on being a minister here if he had an affair with an island girl. He would be kicked out in disgrace, and some stupid old man like Father Mitchell would come to take his place, and Catus would no longer have any problem. Perhaps if he cared enough for her he would stay on the island after his dismissal. He might if she had a child. He might even marry her.

She smiled at her thoughts. That was really imagining things, that was. Still, it wasn't impossible. There were whites in the capital with dark-skinned wives, people said. Not many, but some. She moved her ironing board closer to the doorway to catch some of the breeze that stirred the dust in the yard. She should have gone to the beach with Louis and Dauré and her parents. It was no afternoon to be slaving over her brother's laundry, even if he did have an important service tomorrow night . . .

A horse stopped at the gate in the cactus hedge and Micheline caught her breath sharply in anticipation before remembering that the Father didn't own a horse. Curiosity held her motionless, though, as the man dismounted. *M'sieu* Lemke, from the plantation? What could he want here?

She wiped her moist face with her arm and watched him come into the yard. Did he know himself what he wanted? He seemed confused, peering first at Louis' house and then at the *tonnelle*. At last he saw her and lengthened his stride, stopping at the door. The ironing board stood between them.

"Hello," Lemke said. "I believe we've met before, haven't we?"

"I know who you are, *m'sieu*."

"Good. I hope I'm not intruding. My horse needed some water and I thought——" He let it drop, feeling his pulse quicken as he gazed at her. What he had really thought was that he would find a crowd of people here sitting a Sunday afternoon away, and that he would go through the motions of obtaining water for his horse and actually accomplish nothing. It was hopeless, meeting a girl in the midst of her family. All the way from the plantation he had searched his mind for some better approach and finally resigned himself to the inevitable. The least he could hope for was to make her aware of him and perhaps plant a hint that he would like to know her better.

But, by God, she was alone here, or seemed to be. What a stroke of luck. And what a beauty she was; even the sweat-stained dress she wore couldn't hide the fact. She hadn't a thing on under the dress either; that was obvious. It clung——

"If you would bring the animal here, *m'sieu*," she was saying, "we would not have to carry the water so far."

"Right. I'll get him." He crossed the yard again, urged almost to a run by his thoughts. Then caution curbed his eagerness. What the devil was he to say to her? How was he to manage it? She wasn't like the rest of them, this girl; she was smart. There was her *houngan* brother to be considered too: a devil when aroused, according to all reports. I don't want him for an enemy, Lemke thought. This has to be handled with care.

She was waiting with a pail of water when he led the horse to the doorway. She handed him the pail without comment. All the time the animal was drinking, Lemke was aware of her leaning in the doorway behind him. He thought of and discarded a dozen things to say to her.

He handed back the empty pail. "How is it I never see you at my end of the island? Do all the pretty girls stay in Terre Rouge?"

She laughed. So that was what he wanted, was it? She allowed her gaze to grow bold, passing it over him from head to foot, and laughed again more softly. He had quite a time for himself at his end of the island, according to rumors she had heard. She could see why. He was attractive and had the peasant's way of making himself understood with a few words and a look.

"My parents are very strict," she said.

"I'm sure they are. But you do go swimming sometimes, don't you?"

"Sometimes."

"Then you ought to try the beaches by the plantation some evening. Especially the little one with the *malfini* bushes. That one's the best on the island, really. Especially in the evening." Lemke smiled at her. "I go there often."

"I was there a few days ago," Micheline said.

"I know. I saw you."

She read the unspoken words in his eyes. His eyes were like hands sliding over her body and she felt herself tingling to their touch as though it were real. He was a bigger man than Father Clinton. A more powerful man. He was even better looking. How far away had he been when she stripped off her dress and went striding into the sea to help those stupid women? Close?

"So you see," he was saying, "we're not exactly strangers, are we?"

She continued to return his gaze. "Did you come all the way from the plantation to get water here?"

Lemke was forced to laugh. "No. I'm on my way to the mission."

"Oh? You and Father Clinton are friends?"

Careful, he thought; she's a *houngan's* sister. "We know each other," he shrugged. "But never mind that. Are you going to accept my invitation?"

So he is a friend of the Father, Micheline thought. Probably a very close friend, since they are the only two white men on the island.

They must have known each other when Lemke worked at Fond
Marie. She raised her arms and clasped her hands behind her neck,
gazing over Lemke's head at the tops of the trees beyond the yard,
quite aware that the movement drew her dress tight over her breasts
and that Lemke was devouring her with his eyes. It was an interesting
situation. She wondered how she might turn it to her advantage.
If this man and the Father were good friends——

Lemke took a step toward her. She lowered her arms and he halted,
breathing heavily.

"Tonight?" he said. "Tonight, Micheline?"

"Perhaps. If I can get away."

BARRY HAD GONE to a peasant *caille* to look at a sick girl whose young
husband had come to him pleading for help. She had needed help.
He had extracted no fewer than nine *chigres* from her feet—nasty little
beasts that laid eggs under the skin and could cause real trouble if
neglected. He had given the husband a can of DDT to spray the floor
of the hut, obviously infested with the things. He returned to the
rectory to find Catus Laroche waiting for him.

Catus sat in the office, as poised as a diplomat despite the fact
that he wore only ragged khaki trousers. What a handsome specimen
of savage he was, Barry thought. If only something could be done
about that missing front tooth . . .

"I came to tell you there is to be a service this week," Catus said.
"It will be Thursday evening and will last all night. If you care to
attend, you will be welcome."

"What time shall I be there?"

"It will not be at my place. I'll call for you here about nine."

"This is a special service then?"

"One that will interest you, I think. Just as this book of yours"—
nodding toward a Bible on the desk—"interests me."

Barry took the book in his hands and sat down, frowning. "But this
is in English."

"I looked at the pictures."

"Oh, I see." Barry had forgotten there were pictures in the book.
It was an old Bible given him years ago by his parents, one he seldom
opened. St. Juste had been looking at it.

"Besides," Catus said, "*Père* Mitchell had some paper-covered books
of Bible stories in Creole when he was here, and a friend gave me
one. I can read Creole. Salmador taught me. I have studied *Père*
Mitchell's book a long time."

Oh Lord, Barry thought. He had seen that little book of Mitchell's. It was one used in the capital to instruct children. It contained, perversely, almost everything in the Bible that was hard to explain. Who wrote such books, anyway?

"These pictures in your big book puzzle me," Catus said. "They show men fighting one another, women being dragged off as captives, people being beaten and killed. Is this what your faith is about?"

"If you've studied *Père* Mitchell's book, you must know that our Bible is in two parts," Barry said. "This part you've been looking at is simply a history, very old and perhaps not very accurate, of the people who lived in Christ's part of the world before he was born. With, at the start, an ancient explanation of how the world began."

Catus sat down. "It is not necessary, then, to believe all this?"

"It doesn't matter whether you believe it or not. I wonder sometimes why it is thought important. Actually it's a history book and should be considered as such, quite apart from the story of Christ and his teachings."

Catus nodded. "My people too have a history. Whether it is written down in such a book I don't know, but we know some of the old tales. This Our Father you prayed to in church this morning, is he the same one we salute in *vodun?*"

"The same, Catus."

"I don't understand how that can be. I would like it explained to me."

"Very well, I'll try. When your people were first brought to this country as slaves, St. Joseph was a Catholic island." And still is for the most part, Barry thought, but that's beside the point. "Your ancestors had no Our Father. They had only the gods of Africa. But your people were ordered to go to church. In church they learned about the Catholic religion. The priests talked about a god who was the greatest of all gods, and your people accepted him. Perhaps they associated him in their minds with your own creator of all things, Nananbouclou, or with the great Chango, though I think your conception of the world's beginning is rather vague."

"Go on, please."

"Well, at the same time, your people identified certain Christian saints with *vodun mystères* and adopted those as well. For example, Moses and St. Patrick are associated in Christianity with snakes. You accepted them as likenesses of Damballa, because Damballa's symbol is the snake. The mother of Christ you took to be Maîtresse Erzulie, because both are held in the highest esteem among women. St. Peter, who guards the gates of heaven, was compared by some of your people with Legba, who guards the entrance to the *hounfor*. Others were sure St. Anthony the hermit must be Legba, because Legba is a kind old man."

Barry waited for an answer. None was forthcoming. Catus only stared at him.

"You can see what happened," he went on. "The priests insisted that Catholicism was the only true faith. They, like the planters, were white men, to be feared and respected. So your ancestors took what they could understand of Catholicism—or Christianity, if you will— and down through the years they've borrowed more and more. Some Christian things were adopted through a process of identification. Others found their way into *vodun* because your people thought them attractive or valuable. I'm told that you begin your services with a prayer to Our Father, the *Grand Maître*, that you call on Christian saints as well as the *loa*, that you recite parts of the Lord's Prayer and the Hail Mary. I've been told you really believe in these things. Do you?"

"Perhaps," Catus said. "But I don't think we understand them. In *Père* Mitchell's little book it says, for instance, that your God the Father, God the Son, and God the Holy Spirit are all one person. How can three persons be one?"

Barry's hands tightened on the Bible. *Articles of Religion*, his mind recited, *as established by the Bishops, the Clergy, and the Laity of the Protestant Episcopal Church in the United States of America, in Convention, on the twelfth day of September in the Year of our Lord, 1801. Article I: Of Faith in the Holy Trinity. There is but one living and true God, everlasting, without body, parts, or passions; of infinite power, wisdom, and goodness; the Maker, and Preserver of all things both visible and invisible. And in unity of this Godhead there be three Persons, of one substance, power, and eternity; the Father, the Son, and the Holy Ghost.* He faltered under the *houngan*'s challenging gaze. A man could struggle for hours to explain the holy trinity and still fail, even with listeners to whom all the pat phrases were familiar. How explain it in Creole to a *vodun*-practicing peasant?

"In *vodun*, Catus, you believe in many gods."

"That is so. The *Grand Maître* we do not understand too well, I think—perhaps because he was borrowed from your faith and does not live in the hearts of our people. But we have many gods of our own."

"Christianity is different. We worship *only* the god you call the *Grand Maître* or Our Father. He created the world. He made man and woman, or at least gave them souls. Then when the world became wicked and turned away from him, he came to earth in the form of a man, to set things straight."

"This man was your Jesus Christ?"

"Yes."

"*Père* Mitchell's book says that he called himself the Son of God. If he was God, why did he call himself God's son? How can a man be his own son?"

Barry silently groaned, wishing he could sit the author of Mitchell's book down and make *him* answer the questions. For a moment he was tempted to say what he thought and hang the consequences. Then he sighed. He had been trapped into trying to explain the trinity after all.

He did his best.

Catus frowned at him. "I still do not understand. I find it impossible to believe that the greatest of all gods would change himself into a man and allow other men to kill him."

Which probably explains, Barry thought, why Jesus plays such a small part in *vodun*. The peasants can understand God, the creator and master of all things; they can accept countless saints who have the personal characteristics of *vodun loa*; but Jesus mystifies them and is ignored. He said, shaking his head, "There are some things in Christianity, Catus, that are hard to understand, just as there must be some in *vodun* that you find puzzling. Most Christians believe that Jesus was God himself, though I think some of them don't quite know why they believe it. Others don't believe that he was even the son of God. They say he was only an inspired man who——"

"What do you believe, *mon Père?*"

This time Barry did not compromise. "I don't know. Some day I shall know what I believe, but at this moment I do not." He leaned forward, aware that he was perspiring. "But does it matter, Catus? Think a moment. This man we call Jesus Christ, this inspired teacher or son of God or God himself, was no ordinary person. If he was only a man, he was the most remarkable man who ever lived. That is why the faith he taught did not die with him."

"The teachings of Jesus are what you believe in, then?"

"They are what we believe in. They are all that matters, believe me. The rest of what is in *Père* Mitchell's book, the stories of Adam and Eve, the great flood that drowned the world, the wars and travels and long lists of hard-to-pronounce names are all unimportant. Even the story of the manger and the star and the shepherds and the wise men is unimportant, really. Begin with Christ's teachings. Those are everything. Those are the hope of mankind."

"What are they?"

Barry had to smile. "It would take a little time to cover that. But I can sum them up for you, I think. Love God and love one another."

Catus nodded. "This God you love, where does he live?"

"We don't think of him as living in any specific place."

"In church you say, 'Our Father which art in heaven.'"

"You say the same thing in the *hounfor*. What do *you* mean by it?"

Catus shrugged. "My ancestors borrowed the prayer from your priests. If you don't know what it means, how can you expect me to?"

"Well, heaven is simply a name for God's dwelling place. If it is a specific place we don't know where it is. God is all around us, watching us all the time."

"He was in church this morning?"

"I'm sure he was."

"Did you see him there?"

"No, but we believe he was there."

Catus frowned. "This, too, I find hard to understand. We know where the gods of *vodun* live. They are on their island under the sea or in the Guinea of our ancestors, or in the sacred trees and waterfalls. When they come to a service we know they are present because they enter into our heads and speak to us. You saw that yourself."

Barry nodded, remembering the session in the *tonnelle* two Sundays ago. "I saw it. And if you find it hard to understand my faith, think what a time I have understanding yours. I'd like to talk to that girl," he added, frowning. "There are some questions I'd like to ask her. With your permission, of course."

"Thursday night there will be others you can talk to. If you wish, you may speak with the *loa* themselves." Catus stood up and held out his hand. "I will ask you not to wear any priestly clothing. The *loa* might not like it, though of course they will know what you are in any case. Thank you for answering my questions, Father."

Barry stood in the doorway, watching him go. Had he, in fact, answered any questions? He doubted it. What Catus needed was someone like Peter Ambrose, who played the game strictly according to the rule book. I have too many questions of my own, Barry thought.

TEN MINUTES after the *houngan's* departure, Warner Lemke rode into the mission clearing, wearing a smug smile and looking pleased as punch with himself. "Jeff told me about your new church and asked me to look in on you," he said.

"That's certainly good of him. Of you too."

"Anything I can do to help?"

"I've no doubt there would be if I could get workers. I'm afraid that's impossible, though, until young Toto returns. You've heard the story going around?"

"Alma told me," Lemke said, nodding. "It's fantastic what these people will believe." Especially when Pradon Beliard goes to work on them, he thought with a secret grin. That boy will be magistrate here before he's finished, and I wouldn't be surprised if he's thought of that too. Of course this latest bit of deviltry on Pradon's part would collapse when the injured Toto came back, but it wasn't to be shrugged aside on that account. Little drops of water . . . And if for some reason the lad didn't return, dear Mr. Clinton *would* have a problem. Indeed he would.

"When do you expect the boy?" Lemke asked.

"I should think in about two weeks, unless there are complications."

"Isn't that pretty serious, a punctured lung?"

"It can be. It isn't always."

"Well, if you're able to start sooner, you know where to find me."

"I'm grateful to you for coming," Barry said. "Can I offer you a drink?"

Lemke still had a headache from his last session with the bottle. "No, thanks," he said, swinging himself into the saddle. He wanted a clear head this evening. A clean breath, too. It would never do to let the girl think he had to be drunk to appreciate her. "See you later, padre," he called back, turning to wave.

Barry stood in the office doorway, thoughtfully gazing after his caller. Queer, the fellow's riding all the way from the plantation to offer his services, when he must have known there was nothing he could do. Today, especially. Sunday afternoon was the time a working man would normally take a longer than usual siesta and then go to the beach with his wife.

But something had happened between Lemke and Alma. She had as much as said so. Only this morning, when he had inquired after her husband, she had answered with an odd sort of laugh and changed the subject.

What, really, had Lemke wanted just now?

11

I T WAS EDITH BARNETT who brought the report from the hospital Thursday morning. Crossing the channel from Anse Ange in a native sailboat, she climbed straight to the mission and arrived there just at noon. Barry was in his office, talking to Clement St. Juste.

She took the report from her handbag and gave it to him. "If I had waited for the radio schedule to ask Warner to meet me with the launch, I couldn't have come until tomorrow," she explained. "I knew you'd want to see this right away."

Barry unfolded the paper. He had been talking to St. Juste about the church. Less than an hour ago the Couronne man had discovered a ledge of limestone not far from the building site, just over the ridge toward the edge of the great cliff, and he was bursting with eagerness. They could begin work the moment the injured Toto Anestor returned to the island, he had been saying. Now he was silent, watching Barry's face. Edith, too, was silent.

Barry read the report and felt his hands shaking, felt the paper shaking in them. He shut his eyes and took in a deep, shuddering breath. When he opened his eyes, Edith and St. Juste were still staring, still waiting. St. Juste's face was an uneasy question mark. Edith's was all compassion.

"He's dead."

"Dead!" St. Juste gasped.

"Complications, they call it. They mean post-operative neglect, bad nursing, lack of care." In the wake of shock came a wave of bitterness, and Barry's voice was sandpaper against the office walls. Then weakness overcame him and he groped for a chair.

Edith moved to his side and placed a hand on his shoulder. "It wasn't anything you could have prevented."

"Just a few days ago he was playing in the village."

"He did run behind your mule."

"To pick up my handkerchief. To do me a favor." He pressed his hands to his face in helpless rage. "It isn't fair. A handkerchief drops out of your pocket and a boy dies. A boy nine years old, his whole life ahead of him."

"Darling, stop."

He looked up at her. St. Juste put the paper on the desk and said, "This is awkward, Mr. Clinton. Aside from how you feel, I mean. What's going to happen if you tell the people?"

"I don't know."

"It isn't hard to guess. They won't believe the boy died in the hospital. They'll just be more certain than ever that he was dead when he left here."

Barry was silent. He had spoken angrily in the first heat of emotion and knew that if he spoke again now his voice would break and he would be in tears. When he felt that he had control of himself he raised his head and looked at Edith again.

"Jeff drove you to Anse Ange?" he asked.

She nodded. "He wanted to come across with me. I couldn't see any need for it."

She looked tired and hot, he thought. It was not a hot morning especially, but the very breeze that kept it cool would have made the channel crossing an ordeal, and of course the climb to the mission was always difficult. Her yellow cotton dress looked as though it had been wet by spray. Her hair was dishevelled. He stood up and said, "I'll tell Lucy to set another place for lunch." He went to the door.

He saw two suitcases standing outside the door, and a boy squatting beside them. It wasn't a boy he knew. Turning back, he said with a frown, "You're going to stay?"

"I thought I would for a few days," Edith said. "Do you mind?"

"No, no, of course not."

She was puzzled by his frown. Didn't he *want* her to stay? Didn't he remember what he had said to her on the beach that evening? She was sorry about Toto, of course she was, but actually this report from the hospital, handed to her last evening by Peter Ambrose, was just the excuse they had been waiting for. She could be with him now on his island.

"You'll be going to the Lemkes'," Barry was saying. "Do they know you're here?"

"No, they don't."

"We'd better send the boy along with a note then, hadn't we? He can bring a horse back for you. I haven't one here."

She thought that would be wise. She would write a note at once.

"After lunch you'll want to rest," he said. "Then we can talk."

"I think it's very unkind of you not to have a guest room here," she said.

She meant it as a joke and expected him to smile. He didn't. He only looked at her strangely, as though wondering how she could joke at such a time. The death of the boy had shocked him deeply, she realized. He seemed numb. Her remark had been a mistake.

"If you stay here, someone will have to sleep in the church," he said. He spoke slowly, almost stupidly. He was shaking his head and scowling.

"I'll go to the Lemkes'," she said quickly. "I'll write the note now."

"Yes," Barry said, and went out.

When he returned from the kitchen, he handed the boy her note and told him what to do, wondering what the Lemkes would say when they learned they were to have a guest. Had he better warn Edith that all was not sweetness and light there? He decided not to. It was really none of his business, and the less he seemed to know about it, the better. Besides, he was not up to it. Not after that ghastly report from the hospital. Edith would have to solve her own problems.

While Edith was removing the stains of travel in the little room behind the Christmas tablecloth, he and St. Juste walked in the shade of the campêche tree, talking. Was there any chance, St. Juste asked with a frown, that the boy's body would be brought to the island for burial?

"No. No chance of that."

"Will the aunt be notified? The one he was living with?"

"It isn't likely. I'm supposed to do that, and see that the magistrate has the information for his records."

"Well, then, why do you have to say anything at all about this? It can't do any good, Mr. Clinton."

"No good at all." But it can do me a lot of harm, Barry thought, if I get caught keeping the information to myself. Felix Dufour, for one, could make a mountain of trouble for me.

St. Juste said, "The situation couldn't be much worse than it is."

"True, as far as building the church is concerned. But I've got other problems. I've got to convince these people I'm their friend and persuade them to trust me. If I deceive them about Toto and they find it out, I'm finished."

"You know what I think, Mr. Clinton?"

"No, Clement. What do you think?"

"We ought to start work on the church ourselves, you and I. We could do it. Louis would probably pitch in, and when the others see themselves losing a chance to earn some money they might change their minds. What do you say?"

Barry was astonished. "Are you serious?"

"Certainly I'm serious. You have five or six patients a day at your clinic, don't you? You don't charge them anything. Well, make them pay a day's work—half a day, anyway—for the medicines you hand out. If it's kids you treat, make the fathers pay. I'll put them to work lugging the stone, and once we get the stone we can lay it up ourselves." St. Juste turned to face him. "That's how half the mountain chapels on the mainland are built, Mr. Clinton. You think about it."

BARRY AND EDITH returned to the mission at four o'clock, walking hand in hand, slowly. They had been to the top of the island. For more than an hour they had sat there on the ridge, undisturbed, enjoying the fresh breeze and the view and the nearness of each other. They had not talked much. Barry was thinking of the dead boy, Edith supposed. She herself was content to have his arm around her. There would be time enough for talk later. There would be whole days for talking.

"Shall I be seeing you tonight?" she asked as they entered the clearing.

"I'm afraid not. I'd have to walk it. I haven't ridden a mule since the accident." He thought it best not to mention the *vodun* service he was pledged to attend. She might not approve.

"You should buy a horse."

"The rector in Anse Ange is trying to find me one. There aren't any for sale on the island."

She tightened her grip on his hand. "May I come tomorrow, darling?"

"Of course. I have a hunch you'll find me on the ridge, working."

The boy who had carried her note to the plantation was sitting on a chair by the office door, waiting. Alma Lemke's horse stood near, saddled and ready. The two suitcases were thrust into a palm-fiber saddlebag on the back of a small donkey.

"The boy will walk along with you," Barry said. "I'll go too, as far as the village. There's someone I want to see."

He said good-by to her at the gate in the cactus hedge. When she had gone, he made his way across the yard to Catus' house, but the door was shut and no one answered his knock.

Micheline came from the middle house to speak to him. "Are you looking for my brother, Father?"

"I'd like to speak to him."

"He's out, getting things ready for the service tonight." What did he want to see Catus about, she wondered. Had he changed his mind about going to the service? If so, her brother would be disappointed. Catus had made quite a point of telling people the Father would be there tonight, as though it were a personal triumph.

Barry frowned at her. "Is he likely to be back soon?"

"No, *mon Père*. He left only an hour ago."

"Is it far? Could I go there?"

"I could take you. You'd never find it by yourself. It's a long way, though, if you're going again tonight."

Barry made no effort to hide his disappointment. "I'd better talk to Louis then. He's here, isn't he?"

She walked with him across the yard to Louis' house. At sight of him the little girl, Fifine, cried out in delight and came running to clasp his legs. He picked her up and kissed her, tingling with pleasure at her acceptance of him. At least the children liked him. That was something.

The child's mother took her from him when he reached the doorway. "Fifine is fond of you, Father," she said, smiling.

"I'm fond of her. Any time you want to get rid of her, just send her over to the mission." It wouldn't be long, he noticed again, before Fifine had a brother or sister. Only a few days now. Would he be summoned when the time came? Probably not, unless something went wrong. Shaking hands with Louis, he said, "Can you step outside for a minute, Louis? Something has happened."

They talked under the big mapou that kept the yard so cool and pleasant, and Barry told of the report from the hospital. Louis' ugly-gentle face revealed deep concern.

"This is bad, Father." The speech impediment, always more noticeable when he was agitated, made the words almost unintelligible.

"I know it's bad. But the truth has got to be told."

"You'll never get your church built. Even the few who helped before will turn against you."

"You think I ought to keep silent then?"

The big man tugged at his misshapen mouth for a moment. "No, that would be worse, I think. I don't know. This is very bad. You

should talk to Catus. It would be a mistake to do anything until you
have seen Catus."

Barry had felt the same way. "But the boy's aunt is entitled to know
what happened," he argued.

"That is not important. She cared nothing for him. She only took
him in because she had to."

"Are you sure of that, Louis? He seemed a good boy."

"He was a good boy. But the aunt is not a good woman. Wait,
Father."

Barry made up his mind. "Very well, I will." He placed a hand on
the man's arm. "St. Juste thinks we should start work on the church
ourselves. He wants to begin tomorrow. Can I count on you to help?"

"I will help."

"Good." Barry lifted a hand toward the house in farewell and
turned away. Perhaps tonight he would have a chance to talk to Catus.
He had done all that was possible for the time being.

As he went toward the gate, Micheline Laroche followed him with
her eyes, and a petulant frown formed on her mouth. He hadn't
looked at her. He hadn't even noticed that she had done her hair
for the service tonight and was wearing a dress he had never seen
before. Strange, that he and *M'sieu* Lemke should be such good
friends. They certainly hadn't much in common where girls were
concerned.

Yet they *were* friends, and had been for a long time. Hadn't Lemke
told her so on the beach?

Well, the Father had something on his mind this afternoon, that
was obvious. He had looked at her before, hadn't he? Perhaps that
white woman from the plantation on the mainland, that *M'selle*
Barnett, had brought him bad news.

It had better be only that, she told herself fiercely. He had better
not be in love with her.

NIGHT DESCENDED on Ile du Vent at approximately the same hour
the year around. Soon after six o'clock the sun slid into the sea beyond
the western tip of the island, and for the next ten minutes or so the
ridge blazed as though on fire. Then the crimson fled from the sky
and the stark contours of the land merged with a haze of mauve
streaked with gold, swiftly changing shape and suddenly losing
identity altogether.

By six-thirty the display was over. The island paths were lost in
darkness and the houses of the peasants were distinguishable only as

narrow doorways framing the pale orange-yellow glow of kerosene lamps. Later those doors would be shut against evil spirits.

Promptly at nine, Catus Laroche emerged from the trees at the edge of the mission clearing and crossed swiftly to the rectory. He carried a flashlight and wore dark trousers and a white shirt. His black feet were bare. Barry saw him coming and with a brief "See you later, Clement" to St. Juste, stepped from the rectory to meet him.

"You are ready, Father?"

"Ready, Catus."

"We have a long way to go. I will try not to walk too fast. Have you a flashlight?"

"Yes."

"Good. Come, then."

The path they followed took them up to the ridge, but it was not the route Barry was familiar with. When they emerged on the grassy, windswept peak of the island he sensed they were some distance east of the site selected for the church. Catus stopped to rest a moment.

"Louis told me about the death of young Toto Anestor. That is a very bad thing, Father. What will you do about it?"

"There's only one thing I can do. Tell them."

"They won't believe you. They will only be more certain he was dead when he left here."

"I can't help that."

"There is a better way, I think. Write a letter to the hospital. Have them send a report of the boy's death to the magistrate. That way it will be official; you will have nothing to do with it."

"But that would take several days," Barry protested.

"It's the only way, though. Think about it."

Catus went on again, following the ridge. Presently he turned toward the high cliff which on the north side of the island rose like a wall from the sea. "Be very careful now," he warned. "The path here is steep."

It was no understatement. Cut like a corkscrew in the cliff face, the trail descended among boulders and twisted trees, looping back on itself interminably and at times shooting straight down in slides of shale. The *houngan* felt his way down it with caution, halting every few minutes to turn and point his light at Barry's feet.

No doubt the darkness made the descent more difficult, yet Barry welcomed it. He was not a man who felt comfortable in high places, and guessed that were he able to see what lay below, his heart would be in his mouth. He could hear the deep-throated snarl of the sea as it rushed in among the rocks. After twenty minutes the sound was like a fist smashing at his face, and there was a thin cool mist in the air that must be spray carried on the sea-wind. The very cliff trembled to the impact of the waves.

At the bottom Catus suggested a rest. "We have only a little more to go, but these rocks are difficult." Barry shone his light about and saw that they were a hundred feet or so from the sea's edge, with the cliff looming above them. It looked ready to topple onto their heads. Between cliff and sea lay a nightmare stretch of boulders piled on boulders. Crabs scuttled into secret hiding places as the light touched them.

Again Catus led the way, this time along the base of the cliff, over and around the boulders. There were openings, Barry saw, in the base of the wall, some large, some small. Were these the caves used in the old days for storage of treasure by the pirates who had made Ile du Vent their base? It might be fun to explore them some day. He aimed his light into some as he passed. The walls and ceiling of one were covered with bats. From the depths of another a pair of red eyes, low to the ground, gazed out at him.

After ten minutes Catus halted again, this time at the mouth of a cave. He was smiling. "Are you wondering why we go to all this trouble when we could hold a service in the village, Father?"

"I was, a little."

"As I told you, many of the *loa* live in the sea. We use this grotto because the sea comes into it at high tide. It has been sacred to *vodun* for as long as anyone can remember. Long before anyone now living on Ile du Vent was born."

Barry played his light over the expanse of boulders between the cave mouth and the water's edge and saw that the shore here was a broad depression. Even now at low tide the sea was close to the base of the cliff here. He nodded, and Catus entered the grotto.

The walls were close and wet. The passage was a winding tube floored with smooth stones and shells. The ceiling was beyond reach. For five minutes Catus led the way in silence, without a halt. Then Barry heard drums. They seemed distant, muffled, but a sudden sharp turn in the tunnel loosed the sound like thunder all about him. Directly ahead lay an enormous room filled with people.

The women wore white, and some wore white kerchiefs about their heads. The men wore white shirts, most of them, and their Sunday trousers. The drums throbbed. A score of women danced about a painted wooden post in the center of the chamber, hands on thighs, shoulders undulating. More than a hundred spectators stood about the walls or sat on the floor with their arms looped about their knees. High on the walls, kerosene lanterns had been placed in niches to illuminate the scene.

The drumming ceased as Catus entered. The dancing stopped. Seated spectators rose to their feet and all faces were turned toward the *houngan*. Barry recognized a number of persons. Micheline and her sister Dauré were among the dancers. Big Louis César was one of the drummers. Against the wall stood Pradon Beliard. There were others.

Was he imagining things, or were they staring at him and not at Catus? He was suddenly uneasy. There was something hostile in the silence. Catus must have felt it too. The *houngan* halted, looked about him with a frown and said almost inaudibly, "Wait, Father." He beckoned to Louis. Louis left his drum and came forward.

"What is it?" Catus asked in a low voice. "I told them the Father would be here."

The big man's face was heavy with concern. "It is not that. They know about the boy."

"The boy!" Catus turned impatiently to Barry. "How can they know? Did you tell anyone?"

"Only Louis and St. Juste," Barry said, feeling a nervous perspiration form under his clothes.

"How can they know then? How is it possible?"

Louis said, "Where the Father's affairs are concerned, they seem to know everything. Perhaps the woman from the mainland told someone. Perhaps the Father's housekeeper or St. Juste——" He shook his head. "Anyway, they know. They have been muttering about it for the past hour."

Catus hesitated, then ordered curtly, "Start the drumming." He took hold of Barry's arm. "Come with me," he said, and led Barry back toward the tunnel. An empty wooden bench stood just inside the chamber to the right of the tunnel mouth. He waited for Barry to sit down.

"I will have Micheline sit beside you and explain the service," he said. "There is nothing we can do now about this other thing."

The three drums were creating thunder again. Catus made his way to the central post. Micheline detached herself from the group of white-robed women and came to sit at Barry's side.

12

THE SERVICE, Micheline explained to Barry, was a *kanzo*. Parts of it were secret and would take place in the *hounfor*, which in this case was a small tunnel on the far side of the chamber. Indeed, some of the secret portions of the ceremony had already taken place in the *hounfor* in the village.

When the affair was over, a young woman who was now only a *hounsi bossale*, a neophyte, would have been raised to the rank of *hounsi kanzo* through purification by fire.

While Micheline was talking, the drummers beat on their instruments and the white-clad *hounsis*, seated on a bench behind the drums, sang the traditional chant to Legba, imploring him to "open the gate" so that the *mystères* might come to the service.

"Papa Legba, ouvri barrière pour nous! Ago yé!"

It was beautiful chanting, Barry thought. Not loud, but clear and melodious, it soared to the roof of the great chamber and from there seemed to fall like gentle rain. Through the rain the drums rolled out their thunder. Over and over he heard the name Legba in varied melodies, and then the names of other *loa*. "We salute them all," Micheline said, "but Legba is always first. Papa Legba loves us and intercedes for us. He is a kind old man. We adore him."

S. Peter at the gates of heaven, Barry thought. Who could have told the people about young Toto? Who could have known? Catus, followed from the *hounfor* by men Barry did not know, walked slowly about the chamber scattering water from a jug. "Some *houngans* have come from the mainland to assist him," Micheline said.

The jug was passed from one man to another. The *hounsis* rose and began a slow, dignified *yanvalou* dance about the post, still chanting. It was very impressive, a little like being in church, Barry thought, except that in church one didn't fall to one's knees and kiss the ground every few minutes.

There was much kneeling. "They salute the drums and the *poteau-mitan*," Micheline said. "They show their respect to my brother and the visiting *houngans*. The chanting is for the *loa*." Her brother was raising the right hand of each white-robed *hounsi* and twirling her about in a graceful little pirouette, but the chanting never stopped.

Suddenly one of the women began to dance more rapidly. Her bare feet flew over the rough floor. Her body spun like a spinning top. She threw her arms out for balance and went around and around the post in ever widening circles.

The drummers quickened their tempo. The other women stopped dancing and fell back to make room for the possessed one. Catus and his helpers intently watched her.

She whirled until she lost her balance and fell among the spectators. They helped her to her feet. Reeling, with arms now extended before her and head thrown back, she made her way to the post, sank to her knees and kissed the ground at the base of it. Catus went to her and took her hand, lifting her up.

He looked into her face and spoke to her, his voice so low that Barry could not hear the words even though the drums were now silent. He spoke to the drummers and they bent to a new rhythm, slow in beat. An assisting *houngan* came forward with a rum bottle and the possessed *hounsi* raised it to her lips.

Beside Barry, Micheline frowned. "Guedé?" she said. "This is strange. Perhaps because of young Toto——" She leaned forward, staring. Guedé, Barry knew, was their god of death, their guardian of the cemetery.

With Catus at her side the girl walked about the chamber, halting before the other *houngans*, taking rum into her mouth and spraying it into their faces. "Guedé salutes them," Micheline whispered. Suddenly the bottle itself was thrust at Catus. He put it to his lips and sipped, handed it back with his gaze fixed on the girl's face. The girl turned abruptly and strode across the room to the bench.

The bottle was thrust at Barry. "Take it!" Micheline whispered. "Drink some!"

He rose, accepted the bottle and put it to his mouth. The rum touched his tongue. It was liquid fire. He passed the bottle back and abruptly sat down, feeling that a hot iron had been thrust into his mouth. The girl, gazing down at him, tipped the bottle to her own lips and drank slowly for a full minute, then let the bottle fall. It was empty. It had been almost full when Barry held it; now it was empty. The girl turned away and began dancing. The drums throbbed. The other *hounsis* joined in the dance.

"What—what in heaven's name *was* that?" Barry whispered to his companion. "It wasn't rum!"

"A *trempé* that Guedé is fond of, made of hot peppers and *clairin*."

"But she drank it all!"

"Guedé is able to do that."

Barry watched the girl. *Clairin*, raw rum, taken in such quantity could kill an ordinary person. Spiked with the wickedly hot peppers of St. Joseph, it *must* do irreparable damage. But the girl was dancing as though nothing had happened.

Catus spoke to her. She stopped dancing and looked across the chamber at Barry, shrugged her shoulders, allowed Catus to take her hand and lead her to the bench. Again Barry rose to his feet.

"Papa Guedé will speak to you if you wish," Catus said.

Barry studied the girl's face. It was not normal. There was an emptiness in the eyes, a telltale slackness to the mouth. This was the face of a god? He didn't believe it. She was in a trance of some sort. Under the spell of the drumming and chanting she had hypnotized herself. Questioning her would be ridiculous. What could he ask her? He shook his head. "I'm afraid I——" He caught himself, remembering his manners. "I greet you, Papa Guedé," he forced himself to say. After all, he was a guest here. "I bid you good evening."

"I greet you," the girl said. Her voice in the dark would have been mistaken for a man's. "In the name of the spirits I greet you. I bring you greetings from the boy who died."

She turned away. Now what the devil was that supposed to mean, Barry asked himself.

THERE WERE SEVERAL OTHER POSSESSIONS in the next hour or so, all of them induced, he was certain, by the incessant throbbing of the drums. Micheline told him the names of the *loa* involved, but he recognized none of them. Apparently they were minor *mystères* important only to the persons possessed. Catus did not bring any of them over to talk to him.

Then from the tunnel where the *pé*, or altar, stood, two girls in white robes marched forth bearing handsomely colored flags, to be led briskly about the chamber by a young man with a machete. The chanting was to Papa Sobo, who, it seemed, was the flags' special guardian.

The drums thundered again. Catus, a gourd rattle in hand, performed a graceful dance about the post and the *hounsis* lifted their beautifully blended voices in song after song. At the end of each song, big Louis César brought his wooden hammer crashing down on the largest of the three drums and the congregations shouted "*Abobo!*"

This would never do for Christians, Barry told himself wryly; it takes too long. He looked at his watch. It was after eleven.

Someone brought a plate of cornmeal to Catus and he began drawing designs on the floor around the *poteau-mitan*. Bending from the waist, knees straight, he held the dish in his left hand and created the patterns by letting the cornmeal dribble between the thumb and forefinger of his right. Barry watched, astonished by the *houngan's* artistry.

Catus drew an elaborate steamship with smoking funnels. "For Agué," Micheline whispered. He moved to the right and created an intricate heart—"For Maîtresse Erzulie"—and then the writhing serpents of Damballa and Aïda Ouedo, the machete and flags of Ogoun Badagry, the elaborate crosses of the Guedés. Micheline supplied the gods' names in a whisper.

By now the assisting *houngans* had stepped forward. With their own plates of cornmeal they added to the designs, blending them all into one great picture that completely encircled the post. If *vodun* did nothing else, Barry mused, it certainly brought out the artistic in its followers. The drawings were magnificent.

Catus walked about, sprinkling the designs with water. The *hounsis* fell to their knees and kissed them. Seven small chairs were produced, and Catus lifted each one in salute before placing it on the ground. The drummers played softly as though in a trance. From the altar in the tunnel the white-robed *hounsis* brought bundles of pine sticks and placed them beside a lighted candle at the foot of the post. Then they followed Catus back to the *hounfor*.

Barry had been watching the girl who had consumed the bottle of *clairin*. She was no longer possessed. Nor was she drunk. But how could she not be drunk, he asked himself. His own tongue and lips were still burning, and he had only sipped the stuff. He turned to Micheline.

"The girl who was Guedé—does she remember what she did when she was possessed?"

"No. Of course not."

"If I spoke to her now, would she remember what she said to me?"

Micheline shook her head. "It was not she who said it. It was Guedé."

I don't believe it, Barry told himself. I can't.

Something was about to happen. The people were watching the

little tunnel where stood the altar, a large flat stone partly covered with a white cloth. Suddenly the drums boomed. Out of the tunnel came a procession of priests and *hounsis*. Catus Laroche clutched the yellow legs of two live chickens.

Catus danced about the post, slowly at first, then more and more rapidly as the tempo of the drums quickened. The others followed. The sound of the drums filled the cavern and pressed against Barry's ears. He felt the rhythm inside him stirring his arms and legs to action. The drums, the dancing figures, the flickering light of the kerosene lanterns transformed the cavern into a world of fantasy.

Leaning forward on the bench, he watched the dance become a chase. Catus swung the two chickens wildly about his head as he pursued the *hounsis*. One after another he caught and embraced them, after which they retired to the chairs set out for them.

The drums were still. The *hounsis* were seated. Before each girl lay an iron cook-pot and a plate. The two chickens lay at the foot of the post. Catus stood with his eyes shut while a woman carefully wiped the sweat from his face with a white cloth.

Silence. Barry took in a long slow breath and felt the rhythm of the drums ooze out of him. What a relief after twenty minutes of pure din!

Catus sat down. The chairs, placed in a circle about the *vevé*, were now occupied by six white-robed *hounsis* and the *houngan*. Catus took his gourd rattle in one hand and shook it. His other hand covered his eyes. He stared at the ground. His voice, low, unhurried, rolled out through the chamber.

"Notre Père, qui es aux cieux . . ."

It was impressive.

IT WAS HERE, Barry saw, that Catholicism had penetrated most deeply into the *vodun* ritual. In a strange mixture of Creole and French were recited the Hail Marys, canticles, creeds and prayers which the ancestors of the present congregation had borrowed from the only religion they were permitted to practice. Did the words have any meaning for these people? Did the long list of Catholic saints mean anything? He wondered. The atmosphere was reverent enough. There was no noticeable change when the salutation to the saints ended and the service became *vodun* again. Still . . .

The drummers produced a slow, gentle rhythm from their instruments. *"Lis adolé zo,"* Catus intoned softly. *"Lis adolé zo—zo—zo,"* the *hounsis* repeated. Barry turned to his companion.

"What does that mean?"

"It is *langage*, old African talk. No one knows what it means any more."

Endlessly, one after another, the *mystères* of *vodun* were saluted in prayer. How many gods could there be? It was after midnight and the recitation went on and on, the drums gently throbbing, the little bell affixed to the *houngan's* gourd *asson* softly tinkling. First the voice of Catus, murmuring a *loa's* name and a few words in his honor, then the combined voices of the *hounsis*, hypnotic, like a low humming of bees, and after each invocation the inevitable "*Lis adolé zo—zo—zo—zo.*" The *hounsis* bent to kiss the ground. They touched their fingers to the ground and kissed those. The hundred or more members of the congregation were still as death in the presence of a thing sacred to them. Now and then the ring on Catus' finger caught a glint of lantern light and seemed to glow.

They believe, Barry told himself. But what do they believe?

When it ended at last, Catus was scarcely able to rise from the tiny chair on which he had sat for so long. He seemed exhausted. The spectators awoke as from a trance and began moving about. Cigarettes glowed. But the *hounsis*, still seated, were not finished.

Each of them took three iron spikes from the cook-pot under her chair and with a stone for a hammer pounded them into the ground before her, forming a triangle. When they had finished, Catus poured into each triangle a little water from a jug, adding bits of food from dishes at the base of the post. "Food for the *loa*," Micheline murmured to Barry. Having constructed a similar triangle before his own chair, her brother repeated the ritual there.

The drumming was more vigorous. Barry raised his head to glance at Louis, on the *maman* drum. Did he never tire? He seemed very tired indeed. His eyes were closed. His ugly-gentle face was oily with sweat.

Again Catus distributed offerings to the gods. Then while he intoned other chants, the six women built fires of pine sticks within their triangles of spikes, and the visiting *houngans* moved about the cavern extinguishing the lanterns. Only the light of the fires remained, feeble and flickering. Only Catus and the white-clad *hounsis* could be seen, and the iron pots on their iron spikes, and the painted central post rising from the decorated floor to disappear in darkness.

I am in a grotto in the bowels of a mountain, Barry reminded himself. I am on Ile du Vent. I am an Episcopalian missionary. This is not the heart of Africa and these people are not savages. They are my people. I am here to teach them.

He became aware of a new sound in the chamber, or rather in the depths of the tunnel behind the bench he sat on. It was the sound of the sea crashing against the cliff and pouring into the passage. He looked at his watch. Three o'clock. The tide was high. Panic clutched at him for a moment as he realized that he and the others were trapped in the cave.

But the service was far from finished. No one wished to leave now.

Catus rose, clutching the two chickens. They were still alive. They had recovered from the shock of being whirled about his head earlier. Before each of the fires he knelt and held the birds close to the little piles of food, waiting patiently for them to brave the heat and peck at the offerings. "The chickens must eat," Micheline said, "or the *loa* will not accept them." The sacrifice must indicate its willingness to be sacrificed? Barry shook his head, mystified.

Both chickens ate, and the watchers' murmur of approval was a sound like a soft wind blowing through the cavern. Catus handed one of the birds to an assistant. Together the two *houngans* passed along the line of smoking fires, plucking the birds' necks and letting the feathers fall into the flames.

Catus' strong black fingers closed over the naked necks of the chickens and twisted their heads from their bodies. The *hounsis* leaned back on their little chairs, thrust their bare feet forward, picked up the iron cook-pots between their feet and set them on the spikes. Catus and his helpers poured water and oil into the pots. The drumming became thunder again.

Dancers came forward. They were neophytes, Micheline explained hurriedly; those tending the fires were all *kanzo*, graduates of this very ritual. The learners began a slow *yanvalou* about the post, blurring the handsome cornmeal drawings with their shuffling feet. The *kanzos* added pine sticks to their already blazing fires.

"The chickens will be cooked in the *zins*," Micheline said. "Then— but you will see."

The pots bubbled and smoked and the drums thundered and spectators joined the servitors in a rapid shuffling dance that seemed to bring on possessions. One by one a dozen or more dancers fell out of line. Some threw up their arms and shouted. Some dropped writhing to the ground. Some danced more furiously, clearing a space around them with the speed and violence of their movements.

"Many *loa* are present tonight," Micheline said calmly. "It is always so when Catus draws the *vevés* and Louis beats the *maman* drum."

So these were the gods of *vodun*, these men and women throwing themselves about, waving their arms, squirming on the ground. Barry watched and frowned. Did the gods do nothing else but demonstrate their presence? Did they never talk to their devotees calmly?

He studied faces he knew. Dauré César's was the mask of a sleep-walker. Catus' was old with fatigue. The face of Micheline, who had risen to take part in the dance, was that of a passionate young animal who found in dancing a release for stored-up urges.

I don't know these people, Barry told himself. I only thought I did.

AT A SIGNAL FROM CATUS the sacrificial chickens, now thoroughly cooked, were lifted from the pots and transferred to plates. Into the boiling oil went cornmeal and herbs, to be vigorously stirred by the *hounsis* until once more the pots bubbled and smoked. The drums were only a mutter in the darkness. The dancing had ceased. Micheline, on the bench again, found Barry's knee with her fingers.

"Now," she said.

Catus had disappeared into the *hounfor* tunnel. He came into the light again, leading by the hand a young woman. The girl walked as though unaware of where she was. She wore a sleeveless white dress that came to her knees. Her eyes were open but unseeing. She was about eighteen.

Catus led her to the iron pot in front of his vacant chair. He spoke to her and she knelt. Micheline, leaning toward Barry, said quietly, "On the mainland the initiate is always covered with a white cloth. Here we do it this way."

Catus knelt at the girl's left. Another *houngan* came and knelt at her right. At a signal from Catus the six *hounsis* reached into the bubbling iron pots before them and took out handfuls of the cornmeal mixture. Barry caught his breath.

Had he seen it or imagined it? Had they actually put their hands into the boiling oil?

"It is nothing," Micheline said. "My brother, when possessed, is able to take a red-hot bar of iron in his hands."

Her brother accepted the small cakes of cornmeal passed along to him by the women. He handed them to his assistant, who fed them one by one to the kneeling initiate. Then the two *houngans* stood up and led the girl back to the tunnel. The cakes, Barry supposed, were some sort of god-food. There was no denying the impressiveness of the ceremony or the sincerity of the participants.

The six *hounsis* held his attention now. The iron pots before them glowed red with imprisoned heat. The girls leaned forward, lifted the shimmering containers in their bare hands, and emptied them.

My brother, when possessed, is able to take a red-hot bar of iron in his hands. These pots were red hot and these girls were not possessed. Or were they? I can't believe this, Barry told himself. I won't. But the *hounsis* calmly finished pouring the mixture of cornmeal, herbs and oil out of the pots, cleaned the vessels with handfuls of green leaves, and replaced them on the spikes.

"In *vodun* are many things that cannot easily be explained." He had read that somewhere, in a book by one of the few writers who had seen enough *vodun* to be worth reading. "It is a religion beyond the comprehension of the uninitiated."

Catus, walking along the line of fires, examined each pot and filled it with oil. The *hounsis* thrust fresh pine sticks into their fires, blowing on them to make them burn more rapidly. Presently from each of the pots a column of smoke rose through the firelight to disappear into the darkness under the cavern roof.

The oil in the pots bubbled. The only other sound was the whisper-faint patter of the drums. Once more the girl with the vacant eyes and expressionless face was led from the *hounfor*.

This time when she knelt before the first fire, Catus seized her right wrist and slowly thrust her hand into the boiling oil. The kneeling figure shivered as though a chill or shock had passed through her, then was still again. Seconds passed. Catus withdrew her hand and raised her to her feet. She stared straight ahead, seeing nothing. Oil dripped from her fingers to the ground. The hand seemed unharmed.

At each of the other fires the performance was repeated. It was at the seventh and last fire that Barry saw her face change.

Was it the firelight painting false emotion on a face actually immobile? No. Her mouth had come open. Her eyes were suddenly wide. She was seized by some extravagant joy, some ecstasy. *She sees something. What does she see?* There was no indication of pain from the boiling oil. The girl was exalted.

Catus lifted her for the last time. She walked to the *hounfor* with him as though walking to paradise, head thrown back, lips moving in silent song, eyes bright as the fires of her ordeal.

What had she seen? What had happened to her? *How* had it happened?

With their bare feet the *hounsis* removed the glowing pots and set them aside. They stood up, passing their feet slowly through the flames. From the altar in the *hounfor* tunnel Catus and the assisting *houngans* brought machetes, *assons*, *govis*, and other implements used in the service. These too were passed through the flames—to sanctify them, Barry supposed. Some of the congregation edged forward. The boldest stepped to the fires and held their hands above them.

On an impulse Barry rose and moved toward the post. Halting beside one of the little chairs, he surreptitiously reached down and put his hand against the iron pot beside it. He jerked the hand away quickly, suppressing an exclamation of pain. His finger tips throbbed.

He returned to the bench and sat down, to find Micheline frowning at him.

"Did you think they were not hot?" she asked.

He answered honestly, "I don't know what I thought."

13

THE AFFAIR ENDED AT DAWN, after two hours of social dancing in which nearly all those present took part. When the drums were silent at last, Catus came to the bench.

"We can go now if you wish." The *houngan* was soaked with sweat, exhausted.

It was impossible to talk as they made their way out of the grotto and climbed the difficult path up the face of the cliff. When they had rested awhile at the top, however, Catus said with a smile, "Well, Father, now you have seen a complete *vodun* service."

"Yes. I'm grateful to you."

"And your thoughts on the service itself?"

"I understood very little, of course, even with Micheline explaining it. I shouldn't want to question you until I've had a chance to think it over." Barry hesitated. "I do wonder, though—well, I can't quite see the point of having all your gods come to the service."

"The point, Father?"

"I mean, if you were able to sit down and talk over your problems with them, ask them questions—but it seems rather meaningless, their just possessing someone and then going away again."

Catus lay back on the grass and looked at the sky, frowning. It was odd, the Father's driving straight to the one thing in *vodun* that he himself found so troubling. Of course, it *was* possible sometimes to talk to the *loa*. He had done it. But the Father was right: it was rare indeed when the *loa* had anything to say that would help a man to understand them. And very often, Catus was certain, the gods were not present at all when people were possessed. The drumming and chanting made them think themselves possessed when they were not.

He wished the *mystères would* sit down quietly, like reasonable beings, and discuss things. What was it like, for instance, on their island under the sea and in their secret home in Guinea? What did they do when not answering the call of the drums? If a *houngan* were to help his people to a better life he ought to know these things, not be groping in the dark for answers the *loa* could so easily furnish if they would.

He looked at Barry. "We have things to talk about, you and I, I think. But not now after an all-night service. Shall we go on?"

BARRY SMELLED SMOKE IN THE AIR before they reached the end of the path, but thought nothing of it. The peasants did most of their cooking outdoors, and very often there was smoke in the atmosphere. When he stepped into the clearing a moment later, however, and saw a crowd of people in front of the church, he was alarmed.

He quickened his stride, leaving Catus behind as he hurried across the bare red earth. Near the church the smell of smoke was stronger. The assembled peasants gazed at him in silence.

He halted with a gasp in the church doorway.

There *had* been a fire. As he went down the aisle he saw that the whole altar had been consumed. The beams above it were scorched. The underside of the iron roof was black.

He saw something else. On the floor in front of the ruined altar lay the gray mule that had killed Toto Anestor. St. Juste was bending over it, trying to twist a rope around its hind legs. Lucille was scratching at the hard-packed ground with a shovel.

When they saw him, St. Juste straightened over the mule and the woman stopped work. They watched him come down the aisle. St. Juste said in a low, angry voice, "This was no accident, Mr. Clinton. It was set."

"I'm sure it was. Do you know who set it?"

"No. We were asleep. But he meant to burn the house too. I heard him prowling and called out to him. He ran."

"What is the mule doing here?"

"Look for yourself."

Barry walked around the animal and saw that its throat had been slashed. The ground near its almost severed head was soaked with blood. It was this blood-soaked earth that Lucy had been trying to scrape up with her shovel and put into a bucket.

"I don't understand," he said.

St. Juste said grimly, "It's another filthy trick to turn the people against you, Mr. Clinton."

That was it, of course. Some enemy, knowing he was at the service, had led the mule into the church and slaughtered it here before the altar, then set fire to the church, to make the islanders think the *mystères* were angry about Toto's death. Quite likely the church would have been a smoking ruin if St. Juste had not heard the man prowling. These walls were only wattle under their cracked veneer of mud. The roof-supports were wood. The arsonist had planned a totally destroyed church with the slain animal lying in the wreckage, a spectacle that would have made quite an impression on the superstitious minds of the islanders.

"Who could have done such a thing, Father?" Lucille demanded.

Who *could* have done it? Who *were* his enemies? He turned his head and saw Catus in the doorway, watching. He beckoned, and the *houngan* came silently down the aisle.

"This was no accident, Catus," Barry said. "Who did it?"

Catus frowned at the mule, at the heap of charred timbers that had been the altar. An altar, to Catus, was a sacred thing. V*odun*, too, had its *pé*. "Someone who wishes to drive you from the island, obviously," the *houngan* muttered, scowling. "I don't know who that is."

"Well, we know a number of persons it could not have been. What time did this happen, Clement?"

"About four o'clock. A little before."

"It was no one at the ceremony, then. To get here at four, the fellow would have had to leave the grotto at three, and it was impossible to leave at that time or anywhere near that time. The tide was in. That eliminates a lot of people." It eliminated, Barry told himself, almost too many people. He ticked off in his mind the ones he had had any dealings with: Catus, Micheline, the Césars, Pradon Beliard. Later, no doubt, he would think of others. In any case, it eliminated just about everyone.

Of course, the guilty man might have been at the service and slipped out earlier, before the tunnel became impassable. But that was hardly probable. There would have been no point at all in his waiting until four o'clock to set the fire if he had reached the clearing at, say, two or three. No, the man responsible for this was someone who hadn't been in the grotto at all. But who hadn't been there?

He stopped trying to think. "What are you doing with the mule?" he asked St. Juste.

"It's got to be buried, Mr. Clinton. I've dug a hole just behind the church."

"I see. There wasn't a chance, I suppose, of getting it out of here before the people saw it?"

St. Juste drew his lips thin and glared at Lucy. "There might have been, if some women weren't so stupid. She started running around like a plucked chicken, screaming her fool head off. We had an audience before I could shut her up."

Lucy hung her head. "I thought the church would burn down, *mon Père*."

"It's all right, Lucy. They'd have found out in any event." Barry turned to St. Juste. "Here, let me help you."

Together they finished roping the dead animal's legs.

"I don't suppose I could have dragged the brute out of here anyway," St. Juste said with a shrug. "Not even with her helping me."

It was not an easy task even with Catus hauling at the rope too, but they managed eventually to drag the mule to the hole. Some thirty persons were on hand now, watching every move, but Barry ignored them. At least, he thought while shoveling the red earth into the grave, this answers my problem of what to do with one gray mule. Returning to the church, he applied the shovel to the blood-soaked ground before the altar.

"Will you rebuild the altar, Mr. Clinton?" St. Juste asked.

"No. I'll use a table. As soon as we've had something to eat, I'm going to start building the church on the ridge. We've no time for this one."

That was something the arsonist perhaps hadn't known, he told himself—that he was already planning a new church. He hoped the fellow would be disappointed.

BIG LOUIS CAME AT NINE O'CLOCK, faithful to his promise despite his weariness. Barry was mildly surprised. It was one thing to sit on a bench all night watching a ceremony as he had done; quite another to beat a drum all that time. He could well understand why Louis' shoulders sagged and his speech was thick.

They wouldn't accomplish much on the ridge, he supposed. Still, it was important to make a start. Doubly important after the arson attempt.

He handed Lucy a letter he had written. He was following Catus' advice and requesting the hospital in the capital to send a report of Toto's death to the magistrate, with a copy to himself. It seemed the only thing left to do. He had put the letter into an envelope addressed to Alma Lemke, with a note asking Alma to see that it reached the mainland. If sent the usual way, across the channel to Anse Ange by sailboat, it might not get there.

"A boy named Présilus is coming this morning for medicine, Lucy. Tell him that if he wants it he must take this letter to the plantation at once, and bring back a note from Mrs. Lemke saying she received it. Do you understand?"

"*Oui, mon Père.*"

"There will be others coming around. Tell them the clinic is closed. I no longer intend to help people who try to injure me. If they want to be looked after from now on, they'll have to pay for it. Not in money, of course, but in other ways. I'll be on the ridge if they want to know more about it."

"*Oui, mon Père.* And I'm *glad.*"

He shouldered a bag of cement and nodded to St. Juste and Louis, who were already laden and waiting.

"All right, *compères.* Let's go."

IT WAS AN INTERESTING EXPERIMENT. By the time the first clinic customer arrived on the ridge, the work was already well under way and there was an audience. Barry had anticipated the audience. Nothing of this sort could happen on Ile du Vent without one.

The man sent up by Lucy was not a patient himself; he was the father of a child being treated for hookworm. Barry, stripped to the waist and sweating from his labors, sat on the limestone outcrop and frowned at him.

"You want my help, Léon?"

"*Oui, mon Père.*"

"Very well, I want yours. Help Louis carry stones today and I'll look after your little girl this evening."

Léon was one of those who had watched him drag the mule to the hole, a husky young fellow, not too bright, with a soft, lumpy face that resembled an overripe corossol. He glanced about uneasily, scratching the side of his slack mouth. Louis and St. Juste had stopped work to watch. The dozen peasants seated on the grass under the pomme-rose trees watched too. Barry waited in silence, sensing the importance of the moment.

"Why should I have to pay?" Léon mumbled at last. "No one else does."

"Everyone else does from now on. Everyone who's strong enough to lift a handful of gravel or a *calebasse* of water." Barry pushed himself erect. "Make up your mind, please. I've things to do."

"Well——"

"Good. Louis will show you where the stones are." Barry at once picked up his shovel and returned to work.

At ten-thirty Micheline Laroche came. Louis had told her the Father was starting the new church this morning. She was alone. Nodding to those under the trees, she sat down a little distance away. She was wearing the butterfly dress she had worn that day on the boat.

The Father and St. Juste were digging a trench, she saw, to hold the first course of stones that would support the walls of the church. They had lines strung up to guide them. As she watched, her brother-in-law and Léon Devieux came along the ridge carrying stones. They dropped the stones onto an already large pile outside the trench and at once trudged off again.

Why was Léon helping the Father? Catus had been sure no one would help, with the whole village buzzing about what had happened in the old church last night.

She shrugged. It was no concern of hers, who worked or didn't. She plucked a blade of grass and nibbled at it, watching the Father. It was the first time she had seen him without a shirt on. His skin was much whiter than Lemke's. She hadn't known a white man could sweat so, either. Lemke had been only damp and sticky, unpleasantly so, that night on the plantation beach. The Father looked as though he had been rubbed with cooking oil. It would be interesting to lie in his arms when he was like that . . .

I wonder if Lemke kept his promise to tell the Father how much I like him, she thought. I'll ask him tomorrow night. If he didn't, I'm going to be difficult.

At eleven o'clock Barry stopped work to talk to two more men sent up from the rectory by Lucy. They argued. One stayed to work, the other refused. The one who stayed had an ugly sore on his lower lip and had not been a patient before. I'll treat him when we go down at noon, Barry thought. The other had been dismissed days ago after treatment for an aching tooth but had returned every day since to beg more medicine. Barry had doled out aspirin, one tablet at a time, to get rid of him, and was glad now to see him go.

At noon Barry called a halt and went down to the mission for lunch, taking Louis and St. Juste with him. No one in St. Joseph worked when the sun was high. He found Edith at the rectory. She had arrived half an hour before, on horseback from the plantation, but knowing he would soon be stopping work, had decided to wait for him.

"Must you work all afternoon too?" she asked with a pout.

He laughed. He was in high spirits with the job going so well. "I wouldn't think of not working all afternoon," he told her. "We've got two workers we didn't expect, and every man counts."

He treated the ugly lip-sore and told the fellow he would need daily attention for at least a week. "But you'll have to work for it. I'm through giving you people costly medicines for nothing."

"You want me to keep coming so you can get work out of me," the man grumbled.

"Don't come, then. Suit yourself."

With four at the table the little dining room was sadly crowded and Barry was aware that Edith was not enjoying her visit. It troubled him. She had ridden all the way from the plantation to be with him. But he could see no way to alter the situation.

"There's something I've been wanting to ask you," he said to her. "Did you speak to anyone yesterday about Toto's death?"

"No. Not a soul."

"The people knew about it last night."

She seemed startled. "But how could they?"

"We don't know. It's a mystery."

"I came straight here from the boat."

"You didn't talk to anyone on the boat? Or in Anse Ange?"

"Not a soul."

Barry looked at St. Juste and shrugged. "I suppose it will come out sometime. Meanwhile there's nothing we can do about it."

After lunch he walked with Edith in the yard, unwilling to leave the mission. More patients might arrive, and patients were potential workers. He had to smile at his change of attitude toward those who sought his help. He was a genuine villain, he supposed. But there could be no harm in it, and might even be some good. The average St. Joseph peasant was pretty shrewd, quick to take advantage of anyone who permitted it but more likely to respect a man who wouldn't. They had never held it against Felix Dufour for selling the mule, for example. *He* was the fool for having been outsmarted.

He sat with Edith under the campêche and took her hand. "I'm sorry about this afternoon, really I am. Can't you stay for dinner and spend the evening here? You know your way to the plantation now."

She was still annoyed. "I'm not sure that I should."

"I do have a job to do."

"Of course." She turned to face him and he sensed that she was trying very hard to escape the mood she was in. "Did you think about me last night?" she asked.

He had to smile. "I couldn't very well. I was at a *vodun* service till daylight."

"A what?"

He told her of the affair in the grotto. Just as he finished, a little group of people arrived from the village and he had to excuse himself. When he returned after giving them the medicine they had come for, he was grinning. He had obtained two more workers.

Edith frowned at him as he seated himself beside her again. "Are you sure it's a good thing for you to attend these *vodun* affairs?" she asked.

"Of course it is. How else am I going to understand these people?"

"Surely you don't condone it?"

"At the moment I'm observing, not judging."

"I don't like it," she said.

He thought it wise to change the subject and asked if she were comfortable at the Lemkes'. The question brought another frown to her face.

"I don't think I'm very welcome," she said. "If I'm not mistaken, they were using both bedrooms and I've put one of them out. Warner sleeps on the veranda."

"They've been quarreling, you mean?"

"They hardly speak to each other. When they do, it seems to be always with a double meaning." Her lips tightened and Barry felt her shiver. "I don't like Warner Lemke, Barry. I don't like the way he looks at me or the way he speaks of you. It's always 'dear Mr. Clinton' as though he despised you."

"He feels that way about all clerics. We're a bit queer, he thinks."

"I wish I could stay here at the mission."

"I wish you could too." He squeezed her hand. "But the Bishop wouldn't like it, with things so crowded here."

EDITH INSISTED ON GOING TO THE RIDGE in the afternoon. There must be some way she could help, she said. Her petulance seemed to have vanished, and Barry was delighted at the prospect of her company.

He gave her a trowel and she stood at his side, applying mortar to the wall as he lifted the stones into place.

Soon afterward, Pradon Beliard arrived. He was not dressed for work. At sight of Barry stripped to the waist and toiling with the others, his eyes widened and he had a moment of panic. His job was to help Mr. Clinton. He was being paid for it. But he had no intention of working like a peasant.

It was too late for flight; he had already been seen. He advanced slowly, his glance darting this way and that in frantic search of an escape. What kind of man *was* this Clinton, anyway, to be acting like a common laborer? And what in God's name did the white girl think she was doing, working there beside him? Had the world gone crazy?

Barry, amused by his antics, watched him out of an eye-corner.

"I—I have come to offer my services," Pradon stammered.

Barry solemnly nodded. "We certainly can use you. Do you know how to lay up a wall?"

"I'm afraid I don't."

"You'd better help carry the stones, then."

"Sir, with this leg of mine——"

"Oh, yes, the leg. I'd forgotten. Well"— Barry looked around— "we've a lot more digging to do. The church is to have a concrete floor. Go and help Louis dig, why don't you, if you want to be useful."

Pradon was now actually trembling. "I—I thought I might help with the supervision," he managed weakly.

"What the devil would you supervise?" Barry was thoroughly enjoying the young man's discomfiture. "Come off it and pick up a shovel. You're no better than the rest of us, are you?"

Pradon reluctantly trudged over to where Louis was digging. Louis leered at him. They had all heard the conversation. They were all watching to see what he would do. He picked up a shovel and saw that the audience under the pomme-rose trees was observing him too. His lip curled. He went to work savagely.

"You're going to get that pretty shirt dirty if you don't take it off," Louis said innocently.

Pradon swore under his breath, threw down the shovel, and peeled off his shirt. His eyes blazed. Every few moments, as he dug furiously at the hard ground, he lifted his head to look at Barry, whose back was toward him. There was pure hatred in his gaze.

A little later Catus Laroche came. The work was going well, with Louis and Pradon shoveling, four men now carrying stones, and St. Juste and Barry laying them up. Catus glanced at the audience of peasants and sat down beside his sister, who had gone home at noon but returned soon after the siesta hour. At sight of the white girl working at Barry's side, he frowned. His sister was frowning too.

"Look at her!" Micheline said. "If she is not careful, she'll get her pretty hands dirty! You'd think she would be ashamed to let the whole world know she is after him."

"How do you know she is after him? It could be the church she is interested in."

"The way she looks at him? Don't be stupid."

Catus saw that she was right. As she worked, the woman kept

glancing at the Father. They were not talking much, but she seemed unable to keep her mind and her eyes on what she was doing. He shrugged. The mind of a white woman was something he knew nothing about. He knew the mind of his sister though.

He scowled at Micheline. "The way she looks at him is no concern of yours," he said.

She tossed her head but made no retort.

Catus watched the men at work and was impressed by what they had accomplished in such a short time. When Louis had told him the new church was to be of stone, he had thought of the task as a tremendous undertaking. On Ile du Vent no one built with stone. He saw now that it was relatively easy. You simply placed one chunk of limestone on top of another with a mortar of sand and cement, and if a chunk didn't fit you broke it with a hammer. They would need a certain amount of skill when they came to the doors and windows, he guessed, but the walls were no great problem.

He frowned, running his tongue over the gap in his teeth. Perhaps he should build a stone *hounfor*.

His sister glanced at him sideways. "Why don't you help them?" she asked.

"Why should I help?"

"The Father is your friend, isn't he?"

"It is not up to me to build a church for him. Let him build his own."

"When he does, will you set fire to it?"

Catus turned his head slowly toward her. "That is not amusing."

"Then it wasn't you who destroyed the Father's altar?"

"You know it wasn't."

He wondered who *had* set fire to the Father's church, and, for that matter, who had told the people about young Toto. His gaze fastened on the white girl again, and after a moment he rose. As he strolled toward the Father he was aware that people were watching him. What were they expecting? That he would call on the *loa* to knock this new church to pieces?

"May I speak to you a moment, Father?"

"Certainly." Welcoming the excuse to rest a moment, Barry strolled with him to the edge of the ridge, not failing to appreciate the magnificent view of the sea as he halted. "What is it, Catus?"

"You said you would ask *M'selle* Barnett if she talked to anyone about Toto."

"I asked her at lunch. She didn't."

"Is she positive?"

"Quite. She told no one."

"Well, I won't keep you from your work," Catus said, and returned to his sister.

There was but one answer, he told himself. If the girl had spoken to no one, the news of the boy's death must have reached the island another way. There was only one other way. *M'sieu* Lemke, at the plantation, conversed with Couronne every day on the radio. Someone at Couronne must have told *him*.

This raised another question. The story, it now seemed certain, had first made its appearance at the ceremony in the grotto. Catus had spent the morning making inquiries and was positive on that point. But Lemke had not attended the service. The whispers had been set in motion by someone else then.

By whom?

Catus looped his arms about his knees and scowled at the men working on the church. At one in particular—Pradon Beliard. He had been thinking about Pradon for some days now. There were rumors in Petit Trou, where this young dandy with the limp lived, that he and the magistrate, Felix Dufour, were thick as thieves. It was Dufour who had sold *Père* Clinton that mule.

And what about the curious remark Pradon had made to him on the boat, the day of the Father's arrival? "Don't worry about this one making trouble for you," the dandy had said. "He won't last long." How could Pradon Beliard know how long the Father would last?

One thing was certain: the Father had an enemy here on the island, and that enemy was no ordinary peasant. Only someone with a special knack for intrigue could have set in motion the lie that Toto was dead before he left the island, and convinced the people the Father was to blame. Ordinarily they wouldn't have dreamed of doubting Louis, nor would they have blamed a man for something his mule had done.

As for the mutterings in the grotto last night—well, Pradon had been there, hadn't he?

Had he also set fire to the church? Catus thought it was very probable. The Father, of course, was wrong in believing that no one at the service could have set the fire. The tunnel into which the tide flowed was not the only entrance to that cave, and many people knew it.

He would have to watch Pradon. *Oui.*

He watched him now, and another thought came. What if he did discover proof that Pradon was the Father's enemy? The Father was building this big new church. At the very first service in the old church, before the Toto affair, a surprisingly large number of people had turned out. Far more than old *Père* Mitchell had ever been able to entice. What would happen if Pradon were exposed? The Father would have everyone's sympathy. Already the people admired him for his industry. Just look at him now, half drowned in sweat but working as hard an any black man and laughing while he labored. They went to him for medical help when he, Catus, could not cure them. They were watching to see what kind of vegetables would come up in the model garden he talked so much about.

If I stop Beliard from destroying him he will grow strong, Catus thought. He may soon be strong enough to preach against *vodun*, as old *Père* Mitchell did. And if this man raises his voice against the things I believe in, people may listen to him.

Still, the very things for which the people respected the Father were the things Ile du Vent needed so badly. His interest in their health. His efforts to improve their way of life. The example he set by working so hard.

Perhaps he will not preach against me, Catus reflected. After all, he did come to the *vodun* service. And he doesn't claim that his sacred book holds all the answers. . . .

14

L UCILLE BRISTLED WITH INDIGNATION as she bustled about the breakfast table. She had gone early to the market in Petit Trou this morning, hoping to get her pick of the vegetables and a choice cut of the pig to be slaughtered. She had returned seething.

"That Dufour!" she stormed. "You will have to do something about him, Father! It's all very well for you to be working at the church and killing yourself over a crowd of patients every day, but someone's got to put that man in his place, and who but you can do it? In Anse Ange the *marchandes* are taxed only two cents a basket. Here they must pay ten now!"

"Ten?" Barry was truly concerned. The previous complaints had been about a tax of five.

"He raised it again this morning. He has no right!"

Barry looked at his watch and then across the table at St. Juste. "Perhaps I'd better go down there, Clement. I hate to run out on you, but she's right. Something *has* got to be done."

"You don't need to work on the church every morning, Mr. Clinton," St. Juste said. "We've got quite a crew now. You don't need to go up there at all."

"I like it."

"You go at it too hard. You're losing weight."

"Wrong. I've gained." As a matter of fact he had never felt better in his life. The week of hard physical labor on the ridge had toughened him. He could climb that ridge path now without even puffing, and lift stones that would have broken his back before. He was very nearly as dark as a native too, from the sun. When he undressed at night he looked like a man made of two half bodies, one white and one dark brown, stuck together at the waist.

"I'll go and see Dufour now, Lucy," he said. "If people come for treatment, have them wait. I should be back soon." He had been having her tell them to come back in the evening, unless it was an emergency. Mornings he worked on the church, and in the afternoons Edith usually came.

As he rode to Petit Trou—he had a horse now, a sturdy little animal sent over from Anse Ange by the rector there—he thought about Edith and shook his head. She wasn't having much fun, he supposed. Even though he had arranged his schedule so that he might spend some time with her every day, there was really little they could do together. At Fond Marie there had been the Couronne parties and the beach. Here they could only stroll about the island paths. On the one occasion when they had gone down to the channel shore for a swim, half the people of Ile du Vent, it seemed, had gathered to gawk at a white girl in a bathing suit, and Edith had been furious.

The truth, he supposed, was that Ile du Vent was a pretty deadly place for anyone not concerned with its problems or blessed with a streak of adventure. An adventurous girl might find things to do. Those caves in the great cliff just begged to be explored, for instance. And spear-fishing on the channel reef should be an exciting experience. He wished he had time for such pleasures himself. Some day he would have. But for a woman like Edith there was nothing. She simply wasn't the curious sort. She had come here for one reason, to be with him, and being with him was turning out to be dull.

She wants to be loved, I suppose, he told himself. But confound it, I can't make love to her when I don't feel like it, and there's never a moment when someone isn't watching us, anyway. He had walked with her one day along what had seemed to be a deserted path, and stopped to kiss her, and the kiss had been interrupted by the giggling of two little girls sitting less than ten feet away under a tree. Another time, thinking themselves safe, they had been caught in the act of embracing by Micheline Laroche and her sister Dauré. It was hopeless.

She wouldn't come in the evening, that was the trouble. She disliked the long ride back to the plantation in the dark. He, of course, had been invited to the plantation by the Lemkes, but so far had been able to avoid going. He could foresee no pleasure in a pointless struggle to make conversation with a married pair who were scarcely speaking to each other. Especially when one of them frankly despised him in the bargain.

He dismounted at Dufour's house and climbed the veranda steps. People in the village street stopped to watch as he knocked on the screen door.

"*Père* Clinton!" the little man exclaimed through his bad teeth. "This *is* a surprise!"

"I don't get down here very often, do I?" Barry tried to sound pleasant. "I'll mend my ways when the church is a bit farther along."

Dufour held the door and Barry entered, wondering if the fellow never had his shirts laundered, and how he could possibly stand having his sleeves rolled down with their filthy cuffs buttoned about his wrists. He accepted the chair Dufour gestured him to and waited for the magistrate to stop bustling about, picking things up and putting them down again. The room was just about what he had expected: sisal rugs on the floor, the furniture fashioned of thick mahogany planks layered with varnish, the walls decorated with framed magazine illustrations and calendars advertising Coca Cola, Swiss drugs, and sundry other commodities for sale in the stores of the capital. The females pictured on the calendars were white and alluring, but the Swiss presentation was a striking color photograph of snow-covered mountains.

Dufour sat down, adjusting his black bow tie. "Now, *mon Père*. What can I do for you?"

"I've come to quarrel with you," Barry told him with a smile.

"Quarrel? But no!"

"But yes, my friend. And not about the mule you sold me, either. What's all this I hear about a whopping big tax in the market place?"

Dufour's gray-white eyebrows dropped a fraction of an inch and his bony fingers curled over the edge of his chair-arms. "Tax? There is some complaint, you mean?"

"You're darned right there's some complaint," Barry said, determined to keep the discussion breezy as long as possible. He did not want this man for an enemy; Dufour was too clever and too powerful. "You can't go around slapping taxes on people just because you're a little short of money, you know. It isn't done."

"The money is for a new market," Dufour retorted.

"A worthy project, I'm sure." *If* you were telling the truth, Barry thought, but of course you're not. "But have you the authority?"

"Authority?"

"I realize you're the magistrate here. But a tax increase would have to be approved by the legislature, wouldn't it? I'm quite sure it would. Taxation is a very serious business, you know."

"I have raised the market tax only a little."

"It doesn't seem a small amount to the *marchandes*."

"Those women! They *look* for things to complain about!"

"At the moment they're looking for relief," Barry said, "and I'm bound to say I think they ought to have it. A ten-cent tax is a whopping burden, really. Why, suppose a woman has only a basket of mangoes to sell. Fifty mangoes, say, at two for a penny. After walking here to Petit Trou with them and sitting in the market all day to sell them, she'd get twenty-five cents for the lot. And out of that you demand ten."

"They don't all sell mangoes."

"They don't make a lot of money, any of them. Really, Dufour, you've got to cut this out."

Dufour was squirming. "Well, I'll reduce it to eight."

"That won't do. The legal tax is two, and you know it."

"Five, then."

Barry shook his head, still smiling.

"We need a new market!" Dufour sputtered.

"I'll tell you what," Barry countered. "You have a talk with the deputy for this district. It's Beauvoir, isn't it, over in Anse Ange? Ask him to bring the matter up at the next session of the legislature. If they'll approve an increase, I'll not only shut my mouth; I'll donate a tidy sum toward a new market myself." That ought to hold the old buzzard, he thought. It sounded just plausible enough to be entirely innocent, just the sort of suggestion to be expected from a well-meaning outsider who didn't know how local politics were managed; yet it left Mr. Felix Dufour with only a handful of air. He pushed himself to his feet, smiling again. "Meanwhile, back we go to the legal two-cent tax, hey, until the increase is all proper and above-board. Agreed?"

Dufour rose, scowling.

"Well, I'll be running along." Barry held out his hand. "I'm sure you won't hold this against me. Just trying to do my job, you know."

Dufour shook hands, went to the door, and opened it. Barry saw that he was seething.

When Barry had gone, the little magistrate began to shake. He shook uncontrollably. The hair shimmered on his head and his teeth made a clicking noise. For almost a minute he simply stood there by the door, shaking. Then he flung the door open and spat, aiming his spittle at the back of the man now riding up the village street.

Barry, of course, was unaware of the insult.

Dufour let the door slam and returned to his chair. But he could not sit still. He shot to his feet and paced the floor, clenching and unclenching his hands. He knew why the Father had come this morning. It wasn't to help the *marchandes*. All that talk about the poor suffering *marchandes* was simply pig defecation. The Father was out to settle the score for the mule. Why had he mentioned the mule, if not to make that clear? Why had he been so free with his smiles? Damn!

The worst of it was, he couldn't fight back. That was a clever man, that Father. He had sat up there in his miserable mission like a patient spider, waiting for the web to entangle his victim before he struck. The tax would have to be dropped. If it wasn't, all the Father had to do was file a complaint with the right people and Ile du Vent would have a new magistrate. The stupid *marchandes* wouldn't register an official complaint, but the Father would. He probably had a letter already written and was just hoping for the excuse to send it.

As for an appeal to the legislature, what a stream of horse urine that was. As if those Cadillac-rich politicians in the capital would listen to a plea from the magistrate of Ile du Vent! Why, they didn't know there *was* such a place as Ile du Vent. And even if they did, he would have to guarantee that crooked deputy, Beauvoir, nine tenths of the profits before he would agree to bring the request up.

Damn the Father! Dufour spat again, forgetting where he was. The blob of spittle struck the Swiss calendar on the wall and dribbled like a fat white snail down the side of a snow-covered mountain. He beat his clenched hands against his forehead, squealing with rage.

Then he remembered the letter.

It had come yesterday, a letter from the hospital in the capital, very official, explaining the circumstances of young Toto Anestor's death and instructing him to make the facts known to the populace of Ile du Vent in his capacity of magistrate. It was going to mean a great deal to the Father, that letter. True, the work on the church was proceeding in spite of the people's attitude, but he still hadn't nearly enough workers. And according to Pradon Beliard, the old church had been practically empty at last Sunday's service.

Dufour yanked open a table drawer and read the letter again. His lips curled. He turned and marched through his ornate little dining room into the kitchen. There he crumpled the letter in his fist, dropped it into one of the iron charcoal braziers, and set fire to it.

ON HIS RETURN TO THE MISSION Barry found Alma Lemke waiting with a patient. The man's name was Julio Everaste. He was a fisherman. He had been carried from the plantation end of the island on a stretcher of poles and woven palm fronds by some of his neighbors.

"My cook told me about him," Alma said. "I found him lying on a mat in his *caille*, waiting to die. Can you do anything for him?"

Everaste lay now on the cot in the office. His left foot was a great bloated balloon and he was obviously in pain.

Barry made an examination, then called for hot water and laid out some instruments. Removing his shirt, he said, "Are you sure you want to watch this?"

"You may need help, don't you think?"

"It won't be very pretty."

"It isn't pretty now."

He had no operating table; there wasn't room in the office for one. He would have to do this on his knees, he saw. Having washed the awful-looking foot and put a folded towel under it, he leaned forward to peer into the fellow's face.

"This is going to hurt for a minute, *compère*."

"*Oui.*"

"After it's over, you'll be all right."

"*Merci, mon Père.*"

With his left arm around the leg to hold it, he cut into the side of the foot where the infection seemed to be centered. Everaste made a gasping sound and arched his back convulsively. But the blade had not pierced the skin. The skin was like leather.

Barry tightened the pressure of his arm and cut again in the same place. It was like going through the hard rind of a watermelon into the pulp. There was a great spurt of fluid from the incision. He felt a sticky wetness on his face and saw that the front of his undershirt was yellow. The stench was horrible. Behind him Alma gasped.

The man on the cot was writhing.

Barry dropped the foot and groped to his feet, sickened by the stench, aware that his eyes were smarting. It was a frightful moment. He must wash at once or run the risk of some ghastly infection, but the patient was tossing about in agony, banging his bad foot against the frame of the cot, and the fluid spurting from the wound was getting all over everything.

"Alma!" he said frantically. "Can you hold him?"

"Of course." She stepped past him and went to her knees, pressing her hands down on Everaste's shoulders. "Julio!" she said sharply. "Stop it!"

Barry groped for a basin of water.

He was still scrubbing himself when Alma said from her position beside the cot, "It seems to have stopped spurting now. Is there something I should do?" She seemed completely calm.

"No, I can attend to it. I'm all right now."

She rose to make room for him and, after watching for a moment, opened the door and went out. He didn't blame her. He was on the verge of being ill himself. It was all he could do to hold down the contents of his stomach while he cleaned the open foot and put a dressing on it.

The door opened. Alma came in again with a bucket of steaming hot water and a handful of cloths. At once she began to clean up the mess on the floor. For a moment Barry was too astonished to speak.

"You don't have to do that," he said.

"It isn't the first floor I've scrubbed," she replied with a shrug. "Take care of your patient."

He gave his patient an injection of penicillin and leaned over him. "Does it hurt very much, Julio?"

"A little, *mon Père*."

"Do you want something to make you sleep for a while, or would you rather have a shot of rum?"

The sick man grinned. "What do you think, *mon Père*?"

"Rum it is." Barry put some into a glass and supported the fellow's shoulders while he drank it. "As a matter of fact, I could use a little of this myself."

He poured two small drinks and handed one to Alma. She touched her glass to his.

"To the doctor," she said.

"And to his nurse."

"Shall I go home now, *mon Père*?" Julio asked.

"No. I'll want another look at you when you feel better. You'd better plan on staying here tonight."

"Here in your house?"

"Right where you are. Now, though, I think we'll have your friends put you in the church so we can clean this place up. No one will bother you there." Barry opened the door and told the men outside what he wanted. As they followed instructions and carried the cot from the room, they gazed at the man lying on it as though he had been returned to them from the dead.

With Alma's help Barry put the room to rights. When the job was done, they collapsed onto chairs and looked at each other.

"You should have been a nurse," he said.

She frowned. She was wondering what had happened to her. If

anyone had told her an hour ago that she could be useful in a doctor's office, she would have laughed. The thought of handling a sick person would have made her sick herself. Especially a black one.

She tried to recall what had passed through her mind when Barry looked up from the spurting foot and asked if she could help. Nothing had passed through it; that was the strangest part of the whole business. She hadn't thought at all. She had simply stepped forward and done what she knew had to be done. She was like a person who had lived a lifetime in fear of water, then suddenly was forced to swim and discovered it was a natural, easy thing to do. There on her knees beside the cot she hadn't been conscious of anything except that Julio might hurt himself unless she helped him. She was glad she had helped him. She felt a little proud of herself. She looked at Barry with new understanding. He too must feel something when he helped these people. There *was* a reward.

"I said," he was repeating, "you should have been a nurse."

"You could use a nurse here if this sort of thing happens often."

"All sorts of things happen. What's the story on Julio, do you know? What happened to him?"

"He isn't sure. He was wading in shallow water off the beach one day and something stung him."

It was all Barry ever learned about the cause of Julio's illness.

HE HAD TWO MORE PATIENTS THAT MORNING. Alma stayed to help, and he was astonished at her instinctive understanding of how best to help him. It was a joy to have her at his side.

She remained for lunch, and her presence magically transformed the occasion into a session of fun. St. Juste told some hilarious stories of Pradon Beliard's attempts to avoid work on the ridge. Barry recalled some of the amusing things that had happened at the clinic. Before the meal ended, there was even a smile on the usually hangdog face of Lucille as the old housekeeper served them.

"That Mrs. Lemke is a wonderful woman," St. Juste said when Alma had gone. "I didn't know she was like that."

"I didn't either," Barry said. "She must have enjoyed being a nurse this morning."

Soon afterward, Edith arrived. Barry found her complaints about the heat and the long ride hard to take, then suffered pangs of guilt for his attitude and put himself out to make her visit pleasant. When she left at five, though, he was glad to see her go and wondered what on earth was the matter with him.

THE FOLLOWING DAY Edith told him she was returning to Couronne. The atmosphere at the Lemkes' house, she said, was just too much for her.

"Perhaps I can come again when the church is finished and you're not so busy," she said.

15

ST. JUSTE SAID ONE DAY AT BREAKFAST, "We'll be starting on the rectory this morning, Mr. Clinton. You'll be up to swing the first shovel, won't you?" With Edith's departure Barry had returned to his original schedule, holding clinic in the mornings and working on the ridge in the afternoons. Alma found it more convenient to come in the mornings.

"You couldn't keep me away."

He waited for Alma to arrive, left her in charge, and hurried to the ridge. St. Juste and his handful of workers were putting the finishing touches on the church roof, but stopped and led him to the lines laid out for the rectory near by. St. Juste put a shovel in his hands.

"Just break the ground for us, Mr. Clinton. Then you can run along back to your patients."

They cheered when he swung the shovel.

He turned to admire the church. It was nearly finished. The job had taken longer than St. Juste had predicted, of course—everything in St. Joseph took longer than it ought to—but the result was a structure to make a man proud.

It was large. It had a broad, high entrance and spacious window openings to let in the breeze. Its corrugated iron roof gleaming in the sun could be seen from Anse Ange, across the channel, and probably from many a mountainside far back in the interior of the mainland. Barry had to smile. A lot of people in the mainland mountains, including a number of his fellow missionaries, must be wondering about the strange new glitter atop Ile du Vent.

A few items were lacking. The bell for the handsome little bell-tower had not arrived yet from the capital. For that matter, it probably hadn't arrived in the capital yet from the States. The benches, though cut and sanded, couldn't be assembled until the brackets came. The altar wasn't finished. But he was not impatient.

Things had gone well, he told himself. They might have gone better, of course. If Felix Dufour in his fury over the market-tax business had not denied having received the letter from the hospital—a letter he must have received because Barry had been sent a copy of it—there would have been more workers. It hadn't done much good to produce his own copy and insist that Dufour was lying. The peasants were quite sure that the magistrate, even though they hated him, just wouldn't have the nerve to lie about such a serious matter. Still, St. Juste had never been entirely without help, even if much of it was unwilling and incompetent.

The garden was flourishing. Some of the quick-growing vegetables —radishes, bush beans, leaf lettuce, mustard greens—were ready for harvest, and scarcely a day went by when some of the peasants didn't come for seeds and advice on how to plant them. There would be more and better food for the islanders soon; no question of it.

At the clinic he was always busy and always facing new problems, but there was a difference now. Since helping him that day with Julio Everaste, Alma had come nearly every day. It was a pity she had never studied nursing. She had an amazing knack for it and, surprisingly, just the right temperament; at least it was just right for Ile du Vent. Cheerful no matter what happened, able to scold without being angry and joke without being ridiculous, she could win the co-operation of the most difficult patients. The stubborn ones gave in to her, the stupid ones obeyed her, the frightened ones gained courage from her, the demanding ones trembled before her. She took her work seriously too; it was no mere fad. At home she studied the medical books he had lent her. They were more interesting, she said —"a damned sight more interesting"—than the romances she had used as an antidote for boredom before.

He still did not know why she should be bored at home. She rarely mentioned her husband, and Barry had asked no questions. Warner had ridden up from the plantation once or twice to ask if there was anything he could do to help with the work on the church. On being told there wasn't, he had said politely "Well, let me know if I'm needed" and ridden off again.

There was one real problem. Too few people came to church on Sundays.

He never had more than a dozen in his congregation. Lucy always attended, of course. Alma came when she could. Louis and Dauré were amazingly faithful, and even on the Sunday following the birth of Dauré's second child—it was another girl, born on a Friday—Louis had turned up. Of course he could count on St. Juste, and sometimes

on Catus. But Micheline had stopped coming, and so had Pradon
Beliard, who was in a perpetual sulk these days.

He rarely saw any of the others. There hadn't been a new face
since the first Sunday, or, to put the blame where it belonged, since
the spread of that fantastic story that he had paid Louis to smuggle
a dead boy off the island so he would not be blamed for the boy's
death.

It would not be correct, though, to say that he had accomplished
nothing religionwise. He had accomplished a great deal, he felt. Catus
and he, since their curious discussion of Christianity prompted by
the lurid illustrations in the old Bible, had found much to talk about.
He would not soon forget, for example, the evening Catus had called
on him with a copy of old Mitchell's Creole book.

"I have been reading this again," Catus had said. "As you instructed, I paid small attention to those tales of how the world was
made and the great flood came, and so forth. But I did read about
those two in the garden, and it puzzles me."

"You find the story of Adam and Eve hard to believe?"

"The book says that two people made by God to populate the
earth were given a wonderful garden to live in but were ordered not to
touch a certain fruit. They ate the fruit and were driven from the
garden as punishment. The story seems to me just silly. If God made
these people and wished them to be blameless, why did he put a
temptation in the garden to trap them? You are building a new
church on the ridge. Are you going to build a crack in it so the
church will have a chance to fall down and prove itself bad? Or do I
offend you by questioning this?"

"You don't offend me. Go on."

"Well, then comes the really incredible part of this silly story. Because the first man and woman sinned, all men are sinners. How can
that be? Is Dauré's new baby wicked because her great-great-grand-
mama did a wrong thing one time?" Catus shook his head. "If you
expect me to believe this kind of thing, you must think me a fool.
If you believe it, *you* must be a fool."

"I don't think we're fools, Catus. And if you remember, I asked you
to believe only one thing."

"What is that?"

"The truth of the teachings of Jesus."

Catus thought for a moment. "This Jesus of yours was a good man,
I believe, though I think he was not a god and probably not the son
of one. He may have believed he was, of course. That he had no

earthly father I don't believe either, though I may be wrong. The big thing that troubles me is that since his return to heaven he has never shown himself to you who believe in him. If the *loa* can come to a *vodun* service, why can't Jesus come to yours?"

"We believe he does, Catus, though of course not in the same way. He possesses our minds, so to speak, instead of our bodies."

"Well, if you choose to believe that, without ever seeing him . . . On the whole, as I say, I admire him very much. He said many good things and lived the kind of life he asked others to live. It pleases me that he showed such an interest in the peasants and had no wish to be rich or a politician. Probably the rich would not have accepted him, of course, he being poor himself. How long did he live, this Jesus?"

"A little more than thirty years. But he was a teacher only three."

"Only three?" Catus was astonished. "From only three years' teaching has come a faith so strong? Why, I have heard it said that your religion covers the whole world!"

"There you have proof of its greatness, Catus. Despite all the foolish and hard-to-understand doctrine that misguided men have invented in their efforts to seem wise, there is something in Christianity that people grasp at."

"The hope of living again, you mean?"

"More than that, I'm sure. People feel in their hearts that Jesus found the one way for us to live together here and now without destroying one another."

"Perhaps you are right. But I could wish that the teachings of this man had been kept separate from all those silly stories. It would make everything much easier to understand."

It boiled down, Barry began to see, to the interesting fact that Catus accepted the teachings of Christ but rejected most of the rest. A peasant with a peasant's mind, albeit a shrewd one, he found truth in simplicity but refused to swallow the trappings, less simple, which even the theologians had to interpret as mystic symbols meaning more than they seemed to mean. He would accept the incredible if it contained something worth-while. He wanted no part of it if it didn't.

Well, he was certainly not alone in his reasoning. Many another doubter had been driven the whole way back by theology's learned efforts to make the Christ story all but incomprehensible. That Catus found it the inspiring tale of a great and good man was an interesting start.

Am I teaching him or learning from him, Barry wondered.

Equally interesting had been his attendance at several *vodun* services in the village *tonnelle*. One had been a service to Erzulie at which a woman at least sixty years old, a rack of bones with a face that must have been designed for frightening small children, had got tippled on *clairin*. Nicely drunk, the old girl had gone mincing around the enclosure making obscene gestures at some of the men. Especially at Catus, who had turned from her in disgust.

Then the same impossible creature had become possessed— "mounted" they called it—by the goddess in whose honor the service was being held. And after being drenched in perfume and dressed in what was surely a wedding gown, she had taken Catus by the hand and marched him off into the darkness.

Barry would have been mystified by such a performance a few weeks before. His education in *vodun* was progressing, however, thanks to frequent talks with Catus. Erzulie was the goddess to whom Catus was "married." The green ring on the *houngan's* left hand was the symbol of the union. When Erzulie "came" to an affair, she could demand the services of her husband and must not be denied, no matter how unappetizing the human form she chose to occupy when presenting herself.

Catus and the drunken old witch had been absent from the ceremony a couple of hours. Later, Barry had questioned him about it.

"*Was* that Erzulie you slept with, or did that old bag of bones simply pretend to be Erzulie so she could force you to go with her?"

The question seemed to bewilder Catus. "It was Erzulie, of course."

"Don't say 'of course.' Did she talk to you?"

"She spoke in *langage*, as the gods often do. I was not able to understand what she said."

"Listen to me," Barry requested, and spoke rapidly for a few minutes in what sounded like Creole but was babbled out without thought. It was not a difficult demonstration. To speak Creole properly he had to concentrate. Simply by not concentrating, he achieved the effect he sought.

"What was I saying, Catus?"

Catus shrugged. "Nothing. Nothing that made sense, at any rate."

"It sounded something like *langage* though, didn't it?"

Catus fingered the gap where his front tooth was missing and studied Barry's face. "Are you trying to tell me that *vodun* is a fake?"

"Not necessarily. There may be a real Erzulie. But if a very ugly old woman took me to bed and spoke only a lot of easily faked *langage*, telling me nothing about herself, asking nothing about me,

I'd certainly suspect her of being just a shrewd old girl who craved attention."

Catus gazed into space, scowling.

"It's hard to be sure, isn't it?" Barry murmured.

He had scored again, he was sure, when the *loa* called Zaca turned up at another service. The person possessed was an old fellow from the village, a man whose daughter, Barry knew, sometimes defied him by coming to church on Sundays. As soon as the god's identity was established by the possessed man's speech and behavior, the fellow was led to the *hounfor* by Catus. There he was dressed in Zaca's traditional blue-denim blouse and straw hat, and given a pipe to smoke and a tasseled *halford* to wear over his shoulder. Zaca was a peasant farmer and should look like one. He then stayed an hour, having a gay old time for himself strutting up and down the *tonnelle* and pinching female bottoms while holes were dug in the *tonnelle* floor and food offerings placed in them to honor him. His only vocal contribution, so far as Barry could determine, was an occasional loud announcement to the effect that he was Zaca. "*M'Zaca, oui! M'Zac!*"

When he departed, Barry had some questions ready. "This Zaca is the god who looks after your crops, isn't he, Catus?"

"He takes an interest," Catus said guardedly.

"You offer food and other things to him to insure his aid?"

"Yes, we do that."

"I wonder what he thinks of my garden on the ridge," Barry said, smiling.

All in all, these had been most interesting weeks.

He had expected to be lonely when Edith left. Surprisingly he had not been. His days were full, almost too full, and there was St. Juste to talk to in the evenings. There had been letters from Edith, too, the first one apologizing for what she called her "inexcusably selfish attitude" while on the island, the others very sweet and tender. She was planning another visit when the Bishop came to consecrate the church. If things were less strained at the Lemkes' she would stay two or three weeks.

He was looking forward to her visit and would certainly enjoy having her. But he was not impatient.

SOON AFTER BARRY LEFT THE RIDGE, Clement St. Juste had an argument with Pradon Beliard. It was not the first time.

Industriously wielding a shovel, St. Juste looked up to find Pradon shirking. At another time he might have said nothing, for Pradon's contribution to the job had never amounted to much. Now because of his own eagerness to get the rectory under way, he was annoyed.

"All right, you," he said. "Get your nose out of the air and be useful."

Pradon stood very straight and glared at him. "You can't talk to me like that!"

"I *am* talking to you like that."

"I don't work for you," Pradon retorted. "I work for Mr. Clinton."

Enough was enough. It was time for a showdown, St. Juste decided. He knew, of course, where he stood with Barry in the matter; he and Barry had discussed it a number of times. He knew what the trouble was, too. Coming here to his home island as Barry's "boy," handed his portfolio, so to speak, by none other than Jeff Barnett, Pradon had expected to do precious little actual work and be a big shot in the eyes of the islanders. Well——

St. Juste threw down his shovel, walked over and grasped a handful of the undershirt Pradon always wore. He held the boy helpless and glared at him. Louis and the others had stopped work to await the outcome.

"All right, you puffed-up little piece of donkey dirt," St. Juste said very carefully, "you've been asking for this. Now you listen to me. You don't work for Mr. Clinton. You work for Mr. Barnett at the Plantation Couronne, and at Couronne I'm your boss. Now you either get busy and do your share of the work here, or go back to Couronne in a damned big hurry and tell Mr. Barnett I sent you. Tell him I fired you because you're a worthless, lazy, stuck-up little pig-fart who thinks he's better than I am."

He straightened his arm and Pradon, pushed backward, stumbled over a mound of earth and sat down. St. Juste, turning away, at once took up his shovel again and paid the boy no further attention. The others returned to work too, but with an eye on Pradon as he struggled to get up.

He rose to his feet shaking with fury. His hands curled and his eyes were small, hard, vibrating beetles. For a moment it was a question whether he would snatch up his shovel and attack St. Juste with it, scream at him to continue the argument, or wheel and stalk off the job.

He did none of those things in the end. He went back to work. But he spoke to no one the rest of the day and when the day ended at last, instead of descending from the ridge with the others by the usual path, he limped off in another direction. He muttered as he walked, hobbling along at a pace that beaded his twitching face with sweat.

His destination was an old but larger than average *caille* on the outskirts of the channel-shore village called Tête Kabrit. A woman of sixty, sweeping beach-sand from the doorway, looked up at him and nodded as he entered the yard. When he inquired for her *mari*, she lifted the broom and pointed indifferently with it to a nearby cluster of coconut palms.

Pradon limped over to the trees. In their shade a man about the same age as the woman lay asleep on his back with his hands clasped under his head, his mouth open, and flies buzzing about his face. He wore only ragged trousers. Pradon kicked him lightly in the ribs.

The man sat up, grumbling. "Damn it, woman, can't you leave a man alone, no? What is it you——" He saw who it was and subsided. "Oh-oh. Excuse me, *compère*. What brings you here this morning?"

"It happens to be afternoon," Pradon retorted, "though I doubt if you'd know the difference. Believe me, you'd know it if you had to swing a shovel all day as I do. As for why I'm here, I came because I've changed my mind about waiting for the rectory to be finished. Get a shirt on. We're going to see the magistrate now."

"Now?"

"This very minute."

"I must have time to think about this."

"You've had time enough to think!" Pradon was furious again and began stamping his good foot on the sand. "You've been thinking for two weeks now! You gave me your word and I'm holding you to it!"

Antoine Constant, who had been magistrate of Ile du Vent until four years ago and had done little but lie in the shade of his palm trees since—he was rich, after all, from the sale of valuable property to *Père* Mitchell—let his heavy eyelids droop a little and studied the angry face of his caller. True, he had given his word and he was a man of honor. But it would never do to let this shrewd dandy think him eager. He would get up in a minute, yes, and put on a shirt if his insufferably critical wife had washed one, and go with Beliard to the house of Felix Dufour and do what had to be done. But all in good time. A slow fire cooked a better stew; everyone knew that.

The impatience of his caller disturbed him a little. Something had happened, apparently, for only a few days ago Beliard had advised *him* to be more patient. Besides, he didn't trust this dandy. It was all very well for Beliard to keep saying "You want to be magistrate again,

don't you?" Of course he did, as would any man who'd been cheated
out of his rights by a scheming rascal. But Beliard ought to be honest
enough to say what *he* wanted. Just the privilege of doing an acquaint-
ance a favor, or the pleasure of seeing a wrong righted? Oh-oh. The
pig didn't root up tidbits for the goat; everyone knew that. No man
was going to put himself to this much trouble for nothing.

Well, it was a personal thing, most likely. A feud of some sort
between Pradon and the new Father. There was no sense asking,
because the answer would be only an evasion. The big thing was to
make sure that he, Antoine, was going to get the reward promised him,
meaning the honor of being magistrate again, and that he wasn't
sticking his head into a noose. He'd have to be careful.

He stood up, brushing the sand from the seat of his pants. "Rest
yourself while I make myself presentable," he said.

FELIX DUFOUR WAS SITTING on his veranda when his callers came up the
road. He was surprised and instantly suspicious. Only a matter of real
importance could have induced Antoine Constant to visit him, he
knew. Usually when passing the magistrate's house Antoine spat in
the dirt or muttered insults.

The sun had just set and the village street was in shadow. Dufour
ushered his guests inside and lit a lamp. When they were seated on the
hard mahogany-plank chairs, Pradon Beliard came directly to the
point of the visit.

"I have discovered a most interesting fact, my friend."

"What interesting fact?" Dufour countered warily.

"As you know, a certain piece of land on the top of this island is
now being transformed into a mission."

"I am aware of it."

"Said land was originally purchased by old Father Mitchell from
three of our islanders."

"I was here at the time."

"One of the three was Antoine Constant."

"That I know too."

"Whose particular piece of land now lies under the new church
and will eventually support the rectory."

"I have no reason to doubt your word," Dufour said impatiently.
"What are you driving at?"

"This, my friend." And Pradon leaned forward on his chair, his
eyes shining brightly in the lamplight. "Antoine has sworn to me that
he never signed the papers!"

Dufour gazed at his callers and sighed. He was genuinely disappointed. Their coming here together, their air of secrecy and hint of something tremendous to be divulged had actually had him trembling with eagerness. He sighed again.

"What nonsense is this? Of course he signed."

"Did you witness the signing?" Pradon insisted.

"Well, no. I was attending a cousin's wedding on the mainland that particular day. But there *were* witnesses."

"Two of them," Pradon said, smiling. "And both are dead now. They died last January, you will recall, when the *Dieu Protège* turned over in the channel."

Dufour studied Pradon's confident smile and began to be interested. This young man with the limp was, after all, no fool. "So?" he said, eager again in spite of himself.

"So Antoine here insists that he signed nothing, and the only two men who saw him do it are dead."

Again the little magistrate felt deflated. "It won't do. His name is on the papers no matter what he says. It can be compared with other papers he signed when he was magistrate."

"Give me a piece of paper and a pencil, please."

Puzzled, Dufour did so. Pradon handed them to Antoine, who placed the paper on the table, hunched himself over it and laboriously drew his signature, letter by letter, as though building a fence. It took him almost as long.

"That," Pradon said, thrusting the paper triumphantly at the magistrate, "is the signature that appears on the land transfer. Now go and look at the dozens of official papers Antoine signed when he was magistrate."

Felix Dufour sensed something of great importance again and hurried across the room. From his desk he snatched some dog-eared notebooks and a great handful of papers. He began to flip through them. He put them down and swung himself about, frowning.

"This I don't understand. Explain it, please."

A look of embarrassment settled on Antoine's face. He glanced helplessly at Pradon.

Pradon laughed. "In all the time he was magistrate, he wrote his name only once."

"What?"

"That was the time *Père* Mitchell stood over him and he had to. He was always ashamed of this duck-track signature of his. You saw how long it takes him."

"But these official papers——"

"His wife, who came from Anse Ange and has had some schooling, always signed them for him. Every official paper you have here, and every one of those sent to the capital, was signed by Antoine's wife. But Antoine himself signed the land transfer. You see?"

Suddenly the little magistrate, who had been standing all this time, groped back to his chair and dropped with a thud into it. The possibilities had exploded in him like a swallowed firecracker. He sat with his mouth open, trembling.

Pradon patiently waited, watching him.

Dufour came to at last. Running his fingers through his bushy hair, he leaned forward. Suddenly he jabbed a finger at Antoine.

"You will have to learn to write like your wife, of course. You understand that? They will almost certainly ask you to sign your name."

"I can teach him," Pradon said.

"Mother of God, the Father will have to tear that church down again!"

"And the rectory. Or lose them. Whatever is on the land when Antoine gets it back will be his."

They sat and stared at one another. It was too tremendous to be talked about.

At last, with a shout, the magistrate shot to his feet. "Rum!" he cried. "We must have rum! No, by God, this is an occasion. I have a bottle of gin I have been saving. Antoine, Pradon, we celebrate! We have that meddling prayer-prattler right where the hair grows short. What a time we'll have watching him squirm!"

ANTOINE WAS UNSTEADY ON HIS FEET when he and Pradon left the magistrate's house. Pradon was not much better. It was a dark night. As the two of them stumbled through the village, Pradon decided he had better see his companion home. Otherwise Antoine might fall in with acquaintances and talk too much.

Arm in arm they wobbled along the footpath to Tête Kabrit. Presently Antoine looked at his companion and giggled.

"Tell me again how this affair with Dufour will result in my getting to be magistrate."

"I will explain when you are sober."

Antoine halted. "Tell me now. I don't go another step until I know!"

Pradon sighed. "Very well, this is how. When you have your land back, that will be the end of *Père* Clinton. For his stupidity in building an expensive new church and rectory on land that did not belong to him, he will be the laughing-stock of the island. He will have to leave. That much is clear to you?"

"Of course it is clear. Am I stupid?"

Stupid enough, Pradon thought; and for that I am extremely grateful, my tipsy friend. "Well, in a short while a new Father will be sent here to take *Père* Clinton's place. He will of course have to use the old church because the new one will belong to you. So you will start going to church and you will make friends with this man, which will not be difficult because he will be trying to undo the damage done by *Père* Clinton and will be most anxious to make friends. This is clear?"

"I become the new Father's friend, *oui*. Then what?"

"You become his very *good* friend. Then one day you go to him and say you wish to confess a terrible thing. You say that your statement about not signing the land-transfer papers was untrue, and the land really belongs to the church after all. It was a wicked, wicked thing you did and you are full of shame and sorrow, but really it was not your fault. Felix Dufour made you do it. You are only an ignorant peasant. Dufour threatened you with all sorts of abuses if you refused to say what he told you to say, and you were afraid to anger him. Then there will be another hearing."

Antoine tried to stand on one leg while scratching the other and almost fell down. "But then the church will get back the property, won't it?"

"Certainly it will get back the property. We've been all over that. You don't want the property. You want to be magistrate."

"That's right," Antoine said, brightening. "I want to be magistrate."

"Well, you will be, because Dufour will be packed off to the capital and slapped into jail. You will be named to take his place because you were magistrate before. *Now* will you stop scratching your damned leg and come home to bed?"

They walked a little more and Antoine stopped again, scowling. "How long will this take?" he demanded.

"How long will what take, for God's sake!"

"For me to be magistrate again."

Pradon flung up his arms. "How do I know how long it will take? A month, maybe. Two months. What do you care? You don't have to stand on your head till it happens, do you? You've got a palm tree to sleep under."

Antoine giggled.

"That fool!" Pradon muttered as he walked back alone after shoving Antoine into the arms of his wife. "That ignorant, stupid peasant! Magistrate, for the love of God!" There was going to be a new magistrate on Ile du Vent, all right, but it wouldn't be Antoine Constant. How trusting could the fool be?

"Tell me again how this affair will result in my getting to be magistrate," Pradon mimicked.

He laughed.

"All right, my friend, I'll tell you. Not how you're going to be magistrate, because you're not going to be, but how you and Felix Dufour are going to find yourselves skipping out of here some dark night for the mainland, with scared looks over your shoulders to make sure you aren't being followed.

"You're going through with this business of the papers, see? And it will work because Felix is smart enough to make it work. When it's over, that white-skinned priest who thinks I'm only a laborer will be finished here and you, my dumb friend, will own a church and a rectory. And then Pradon Beliard, who is *much* smarter than you and Felix think he is, and whose name will not have been mixed up in the affair at all, is going to call on both of you one day and threaten to expose you. And you and Felix, knowing very well that he can do it, are going to be scared out of your wits.

"That's what's going to happen, friend, if you want to know the truth of it. You think *you're* going to be magistrate? You think *you're* going to take Dufour's place? Don't make me laugh. To quote one of your own peasant proverbs, my trusting idiot friend, 'The stone you don't see is the one you trip over.' Only this stone will be big enough to break your neck."

And beginning to chuckle because he was a little drunk, Pradon kept it up all the way home.

16

WARNER LEMKE, TOO, was drinking that evening. He had begun earlier than usual and was unsteady on his feet when he let the screen door of the plantation house slam behind him and headed for the beach.

He carried a bottle. The night was very dark.

Arriving at the beach just before eight, he looked eagerly along it as he staggered through the screen of *malfini* bushes. It was deserted. A crab scuttled over his foot in the darkness and he lurched backward, letting the bottle fall. Retrieving it, he unscrewed the cap and drank, only to choke on the rum and spit most of it out.

Where was she? Why didn't she come?

For three evenings he had walked the beach, cursing her. She *had* to come tonight. Sure, sure, she had a hard time escaping her brother's vigilance; he could appreciate that. But four nights in a row was too much.

He walked up and down the beach, clutching the bottle by its neck, halting every little while to peer at the screen of bushes and listen for footsteps. With every halt his anger increased. Damn it, he was a white man. He was manager of a plantation. No native bitch could do this to him.

He had another drink. The rum warmed him at last and his anger momentarily receded. What the hell, he was better off here, listening to the sound of the sea, than cooped up in the house with nothing to do but fiddle with the radio or read a book. Waiting for Micheline was better than sitting in the same deadly room with a wife who didn't know he existed. At least *something* might happen here.

There was no longer any possibility of a reconciliation with Alma, Lemke realized. If there ever had been, he had let it slip past him. To hell with it. No, that wasn't the way he felt. He wished there could be a reconciliation. At times he wished it very much, and felt that if she didn't stop poring over her damned medical books and pay some attention to him, he would start screaming. He knew it was hopeless, that was all.

She never looked at him any more. She never spoke except in the polite, impersonal way she would speak to a fellow guest at a hotel. They met at breakfast with indifferent nods of recognition, got through the days somehow, and after the long, murderous evenings of silence they nodded good night and went to their rooms. It was torture.

He longed sometimes for the flare-ups of the period following their return from Fond Marie. But she managed somehow to deny him even that. What was she made of, anyway?

Something very strange had happened to Alma. He didn't understand it. She wore the same clothes but wore them differently, walked differently in them, talked differently. She had changed completely. Was she in love with Clinton? Had she got religion? Maybe both. Either would explain the change in her, he realized. Either would explain why she went to that miserable clinic every morning to help dear Mr. Clinton look after a lot of filthy peasants.

He didn't get it at all. A nurse, for God's sake. Why, before the start of this clinic business, Alma wouldn't have touched a sick peasant with a twenty-foot pole. Disease of any sort repelled her. Now if she condescended to talk to him at all, it was likely to be about some "interesting" or "pathetic" case of something with a long name. She spouted those Latin names as though she'd invented them.

He tipped the bottle to his mouth again, beginning to be very drunk as the straight rum took effect. He pawed at his watch and looked up and down the beach again and swore. What a fool he was, coming here night after night when he knew damned well the girl had no intention of showing up again. She'd as much as told him, hadn't she? "I'll see you when I can," she'd said. "If I change my mind about not wanting to" was what she had meant.

She wasn't interested in him and never had been. Face it. What she really wanted was a thing he couldn't give her. How did she expect him to give it? Was he supposed to invent a drug that would make Clinton break out in a rash of desire? They had potions of their own for that, if you believed the tales. Why didn't she use one herself?

A crab investigated his feet again. Lemke kicked out savagely and sent it flying, heard it fall with a plop into the water, then drank again. The bottle was empty. He tossed it away and wiped his mouth on the back of his hand.

Micheline wasn't coming. All right, he'd show her. He'd prove to her he didn't have to hang around here night after night waiting for her to make up her mind. There was a *bamboche* up at the fishermen's shacks tonight. He'd heard the cook telling Alberse about it when she came back from there this morning with some lobsters.

HE WAS REALLY DRUNK NOW. Half a dozen times he lost the path and stumbled blindly about in the dark, tearing his clothes on the bushes. Once he blundered into some mangroves and sank to his knees in mud. The trip should have taken him a quarter hour at the most, but an hour passed before he heard the throbbing of the Congos.

The dance was in full swing when he located it. It was being held in a yard near the shore, under lanterns suspended from the limbs of an old tamarind tree. Fifty or more persons were present. Had he been sober he would not have thought of intruding; would only have voiced a polite greeting and walked on. He was white, after all. He was the plantation boss. But he halted now by the refreshment table and demanded a glass of *clairin*, slapping a coin down to pay for it. He staggered through the gate and pushed in among them, leered at a good-looking girl of eighteen or so and invited her to dance.

She hesitated, but after a quick look around she stepped toward him. When he pulled her into his arms there was a sudden stillness, as though the scene were on film and the film had snapped. In St. Joseph a man did not wrap his arms around the woman he danced with. He did not touch her at all. Dancers simply faced each other, hands on hips, and moved their feet and bodies to the rhythm of the drumbeats.

The drums were silent. Lemke realized what he had done and released the girl. "Sorry," he mumbled, foolishly grinning. But the girl had turned away from him in disgust, repelled by his drunkenness. He had to go lurching through the crowd in search of another.

Some of them danced with him for a moment or two, but not the way they had danced with their own men. Not with laughter on their lips and an invitation in their flashing eyes. They simply went through the motions to be polite and escaped as quickly as they could. The men watched him, every move he made. There were whispers.

He stopped trying at last. Hands clenched at his sides, he glared around him, cursed them under his breath, then flung himself about and walked out. To hell with them if that was how they felt. He stumbled toward the beach, out of the lantern light. He found an overturned dugout and sat on it. What was he going to do? Where could he go?

He remembered Tina then. Tina Nerette. He remembered going to her house the day of his return to the island. She had been visiting a sister, her mother had said. Some sister who was expecting a baby. He hadn't looked her up since then. There'd been no need to, with Micheline taking her place.

He hadn't seen Tina at the *bamboche*. She must be at home, then. Muttering to himself, he stumbled along the path to her house.

The door was shut. When he knocked, there was a stirring inside and a sound of whispering. He became impatient and hit the door hard with his fist. Then a voice demanded, *"Qui moun la?"*

"M'sieu Lemke!" he said angrily.

The door was opened by the woman he had talked to on his previous visit. She peered into his face, obviously bewildered. "My daughter and I were in bed, *m'sieu*. What is it you want?"

"Tell Tina to step out here. I want to speak to her."

"M'sieu, she can't do that, no. She is not well. She is really very sick."

"Sick?" Lemke muttered. He had not foreseen this; it confused him. "What do you mean, sick? What's wrong with her?"

"She coughs all the time, *m'sieu*. She has a bad cold, maybe something worse than a cold. She has been coughing for days. She can't get out of bed to talk to you, no. She really can't."

"What the hell," Lemke said, swaying. "Let me have a look at her."

He stepped into the *caille* and struck a match. They had a bed, these people. The girl lay on it under an old gray blanket. He lit a lamp and leaned over her, peering into her face. Her eyes were wide, gazing up at him. She tried to speak to him and began to cough. He wondered if she had T.B.

"What—what do you want with me, *m'sieu?*" she whispered when she could manage her voice.

"Want?" Lemke mumbled. "I don't want anything. Not now. Not with you like this." He scowled at her. "Look—what are you doing for this? Are you doing anything?"

"It will go away, *m'sieu*."

"Not if you don't do something about it, it won't." He put a hand out and began to stroke her face. Her face was hot. She had a high fever. "You take yourself to the clinic," he said, "and let *Père* Clinton give you some medicine for this. You hear? You won't get better just lying here."

She caught his hand and held it. "If I go to the clinic, will you come to see me again, *m'sieu?*"

"Of course I will, when you're well."

"Then I'll go. I'll go tomorrow. I promise."

Outside the hut Lemke wondered what to do next. He felt cheated. He was desperately lonely. Maybe if he returned to the beach, Micheline would show up after all. He stumbled away into the darkness.

TINA WALKED SLOWLY across the red earth of the mission clearing, tired from her long journey. Halting in the office doorway, she said in a whisper, "Mon Père."

"Hello," Barry said cheerfully, turning toward her. "What can I do for you?"

"I—I'm not well, mon Père."

Barry nodded and stepped forward. He was a head taller than she; he had to look down at her. She was a pretty little thing, not more than eighteen. He took her by the hand and led her to a chair, then sat on a corner of his desk, one leg swinging, and looked at her. He was alone in the clinic. Alma had left just a little while ago.

"You haven't been here before, have you? Suppose you begin by telling me your name and where you're from."

Before she finished giving him the information for his file card, she was coughing. He frowned at her.

"Is that the sickness you mean? That cough?"

She nodded, struggling to get her breath.

"It's a bad one," Barry said, frowning. "How long have you had it?"

"A long time, mon Père. But not like this. It's getting worse."

Barry examined her, calling Lucy in from the kitchen so the girl would not be frightened. It was not tuberculosis, he told himself. It might be, of course—he couldn't be sure without X rays, and there certainly was T.B. among the four thousand people on his island— but he guessed it was only a bad cold or bronchial infection, probably aggravated by dust. They lived in those miserable dirt-floored huts and stirred up clouds of dust every time they plied a broom. He dismissed Lucy and sat the girl down to finish filling out her card.

"I haven't had many patients from your end of the island," he said to make conversation. "Who sent you to me?"

"M'sieu Lemke, mon Père."

"Oh? You work for him?"

"No." She shook her head. "I'm his girl."

"You're what?"

"His girl. At least, I was for a time."

He stared at her, knowing his mouth had dropped open. She had said it so matter-of-factly. No preamble. No warning. *I'm his girl.* He felt as though a bolt of lightning had penetrated his skull and was crackling around inside. Lemke's girl! No wonder there was trouble between Lemke and Alma!

Did Alma know about it though? She must. She did. That night of the farewell party at the plantation—this was the reason for her strange behavior, her brazen flirting with the men as though she were determined to shame her husband in front of them all. It must be. A native girl. Good Lord!

He took in a breath. "What do you mean, you were for a time? Aren't you now?"

For the first time since she had stepped through the doorway, the girl showed some spirit. "He didn't come near me for weeks until last night," she said in a sudden outburst of bitterness. "That Micheline Laroche put a spell on him!"

Another lightning bolt. Careful, Barry warned himself. Be careful here. "You mean he's been seeing Micheline?"

"He couldn't help himself. She made him."

"Where have they been meeting?"

"On a beach near the plantation."

"Does anyone else know this?"

"If you mean have I told anyone, no. But I'm not the only one with a pair of eyes."

Sooner or later, Barry thought, Catus will hear about it. What will he do?

He gave the girl medicine and instructed her to come again. When she had gone, he stayed at his desk, thinking. It threw a new light on Alma Lemke, this did. He had been sure for some time, of course, that she and her husband were seriously on the outs, and had wondered about it. He had wondered about the change in her too, but had attributed that to the fact that in coming daily to the clinic, working with people who so badly needed help, she had found a relief from boredom.

The truth was, he had never quite *believed* in the change, wonderful as she was with the peasants. The memory of the other Alma Lemke, sardonic, a little cheap, a kind of genteel street-walker in speech and attitude, had kept rising to disturb the picture, like bubbles rising from the dark bottom of a clear pool.

Not once had she mentioned the real cause of her trouble. Those first sarcastic hints had led to nothing. Morning after morning here in the clinic they had talked of other things, he of his boyhood in the hot countries, his reasons for wanting to be a missionary, his struggle to be one; she of her Louisiana childhood, her parents, her marriage. All sorts of subjects had bounced off these whitewashed walls in the past month. They had played catch with theology, philosophy, medicine. They had discussed the possibility of turning the old church and rectory into a school when the mission was moved to the ridge. They had argued about the probable origins of *vodun*, weighed the possibilities of improving and expanding the island coffee crop so the natives would have a chance to make some real money, even pretended to take sides in the old mock battle of tropic heat versus temperate-zone winters. He could not even remember all the things they had talked about while working together.

But she had never mentioned her husband's affair with this native girl. She was certainly a strange woman.

17

THREE DAYS AFTER Tina Nerette's startling revelation, Barry and Alma were just finishing their morning's work at the clinic when a young woman appeared at the door. Barry had seen her in church and knew her name: Yolande Desinor. Her husband had met death by drowning the year before. She and her little girl lived with her parents in the village.

Yolande flung herself at him with a babble of Creole, pawing at him like one possessed.

Her child was desperately ill, he gathered. (Would he *ever* learn to understand their Creole when it was hurled at him with such speed?) He must come at once. No matter what her parents said, he must come and save the little girl from death.

"You saved Fifine César!" she wailed. "Please, *mon Père*, save my daughter!"

He turned to ask Alma to stay for lunch—he would probably not be long in the village—and found her at his side, with his bag in her hand.

"We're through here," she said. "I'll go with you."

"Good."

The house was an average *caille* only a little distance from the Laroche place: one of those where people had stood in the yard, staring at him but not returning his greeting, his first day on the island. On his entering the yard now, Yolande's parents came from the hut and glared at him. The man was the fellow who had been possessed by Zaca at the planting ceremony. The woman croaked hoarsely at Yolande, "You will be sorry for this! You'll see!"

The child lay on a rude bed inside, half covered with a ragged blanket. He knew at once that he had been summoned too late. He glanced at Alma and shook his head. Then he became aware that someone was standing at the entrance to an inner room, watching him. Startled, he rose to his feet.

"Catus!"

Catus Laroche quietly came forward. "I told them you could do nothing," he said with a shrug. "She was dead before her mother left to go for you."

Yolande Desinor threw herself on the bed and began a hideous wailing. Her parents came into the *caille* and stood against the wall, silent as rag-draped black statues.

"I have been treating the child for days," Catus said. "You see for yourself it was hopeless." The words were a question, though not put as such.

Barry looked at the child again and nodded. "I agree. It was hopeless."

He saw Alma frown and sent her a warning glance. It was a delicate situation. There had been a family conflict here, obviously. Yolande, who went to church occasionally, had wanted to ask his help. Her parents were faithful followers of *vodun* who believed that any sickness was a matter for the *houngan*. Not until this morning had Yolande in desperation dared to defy them and seek assistance at the mission.

Suddenly the child's mother came off the bed and clung to him. "*Mon Père,* you can save her!" she cried. "She is not dead yet! I know she is not! For the love of God, *mon Père,* I am a Christian! I go to your church. Even before you came here I went to church and believed in God as *Père* Mitchell said to!"

He could find no words to comfort her. Alma had to come to his rescue. "Let me," she said quietly, and led the hysterical girl to a chair.

After a while the wailing stopped.

There were things to be done then. Names to be written down. Arrangements to be made for a funeral. The information Barry sought was grudgingly given by the old couple while the child's mother sobbed in Alma's arms. Catus Laroche stood by in silence.

Finished, Barry returned pencil and paper to his pocket and turned to the *houngan*. "If I may, I'd like to go along to your place."

"Certainly, Father."

He spoke to Alma. "Will you go back to the clinic and wait for me?"

"When I've finished here."

"This needs talking about. We have a serious problem." He spoke in English. When she nodded, showing him she understood, he turned away, murmured his farewells and went out. Catus followed. In silence, side by side, Barry and the *vodun* priest walked up through the village.

FROM THE DOOR of the *hounfor*, which was part of Catus' house and opened into the *tonnelle*, Micheline saw them coming. She was cleaning the inner sanctum for a ceremony that evening. Already she had taken up and dusted the assorted objects on the concrete altar: the painted *govis* and *pierres-loas* in which the spirits of the gods were known to dwell, the *assons* with their windings of snake vertebrae and colored beads, the flags, *trempé* bottles, Catholic statuettes, and all the curious paraphernalia accumulated by her brother in the course of his career. Now she was vigorously sweeping the floor.

At sight of the Father she stopped sweeping and looked at herself. The dress she wore was a soiled black rag saved for just such occasions. Sweat trickled through the film of dust on her arms and legs. The Father must never see her like this!

She stepped back and quickly shut the door. They had not seen her, she was certain. Careful to make no sound, for the wall behind the altar, separating the *hounfor* from Catus' sitting room, was only the usual whitewashed mud pack over a frame of wything, she seated herself on a chair and resigned herself to waiting.

In a moment she heard voices.

BARRY HAD WONDERED how to say what must be said. Now, seated in Catus' house with the door closed, he accepted the tiny glass of rum the *houngan* handed him and realized there was but one way to say it. He waited for Catus to sit down.

"That child should not have died, Catus."

Catus frowned. "I did everything possible."

"Not everything, I'm afraid. Not the most important thing. May I ask what you did do, exactly?"

"When I was sent for, I saw she was suffering from *la fièvre*. I don't believe, as many *houngans* do, that all sicknesses are punishments sent by the *loa*. Some are, perhaps, but not all. For fevers there are certain known remedies. An infusion of corossol leaves will sometimes cure a mild one. Or basilique. I spent an entire day gathering leaves, barks, roots, then carried them into the *hounfor* and asked the *loa* to bless them, to be doubly sure. Unfortunately the child did not respond."

"Then?"

"Apparently in this case she *was* being punished. Or rather, her mother was being punished through her. I consulted Yolande and her parents. The parents were convinced that the mother had brought sickness upon the child by going to your church."

"You believed that?"

"No, for two reasons. First because you have never said or done anything to make the *mystères* angry. Second because no one else attending your services has been punished. Nevertheless it was possible that Yolande was being punished for something. So I held a service to find out what was needed to put things straight."

"What did you find out?"

"Nothing. The *loa* did not come. I suspect Yolande no longer believes in them, even though she consented to the service. Even before you came here she had turned away from the faith of her ancestors. *Père* Mitchell won her over. She was one of the few he was able to convince."

"Do you think the child died because of *Père* Mitchell's success, Catus?"

"With the proper guidance I might have saved her."

"I could have guided you."

Catus sat straighter on his chair. "You, Father?"

"Listen to me, Catus. Back there at the *caille* I said I agreed with you that it was hopeless. I said that because I knew you had done your best, and because we are two men struggling to find a way to work together to help your people. I might even say 'our people.' In matters of religion we seem to have achieved an unusual degree of understanding. I won't go into that now. But we need a working arrangement in other matters as well."

Catus said nothing.

"I respect your knowledge of native medicines," Barry went on, turning the empty rum glass slowly in his fingers. "I hope some day you'll share it with me. It's a knowledge handed down to you, I know, by wise and devoted men, a very old knowledge, very precious. In a way it's also quite modern. Whether you know it or not, today's scientific cures are more closely related to your so-called primitive knowledge of medicinal roots, leaves, and barks than to—well, to the fantastic things doctors thought scientific in the Middle Ages. But it has limitations, Catus. That little girl died of malaria, and she shouldn't have."

"You could have saved her?"

"With a handful of pills."

Catus sat very still. "You accuse me, then, of having killed her?"

"No. Only of failing to keep her alive. And I'm informing, not accusing. There are times when I need your help and times when you need mine. If we're to accomplish anything good here, we must recognize that." Barry stood up. "Only you and I and Mrs. Lemke know about this, Catus. No one else will ever be told, believe me."

"I believe you."

Before Barry departed, they shook hands.

IT WAS NEARLY TWO O'CLOCK when Barry reached the mission. Alma Lemke had finished straightening up the clinic and was waiting for him. St. Juste, she told him, had come for lunch and returned to the ridge.

"It was malaria, wasn't it?" she said.

"Yes."

"What did you say to Catus?"

He told her. When he had finished, she gave her head a little shake and quizzically frowned at him.

"Do you realize how odd it is, the way you two have managed to understand each other? The way you've become friends in spite of everything, when by all the rules you should be sworn enemies?"

"I'm afraid it was only by the rules laid down for *me* that we were supposed to be enemies. Catus was ready enough to take me as he found me."

"Meaning you've broken the rules to win him over?"

"Let's say I'm ignoring some of them. Can I do anything else?"

"Aren't you supposed to have unwavering convictions?"

Barry leaned on the desk. "They waver on occasions. You know they do, I'm sure. I suspect Catus is sharp enough to have guessed it too, just as I've discovered that his convictions aren't unshakable." He was amused by her line of questioning. "We may wind up admitting to each other that we know practically nothing."

"A clean slate?"

"Waiting for the unknown hand to write. If it will. I've had the peculiar notion, ever since coming here, that on Ile du Vent it might."

Alma had seated herself and was gazing at him. She let a few seconds of silence go by, then said quietly, "I had a caller while I was waiting for you."

"Oh?"

"Tina Nerette came for her medicine. She was scared half to death when she found me here. It didn't take me long to find out why. She thought you'd already told me."

Barry felt himself twitch. "I forgot about her." He made a face. "I didn't want you to know that I knew."

"I'm glad she came. There's something I should have told you long ago. Shall we have lunch while I tell you? No, that wouldn't be safe, would it? Lucille understands just enough English to hear too much."

"Mitchell taught her." He got off the desk and walked about the room. This was awkward. He felt she must be embarrassed. Abruptly he faced her. "You don't have to talk about it if you'd rather not," he blurted. "I mean—well, I don't mean I'm not interested. Of course I am. For weeks I wondered what was wrong between you and Warner. You were so decent, coming here day after day, helping out. I couldn't understand. I wanted to help. No, confound it, I didn't— at least not him. I did want to help *you* if I could, if there were some way to do it without——" He caught himself.

"Without what?" she asked quietly.

He shook his head. The words were still there, unspoken. *Without sending you back to him,* he had been going to say. What had he been thinking of? What had come over him?

He sat on the desk again, staring at her, afraid now to say anything at all. He was shaking. He waited for her to speak.

She did, presently.

"It may surprise you," she said, "but I didn't know about my husband and Tina. I did know about the other girl, the one at Fond Marie."

"Fond Marie?" Barry said, confused.

She smiled. "We seem to be going around in circles, don't we? There were other girls before Tina. One, at least. She was at Fond Marie when Warner and I went there. Her name was Anita. She worked for you and Peter Ambrose."

"Anita!"

"What you ought to know," she said, "is that my husband blames *you* for telling me. You see, I didn't know there were native girls until we went to Fond Marie. I knew there'd been other women in the States, but—well, at Fond Marie I found out about Anita and threw it up to him. It was the night of the party. He thinks you're the one who told me."

Barry shook his head in bewilderment. "How could it have been I?"

"It couldn't have been anyone else, according to his way of thinking. The girl worked for you and Peter. Peter never would have told me. Therefore, you're the villain."

"I didn't even know. Nor did Peter, I'm positive. The girl only worked in the kitchen."

"What happened was my fault, really." Alma was speaking slowly now, gazing at the floor. "I didn't care about you or anyone else then. I simply despised him and hated myself for having married him. It wasn't until long after we came back here to the island—until I began to suspect he was trying to break you—that I told him the truth. Then it was too late. He wouldn't believe me."

"How *did* you get the information?"

"From the girl herself. Jeff borrowed her that night, you remember. He needed some extra servants for the party. She was wearing a piece of costume jewelry Warner had given her, a rhinestone clip of mine that I thought had been stolen. I accused her of stealing it and she laughed at me. It was quite a scene. We were in the kitchen at the time. I remember thinking the whole place must have heard us. Apparently Warner didn't. Now I wish he had."

"He wouldn't believe you when you told him?"

"He didn't want to believe me. He wants an enemy he can fight. You. When I tried to tell him how I knew, he insisted I describe the clip. I couldn't, of course—not to his satisfaction, at any rate. I hardly ever wore it."

Barry soberly nodded. "You say you didn't tell him the truth until you learned he was trying to break me. What do you mean by that?"

"First, the mule Dufour sold you. Pradon Beliard came to the house one day. The day we returned to the island, in fact. He told Warner something about a *bête diable*. I didn't understand, and Warner wouldn't discuss it. It wasn't until later that I heard the natives referring to your mule as a *bête diable*, and guessed what had happened."

"You think Pradon put Dufour up to selling me the mule?"

"I think my husband arranged with Pradon to make trouble for you even before you left Fond Marie. The night before we left there he asked me again who had told me about his affair with Anita. When I refused to tell him he said I needn't bother, he already knew."

Barry remembered some of the little things: Pradon's attempt to overcharge him, the boy's pretense at being helpful while shirking on every possible occasion. "Any other proof?" he asked. "Any proof that Pradon started the rumor that Toto was dead when we took him to the mainland?"

"Only that he was at the house again that night."

"It couldn't have been he who slaughtered the mule in the church and set fire to the altar."

"No, but it could have been Warner."

"I can't picture your husband slashing a mule's throat with a machete," Barry argued. "You're only guessing."

She smiled wanly. "I have no real proof of anything, do I? But I should have told you how he hates you."

"I think you did. At least you tried to."

"Yes, I think I tried. You said you knew he despised you. But despising and hating aren't the same thing, are they? Well, now you know." She stood up. "Shall we have some lunch before I ride back?"

He took her hand as they went across the rectory yard to the dining room. It seemed a natural thing to do. She was the girl who worked with him at the clinic and shared a great many secrets with him, including the possibly dangerous secret that Catus Laroche was responsible for the Desinor child's death.

It was hard to think of her as being another man's wife.

"o god, whose most dear Son did take little children into his arms and bless them; Give us grace, we beseech thee, to entrust the soul of this child to thy never-failing care and love, and bring us all to thy heavenly kingdom; through the same thy Son, Jesus Christ our Lord. Amen."

Rising from his knees and closing his prayer book as a sign to the congregation that the service was finished, Barry gazed down at the small plain box before the altar rail. His eyes closed for an instant. A child, he thought. A child that need not have died. He looked across the coffin at the mourners. Only a handful had come into the church. Only the child's mother, a few neighbors, and near the door, kneeling, Catus Laroche. What was Catus thinking?

Barry was suddenly bitter—not at Catus, who after all had done his best, but at the two persons who were even more to blame. The mother and father of Yolande Desinor were not present. Not even to comfort their weeping daughter would they set foot in the accursed church of the white missionary. They waited in the crowd outside.

A man came forward, lifted the small box and carried it down the aisle. At the door he raised it to his head. So far as Barry was concerned the service was finished. Not even Yolande wished him to accompany the body to the cemetery.

It was Catus who led the procession. Barry stood in the church doorway and watched. Like the Pied Piper followed by the children of Hamelin, Catus marched across the mission clearing in the golden brightness of the afternoon, the others strung out in single file behind. Catus alone seemed aware of the solemnity of the occasion. The others jerked and swayed from side to side to ward off the evil spirits known to be ever eager to snatch the souls of the departed. Even the man with the box on his head—that pathetic little box hurriedly knocked together within the past hour by the village coffin maker— leaped and pranced with his burden.

The women wailed. The men yelled and shrieked. There were some who, losing their balance, laughed at their own clumsiness as they picked themselves up.

When the procession had disappeared at last, Barry bowed his head and moved his lips.

"In sure and certain hope of the Resurrection to eternal life through our Lord Jesus Christ, we commit the body of this child to the ground. The Lord bless her and keep her, the Lord make his face to shine upon her and be gracious unto her, the Lord lift up his countenance upon her, and give her peace, both now and evermore."

It seemed a pity, he thought, that this last service in old Mr. Mitchell's church had to be for the dead. Yet it was sadly appropriate. On Sunday the Bishop was coming to consecrate the new church on the ridge.

18

THE RIGHT REVEREND ERNEST LAXSON, Bishop of St. Joseph, was not completely a stranger to Ile du Vent. He had made two previous visits to the island, one to consecrate the church erected by Leander Mitchell, the other to pay Mr. Mitchell an official visit many months later. He did not recall either visit with much pleasure, nor did he look forward with pleasure to the one now confronting him.

As he bumped along the road to Anse Ange in the Fond Marie jeep, with Peter Ambrose at the wheel and Jeff Barnett and Jeff's daughter Edith sitting behind, the Bishop found himself wondering about the letter he had received from Warner Lemke.

Odd, that letter. He didn't question its contents, of course; as a matter of fact he had rather expected something of this sort to happen when young Clinton took the island over. The surprise lay in the fact that Lemke had bothered to write him. He hadn't known the plantation man was interested in church affairs to that extent. It would be enlightening to talk to him. The fellow knew a great deal about his islanders, obviously. Much more than Clinton did.

Though the sun was only just up, the morning was hot and the Bishop wiped his face frequently with a large linen handkerchief. He was a large man, badly proportioned for riding in a jeep, even in front. The two small shift-sticks bristling from the floor kept thumping his left leg. He tried moving that leg to the right and resting his right foot on the little metal step outside, but found the position uncomfortable and resigned himself at last to sitting very straight with his plump red hands folded in his lap. He had long since given up trying to sit sideways so as to talk to Jeff and Edith, on the seat behind him. As for conversing with Peter, the growl of the engine made it all but impossible. He could shout when he had to, but preferred to save his voice for occasions that justified the effort.

He was greatly relieved when at eight o'clock the jeep rolled into Anse Ange, where Barry and Warner Lemke were waiting with the local rector. At sight of a huge pitcher of iced citronade on the veranda table, the Bishop smiled for the first time since dragging himself out of bed that morning in the dark.

Stoop-shouldered Peter Ambrose was glad to get out of the jeep too. The Bishop had been his guest at Fond Marie the night before, and Peter was puzzled by certain references to an "interesting" letter from Warner Lemke. What was in the letter he did not know; the Bishop had not chosen to show it to him. But apparently it had to do with Barry, and Peter was worried.

He watched closely as Barry greeted the Bishop, and was relieved when nothing happened. You never knew with Bishop Laxson. He might blow up in your face; he might say nothing at all. Of course, if he said nothing when there were things that ought to be said, you could be sure of getting your comeuppance later, in some form perhaps harder to take than the postponed explosion. But this first potential crisis was past, at any rate.

Peter shook Barry's hand. "It's good to see you, boy. You look as though you'd been on vacation rather than working harder than ever before in your life."

"I've never felt better in my life. Wait till you see my island, Peter." The bright blue eyes twinkled. "It's *your* island now, eh?"

"I hope it always will be."

Peter wondered at the remarkable change in his former assistant. Had Barry got religion, by any chance? Whatever it was, it was a good thing, he was sure. No bad thing could light up a man's face this way.

He saw the Bishop glancing at them and offered a prayer that Barry's hope of staying on Ile du Vent was not doomed to disappointment.

WHEN THEY WERE WALKING to the beach to go aboard the plantation launch, which Lemke had brought over on radioed instructions from Jeff Barnett, Barry had a chance to talk to Edith alone. He and she dropped back to the tail of the procession, and her hand found his and squeezed it.

"Am I forgiven for being so selfish the last time I came?" she asked.

He smiled at her. She wore a plain white dress, dusty now from the jeep ride but still most attractive, and a white cloth about her hair, and white shoes that were little more than straps. The costume made her seem very slight and young.

"You know there's nothing to forgive," Barry said.

"I never should have come at such a time. You're not so busy now, are you?"

"I'll try very hard not to be, after the Bishop goes."

"Are things any better at the Lemkes', do you suppose?"

"Well, I think you'll find that Alma has changed a good deal."

"Oh? With helping you at the clinic, you mean?" He had, of course, written her about that. Possibly the enthusiasm of his written remarks was responsible for the way she now looked at him, with a little frown, as she put her question.

"She's a different person, really," Barry said. "You'll see."

Edith changed the subject.

Her father, she told him, would be going back with the Bishop and Peter that afternoon. She could stay as long as she liked. "Perhaps I can be useful at the clinic, too," she suggested. "I'd like to try, if you think you could stand having me underfoot."

Barry smiled and pressed her fingers.

ON THE WAY ACROSS THE CHANNEL Warner Lemke wondered if the Bishop would question him about his letter. He was proud of that letter. Of course, he had a knack with words; everyone said so. One of these days he ought to sit down and write a book about life in the tropics. A real book, not the moonlight-and-palm-trees pap passed off as truth by the travel writers. He certainly could do it.

He sent a triumphant glance at Barry. *There* was a story to make readers sit up and take notice, by God. The angelic do-gooder sleeping with another man's wife while pretending to be a saint. Clinton *was* sleeping with Alma, he was positive. She wasn't visiting his clinic every day just to look after a lot of sick peasants.

Yes, that letter to the Bishop had been an inspiration. There was nothing in it about Alma, of course. If he made that charge he would have to prove it. But there was plenty about Catus Laroche and *vodun*, and the Reverend Mr. Clinton's attendance at *vodun* services. *That* could be proved. The Bishop must have sat up straight when he read it. Everyone in St. Joseph knew what Laxson thought about *vodun*.

It served Clinton right. The trouble with Alma was all his fault. If he'd kept his meddling mouth shut, she never would have known a thing.

Cupping a match in his hands to shield it from the brisk wind blowing down the channel, Lemke lit a cigarette and glanced at the sky. A beautiful morning. No sign of the storm the radio had reported last night, supposed to be picking up speed in the vicinity of Saint Lucia and heading this way. It was too soon, of course. There might be some wind tonight or tomorrow.

With satisfaction he eyed his companions. Dear Mr. Clinton and Edith Barnett had their heads together, talking. Alma ought to see that; Clinton would find out then what a jealous bitch she could be. Laxson and Jeff Barnett were gazing ahead at the green slopes of the island. Old Ambrose sat with his hands against his stomach and his eyes shut, looking as though he could do with some of his own pills. The boat boy ignored them all.

The next time dear Mr. Clinton crossed the Channel of the Wind would probably be his last. A one-way trip out. And good riddance.

BARRY HAD BORROWED HORSES from the plantation, but there were not enough for everyone. The Bishop rode, of course, and there were mounts for Edith, Peter, and Jeff. Barry and Warner Lemke climbed the trail to the mission on foot, followed by boys burdened with suitcases. Two of the cases were Edith's. The others contained Peter's and the Bishop's vestments.

Leading the way, Barry set a fast pace, aware that the Bishop had a tight schedule. He was grateful for that, really. It might have been flattering to have such an important guest stay overnight, and certainly it would have impressed the islanders, but a brief visit was a good deal safer. Bishop Laxson had a well-developed talent for asking embarrassing questions.

On entering the clearing he saw the Bishop talking to Clement St. Juste in front of the old church. St. Juste looked uncomfortable. With his hands clasped behind his back he kept glancing at the Bishop's face and away again, as though he felt trapped and longed to escape. Barry frowned, wondering what they could be talking about, or rather what sort of questions the Bishop was asking. He hurried toward them but the clearing was crowded with people. The whole island, it seemed, knew that the fine new church was to be "blessed" this morning.

Before he could reach them, the Bishop turned from St. Juste with a brisk nod and walked toward the rectory, where Jeff Barnett and others from the boat were talking to Alma. St. Juste came forward to look after the luggage. Halting beside Barry, he spoke quickly under his breath.

"He was pumping me for information, Mr. Clinton. I don't like it."

"What did he ask you?"

"About the *vodun* here. How many services you've been to. If you and Laroche are friendly."

"I see."

"I couldn't avoid telling him something. He's too sharp. I hope I haven't hurt you." St. Juste looked distressed.

"I'm sure it's all right," Barry said.

Was it?

When he joined the group at the rectory, the Bishop's gaze lingered on his face longer than was necessary, he thought. Still, the big man seemed entirely matter-of-fact when he spoke.

"We should ascend to the ridge on foot, I think. That way the people will be able to fall in behind and make a procession of it. We want this to be impressive, something they will remember. I suggest we make ourselves ready."

There was no clinic this morning. The three men donned their vestments in the crowded little office where, with the door shut, the stifling air smelled of alcohol and iodine. When they emerged, the Bishop said, "It might be best if you went on ahead, Mr. Clinton, to greet us at the church. We'll give you a few minutes' start."

Barry hurried across the clearing, aware that all eyes were on him. He was breathing hard. Was the morning really this hot or was he sweating from nervousness? His vestments seemed heavy as a set of chains dangling from his shoulders. He would be glad when this was over. He wanted the church consecrated, of course—he was eager to use it—but he would be relieved when Bishop Laxson was safely off the island. There was something in the air this morning. A threat of disaster. Or was he only imagining things?

He was half way to the ridge-top, passing the steep gardens now planted with good seed and producing respectable vegetables, when he became aware of someone in white on the path ahead of him. It was Edith.

"I guessed you'd be the first one along," she said brightly, "so I slipped away." Her happy smile exorcised some of his apprehension. Surely if there were anything really wrong, she would know it. The Bishop would have made some comment on the journey from Fond Marie.

At the top of the trail Edith caught her breath and gave a start. "Oh!" she exclaimed. "It's beautiful, Barry!"

"It does look a little better than the old one, doesn't it?"

"And the new rectory!" This, of course, was still under construction, but the work was far enough along so that she could visualize the house as it would look when completed. "Darling, it *will* be nice for you here, won't it?" She looked at him with shining eyes. "It's a *big* house, and you'll have so much more privacy here away from the village."

He was startled for a moment, then had a mental picture of the peasants who would be trooping up here when he moved the clinic. "It won't seem so crowded, anyway, with all this fresh air and space," he conceded.

"You can have guests."

"Yes, there'll be room for visitors."

She leaned against him as they walked toward the church. "Do you know what was the matter with me before, darling? I was frightened for you. The thought of you living here on such a small island terrified me. I was foolish, wasn't I? You won't be *buried* here. You do get vacations."

He felt the weight of his vestments again.

"And it won't be forever, will it?" she went on, smiling at him. No doubt she thought it a brave smile. "You *will* be transferred eventually, won't you?"

"I suppose I will."

"I ought to disappear now, hadn't I? They'll be coming."

"Yes. I'd better meet them alone."

She went off through the pomme-rose trees, and he stationed himself in the wide doorway of the church. Why *was* he sweating so this morning? It was never really hot up here. There was a breeze. Yet as he looked along the ridge, waiting for the Bishop's formidable figure to appear, he could feel a dozen separate streams of moisture running down his body.

What had come over Edith? Did she think he *wanted* to leave Ile du Vent? Didn't she know yet what the island meant to him?

Here came the Bishop . . .

He watched them approach along the ridge and was impressed. It was a stirring climax to the weeks of toil, the days on end when he had labored here stripped to the waist under a fiery sun, the endless trips to Anse Ange for tools and materials, the thousand and one petty annoyances, the long nights when he and St. Juste had stared hollow-eyed at each other, struggling to find solutions to seemingly insoluble problems. His spirits soared.

The Bishop led the parade, followed by little Peter Ambrose, Jeff Barnett, Edith, Alma, Alma's husband (he *would* walk with a slouch), and St. Juste. Barry had to smile at the careful attention to rank, but felt a touch of annoyance that St. Juste should be at the end of the line. Without him there would be no church to consecrate.

Then came the islanders. No protocol there. No single line carefully spaced. They flowed after the procession like a Mardi Gras crowd after a line of slow-moving floats. Colorful as Mardi Gras too, in their Sunday attire. Never before, he was sure, had so many of them been on the ridge at one time. He ought to have a picture of this in color, one that could be enlarged and hung in the rectory.

He stepped forward. On an occasion such as this the Bishop should be received by wardens and vestrymen, of course, but when you had none . . . He smiled a greeting. They went slowly up the aisle over the clean, smooth concrete floor, their shoe soles whispering an accompaniment to the words of the psalm.

"The earth is the Lord's, and all that therein is . . ."

"Lift up your heads, O ye gates; and be ye lift up, ye everlasting doors; and the King of Glory shall come in . . ."

The Bishop's voice was loud and clear. Those of Barry and Peter Ambrose, reciting the alternate verses, were less so. In Peter's there was a quavering that to Barry sounded strangely like a sob.

It was the Bishop's service now.

"Dearly beloved in the Lord; forasmuch as devout and holy men . . . have erected houses for the public worship of God, and separated them from all unhallowed, worldly, and common uses . . . let us faithfully and devoutly beg his blessing on this our undertaking."

"O Eternal God, mighty in power . . ."

On his knees Barry looked under lowered lids at the congregation. They had all entered the church. Those for whom there was not room in the pews were standing at the rear. How many? More than a hundred; more nearly two hundred. He was startled. Last Sunday at the old church there had been eleven.

Their curiosity had brought them, of course. He had no illusions. This was an event—a new church to be blessed, the great Christian *houngan* here from the world outside. In days to come it would be a thing to talk about. "I was there. I saw it." Yet they must be aware too of the true significance of the occasion. Even in *vodun* the drums had to be consecrated before use.

The Bishop had risen. His voice filled the church.

"And grant that whosoever in this house shall be received by Baptism into the congregation of Christ's flock, may be sanctified . . ."

Had Catus come? Yes, there he was on the aisle, toward the rear, with Louis and Dauré. He sat like a statue, gazing at the Bishop.

What was he thinking? That this new church might be a challenge to him that the old one had never been? Or had he realized at last that the Reverend Arthur Barry Clinton had no wish to destroy him but desired his help?

"Grant, O Lord, that they who at this place shall . . . renew the promises and vows of their Baptism, and be Confirmed . . ."

How proud Edith looked. How lovely in her white dress. Like a little girl at confirmation.

"Grant, O Lord, that by thy hold Word which shall be read and blessed Sacrament of the Body and Blood of Christ . . ."

And Alma. Was she happy for him too? He could not help comparing her with Edith; they sat next to each other. Two such different women, one a child, bright-eyed, taking everything in with quick movements of her head; the other so still, so grave. A stranger might have mistaken them for mother and daughter, though they were nearly the same age. That comes of suffering, Barry thought.

"Grant, O Lord, that by thy holy Word which shall be read and preached in this place . . . the hearers thereof may both perceive and know what things they ought to do . . ."

What ought Alma to do about the man sitting on the other side of her? Should she divorce him? The situation was hopeless the way it was. Dangerous, too. Sooner or later he was bound to get drunk enough to force himself upon her, or try to.

"Grant, O Lord, that whosoever shall be joined together in this place in the holy estate of Matrimony . . . may remain in perfect love together unto their life's end."

Edith was looking straight at him, her thoughts in the brightness of her eyes, as though she would compel him to see her at that special moment. Her lips were parted. He could almost hear her say, "We shall be joined together here, darling. In your church. Soon!" He kept his head down until the Bishop's prayers came to an end. It was so hot in here. What had happened to the breeze?

Peter Ambrose read the Sentence of Consecration. The congregation was very quiet through the prayers that followed. The Bishop rose from his chair and stepped forward. Barry saw him wet his lips.

"My friends, this is an occasion of great meaning to all of us, but especially to you who dwell here on Ile du Vent." The Bishop's Creole was rich and fluent, his voice a little louder than it had been. "I wish to talk to you for a few moments about what has happened here, so that you may more fully understand it.

"As you know, the Reverend Mr. Mitchell came to this island to establish a mission and bring you the word of God. He worked hard in your interests, and though he wrought no miracles here, he did lay a foundation. You know, I think, why he was not able to do more. To put it very simply, you would not let him.

"Now you have a new minister. He is a younger man than Mr. Mitchell. He is stronger, more energetic. Since his coming he has made great progress here. You have a clinic. You have been taught how to farm your land more profitably. I was told this morning that Mr. Clinton has ambitious plans for turning the old church and rectory into a school for your children and asking the government to send teachers."

Barry caught his breath. Who had told the Bishop that? Probably St. Juste, in a desperate effort to fend off those questions about *vodun*.

"But——"

He sensed a change in the Bishop's tone. His hands gripped his knees.

"But," the Bishop went on, grimly now, "this progress I speak of was not made without cost, and the cost was great. I do not refer to a cost of *gourdes* and *centimes*. I mean something much more. In order to achieve the goals he set for himself, your minister has had to ignore, temporarily, his sworn duty to make war on the forces of evil in your midst."

Oh God, Barry thought.

Inexorably the Bishop's voice boomed on.

"Perhaps this was necessary. I do not know. I myself would never have pursued such a compromise even to win your allegiance and build this fine new church for you. No matter. Your minister followed the course of action he thought best. But now you have your fine new church, and from this dedicated house of God the war against evil will be waged without mercy, I give you fair warning. No man among you can follow both God and the false deities. No man can believe in both Christ and *vodun* superstitions. None can kneel at this rail and obey the commands of the *houngan*. The period of compromise is over. You come to Christ with clean hands and hearts or you do not come at all."

There was a sound of movement in the pews and Barry opened the eyes he had closed in torment. Catus Laroche had risen. He was in the aisle, on his feet, glaring. Barry had never seen such naked hate and fury on a human face before. If a man's gaze could destroy, the Bishop's legs would melt under him. But they did not melt. The

Bishop stood as straight as Catus, stone against stone, will against will. Catus moved his head and directed his gaze at Barry.

This was the end, Barry realized. The end of understanding, of hope, of everything he had worked for. He felt weak. His mind was overwhelmed, incapable of clear thought. He had the sensation of being in a huge empty room with the Bishop's words hurling themselves at him from the bare walls, stoning him. The layer of sweat under his vestments had turned cold and he was shivering. He could not stop shivering.

Catus flung himself about and strode down the aisle. Almost to a man the congregation rose and followed him.

The Bishop, as though nothing had happened, calmly concluded the service.

"The Peace of God, which passeth all understanding, keep your hearts and minds in the knowledge and love of God . . ."

The Peace of God, Barry thought in an agony of bitterness. *And this man thunders for war.*

19

CATUS MUST HAVE GONE STRAIGHT to the *hounfor*. The drums began throbbing while Barry and the other clerics were taking off their vestments.

The Bishop listened to the sound for a moment, then turned a cold eye on Barry. "You see, he was no true friend."

Barry was silent.

"I know his sort," the Bishop went on. "He was only waiting to turn on you when you would least expect it. You're better off with your sword unsheathed, ready for combat."

Do you have to talk like a Sunday-school pamphlet? Barry thought in his bitterness. Nevertheless he nodded. A response of some sort was required of him.

He pushed aside the drape at his bedroom door—for the Bishop's coming the old Christmas tablecloth had at last been replaced—hung up his cassock, and went out to check on Lucy. His guests would have lunch here and then return to the mainland. Edith was waiting outside.

She caught his hand. "Will it make a great deal of difference to you, darling?" she asked.

He looked at her blankly. "Good God!"

"But he had to say it, didn't he? I mean he *is* a Bishop, and the church does take a stand against these things. You'd have been obliged to declare yourself sooner or later."

"Bishop Laxson," Barry said in a controlled voice, "is the biggest fool God ever made."

"Barry!"

"And if you are shocked by that statement, you haven't the faintest notion of what I've been trying to do here."

She *was* shocked. "Barry, I don't understand you. It isn't like you——"

"If there is such a place as hell, I wish your precious Bishop were in it right now, suffering all the assorted torments he deserves. You'll have to excuse me now, Edith. I've got to see that he's fed."

He left her standing there, mouth and eyes wide in astonishment, and went into the kitchen. Lucy sat on a chair, weeping. Alma was the one looking after the lunch.

She turned to face him, in one hand a knife with which she had been slicing tomatoes. "I'm sorry," she said quietly. "Would it do any good to cut his throat?"

He almost smiled. "I'm afraid not. Would you like to?"

"It would give me the greatest pleasure."

"Thanks." He touched her arm, went past her, and put a hand under Lucy's chin. The housekeeper's crying surprised him a little. He hadn't known she had any feeling for him. Now he realized suddenly that she had not mentioned old Mitchell in quite a while.

"Tears won't do much good, will they?" he said gently. "Hadn't you better set the table, Lucy?"

NOTHING WAS SAID AT LUNCH about the Bishop's bombshell. The Bishop himself did not bring up the subject and the others were only too glad to leave it alone. The only person who appeared to be enjoying the meal was Warner Lemke. He, with a slight but unwholesome sort of smile, kept glancing across the table at his wife as though waiting for her applause.

There had to be talk of some sort, if only because the table had been set in the yard—the rectory's tiny dining room was hopelessly inadequate—and people were curiously watching from the edge of the clearing. Peter directed it by asking about the proposed school. Barry answered with feigned enthusiasm and a desolate feeling that the project, now, would never get beyond the words with which he explained it. When that subject was exhausted he told of his plan to introduce more and better coffee. The Bishop listened, ate and nodded, with the fixed smile of a crusader who had just destroyed a city of sin and was resting amid the ruins.

On the way down to the launch, after lunch, Peter Ambrose contrived to drop back in line and speak to Barry alone.

"I had a feeling something unpleasant would happen, Barry. I'm really sorry. The Bishop had a long letter from Lemke. It's fairly obvious now what was in it."

"I see." So Alma had been right. Lemke *was* out to smash him.

"I don't know what that man has against you," Peter said, shaking his head.

"He had an affair with Anita before she came to work for you at Fond Marie. He thinks we found out about it and I told his wife."

"Oh? Perhaps I should tell the Bishop that."

"Perhaps you should, though it's too late now to do any good, isn't it? Anyway, I imagine Lemke was careful enough to stick to facts in denouncing me. Distorted to suit his purpose, no doubt, but still facts."

Peter seemed old and very tired. The bright blue eyes had lost their luster. "It's a shame, a great shame," he said, sighing. "You were doing such a fine job here, boy."

"Was I, Peter? Coming from you——"

"I know, I know. At Fond Marie I called you immature and head-strong. I said you were wrong about a lot of things. But I've been thinking about you a good deal lately and I keep coming back to the greatest of all sermons and find you doing just as *He* instructed. 'But I say unto you, Love your enemies, bless them that curse you, do good to them that hate you . . .' All this time you've known Him better than I, it seems."

Barry had to smile. *It's in the Bible if you'll look for it*, he thought. "Thank you, Peter. You're wrong, of course."

The bony fingers clasped his hand. "I'm not wrong. You mustn't give up, boy. No matter what happens, you mustn't give up."

THE BOAT BOY DROPPED HIS GAZE from an anxious examination of the sky and turned to Lemke.

"*Li pa bon, m'sieu.* A bad storm may be coming, I think."

Lemke thought so too, and revised his opinion of the radio warning. There was no danger, though. "We'll be back long before it hits," he said. "Get that line in and let's go."

The channel was quite calm. Not even Peter Ambrose suffered as the launch sped toward the mainland. Barry sat as far from the Bishop as possible, longing to get the trip over with. He had already made up his mind not to return to the island with Lemke. A native sailboat was preferable to a return trip alone with this man who had defeated him and was now openly gloating.

The boy took the craft as close to the mainland beach as he dared, and Barry dropped over the side into knee-deep water, lifting a hand to help the others. To Lemke he said, "Don't wait for me. I have some things to do in Anse Ange."

Lemke only laughed.

At the village rectory Barry said good-by to the Bishop, Peter, and

Jeff, and emptied himself of a sigh of relief as the Fond Marie jeep rolled out through the gate. Courtesy demanded he spend a few moments with the Anse Ange rector, then he departed and walked alone through the village.

What was he to do now on his island?

Catus, he realized, would probably not remain angry. At least not as violently angry as he must be at the moment. The understanding between them was built on too firm a foundation to be shattered by a third man's words. Sooner or later the *houngan's* rage would subside and he would wait to see what would happen next.

For Barry there were two roads open. He could ignore the Bishop's thundering threat and go on as before, with the certain knowledge that if he did so, the Bishop would be informed of his disobedience by Lemke. Or he could unsheathe his sword, as the Bishop had so colorfully put it, and destroy himself and all he had thus far accomplished in a crusade against phantoms. Don Quixote charging the windmill.

Two roads. Only two. Either led to destruction.

He strolled through the market place, which on Sundays was a ghost city of small thatch shelters on crooked poles, inhabited only by a few scavenging dogs, dirty white and half starved like all the native dogs in St. Joseph. He trudged through Anse Ange's narrow, crooked streets with their open gutters and foolishly tight-packed houses and shops. The shops were closed. At this hour on a Sunday afternoon there were scarcely a dozen people abroad in the whole village. He lost track of the time.

It was very hot in Anse Ange, hotter than it should be, he thought. Not a breath of breeze came off the channel or down from the mountains. The mountains had surrendered their sharp contours to something hazy in the atmosphere, like pictures drawn with pastels and then smudged. Even the sun seemed smudged. As he plodded through the town his shoes stirred up little puffs of dust that fell to the ground behind him as though weighted.

A house door opened. A girl came out backward, laughing gaily and calling farewells to those within. At the sound of her voice Barry turned his head. She bounced down the steps and saw him.

"*Père* Clinton!"

It was Micheline.

"What are you doing here?" he asked.

"Oh, visiting one of my cousins." Her dark eyes regarded him curiously. "I'm going home now. Are you? You'd better if you don't want to spend the night here."

It *was* late, he realized. Most of the boats would be gone. Their owners never liked to stay in Anse Ange much after midday.

"I suppose I should." He had nothing to do in the village. He had stayed only to avoid the return passage with Lemke.

They walked to the beach together, Micheline chattering about her visit. It was his turn to look curiously at her. Was it possible, really, that this child was or had been Warner Lemke's mistress? He found it hard to believe. Then he remembered his visits to the César house and the way she had looked at him, the way he had *felt* when she looked at him. She was no child. Whatever else she was, and he suspected she was many things, she was no child.

There were three boats at the shore. The owners of two flatly refused to make the trip. The third man, torn between his reluctance and the chance to earn money, peered dubiously at the sky and the distant island. His boat was one of the poorer craft, small and crudely made, with a sail that appeared to be little more than patches sewn together.

"I am not sure," he said. "The other men think a bad storm may be coming."

Barry awaited the decision in silence. He knew nothing of sailing and even less about weather signs. If a storm threatened, he preferred to spend the night at the rectory in Anse Ange rather than take a chance on this channel with its ugly reputation.

Micheline reacted differently. Hands on hips, she bestowed on the poor fellow a grimace of disgust. "A storm! Why, there isn't enough wind to fill your sail, if you call that puzzle of patches a sail!"

"That's the trouble," he grumbled. "If we start, we may be a long time getting there. Anything could happen."

"What can happen? This sorry-looking boat of yours doesn't leak, does it?"

"No, it doesn't leak."

"Then what are you afraid of? If a wind comes up, we'll get there that much sooner."

Two other women seeking passage across the channel had come along the black-sand beach to listen to the argument. They added their voices to Micheline's. It was important for them to get home, they insisted. Were they expected to remain here all night just because a cowardly boatman thought the sun looked a little queer? What would their men say?

Barry listened and frowned. Had the fellow remained undecided a moment longer he would have turned away. But the man yielded. With misgivings, Barry waded out to the craft with the others and pulled himself aboard.

He settled himself with his back against the weathered plank that served for a rail and hoped his apprehension was unwarranted. Micheline sat beside him, delighted with her victory. The other two, both older than she, both in white dresses he guessed were their Sunday best, smiled at her from the opposite side of the warped deck and at once began chattering to each other, bobbing their heads like a pair of birds.

The boatman—his name was Telemaque, Barry had gathered from the conversation on the beach—reluctantly ran up his sail. He had no helper. Perhaps on a craft this small he had no need of one, but the presence of a crew would have made Barry feel a good deal safer.

With its crazy-quilt sail barely flapping in a ghost of wind, the craft crept away from the shore. Not another sail was to be seen between Ile du Vent and the mainland. The water looked dark and stealthy. The heat was intense.

"Well!" Micheline, lifting her bare arms, contentedly stretched herself. "Aren't you glad I was with you, *mon Père?*"

"I'm sure I should be. I can't say I like the feel of this weather, though."

"Oh, that Telemaque. He's crazy."

"I hope you're right."

"Do you like my dress, *mon Père?* It's new."

Barry could see no polite way of refusing the invitation to look at her. It *was* a new dress, obviously. She must be very fond of new dresses, he told himself. This one was white and quite snug, with a wide belt of red plastic. She wore the green stone at her throat, he noticed, and a pair of rather large gold-plated hoop earrings.

"You look very nice in it."

"I bought it for the blessing of your church this morning. Then my cousin in Anse Ange sent word that another cousin would be visiting her today, one from Raphael that I hadn't seen for ages, so I couldn't go to the blessing after all. Was it a nice service?"

"It was in the beginning," Barry said with a shrug.

"Oh? Did something go wrong?"

"The Bishop spoke very strongly against *vodun* and your brother walked out in anger. I'm afraid most of the people followed him."

Micheline gazed at him in astonishment. "The Bishop offended my brother? Did he have a right to do that in your church?"

"I'm afraid a Bishop can do what he pleases," Barry said unhappily.

She took time to think about it while the boat continued its creeping, creaking progress and the two older women went on with their gossip. "You didn't speak out against *vodun*, did you?" she asked then.

"No."

"But now you must?"

He glanced at her sharply. She was intelligent, this girl. She had her brother's knack of going straight to the crux of a thing.

"Let's just say I have a problem," he replied. "A very troublesome problem. Unhappily it's one that I'll have to find the answer to by myself."

"You don't want to talk about it, you mean?"

"Not until I've had time to think it over, if you don't mind."

She subsided. Barry took a handkerchief from his pocket and wiped his face. The heat this time was real, not a product of his nerves as it had been in church this morning. He was beginning to feel suffocated.

THEY WERE IN THE CENTER of the channel. The terrible heat and weight of the air had at last oppressed even the two chattering women by the opposite rail, and there was no sound other than the slapping of the sail and the oily murmur of the water along the boat's side. The journey thus far had required an hour and twenty minutes by Barry's watch. Telemaque, at the tiller, was plainly nervous.

Suddenly the boatman's roving gaze fastened on something at the eastern end of the passage and Barry turned to see what had caught his attention. An odd black object moved on the sea's surface there: a shadow of some sort, arrow-shaped, with its point toward them. It approached rapidly, growing in size as it came. The boatman shielded his eyes from the hazy sun to peer at it.

Bewildered, Barry scrambled to his feet. Something else was happening. The sultry air vibrated now to a high, thin whistling sound, faint but growing louder. He wheeled on Telemaque.

"What is it?"

"Wind!"

Isle of the Wind, Barry thought. Channel of the Wind. But this was no ordinary breeze. The approaching blackness was a sea in upheaval, churned out of its lethargy by some tremendous force. He shouted at Micheline and the women to get hold of something and raced to the tiller to help the boatman.

The whistling grew louder. It was a prolonged, ear-splitting shriek now, a sound to fill a man with panic. Suddenly it was directly overhead, an invisible train on a phantom trestle. With a single sharp explosion the sail filled and was torn to shreds. The boat heeled far over. Rain and sea struck at the same instant.

Had he not reached the tiller at that moment, Barry would have been swept overboard in the mass of water that crashed against the vessel. Only the strength of his hands saved him. He felt himself horizontal in the sea's smothering rush, buried under tons of foam. Felt his arms being torn from his shoulders. Felt himself strangling.

He heard, close to him, a cry of anguish and terror. Something grabbed at his face for a second.

With awful slowness the boat began to right itself. He opened his mouth to gasp for air and the wind filled it with unbearable pressure. He turned his head for relief as the craft, like a living thing, continued its desperate struggle to reach an even keel. The tiller was against his chest. Somehow his arms had wrapped themselves around it. He pulled himself up by it.

Ile du Vent and the mainland had disappeared behind a blinding wall of wind-driven rain. He saw with horror that Telemaque and the two chattering women had vanished too. Micheline, on her knees, clung to the base of the mast. The Channel of the Wind was a boundless fury under a sky filled with tumult.

We're going to drown, he thought. He could feel the boat's timbers trembling beneath his feet, shaking themselves apart. Then it occurred to him that with the tiller in his hands he might turn the craft so that the sea would not pound it to pieces so soon. He pushed against the clumsy, hand-hewn timber and the boat's bow slowly came around.

There was nothing he could do then but hold the tiller steady as the wind and sea swept the craft along and the rain roared down on it. At least he had no sail to contend with; he would have been quite helpless had there been canvas on the mast. This was bad enough. The boat rose and fell, lifted and plunged, in mountainous waves that seemed certain to shake it to pieces. The tiller burned his hands cruelly, though most of the time they were under the water that foamed about him, submerging all but his head and chest.

There was a terrible moment when the boat struck something, when it stopped with a monstrous convulsion, swung half about, heeled far over and then was hurled free on a great wave. He knew then that they must be close to shore—the island shore, probably—and was seized with a wild impulse to throw himself overboard and swim for it. But even he knew that no man could last a moment in such a sea, and besides, there was Micheline, still clinging to the mast. Every wave that boiled over the boat seemed certain to carry her away, yet every time he was able to look, she was still there.

The wind seemed to be abating a little. He thought he heard waves thundering against a shore and wondered whether he and Micheline would survive if the boat were hurled up on the sand or into a patch of mangroves. Perhaps the wind would carry them past the island. If it did, there was supposed to be a current at the western end that turned the island's tip and followed the outer, rocky coast eastward. Would an ocean current influence the direction of a craft being hurled along by such a tremendous wind? He had no idea.

There was a dull pain in his left leg now and a sharper one in his chest, and his head felt heavier by the moment. He was not used to this sort of thing. He was even a poor swimmer. He wondered what time it was and how long he had been clinging to the tiller, enduring the endless battering of the seas that broke over him. He was very tired. He could not hold on much longer. . . .

20

HE MUST HAVE BEEN UNCONSCIOUS a long time, unless the storm had brought darkness prematurely. Daylight was gone when he opened his eyes and became aware that the boat had stopped its wild pitching. The sea seemed pounded flat by the relentless rain still falling into it. Micheline sat close to him. His head was in her lap. He could feel the wetness of her dress and the shape of her legs. Her hands mechanically stroked his face.

He looked up at her. "Where are we?"

"I am not sure, *mon Père*." She spoke quite calmly, as though she had never been afraid. "A moment ago I thought I heard a sound of waves on a rocky shore, but I hear nothing now."

He struggled to sit up. The pain in his left leg, just below the knee, made him wince.

"I let go the tiller," he remembered aloud, frowning at her. "You must have crawled back to me from the mast, or the next wave would have taken me overboard."

"I was watching you."

"Thank you for saving my life." He groped for her hand, failed to find it, and patted her leg instead.

"Listen."

He listened and heard something. By clinging to the tiller he was able to stand up. Was that dark mass to their right the island or only a night sky tortured by the downpour? The sound reached him again: surf crashing on rocks, surely.

"I think you're right," he said. "We're near shore. But we may be drifting past."

"No. If we are not too far out we'll drift onto the rocks. The current swings in close where the sea runs into the *vodun* cave."

His leg was hurting. He had to sit again. "Are you all right?" he asked her.

"I think so, except for some bruises."

He shut his eyes, remembering the awful moment when the storm or squall or whatever it was had all but torn the boat to pieces. "Telemaque grabbed at me as he went overboard. If I had been quicker I might have saved him."

"It was not your fault."

"Did you know him?"

"Not very well. His home is in Tête Cabrit."

"He leaves a wife? Children?"

"No. He had no family."

Thank God for that, Barry thought. "And the women. Who were they?"

"*Marchandes* from Petit Trou." She told him their names.

I saved them a few pennies in taxes, he thought, and then caused their deaths by allowing them to take a needless risk.

"You are not to blame for what happened," Micheline said. "I am."

"You?"

"I knew there was danger. You didn't. I thought it would be interesting to see you frightened."

"Why?"

"I had my reasons."

Puzzled, he tried to read her expression but could see too little of her face in the rain and darkness. He eased himself into a more comfortable position and drew up his trouser leg, feeling for the hurt below his knee. There was a lump, tender to the touch, but no break in the skin. The tiller must have slammed back against him when he lost his grip on it. He turned his head to the sound of breaking seas, now much louder. Micheline was right. They were drifting ashore.

"I'll never be able to climb that cliff in the dark, even if we make a safe landing," he said. "Not with this leg."

"We can go into the cave." She gripped his arm. "Hang on, *mon Père!*"

His ears filled with a roaring and he braced himself, anticipating a great crash that would shatter the boat and hurl them into the sea. The bow swung in a wide arc, rose on a wave and surged forward.

There was no crash. The craft rode in among the rocks and came to rest with a gentle grating sound. Very slowly it slid over on its side.

They clambered onto the rocks. Micheline gazed into the darkness for a moment and then nodded. "Follow me," she said confidently.

He never could have found the grotto by himself. Even in daylight, from the top of the ridge, this whole stretch of inhospitable shore

looked the same to him. But Micheline led him to the entrance with
only a few brief halts to orient herself, and once more he found
himself following a guide along that strange passageway into the cliff.
The tide was low, apparently. There was ankle-deep water at the
entrance, but they soon left it behind. It was a relief to be out of the
rain.

When they reached the big room, Micheline led him unerringly to
the bench from which he had watched the *kanzo* service. "Sit here,
mon Père, while I find a lantern," she instructed. He heard her going
across the chamber to the tunnel where the *hounfor* was.

A light flickered in the far darkness.

She lit two lanterns. One she left burning on the altar; the other
she carried back across the chamber. As she came, he saw that the
white dress she had worn so proudly was torn now and barely covered
her. She reminded him of the inevitable female figure in South Sea
films, one dusky shoulder bare, her breasts only half covered, the
ripped skirt revealing a smooth, bare thigh as she walked.

She halted before him, smiling. "Well, *mon Père*. This isn't so bad,
is it?"

"It's a good deal more than I expected," Barry said. "We've a lot
to be thankful for."

"There is some rum on the altar over there. Would you like me to
get you some?"

"No. No, thanks."

"A drink of water?"

He made a face. "I've had enough water to last for a while, thank
you."

She placed the lantern on the floor and sat beside it, facing him,
with her arms about her drawn-up knees. For a moment she appraised
him in silence and he wondered what she was thinking about. He
found out soon enough.

"I have a bad cut on my side, *mon Père*," she said.

"Have you? How bad?"

She stood up and drew down the torn shoulder of her dress. She
could not get it down far enough. She pulled the dress off and tossed
it onto the bench. She stepped toward him. "See?"

If she had hoped to shock him by standing before him in only thin
panties through which the darkness of her body was clearly visible,
she failed. He had examined too many women at the clinic. Even
with Alma looking on it no longer embarrassed him to see a woman
nearly naked. He leaned forward to look at the four-inch welt on her

side where a timber on the boat must have rubbed against her. When his fingers touched her, she gave a little start.

"It's only a bruise, I'm sure. It must hurt, though."

"I got it when I was crawling to the tiller to help you, *mon Père.*"

Meaning what, he wondered, scowling. That I ought to kiss it better? "There's really nothing I can do now," he said firmly. "If you'll come to the clinic tomorrow I'll give you some salve for it."

"Have you looked at yourself?"

"I will presently. You can put your dress on." He leaned away from her and settled himself on the bench again.

She frowned at him. "I don't like wet clothes," she complained.

"Nevertheless you'd better put it on. It will dry soon enough in here."

"Are you afraid someone might come here and find us?"

"I hardly think anyone's likely to." He smiled.

"Then the dress can dry first."

Barry was annoyed. Rising, he picked the dress up and put it in her hands. "I looked at you because I'm a doctor," he said. "Try to understand that, will you? I haven't any intention of making love to you just because we're alone here. Your brother is my friend." He walked away, toward the lantern she had left burning in the *hounfor.* Turning his head, he said sharply over his shoulder, "Please get dressed, Micheline."

At the altar he unscrewed the cap from a rum bottle and took a small drink, being careful to smell the bottle's contents first to be sure he would not swallow a mouthful of the hot-pepper *trempé* prepared for Guedé. When he returned after a quick look at his own bruises by the light of the altar lantern, he found Micheline sitting on the bench, gazing glumly at the floor. The dress was on.

She had nothing to say. When the silence became awkward, he sat beside her and touched her hand. "I didn't mean to scold you," he said. "I'm sorry, Micheline."

She lifted her head.

"I'm very fond of you, really," Barry went on. "But we can't possibly become involved in a love affair."

"Why?" she asked in a low voice. "Because I'm black?"

"No. Because I'm not."

"What is that supposed to mean?"

"It means that I don't think of you or anyone else as being black. It makes absolutely no difference to me. I mean that. But it makes a great deal of difference to a lot of other people, both black and white, including those I work for and your own brother."

His hand was resting on hers. She suddenly turned hers and gripped his wrist fiercely, moving closer to him on the bench. She was not sulking now.

"No one need ever know, *mon Père!*" she whispered.

Barry shook his head. "They'd find out. In a place like this, people know everything."

"But they don't! Lots of things happen that even my brother doesn't know about."

He shrugged. "If you mean your affair with Lemke—no. And I hope to heaven he never finds out about it. But *I* know."

She was suddenly on her feet, her dark eyes glowing like two new lantern flames. "You know about Lemke? So that's why you push me away!"

"No, that isn't why." He shook his head at her, knowing it was hopeless. He could never make her understand. "Lemke means nothing to me," he said. "What you did with him means nothing, except that I know something terrible is bound to happen if Catus finds out about it."

She said, staring down into his face, "I went with that man because I wanted *you*, *mon Père*. He said he was your friend. He promised to tell you how I felt."

"He's no friend of mine, believe me."

"Then I did it for nothing?"

"I'm afraid you made a mistake."

Barry saw tears in her eyes and stood up, putting his hands on her shoulders. "We need sleep, both of us," he said. "We need to forget all this. Good God, girl, we've just been through a terrible storm. We were nearly drowned. Three people on that boat with us *were* drowned. Even if I *wanted* to make love to you—even if it were possible—do you think I could possibly be in a mood for it now, here, at a time like this?"

"We—we have never been alone together before, *mon Père*," she whispered.

"Well, we're not alone now. At least I'm not. All I have to do is close my eyes for a second and Telemaque and those two women are here with us."

He walked away from her, out of the lantern's glow into darkness, limping a little because his leg was stiff. Thirty feet from the bench he eased himself to the floor of the cave.

There was no sound from the bench. When he raised himself on an elbow and looked in that direction a moment later, Micheline was nowhere to be seen. The lantern still burned on the floor.

He called experimentally, "Micheline?"

Her voice came from the darkness beyond the bench. "Yes, *mon Père?*"

"Good night."

"Good night, *mon Père.*"

He closed his eyes.

HE AWOKE without realizing where he was. He was no more conscious of his surroundings than on many a night when the heat of his stuffy little bedroom at the rectory had interrupted his slumber.

He felt a stirring beside him and turned sleepily to face it. A hand touched his cheek. He still was not sufficiently awake to be aware of what was going on. He moved an arm without knowing he moved it. It fell across something warm and smooth that instantly began quivering.

Micheline, he thought vaguely. Then before the thought could crystallize, her mouth was hot against his and she was forcing herself violently into his embrace. She must have been lying there at his side waiting for him to wake.

He was too startled to move. In an instant she had made herself as completely one with him as his position on the floor would permit. Even when he struggled to his knees she clung to him.

He broke the grip of her arms and pushed her away, shocked by the realization that she was undressed. "Stop it!" he said hoarsely. Then more quietly but still in anger, "Don't be a fool, Micheline."

He stood up, aware that the harsh, heavy sound in the darkness was the sound of her breathing. He was shaken, not so much by what she had done as by the violence of it. He waited for her to get up but she remained where his push had left her, looking up at him. Except for the distant gleam of the lantern on the altar the chamber was dark. The nearer lantern, by the bench, was out. He could see clearly only the whites of her eyes. She gazed at him without blinking.

"Please get up," he said. "Please put your clothes on, Micheline." He spoke gently now, wanting her not to hate him. After all, she had done this because she felt something for him. She was very young. Perhaps she did not understand that what she felt was only passion. He was no prude. At least he hoped he wasn't. He too had felt something in the past when this girl was close to him. He'd be the last to deny it. She was unusually attractive. Even now he found it hard not to stare at her. Something quite different might have happened here tonight if he were not a minister, or even if he had not known about her affair with Lemke.

Unexpectedly she spoke. "Is this your answer?"

"It has to be. I'm sorry, Micheline."

She rose to her feet before him and looked down at herself, as though her beautifully formed body belonged to some other woman and she were dispassionately appraising it. Her gaze fastened on his face again, appraising *that*. Then abruptly she turned away.

He watched her disappear into the darkness where the bench was, and then could follow her movements only by sound. A soft rustling told him she was putting her clothes on. He heard her pick up the lantern—which, he guessed, she had extinguished before lying down beside him—and go across the chamber toward the altar.

She returned carrying both lanterns. She handed him one. "We can go now, *Père* Clinton."

His watch had stopped and he had no idea of the time. He frowned at her. "It can't be daylight yet."

"We're not going up the cliff."

She walked away and he followed in bewilderment. What did she mean? Was there another way out of here? She led him across the chamber and into the altar tunnel which he had been led to believe, or at any rate *had* believed, was only a niche. At the rear of the altar it curved and became a steep, narrow passageway.

He had no chance to question her. She set a fast pace, no doubt because she was angry with him, and with the pain increasing in his leg he had trouble keeping up. The tunnel branched. She turned her head, called sharply "A *gauche!*" and took the steeper fork. As he hurried after her he was surprised to see an empty cigarette package on the floor. On an impulse he picked it up.

Did they all use this passage then? If so, why had Catus taken him down the face of the cliff?

Twice more the tunnel branched. The route she chose was a steady climb. They had been climbing since leaving the *vodun* room. Barry took the cigarette package from his pocket and looked at it. The thought came to him that he could have been mistaken about the fire in the old church.

Someone at the ceremony *could* have set the fire, simply by slipping out this way when the others were too busy to notice. Why hadn't

Catus mentioned that possibility? Or was the existence of this route a secret not to be shared with outsiders?

Who on Ile du Vent smoked American cigarettes?

The passage began to level off. They were only about halfway to the top of the cliff, he guessed, so it was not a route to the top after all. It must come out on the other side of the ridge, perhaps near the village. Was the whole of Ile du Vent honeycombed with tunnels like this? Parts of the mainland were, he knew. In the old days, before the coming of Columbus, the Arawaks had used these underworlds for ceremonies . . .

The roof dipped. Now for long stretches there was not room for him to walk erect and he had to proceed at a crouch. Micheline was far ahead, the light of her lantern disappearing whenever the tunnel curved. He tried to quicken his pace.

His leg hurt. He was very tired.

A sudden sharp bend in the passage revealed a flight of steps fashioned of logs imbedded horizontally in familiar red earth. Micheline was waiting. When she saw him coming she turned at once and began climbing.

With his stiff leg he found the logs difficult and was out of breath when he completed the ascent. To his astonishment he was standing inside a *caille*, one that he recognized at once as a special kind of *caille* used in *vodun*. It contained a stone altar littered with paraphernalia. The door to the outside was open and Micheline waited there in a rectangle of daylight for him to follow her. When he did, he found himself in the *tonnelle* where he had witnessed so many of her brother's ceremonies.

A light, steady rain was falling. The day was about two hours old.

Still clutching the lantern that had lighted his way from the grotto, he followed the girl across the compound, now a sea of mud from the hours of rain. She was halfway to her house when the door of Catus' *caille* opened and Catus saw her. Astonishment stopped the *houngan* in his tracks for an instant. Then he spoke her name with a gasp and hurried toward her.

She brushed him aside with a curt comment and went past him without pausing. Catus gazed after her, frowning. He turned to look at Barry.

At sight of Barry a change came over the *houngan's* face. It might have turned to stone. He thrust his thumbs into his belt and put his bare feet wide apart in the mud, filling his chest with a slow, deep breath. The rain danced on his shoulders.

Barry halted. He understood the man's anger but not what he ought to do about it. In Anse Ange he had not reached a decision. There had been no time for thinking since. He put his lantern down and stepped forward.

"May we talk for a moment, Catus?"

"I have nothing to say to you."

"I know how you feel. But if we could thrash this thing out, we might find that we have a few thoughts in common."

Catus returned his gaze without replying.

Barry tried once more. "It wasn't I who spoke out against you. You know that."

Still no answer.

Barry sighed and turned away. It was too soon, he supposed. Despite all that had happened since the consecration of the church, it was actually less than twenty-four hours ago that the Bishop had thundered his challenge.

Much too tired to tackle such a weighty problem, Barry limped across the inundated clearing to the gate in the cactus hedge.

CATUS WATCHED HIM GO. The stone face softened a little.

Was it possible, Catus wondered, that the Father wished things to be as they had been, and did not mean to carry out the Bishop's threat? He had been thinking about it ever since striding out of the church yesterday morning. All afternoon he had thought about it, while the island was being battered by wind and rain. He had sat up the best part of the night thinking, while the rain drowned the clearing and all but washed the houses away.

He wished to be fair. He did not think the Father had plotted with the Bishop to turn the church service into a denunciation of *vodun*. He was certain he had seen a look of disbelief on the Father's face while the Bishop was speaking.

Still, a Bishop was High Authority. Would *Père* Clinton dare disobey him? Could he, even if he wished?

Catus frowned. Perhaps when the rain stopped he would go down to the mission and hear what the Father had to say. At the moment he had something else to settle. He turned and walked rapidly across the compound to the *caille* occupied by Micheline and his parents.

Micheline, seated on a chair, lifted her head to look at him as he entered. The two old people stood together by a little table in the center of the room, staring at her. Catus saw that his sister was angry. He nodded to his parents and sat down.

"You and the Father came from the *hounfor* with lanterns. Does that mean you came up from the grotto?"

"Yes."

"Why were you there?"

"Our boat was caught in the storm. It went ashore there."

Catus gripped his knees. "You came across from the mainland *yesterday*? I thought you stayed in Anse Ange last night!"

"We came across yesterday. The storm caught us and we spent the night in the grotto."

He sucked in a breath. "The two of you alone?"

She shrugged. In a voice she might have used to describe a walk in the village, she told him what had happened. "I thought if we stayed in the grotto until morning his leg would be stronger and we could climb the cliff," she lied. "But it was still stiff and I had to bring him out by the inside passage."

Catus' thoughts were whirling. He stood up quickly and began to pace. So his sister and the Father had spent the night alone together in a place where both knew they would not be disturbed. Had anything happened? He knew how his sister felt about the Father. But would the Father have *let* anything happen? He stopped pacing and tried to read Micheline's face. What was she so angry about? He could tell by her eyes and the set of her mouth that she was furious.

"Have you told me all that happened?" he demanded suddenly.

"I've told you everything."

"Why are you angry?"

"Who says I'm angry? I'm tired. Do you expect me to be gay when I was nearly drowned? When three people I know *were* drowned?"

"When the Father found out there was another way out of the grotto, did he say anything?"

"We didn't talk. We were too tired to talk."

Catus ran his tongue over the gap in his teeth. She would not hesitate to lie to him; he knew that. "How did your dress get torn like that?" he demanded.

"I tore it on the boat."

"Very well." He glanced at the two old people and moved toward the door. "When you've rested, I want to talk to you again."

"I've told you everything," she said sullenly.

"Perhaps. But I have something to tell you."

BARRY SLEPT FOR TWO HOURS and was having a late breakfast, with Lucy fussing over him, when Alma and Edith arrived at the mission.

They had come from the plantation together. Both thought that he had stayed on the mainland overnight and were astonished when he told them what had happened. Edith looked at him strangely.

"You spent the night in a *vodun* cave with that man's sister?"

He had to smile at her concern. "I don't think Catus will hold it against me. It wasn't exactly prearranged, you know."

"But what will the people say?"

"All sorts of things, probably, if they find out about it. I don't think they're very likely to find out. They won't get the story from me, you can be sure."

Edith had come at this early hour to help at the clinic. When she said so, Barry shook his head.

"There won't be any clinic."

She was shocked. "You mean you're discontinuing it? Just because you're angry with the Bishop?"

"I mean no one will come. The Bishop has made them angry with me."

"I'm sure you're wrong, Barry."

He hoped he was, but it was a small hope. "Anyway, I've got to call on the families of those two women who were drowned, and then on the magistrate to report the deaths. I'll leave you two in charge here."

Would anyone come to the clinic, he wondered as he set out on his depressing errand. He doubted it, after the way Catus had stormed out of the church. He doubted, too, that St. Juste would have any help at the rectory from now on, though Lucy had reported he had gone up the ridge as usual right after having his breakfast. The situation was grave, Barry realized. Catus had become an enemy, and unless he could do something about that he was finished. Oh, in time he might manage to baptize a handful of islanders in the fine new church, but there was no use fooling himself. Catus Laroche was king of Ile du Vent, not he. What Catus told the people to do they would do.

It was after eleven when he rode up the main street of Petit Trou and dismounted at Felix Dufour's house. The rain had stopped an hour ago but the village lay steaming in the heat, with mud on everything. Dufour opened the door at his knock. The little man with the untrimmed hair and bad teeth wore faded pink pajamas and showed his surprise by widening his eyes.

"*Père* Clinton! Why, I was planning to visit *you* today!"

"I've come to report a tragedy," Barry said.

"Sit down, please. Sit down."

When the tale was told and the magistrate had taken down the names of the victims, Barry frowned at him. "What did you want to see me about?"

Dufour drew a long face. "A most important matter. One that will make you terribly unhappy, I am afraid."

Barry waited.

"It has to do with *Père* Mitchell's purchase of the land on which you have built your church," the magistrate said.

"Well?"

"A mistake has been made."

Barry leaned back on his uncomfortable chair and eyed the man. He was in for a long session, he realized, and resigned himself to it. There was no use trying to hurry the fellow. Dufour had something on his mind and obviously intended to give it the full treatment. He might at least offer me a drink, Barry thought. Dufour's failure to do so was significant.

The magistrate lisped his way slowly and painfully through the story, covering all the important details at least twice. By the time he was finished, Barry's hands were clenched on the chair arms.

"Dufour, I don't believe this. You're up to something."

The magistrate waved his arms in protest. "But I have Antoine Constant's sworn statement, *mon Père*. He did *not* sign any land transfer. He *refused* to sell the land on the ridge. *Père* Mitchell must have signed his name without his knowledge."

Barry knew he was pale. He stood up. "Just what do you propose to do about it?"

"As Antoine's representative, it is my duty to see that justice is done, *mon Père*."

Barry looked at him, not failing to note a flicker of triumph in the beady eyes. This, he supposed, was an attempt to get even for the tax business. Dufour had been enormously angry that day. But unless the magistrate could back up his claims with some proof, the thing was fantastic.

Was it fantastic? Whatever else Dufour was, he was no fool. He must have planned this with great care. He *must* have some evidence.

What sort of evidence could he have? Barry tried desperately to reduce the lisped repetitions of the past half hour to something comprehensible. The claim was that old Mitchell, unable to get the land away from Antoine Constant by persuasion, had forged Constant's name to a land transfer. As proof, Dufour would offer various books and papers Constant had signed while magistrate. The "official" signatures would prove the land-transfer signature a forgery.

It didn't hold water. Even if old Mitchell had done anything so dishonest, which of course he hadn't, he at least would have obtained a genuine signature in some way, or such a carefully forged copy that the forgery couldn't be detected except by experts. It certainly wouldn't be anything "obvious to a child," as Dufour claimed.

What the devil was the fellow up to?

Barry decided to play the game on the chance of obtaining more information. "You're not a lawyer, Dufour," he said quietly.

"No," with a shrug. "But as magistrate here I can request legal counsel from the capital. A lawyer will come here and make an investigation. Then he will return to the capital and file charges."

And I, Barry thought, will have to go there and answer them. "I think I'd like to have a talk with this Antoine Constant," he said. "Where can I find him?"

"You would be wasting your time, *mon Père*. He will not talk to you."

"I see. You've laid your groundwork pretty thoroughly, haven't you?"

"I must see justice done."

"Of course. You're a great one for justice, Dufour. If this does go before a court, I imagine the judge will be interested in the justice of your selling me a man-killing mule and robbing the market women."

Dufour smiled, showing the black tops of his teeth. "Are you threatening me, *Père* Clinton?"

"No. But I'll fight you right down to the finish."

And God help me if I lose, Barry thought, for if the church goes, the Bishop won't blame old Mitchell for blundering; he'll blame me for not finding out before I began to build.

On the way back to the mission he totaled up his troubles and the burden seemed unbearable. Catus Laroche had declared war. Micheline was savagely angry with him and very likely to do something about it. Edith was annoyed with him. Now Felix Dufour, with this fantastic but apparently well-thought-out legal claim, was threatening to seize the church.

What would happen next?

He found out soon enough. As he rode into the clearing, St. Juste came from the rectory to help with the horse. The man had a long, glum face.

"No one turned up on the ridge this morning, Mr. Clinton. Not even Louis."

"I see."

"And the girls tell me there hasn't been a soul at the clinic."

So now we sit, Barry thought, and twiddle our thumbs. Unless, somehow, I can persuade Catus to listen to me.

21

THREE TIMES IN THE NEXT THREE DAYS Barry trudged through the gate in the cactus hedge and requested an audience with Catus Laroche. Three times the *houngan* refused to see him. On the fourth try Catus hesitated, shrugged, and motioned him into the house.

They talked the whole morning.

When Barry had departed, Catus summoned his two sisters and big Louis César for a conference. "I must make up my mind on a matter of grave importance," he said. "I wish your advice."

He told them of his talk with Barry. "The Father assured me he will not try to destroy us in spite of what the Bishop said. We had a long talk about what we believe in. With some of the things done in *vodun* he is impatient, and he will speak out against them. At the same time he is equally impatient with some things taught by his own church, and he will not try to make us believe anything he does not believe himself. He asked me to help him teach our people to respect and help one another, to stop lying and cheating and taking advantage of one another. He would make us one big family here, with better crops on our land, coffee to sell, a school for our children, and a great many other things we sorely need but can't possibly have unless we accept him. What do you think?"

He folded his arms and looked at Louis, at Dauré, at Micheline, studying their expressions. It was Micheline who answered first.

"If the Father disobeys the Bishop he will be ordered to leave this island."

"I have an answer to that. We will discuss it later."

"If he stays, he will grow to be dangerous," Micheline persisted. "Our people will become fond of him. They will learn to rely on him instead of you, first for advice on how to keep well and improve their farms, then for other things. They will turn away from the *loa* to worship his god."

"A possibility," Catus acknowledged with a scowl. "Yet much of what we do in *vodun* is of doubtful value. I am convinced of it. We would not lose our belief in the *mystères*, however; we would only see them in a different light. As a matter of fact, the *mystères* might be more useful to us if we changed our way of thinking about them."

Louis said, shaking his head, "Those sound like dangerous words, Catus."

"Do they? Let me ask you a question. At a service for Guedé we expect certain things of him. We expect him to drink *trempés* and generally misbehave, to insult us and make fools of us. Now I ask you, does Guedé do these things because they please him or because we expect it? Suppose we expected him to be understanding and dignified?"

"Guedé would never change," Louis said.

"Have we ever given him the chance?" Catus frowned, aware that he was perilously close to being a mere mouthpiece for disturbing thoughts put into his head by the Father. Still, they were thoughts worth pondering. Over the past several weeks the Father had put forth many such ideas, and this morning he had summed them up.

Dauré said quietly, "I do not think the Father would do anything to make the *loa* angry with us. He truly wants to help us."

"He will do what the Bishop tells him to!" Micheline declared fiercely.

Big Louis looked at Catus and shrugged. "This is a thing you will have to decide for yourself, Catus. You're wiser than we are."

Am I, Catus wondered uneasily. Or have I fallen under the spell of that man and only think myself wise? There is a strange force at work here somewhere. That man's coming to Ile du Vent was no accident. I knew it the moment I saw him.

If only old Salmador were alive, so he could go to him for advice. And especially so he could question him about that old Guinea belief that every man had a *marassa*. Why did the thought keep returning to him that *Père* Clinton and he were men with a single mind who must eventually find a way to work together? Why did the word "brother" hang between them like a white-hot bar of iron waiting for them to grasp it?

He sighed. "Very well, I will think about it some more. Now I wish to tell you why I feel sure the Father will not be ordered to leave this island even if he does not completely obey the Bishop."

He was tired of sitting. He stood up and leaned against the wall.

"When the altar in the old church was set on fire and the Father's mule was slain in front of it," he went on, "I thought very hard about who might have done such a thing. The Father was sure no one at the service could have done it because of the tide in the tunnel. I let him think so. I didn't want any outsider to know about our inner passage. But I personally suspected Pradon Beliard, and I assigned spies to watch him. Now I'm convinced he has done many things to discredit the Father here, and I think I know why."

Louis fingered his ugly-gentle face. "What other things has he done?"

"Certain people in the village remember talking to him the day you and the Father took young Toto Anestor to the mainland. It could be Pradon who spread the lie that Toto was dead and you were paid by the Father to keep still about it."

"If you know that for a fact," Louis said, his voice thickening, "I'll kill him!"

"Wait. Pradon may be the Father's enemy, but the Father has a greater one. My spies tell me that Pradon goes nearly every night to the plantation to talk to M'sieu Lemke."

Micheline said with an exaggerated shrug, "Why shouldn't he go there? He works for Couronne, doesn't he?"

"On this island he is supposed to be working for the Father, not for Lemke. But it would seem he is working for Lemke *against* the Father. In other words, Lemke is the Father's real enemy."

"You can't be sure of that," Micheline retorted.

"My dear sister," Catus said patiently, "the only one on this island who would report *Père* Clinton's interest in *vodun* to the Bishop is the same enemy who has been trying to harm him in other ways. I have given this a lot of thought. *Père* Clinton didn't ask the Bishop to preach that sermon. He was shocked when he heard the Bishop's words. Now consider. The Bishop spoke out against *vodun* because he knew *Père* Clinton had *not* taken a stand against it. But where and when did he get that information? Not here on the island. He was not here long enough. He knew before he came here. He knew because the Father's enemy informed him. Not Pradon Beliard— Pradon would never write a letter to a Bishop—but Lemke."

"And how," Micheline demanded, "will you prevent Lemke from writing to him again if he has something to report?"

"There are ways."

She gasped. "You would kill *M'sieu* Lemke?"

"I said there are ways. But of course I haven't yet made up my mind what ought to be done. I thought you three might advise me."

Big Louis stood up. "This is a big matter, Catus. You must decide it for yourself or ask the *loa* for guidance. Perhaps it might be best to hold a service. The *mystères* will tell you what to do."

Will they, Catus wondered as he opened the door and watched them depart. Or if the drums are beaten and the *vevés* are drawn and the gods come to the service, will I only *think* they are advising me? For that matter, will I even be able to convince myself they are gods?

He had not solved his problem, he realized. As a matter of fact he had only added another one, for now he was puzzled by Micheline's behavior. Knowing how she felt about *Père* Clinton, he had expected her to speak up for him. Instead, she had attacked him. Now why was that?

FOR TWO MORE DAYS Catus thought it over. He knew what his silence was doing to the Father but he had to be sure he was right before making a move. No permanent harm would result from a few days' delay in the work on the rectory, or the fact that the clinic was out of bounds to a few people with ailments. On the other hand, the damage caused by a wrong decision on his part might be irreparable.

Sunday evening he made up his mind and set out for the mission. It was good to have reached a decision. A weight had dropped from his back. His step was brisk.

As he passed the house of Yolande Desinor, the death of whose child he had almost forgotten with all these new problems, Yolande saw him from her doorway. She rushed into the yard and flung out her hand, pointing at him.

"My child should not have died!" she shrieked. "You killed her!"

Catus came to a dead stop.

"You killed her! You killed her!" she accused in a voice that could be heard through half the village. Then her father, who had been Zaca at the planting ceremony, ran from the house and clapped a hand over her mouth, dragging her back inside.

Catus walked into the yard. He waited while the two old people furiously berated the woman for what she had done, then when the noise from the *caille* subsided he stepped to the door.

"Come outside," he ordered.

The old grandmother wrung her hands. "My daughter did not mean it, Catus! She is out of her mind! She has been possessed by some evil *loa!*"

"Never mind her. I wish to speak to you and your husband." Catus turned away, walked to the edge of the yard and waited.

Timidly they approached him. Inside the *caille* the mother of the dead child was sobbing. Catus folded his arms on his chest.

"Who told your daughter I killed her child?"

They looked at each other. Both were believers in *vodun*, and in the presence of an enraged *houngan* they were terrified. "We don't know," the woman babbled. "She heard it in the village this afternoon. The whole village is discussing it, she says. She has talked about nothing else since she came home!"

"What, exactly, did she hear? What am I accused of?"

"Of—of letting the child die when *Père* Clinton could have saved her," the woman said fearfully.

"I see." Catus walked out of the yard, looked down the path toward the mission and turned in the other direction. In the village he entered yard after yard and spoke to their occupants. They shrank from him in fear, most of them. They could tell by his face, if not by his voice, that he was dangerously angry.

Yes, they told him, it was true. People everywhere were whispering a fantastic story that *Père* Clinton could have saved Yolande's child if he had been sent for sooner. Of course *they* did not believe it, certainly not, but people were saying it.

"Has *Père* Clinton himself been here telling this story?" Catus demanded.

Père Clinton? Here in the village? No, they had not seen him. But of course the story must have started with him. Who else would tell such an awful lie?

Catus went home. A little later he stepped out of his house and went into the *hounfor,* closing the door behind him. He did not see his sister, Micheline, come across the compound into the deserted *tonnelle.*

Micheline stood under the thatched roof, in the gloom of the deserted dancing place, gazing at the door behind which her brother had disappeared. Presently she heard the rhythmic rattle of his *asson* and the sound of his voice as he conversed with the spirits in the *govis.*

She tightened her lips in triumph as she strolled out of the *tonnelle* and seated herself under the big mapou in the yard. Her brother had been quite right about Pradon Beliard. He *was* the Father's enemy. Moreover, that boy from the plantation was far from being a fool. It hadn't taken him long to use the information she had whispered to him. The whole village was buzzing this evening.

Well, *now* let her misguided brother talk about being the Father's friend. Or was he at this very moment, with the help of the *mystères*, planning some awful revenge?

She shivered, though the night was unusually warm and no whisper of a breeze could be felt in the compound. She would not like to be standing in *Père* Clinton's footprints now, she told herself. If she were *Père* Clinton she would be burning candles behind a locked door and packing a suitcase for the earliest possible flight to the mainland.

It served him right.

BARRY HAD BEEN COUNTING THE DAYS with growing uneasiness, wondering why Catus did not come to see him. After their long talk in which he and the *houngan* had so thoroughly explored their differences, he had been sure Catus would at least agree to a truce. But nothing had happened.

The waiting had brought one thing home to him quite clearly. He knew now that he and Edith could never make a go of things.

She had been talking to him by the hour. With the clinic deserted and the work on the ridge at a standstill, there had been endless opportunities for him to be with her. She came alone to the mission now. With no patients to look after, Alma did not bother. Arriving in the morning, Edith usually stayed the best part of the day and went back to the Lemkes' about four.

She had talked and talked about the Bishop's sermon. The Bishop was right, she insisted. There could be no possible compromise with *vodun* in a place like this. She implied that Barry's failure on the island was his own fault, a direct result of his having tried to compromise.

She seemed to have decided that it was her duty to save him from himself. "Darling," she argued, "I can't see why you think it important to have that Laroche man on your side. Why *is* it? If you do strike some sort of bargain with him, how will you ever keep it without betraying your trust? You'll never convert him. There might even be some danger of his converting you."

"I don't think I'd be very convincing, prancing around a painted post and singing chants in Creole."

"Darling, I'm not joking. He's a very strong-minded person. And you *don't* have the firm convictions you ought to have; you know you don't. I can't see why you want him for a friend. Your job here is to teach Christianity. If they won't listen to you, is that your fault? In time *some* of them will begin to listen, won't they? Then little by little you'll win them over."

"The flaw in that argument is that I don't expect to live more than the usual number of years."

"Well, I still can't see why all this upsets you so."

She understood nothing, of course, of what he was trying to do. In her eyes all that mattered was the picture he presented to the world, a picture she now found tragically shabby and one she was determined to do over. What she wanted, he supposed, was a dashing young missionary who would stand up in church every Sunday and thunder God's word to the heathen, knowing she stood there at his side to comfort him when the heathen stupidly refused to listen. "My poor, poor boy," she would murmur then, holding him ever so tenderly in her arms. "You mustn't blame yourself. No man could do more than you do."

She was simply incapable of seeing that a man *must* do more or be nothing.

He had walked with her one morning to the ridge, where the half-finished rectory now stood like a historic ruin and the empty church cried out for the sound of voices. Even there she had somehow managed to say exactly the wrong thing.

"You'll never get it finished this way," she scolded. "They won't help you unless Catus gives his permission, and he has no intention of giving it. I don't see why you can't bring some workers over from the mainland."

He tried not to be angry, or at least not to show it. "There are three reasons, Edith. First, I have nowhere to put them up. Second, the islanders would make things too unpleasant for them. Third, if the mission here is to be for the people of Ile du Vent, they ought to be the ones to build it." And he reminded her of the village in the mainland mountains that people for miles around insisted had been built by zombies, those mysterious living-dead of the island's mythology, simply because strange workmen from outside had been brought in to create it.

There on the ridge that morning she had had one of her rare moments of tenderness. Putting her head against his shoulder she had said with a sob, "Barry, Barry darling, I did so look forward to your living up here. Aren't you ever going to be able to?"

He found himself peculiarly unable to respond. "I wonder if anyone will ever live here," he answered from his weariness.

"It would be heaven. If only you'd think of yourself just once, instead of them and what *they* want."

Meaning what, he wondered. If only he would think of her and what she wanted? He held her close, feeling somehow guilty, yet knowing he had never really encouraged her. At least he had never attempted to deceive her about himself. Even at Fond Marie she must have known what he believed in and the kind of life he was likely to have.

"I'll find a solution somehow," he had said, trying very hard to be responsive when she lifted her head to kiss him.

On the Sunday following the Bishop's sermon only four persons came to church. He felt himself preaching less to them than to the ghostly congregation that had marched out after Catus Laroche the week before. The four who listened were Edith and Alma, St. Juste and Lucy. Lucy wept openly all through the service.

The next morning Lucy went to Terre Rouge to buy vegetables. On hearing what was being said in the village, she hurried back with her basket still empty.

She found Barry in the office, writing a letter to Peter Ambrose. Edith had not yet arrived.

"*Mon Père, mon Père!*" Rushing in without waiting for a nod, a breach of routine that in itself told him something was seriously wrong, Lucy stumbled to the desk. "They are saying you have accused Catus of killing the Desinor child!"

He put aside his pen, feeling the blood run out of his face. "Saying *what?*"

"That Yolande Desinor's child need not have died!" she wailed. "That you have been telling people you could have saved her, and Catus let her die! Oh, *mon Père*, that man will do terrible things now! *Did* you say that about him?"

"No. Of course not." He stood up. She was even more upset than he, and forcing her onto a chair he filled a glass of water from the pitcher on the desk and made her drink it. "Now tell me exactly what you've heard," he said. "Slowly, please. This is important."

The whole market, she said, was talking about it. The whole village. Probably, by now, the whole island. Last night when Catus was walking through Terre Rouge, the mother of the dead child had screamed accusations at him. Catus had been so furious he could scarcely speak. He had gone from house to house questioning people, and then spent the night in his *hounfor*. He was still there. The whole village was waiting to see what he would do next.

"*Mon Père*," Lucy sobbed, "you must go away! That man will surely kill you now!"

22

BARRY SAT ON HIS DESK, gazing at her. So the days of waiting had all been wasted, and he had been living in false hopes. He felt as though he were being squeezed in a vise. As though the sweat oozing from his pores were blood. His hands clenched and the knuckles began to ache.

Who could have started *this* lie? The day of the little girl's death, he and Catus had gone straight to Catus' house and talked behind a closed door. No one could possibly have overheard what was said in that room. He felt bewitched, as though an invisible someone were standing behind him. He had an idiotic impulse to twist himself about in the hope of discovering who it was.

No one could have known. The secret had been locked up behind the sealed lips of three persons, himself, Catus, and Alma Lemke. He dismissed Alma from his mind instantly. She would never do this to him. She had no reason. Had she told her husband? No, no, she knew all too well what use her husband would make of such a weapon. Who, then?

Had he and Catus been alone in the *caille* that day? Perhaps someone else had been present. There were two rooms. He had not looked in the second room. Someone must have been there.

What was he to do now?

He remembered his vow to Catus, and the jaws of the vise closed tighter. "Nothing we have said in this room will be repeated outside," he had said. What must Catus be thinking now?

He pushed himself off the desk. Lucy watched him with tears streaming down her homely face. "What will you do, *mon Père?*" she whispered.

"I'm going to call on him."

"No, no! He'll kill you! You don't know that man!"

"We *were* friends before all these things happened. Perhaps I can make him understand. At any rate I've got to try."

He went on horseback. He would have preferred to walk, to think the thing out as he walked, but knew it was dangerous. If he were on foot and one fanatical villager took a notion to throw a stone at him, an orgy of stone-throwing could follow. But he rode slowly.

It was like his first day on the island. He followed the narrow, climbing footpath to the village, past the fenced-in yards and gardens, and people stopped what they were doing to stare at him. But they had been only curious then. Now they sensed the drama behind his journey and by the time he had passed through the village he had a following. They kept their distance but they were there, padding along behind on their bare feet, silent as phantoms. When he rode through the gate in the cactus hedge, into the Laroche compound with its *tonnelle* and three houses, they stopped outside to watch.

He dismounted, aware that he was afraid. It was a strange feeling. He remembered a story Peter Ambrose had told him one night on the veranda at Fond Marie, about a missionary on the mainland who had been attacked and badly beaten for chopping down a mapou tree his parishioners held sacred. The sun beat down on him and he realized he had forgotten his hat. He walked slowly toward the closed door of Catus' *caille*.

Before he reached it, other doors opened. Louis and Dauré stepped from theirs to stand in the shadow cast by the thatch above them. The little girl, Fifine, whose life he had saved, clung to Dauré's hand. Micheline appeared in *her* doorway, silently watching, and he saw the shadowed forms of her parents close behind her. He felt himself in the vise again, with its jaws closing. The distance to Catus' house seemed ten times as long as it ever had before.

He reached it at last and knocked. There was no response. He saw Micheline coming across the compound toward him and noticed she was wearing a black dress. Why black? Black was for mourning. She stopped a few feet from him and he saw on her lips a twisted smile that bewildered him, in her eyes a look of triumph that sent a chill through him.

"My brother is in the *hounfor*," she said.

He turned away from her and entered the *tonnelle*. It was a relief. The roof of thatch blocked off the stinging blaze of the sun and the shadows were a screen against the scores of eyes watching him. He lifted a hand and brought his knuckles against the *hounfor* door and said quietly, "Catus." Then after waiting a moment he knocked again.

The door opened. Catus, hands on hips, wearing dark trousers and a bright red shirt, stood facing him. Their eyes met. The *houngan's*

face, gaunt with fatigue, sunken-cheeked, was like a mask carved
from a chunk of dark driftwood.

"What do you want here?"

"I want to talk to you," Barry said.

"We have nothing to discuss."

"Listen to me. I have only just heard what the people are saying. I
came the moment I heard. It was not I who spread this story. I said
nothing to anyone. Who did this I don't know. I can't even guess,
unless there was someone else in your house the day we talked. But
it was not I."

"There was no one else in my house that day."

"What I'm telling you is the truth. Have I ever lied to you?"

"You are lying now."

"If I had done this thing, to turn your people against you, would I
be here now denying it?"

"You have made me your enemy and you are afraid."

"It wasn't fear that brought me here, Catus. I'm not afraid of you."

"We are enemies." Catus made it sound like a simple statement,
but his eyes left no doubt that the words were a threat. "I bid you good
day and warn you not to come here again."

He shut the door.

Barry turned away, feeling weak, drained of energy. The eyes were
on him as he walked to his horse and swung himself into the saddle.
He saw Micheline again as the horse wheeled half about before heading
for the gate. Her mouth wore the same triumphant smile.

Was this *her* doing, to punish him for having refused her in the
grotto? How could it be?

LATE THAT AFTERNOON Catus emerged from the *hounfor* and returned
to his house. The others had been watching and waiting for hours.
Dauré at once took him a tray of food.

He ate as though he had no appetite, though he had eaten nothing
since shutting himself up in the *hounfor* the evening before. Dauré
sat on a chair and sadly shook her head at him. Micheline came and
leaned in the doorway.

"What's the matter?" Micheline taunted. "Aren't you hungry?
Haven't you made up your mind what to do yet? I thought *griot*
and *djon-djon* were your favorite foods."

Paying no attention, Catus poked with his fork at the chunks of
fried pig and the mound of rice and mushrooms.

"Leave him alone," Dauré said.

"What did the Father say to you?" Micheline persisted. "That he didn't do this thing? Did he tell you again that he was really your best friend?"

"Be quiet, Micheline!" Dauré snapped. "What's the matter with you lately anyway?"

"I suppose *you* think he *didn't* do it!"

"As a matter of fact, yes, that's right. I *do* think he didn't do it. You can say what you like, all of you, but the Father is a good man."

"Because he saved your child? Because Fifine likes him?"

"Yes. And because he has done a lot of other good things. You know he has."

Catus raised his head to look at her. "Are you taking his side against me?"

"Am I what? No." She seemed puzzled by his question. "No, of course I'm not. Would I take any man's side against my own brother? But you don't know for certain he did this thing. People say he accused you, but I haven't heard any of them say that *he* talked to them about it."

"Do you believe I let the child die?" Catus asked her.

Dauré frowned. "If I heard the Father say it I might believe it. Fifine would have died, wouldn't she? But I have not heard him say it, and I don't believe he did. I think someone must have said it for him, to make you hate him."

Micheline gave her sister a pitying look. "How generous of you. And who do you think must have said it for him? Who on this island would dare tell such a lie about Catus?"

"I don't know. But the Father is a good man."

"Good! Good! You said that before. *Why* is he good?"

"He wants to help us. He *has* helped us."

"He did that so we would build his fine new church. Perhaps you noticed that as soon as the church was finished he stood up and said we couldn't go to it unless we had 'clean hearts.'"

"The Bishop said that, not *Père* Clinton," Dauré argued.

"They planned it between them, don't think they didn't. Oh, he's a shrewd one, *Père* Clinton is. His trouble is that he never learned the old proverb, you can't speak evil of a friend's house and expect to be invited to it again. He thought he could have us for friends and we wouldn't guess what he was up to. And now when he finds out we are too smart for him, he tries to shake our faith in Catus with this filthy lie!"

"Be quiet, both of you," Catus said. He frowned at Micheline, wondering again what had happened between her and the Father to make her hate him so. The very intensity of her hate made it open to suspicion.

He shifted his gaze to the face of Dauré. It was not strange, of course, that this sister of his defended the Father. Still, she *was* his sister, and you would think that when a man was wronged, his own family would stand up for him. Did she really think *Père* Clinton was innocent? That someone else had spread this story? Who else could have spread it? Was it possible someone had overheard the conversation in this room the day of the child's death?

Catus glowered at the plate of food before him. The trouble was, he still wanted to believe the Father innocent. He still wanted that man for a friend. He couldn't understand himself. All the evidence pointed to *Père* Clinton's being guilty of the worst possible breach of faith, and yet he wanted to disregard it. The Father was guilty. He had to be guilty. Yet why had he come to the *hounfor* just now, swearing he was not? If he were guilty he ought to be gloating over the knowledge that he had done his enemy great harm. Catus did not understand that.

Another thing. Since yesterday evening he had stood before the altar in the *hounfor*, seeking counsel from the *mystères*. All night long he had performed the most secret and sacred rituals, begging the *loa* to make their wishes known to him. But none of them had come, none had spoken. Why? Because the Father's god was more powerful than they, and they did not wish to become involved in this quarrel? Or was it because he, Catus Laroche, the protégé of the great Salmador, no longer believed in what he was doing?

Perhaps this is not a conflict between the Father and me, Catus thought, but one between his faith and mine.

"Well," Micheline was saying, "are you going to tell us what you've decided to do?"

He looked up at her. "What should I do?"

"You're asking me? It isn't *me* he has made the laughingstock of Ile du Vent!"

"Nevertheless I am asking you. Both of you."

Dauré said timidly, "I wish you would wait. What harm can there be in waiting a little while to be sure you are right?"

Micheline, tossing her head, said with a sneer, "If I were the great Catus Laroche and a two-faced white man set out to destroy me and what I believed in, I would show him things about *vodun* he never dreamed of."

Catus sighed. "Go away, both of you, and let me think."

Micheline sent a look of pure hate at her sister and strode from the *caille*.

ALL THE REST OF THAT HOT, airless afternoon Micheline watched the door of her brother's house, waiting for it to open. She could do no work. When she was not standing in the doorway of her own house she was pacing the hard-packed red earth of the compound. Her parents watched her in uneasy wonder, disturbed by her behavior. Dauré and Louis César noticed and whispered. Little Fifine sucked a thumb and stared.

"Something has come over that sister of yours lately," Louis said to his wife. "What is it?"

"I don't know. But I've certainly noticed it."

Evening came. The sun performed its nightly ritual over the island and the blazing colors faded from the sky. The shadows deepened. Micheline in her black dress was scarcely visible as she walked back and forth, back and forth, with her gaze on her brother's door.

Suddenly she strode to the door and jerked it open.

Catus occupied the same chair, the tray of food still scarcely touched before him. He raised his head from his hands as though it were very heavy. His sunken eyes regarded her without interest.

"What do you want?"

"I have something to say to you." She shut the door and stepped forward. Snatching up a box of matches from the table, she lit a lamp and turned to face him. "Something you won't like to hear."

"All I hear lately is things I don't want to," he muttered. "So say it and get out."

She looked at him and her mouth twitched. She was breathing hard. The front of the black dress rose and fell and the noise of her breathing was loud in the room's hot stillness. She said, "I didn't want to tell you this yet. Not until I had to. But in a few weeks I would have had to, so it doesn't matter, does it? I'm going to have a baby."

The shock was too abrupt. Catus was too tired. "What?" he said.

"Can't you listen? I said I'm going to have a baby. *His* baby."

He began to understand. He took in a quick, noisy breath. His body straightened from its slouch and hardened like a thing of rubber suddenly shot full of air.

"A baby!"

"Yes," she said. "His. The Father's."

He sprang to his feet, upsetting the tray of food on the little table before him. "You lie!"

"Would I lie about such a thing? Do you think I enjoy telling you this?"

"How could you know so soon? It was only a few days ago that you spent the night in the grotto with him!"

"I slept with him the first week he came here. We've been meeting ever since."

Catus stood before her with his body heaving. He had thrown off his red shirt hours before and was clad only in the dark trousers. His shoulders jerked. His arms were like hard black earth with tree-roots growing just under the surface. "A white man!" he shouted. "You've been sleeping with a white man!"

She shrank from his fury. "He wanted me. I didn't know how to refuse him."

"My sister, going with a white man! Having a white baby!"

"I thought he was a good man. You thought so yourself. Dauré, just this afternoon——"

"Get out!" Catus thundered.

She was frightened. She backed away from him. Her eyes opened wide.

"Get out!" Catus kicked the overturned table aside and lunged for her, then stopped and looked wildly about him. He stumbled across the room and snatched up a *cocomacaque* stick, long, slender, tough as steel. It was the kind of stick used in slave days by brutal overseers to beat defiant slaves into submission. The kind of stick used by the slaves themselves on their white masters when they rose in bloody revolt and won their freedom. Catus swung it over his head. "Get out! Out! Out!"

Micheline ran screaming through a barrage of blows and flung the door open.

He pursued her across the clearing, flailing the air with his stick and every few strides catching her across the back or shoulders with it. "Sleeping with a white man!" he howled. "My own sister! A Laroche!" Through the gate in the cactus hedge he raced after her. Down the path to the village. The stick rose and fell. Micheline screamed in pain and terror. Long before they reached the village her black dress was in ribbons, her back and arms streaming with blood.

The whole village heard them coming. People ran from lamplit *cailles* to line the sides of the path. Micheline shrieked at them to help her but they only shrank back and watched. When she snatched at them they tore themselves free. She ran into a yard and Catus followed. The stick rose and fell, whistling in the air, thudding against its target. Whistle, thud, whistle, thud. The sound pouring from the girl's throat was now a continuous scream.

Halfway across the yard she stumbled and fell, struggled to her knees, rolled onto her back and lay moaning. Only remnants of the dress remained. Her naked, bleeding body writhed on the ground and her hands fluttered over her face to deflect the blows of the stick. The stick fell once more. It smashed her hands aside. Catus looked down at her, his own face contorted and unrecognizable.

"Get up!" he shouted.

"No, no! Mother of God——"

"Get up!" He seized her by the wrist and jerked her to her feet, then threw down his stick and with both hands whirled her to face the crowd of people in the yard and on the village path.

"Look at her!" he commanded hoarsely. "Look at this slut who was my sister! By her own confession she has been sleeping with *Père* Clinton—not just once but for weeks! She is going to have a baby. *His* baby. Look at her!"

He suddenly flung her away from him and watched her stumble to her knees. "Get out!" he screamed. "Take your baby and get out, before I forget myself and kill you!"

She staggered to her feet and turned toward him, lifting her bruised arms in supplication.

"Get out!"

Moaning, she covered her face with her hands and went reeling across the yard into darkness.

Catus picked up the *cocomacaque* and curled his hands around the ends of it. He bent his hands downward. The stick snapped. A *cocomacaque* is tough as steel, but it snapped. He let the pieces fall and walked slowly out to the road.

The crowd made way, silently staring at him.

23

The *Télédiol* WAS IN MOTION even before Catus disappeared into his house. During the night it functioned through the village and at daylight it spread outward. Women from Terre Rouge, carrying their wash to a nearby stream, whispered the story to those who came from Petit Trou to fill the family *calebasses*. At the Petit Trou market it was heard by women from Tête Cabrit. Fishermen walking the shore with their sardine nets told it to other fishermen. A cousin of Lucy's heard it and ran breathless to the mission.

A little after ten o'clock that morning Barry dismounted by the gate in the cactus hedge. The gate was closed. He opened it and entered. Big Louis came from the nearest house and stood before him, barring his way.

"I must see Catus."

Louis shook his head, not moving his enormous bare feet. His great ugly-gentle face was now only ugly.

"I tell you I must see him," Barry insisted. "This thing is a lie, Louis. I am not the father of Micheline's child."

Louis said nothing. He only stood there. It was impossible to go around him. Barry looked into the soot-black face with its misshapen mouth and nose and knew that if he tried to force his way past, Louis would stop him. Those powerful hands might do serious damage.

The child, Fifine, appeared in the doorway of Louis' house and saw him. She cried out in delight and ran across the yard toward him, her small feet flying. Louis thrust out a hand and stopped her.

"Dauré!"

Dauré came from the house. Louis thrust the child at her. She caught the little girl by the arm, glanced fearfully at Barry, turned without a word and hurried the child back into the house.

"If you won't let me see him," Barry said, "at least tell me where Micheline is. Perhaps I can find out why she did this."

Louis hesitated. "We do not know where she is." The impediment was back in his speech. The words were half hiss, half rumble.

"Very well," Barry said with a shrug. "I don't blame you, but you are wrong."

He turned away.

The village held its breath as he rode through. Then the whispers began again. *The Father went to see Catus. Catus would not talk to him.*

St. Juste was waiting outside the rectory. He had been standing there since Barry's departure. At sight of Barry, unharmed, relief flowed through him like warm water through a man half frozen, but his hands began to shake as he helped Barry dismount.

"Would he talk to you, Mr. Clinton?"

"No. Nor would Louis. Even the child was forbidden to speak to me."

St. Juste looked at Barry's stricken face and shook his head.

Lucille sat at the table in the kitchen, weeping. Barry entered and laid a hand on her shoulder. "Will you do something for me, Lucy?"

She lifted her head. The movement brought a fresh flow of tears and he had to wait. When her convulsive sobbing subsided a little and her head moved up and down, he said, "I must talk to Micheline. Can you try to find out where she is?"

She stood up, nodding through her sobs. She went out.

He walked slowly back to the office and sat at his desk. St. Juste was there, sitting on the cot where so many of the islanders had sat to describe their ailments. Nothing was said for a time. Then St. Juste stopped staring at the floor and looked up.

"I wish there were something we could do, Mr. Clinton."

"There isn't. At least nothing I can think of."

"Can I get you a drink?"

"No, thanks. Not now."

"Do you mind if I have one?"

"Help yourself."

St. Juste filled a water glass with straight rum, drank half of it down, and sat again to sip the rest. He seldom drank. When he did, he watered his rum until the mixture was almost colorless. He said now, "We've been through a lot together since I came here. I want you to know I appreciate the way you've treated me, Mr. Clinton. No matter what happens you can count on me."

Barry looked at him and nodded. "I know."

"You've been a wonderful friend. I've never had a friend like you before. Not even a colored one."

"I believe I will have a drink," Barry said.

St. Juste jumped up and poured it. They drank together. They were drinking when Edith arrived.

She stopped short in the office doorway and widened her eyes at them in astonishment. "Good heavens!" she laughed. "At this hour in the morning?" She was very attractive in a pale blue skirt and white blouse and had done something to her hair, drawing it back tight against her ears. She had ridden slowly from the plantation to avoid becoming overheated. She held in her hand a small orange-red fruit with a few glossy leaves attached.

"Look at what I found," she said. "Isn't it lovely? I can't think what it might be. There aren't any near Fond Marie, I'm certain. Do you know the name of it?" She put the fruit on the desk between Barry's hands.

Barry turned the stem in his fingers and silently shook his head.

Edith frowned. "What's the matter? Is something wrong?"

He put her treasure down. "If you haven't heard, you must be the only living soul on the island who hasn't. I suppose the plantation *is* the end of the line for the *télédiol.*"

"Heard what?"

"I am now accused"—he turned his head toward her—"of being the father of Micheline Laroche's expected child."

The color fled from Edith's face. She groped for a chair and sat down. "No," she said slowly. "No, Barry. Oh, no!"

He shrugged. The drink had warmed him a little. Not that he was drunk or even partly drunk. He emptied his glass and put it on the edge of the desk, with a glance at St. Juste who rose without comment to refill it.

"It's like a play, isn't it?" Barry said then. "I came here thinking I was only a harmless missionary with a job to do, and if I tried very hard and was very careful, I might make friends and get the job done. I *was* careful according to my own lights, and I even did make friends. A few, anyway. But it seems I have enemies too, and they are resourceful."

He managed a smile. The drink was back in his hand and he sipped it, nodding his thanks at St. Juste.

"You have to admire my enemies, don't you?" he went on. "See how carefully they've turned me into a monster. First the death of young Toto—that wasn't my fault exactly, except that I was stupid enough to buy a *bête diable*. But I was dishonest about it, you see; I tried to conceal the fact that the boy *was* dead. Then when the little Desinor child died of malaria, I used her death as a weapon to destroy Catus after promising him I wouldn't. There were other things, I seem to remember. I can't think of them now. And finally this. The monster is now full-blown and frightful. He has seduced the young sister of the great man of the island. She is to have his child."

"Barry," Edith said, "are you drunk?"

"No, my dear, I'm not."

"But I don't understand what you're telling me!"

"You can't have been listening. I'll repeat it. Micheline Laroche is going to have a baby. I am accused of being its father. I am accused by her."

"But *how* can she accuse you? The night of the storm——"

"I follow your line of reasoning. True, we spent the night together only a short time ago. But the accusation is not based on what took place that night, or what she says took place. I have been her lover for weeks." He laughed, abruptly stopped laughing and frowned at the glass in his hand. "Perhaps I am a little drunk." He knew he wasn't. It was simply nerves. Gazing at Edith again, he said grimly, "Catus drove his sister out of the house last night with the whole village watching. He is now shut up in his own house deciding, I suppose, what he will do next. Surely you felt the tension in the village when you rode through. The place is like a time bomb."

"I didn't notice anything," she said.

"Like a volcano about to erupt."

"But surely you've denied the girl's wild story!"

"My dear, I can deny it until I'm hoarse, but if I'm not able to convince Catus what good will my shouting do? Catus knows that the girl and I spent a night together in the grotto. He knows we *could* have come up through the inner tunnel if we had wanted to."

"You didn't know there *was* an inner tunnel."

"His sister knew. Put yourself in Catus' place for a moment, though heaven knows there's no comfort in doing so; I've tried it and I can only see how devastating the evidence is. His sister and I sought shelter in the grotto. With no reason to remain in the cave all night, she would have led me up through the inner tunnel at once. But she did not. Therefore she wished to stay in the cave. *Why* did she wish to stay? To a man like Catus, whose mind goes straight to the heart of things, there is not even any question."

Edith was pale and tense. "Why *did* she wish to stay?"

"She hoped I would make love to her."

"Barry! Really!"

He shrugged. "Does it shock you? I'm sorry. The truth is that Micheline has been wanting me to make love to her ever since I came here. Since before I even set foot on the island, in fact. We met on the boat, the first day."

"You can't be serious. Why, she's black!"

Barry gazed sadly at St. Juste, who lowered his head and studied the floor. "I'm sorry, Clement. Miss Barnett is upset."

St. Juste said nothing.

Edith looked annoyed. "Well," she said, "if Catus won't believe you, what *are* you going to do about it? You can't let such a fantastic story go unstopped. Why, the whole island—even the mainland——" Suddenly she was frightened. "Good heavens! A story like that will even reach the capital! They'll be tossing it around at the club!"

"I'm sure they will. With relish. And there will certainly be 'reports that' and 'rumors of' in the capital's gossipy little newspapers."

She looked horrified. "Then you must *do* something!"

"I must do something. Agreed. But I don't know what to do."

They were silent, the three of them. Barry studied Edith's face. He was not surprised by her reaction. He was learning to understand people, he supposed, and to foresee just how they *would* react in certain situations. She was thinking of herself, and of course to some extent of him because whatever happened to him would effect her unless her plans for the future were revised. She was not thinking at all of his work on the island and what this latest blow would mean to that. She was annoyed with him for getting into such a mess. It needn't have happened, she was telling herself. He had brought it on himself by being too friendly with these people, by getting involved with them. He should have remained aloof. She thought him stupid and a little vulgar for thinking Micheline desired him. No girl with a black skin would dare to want a white man. Most of all she was thinking of what people she knew would say about him, and about her, when the story reached the mainland as it certainly would.

She stood up. "I think I'd better go back," she said. "Unless, of course, there's something I can do here? Is there?"

"Lucille is trying to find out for me where Micheline is. Until she does, I expect to sit and wait."

"Then I'll go. I don't want to be here when you talk to Micheline."

He walked out with her and helped her into the saddle. As he watched her ride across the red-earth clearing he shook his head. She might come once more, he supposed, but it would be only to say good-by. This was the end, really.

He re-entered the office and picked up the twig with its attached red fruit. "Do you know the name of this, Clement?"

"Not the botanical name, Mr. Clinton. The natives call it Tété Ti-fi, the Young Girl's Breast."

She *is* young, Barry thought sadly. She isn't to blame. He was thinking of Edith, but the thought applied to Micheline as well, he realized.

IN THE PLANTATION BUNGALOW at the end of the island Alma Lemke stood outside the door of Edith's room, listening. Actually it was her husband's room that the girl had. With plastic screening and a curtain of woven palm-fronds, Warner had transformed one end of the veranda into a sleeping chamber for himself.

The door was shut now. It had been shut since the evening meal, an hour ago. Edith had not eaten much dinner. In the middle of the meal she had pushed back her chair and fled weeping to her room. She was still sobbing.

Alma walked out onto the veranda. Her husband sat there with a drink. She leaned against the rail, facing him.

"I suppose this is your doing too," she said.

Lemke looked at her with an amused smile. "Do you mean the girl's having a baby or dear Mr. Clinton's being accused of fathering it?"

"You know what I mean. As a matter of fact the baby is yours, isn't it?"

"I haven't the faintest idea."

"What are you going to do if she changes her mind and tells the truth?"

Lemke grinned. "She's told her story now. Even if she were to scream a denial from the top of Mr. Clinton's magnificent new church, not a soul would believe her."

He was probably right, Alma told herself, despising him from the depths of her being and wishing she knew some way to turn the tables on him. How, she wondered, had he contrived to make Barry the victim of this latest lie? Or had he? Perhaps this time he was innocent. Perhaps the girl herself had turned on Barry. The woman scorned. But Warner was the father of the expected child; of that she was certain.

"I suppose you feel just wonderful about this," she said.

"There are no tears in my eyes, if that's what you're waiting for."

"I don't expect any. A little insane laughter wouldn't surprise me though. You won't believe me, will you, that Barry has never done a thing to hurt you? That this whole hellish campaign of yours has been unjustified?"

"I have a very good reason for not believing you."

"What reason?"

"You didn't try to defend him until you'd fallen in love with him. Your feeble attempt at throwing me off the track came too late."

She felt herself tremble at his words. In love? She, in love with Barry? The word had never entered her thoughts. Was she in love? What was love, anyway?

She considered the man sprawled on the veranda chair in front of her. Was it possible she had ever loved him, or thought she did? He had changed, of course. He had not always been like this. But even in the beginning he had been selfish, demanding, conceited. Even then he had judged all men, including himself, by their capacity for drink and ability to make women notice them.

No, she had never loved Warner Lemke. Whatever love was, it must be something better than the feeling she had had for him even then. She might never have married him but for that trip to Ohio when she had met his folks.

Perhaps that was what she had really wanted: parents like his. A gentle, well-mannered mother who spoke in soft tones and had the gift of understanding, unlike her own mother whose everlasting fault-finding had finally driven her from home. And his father, kind and respectable. Her own father had drunk himself into disgrace to escape her mother's nagging.

Was that what she had wanted? Was that why she had married Warner? She looked at him now, half drunk, leering at her in his triumph, waiting for the rum to jog him out of his inertia and send him stumbling through the dark to some native *caille*. Her mouth trembled. She turned suddenly and went inside.

Lemke's drunken laughter followed her.

LEMKE FINISHED HIS DRINK. It was very dark on the veranda now. Very quiet except for the singing of the cicadas and the distant mutter of waves on the shore. He put his feet up on the rail and watched the fireflies, wondering languidly if they were as numerous as they seemed to be or if the rum had affected his vision. One of them landed on

his leg. He watched it crawl over his trousers, the green fire rhythmi-
cally pulsing. He put his thumb on it.

So Micheline was pregnant. He wondered idly what the baby would
look like. Would it look like him? It *was* his, of course. Would it be
light or dark? By God, he'd like to see it when it arrived. Not that he
would try to. God no. The farther he kept away from that situation
the better. But if the child was his, why the devil had she accused
Clinton?

He wanted a drink. His glass was empty. He pushed himself out
of his chair and considered the distance to the bar inside, decided
the reward was not worth the required effort, and let himself drop
heavily back again. The chair started to tip sideways. He righted it by
grabbing at the railing. The glass fell from his hand and rolled
along the veranda.

Why *had* she accused Clinton? Had she been sleeping with him
too? By God, maybe she had. Maybe she had been Clinton's mistress
before he talked her into that first meeting on the beach.

Lemke's hands tightened fiercely on the arms of his chair. Was that
why she had talked about Clinton all the time? Because she'd had
him and lost him and wanted him back again? No, by God, he
wouldn't believe it. If that were true, Clinton had got the best of him
even with her. It wasn't true. It was a damned lie.

But why had she accused Clinton of fathering her baby? Why?
Why?

Lemke took his right hand from the chair and made a fist of it.
He beat the fist slowly and savagely against his knee.

"No!" he shouted. "It's a damned dirty lie! No! No! No!" His
voice in the quiet night was like the scream of a tortured animal.
Tears streamed down his face.

Alma, inside, looked up from the book she was reading, closed the
book quickly, and went to her room. She shut the door behind her
and locked it. When, she wondered, did drunkenness cease to be
drunkenness and become insanity?

LUCILLE RETURNED TO THE MISSION just before dark with a basket on
her head and a small black and white dog under her arm. She went
straight to the kitchen and tied the dog to a chair leg and set a bowl
of meat scraps in front of it. Then she looked for Barry and found
him in the office, finishing his letter to Peter Ambrose. The letter
had become a detailed report of recent events on the island.

"Have I been gone too long, *mon Père?* Did you and *M'sieu* St.
Juste have your lunch?"

"We had something, Lucy. Please sit down." She was tired, Barry saw. She was not young any more. "Were you able to find out where she is?"

She shook her head. "I think she has left the island."

"Left the island!"

"Some people in Tête Cabrit say they saw her on the beach very early this morning, talking to Ti-Jean Bazin. Ti-Jean has one of the small sailboats. A little later on he took his boat across to the mainland. They are not sure Micheline was on board, but they think she must have been because he had no other passengers and had not planned to go to the mainland today." She shook her head in sadness. "I'm sorry it took me so long to find this out, *mon Père*. I'll get supper now. I bought some fish."

"Wait." Barry frowned at her. "I can't believe this, Lucy. I can't let myself believe it. If Micheline is gone, I'm beaten."

"*Mon Père*, I'm sure she is. I'm sorry. Even before I went to look for her I had a feeling she would be gone. You knew her, *mon Père*. She was a girl of spirit, very proud, really a fine girl until this thing happened. She would never have stayed here on the island after what her brother did."

Barry knew she was right. He got up with a sigh and went around the desk to her. "I'm very grateful," he said. "Why don't you go and rest a little now? St. Juste and I can manage supper by ourselves."

"No, no, *mon Père!*"

"Good heavens, we're not children. You go and rest."

"No!" She was at the door before he could stop her. "I am not at all tired. Not in the least. I will have something on the table in half an hour."

He shook his head after her in bewilderment. Of all the people on the island, she was the one he understood the least, he thought. Yet he liked her and would be desolate now if she left him. Of course, she would not leave him. Not now. In the beginning she had been obsessed with that odd notion that old Mitchell needed her and would send for her. She never mentioned Mitchell any more. Somehow her intense loyalty had fastened itself on him, and she was now equally certain that *he* needed her.

Well, he did.

But this news of Micheline was staggering. Had she left the island? She probably had. Lucy had sized up the situation with surprising insight. A proud young girl, humiliated that way, would never stay to be stared and laughed at.

What would he do now? Wait? There was nothing else he *could* do, was there?

But wait for what?

ST. JUSTE HAD BEEN TO THE VILLAGE. He returned just as Lucy announced supper ready, and he and Barry sat down together to a meal of fried red snapper and vegetables. Lucy hovered over them.

There was nothing to report from the village, St. Juste said. "It's quiet. Too quiet. Nobody's working. People are just sitting around in their yards, waiting. They know this thing isn't over. They know something more has to happen."

"Did you go up to the Laroches'?"

"I walked by. The gate was shut. Louis was in the yard with the little girl but he didn't speak. He saw me, looked right at me, but didn't blink an eye. Catus' door was closed. I suppose he was inside."

"Or in the *hounfor*."

"Yes, or in the *hounfor*." St. Juste put a spoon into his coffee and moved it round and round, apparently unaware that he did so. "It's strange we don't hear any drums," he said. "When there's *vodun* business afoot the drums usually give it away. Maybe they'll start later."

A movement in the corner of the kitchen caught Barry's eye. He turned on his chair and was surprised to see a small black and white dog crawl out from under a chair, yawning.

"Hello," he said. "What's this?"

Lucy said quickly, "Some people I know in Tête Cabrit gave it to me, *mon Père*."

"Cute little rascal." Barry scratched a leg of the table and the animal came timidly to the end of its rope to investigate. He put out a hand. The dog backed away, looked at him, then advanced one step at a time and allowed him to rub it behind an ear.

"What's its name?"

"Name, *mon Père*?"

St. Juste laughed. "Dogs in St. Joseph don't have names, Mr. Clinton."

"Don't they? Well, no, I suppose they don't. This one ought to, though." Barry wrinkled his brow in thought. "Of course. Ti Cadeau, Little Gift. Maybe he'll bring us the gift of a change in fortune."

Lucy solemnly nodded. "It is my hope that he will protect you, *mon Père*."

"A dog that size?" St. Juste said, making a face.

"Sometimes, *m'sieu*, size does not matter."

24

THE DRUMS BEGAN LATE THAT NIGHT. The sound awakened Barry and he was puzzled. Then he remembered. He sat on the edge of his bed and fumbled for a box of matches on the table. He lit the lamp. It was quarter to one. He remembered being awake at half past eleven, using his flashlight then to see the face of the clock. He had thought he would never get to sleep. He must have dozed.

He dressed and went out, remembering to pick up the flashlight as he left the room. It was a dark night. He stood in the office doorway and listened to the throbbing. There was no rhythm to the sound. None that could be distinguished at this distance, at any rate. It was only a rumble, as though the dark earth were struggling to talk. As though the buried roots of the trees around the clearing were in motion, pushing their way through the ground. He walked part way across the clearing and glanced back at the rectory. It looked forlorn and deserted. The old church might have been there a thousand years.

He knew he would not sleep if he went back to bed. He would only lie there on his back staring up at the iron roof, feeling himself shut up in a prison. He took the path to the ridge. The moon broke through as he climbed. The path was like something in a child's painting, done with a finger, a streak of yellow and red against background smudges of dark green and black. He felt unreal on it. The night and the island were unreal. The sound of the drums was an angry mutter from another world.

At the top of the ridge the feeling of unreality was even more vivid. He had not been up here at night in a long time; he had forgotten the eerie brightness of everything when the moon was out. The trees glistened. The grass seemed splashed with aluminum paint. The church and unfinished rectory were props for one of those films about men who became vampires or werewolves when the moon rose, and you never knew quite what was happening because the photography was blurred and the people were only gliding shadows.

What am I here for, he wondered.

He went along to the church and into it, and up the aisle through pale shafts of moonlight to the rail. He stood there frowning at the altar. His church. Or did it belong to that fellow Dufour had talked about, the one who claimed to own the land? In any case the people it was intended for had been driven out by the Bishop and the structure had become a monument to man's stupidity, a mausoleum in which love and understanding lay buried.

He turned to look at the empty benches, recalling the people who had occupied them that day. Catus Laroche, now shut up in his house or *hounfor* planning some dark and terrible vengeance. Micheline, an outcast probably destined to end up a prostitute in the capital. Edith, disillusioned and unhappy. Alma Lemke, burdened with a beast of a husband. All the others.

The drums went on and on.

What was it he had said to Catus about God's being in church even though invisible? "We believe it." Very well, he believed. There were points of doctrine he disputed, being unable to recognize their validity or see that they served any useful purpose, but he believed in a creator of all things, and the name "God" was as good as any other for a mystery no man could understand. But did God know or care what was happening on Ile du Vent?

The universe was a master plan, certainly. Stars, moons, planets, all whirling about through space in perfect order—it was no accident. But with even the most sympathetic interest in the welfare of its inhabitants, could God be aware of all that happened? Of the movements of a handful of people on one small planet? One tiny fragment of one small planet? Wasn't it more likely the Master Mind concerned itself only with long-range results?

An architect didn't look at every nail, brick, grain of sand and speck of cement that went into the building of a house. He paid no attention to nails bent or lost, sand scattered, bricks broken, cement stepped into the ground. He stopped by every little while to see how the house was progressing. The house was what mattered.

Dear God, some of your people are in trouble here on Ile du Vent. Have you noticed?

He waited for a sign. The Bible was full of such signs, wasn't it? An angel had appeared to Mary. Zacharias had seen one in the temple. The disciples had been addressed by strange figures in white at the ascension. God himself had appeared to Moses and spoken to Jesus.

The answer to every problem is in the Bible if you'll look for it, boy.

He saw only the Bishop gesticulating and heard only the drums. When he got back to the mission the drums were still throbbing and St. Juste was pacing up and down in front of the rectory door with a cigarette.

"The racket woke me up, Mr. Clinton. I looked in to see if you were asleep." He peered anxiously at Barry's face. "You haven't been up there to Laroche's place?"

"No. I didn't think it wise."

"Stay away from there, please. With those drums pounding away, the whole village will be on edge. There's no telling what might happen."

"Are they having a ceremony, do you think?"

"Mr. Clinton, you know as much about *vodun* as I do. Probably a whole lot more. You know what those drums mean, if you'll think about it. They mean Catus Laroche has made up his mind what's to be done about you and is calling on his *vodun* gods to help him do it."

"And we can expect trouble of some sort in the morning? Is that what you think?"

"When the drums stop."

The drums did not stop that night. The sound was a deepening flood that flowed down from the village to inundate the mission clearing and lap against the walls of the rectory. Barry could not sleep through it. He was able to achieve only moments of half sleep in which his mind saw big Louis César hunched over a drumhead and the sweat-burnished figure of Catus Laroche whirling in a lantern-lit dimness surrounded by hypnotized eyes.

When he rose at dawn the drums were still pounding. The sound throbbed in his head while he washed and caused his hand to shake while he shaved. At breakfast it was an invisible sheet of glass between him and St. Juste, interfering with their attempts to make conversation. There was no escaping it.

He tried to ignore it. He was no believer in the fanciful notion that a continued beating of drums could drive a man out of his mind. Perhaps in a week or a month it might have some effect. He might want to scream out against it by then, as he would at any other annoyance. But this was terrifying now only because of what it stood for. "When it stops," St. Juste had said. He kept listening for it to stop, interrupting what he was doing to hear if it had.

It didn't.

Edith did not come. He had not expected her. When he did have visitors, just before noon, he was almost pleased to see them, though one of the pair was the strutting little magistrate, Felix Dufour, with a battered briefcase under his arm, and the other had every appearance of being a St. Joseph lawyer.

Barry seated them in the office, retired behind his desk and took a moment to look them over. The stranger was a man of thirty or so, small, wearing a wrinkled gray business suit and gleaming black shoes. The shoes must have been polished within the past few minutes if the pair had walked up from Petit Trou. To complete his costume the fellow wore a white shirt and black tie, and held in his hands a dark felt hat that had seen better days. He looked like a funeral director. His name was Henri LeGrand.

"*M'sieu* LeGrand," Felix said, happily smiling, "is a lawyer from the capital. He represents my constituent, Antoine Constant."

"I take you've come about the land transfer."

LeGrand bobbed his head. "Precisely, Mr. Clinton."

"Why haven't you brought Constant, then?"

"Antoine is indisposed," Felix lisped.

"Is he? Then you've had your walk for nothing, believe me. There's no point in our discussing the matter without him. If it's his land the church is built on, I intend to hear the claim from his own lips."

Felix looked annoyed. "But *M'sieu* LeGrand is here to speak for him, *mon Père!*"

"Not to me, he isn't. Until *M'sieu* LeGrand walked in here just now, I'd never set eyes on him. For all I know he may be an Anse Ange fisherman dressed up to fool me."

The lawyer sat bolt upright, bristling. His hand shot to the inner pocket of his jacket and came out clutching a wallet. From it he extracted a card. "My credentials, Mr. Clinton!"

Barry glanced at the card and shrugged. "Very well, you're a lawyer. I still have no assurance that you represent Antoine Constant."

"I have told you he does!" Felix sputtered.

"You've told me? I bought a mule on your word once. I've learned my lesson."

Anger made Dufour's face twitch. I'm probably a fool to be doing this, Barry told himself, but, damn it, I want to. Let them fume. If they're going to get the church away from me they'll fight for it.

In the pleasure of open conflict he had forgotten the drums for a few minutes. He listened for them now while Dufour and the lawyer put their heads together, whispering.

The sound was still in the air.

Dufour stood up. "Since you insist on it, I will go for Antoine. M'sieu LeGrand will wait here."

"If I may," LeGrand said coldly.

"Suit yourself. Ordinarily this is a clinic, but today I have no patients." Barry watched Dufour hand the battered briefcase to the lawyer and stride from the office. After a moment, he said, "Would you like a drink, m'sieu?"

The fellow seemed startled. "A drink? But yes, please!"

Barry poured him one. Wondering where St. Juste had got to, he put his head out the door to look. The Couronne man was sitting in the kitchen doorway, playing with Lucy's little dog.

Barry leaned against the desk. "Have you known Felix Dufour very long, M'sieu LeGrand?"

The lawyer shrugged. "I met him this morning."

"Oh?"

"I am here at the request of the deputy in Anse Ange. Him I know well."

"I see. You can't possibly be aware, then, that Dufour is a thief and a liar."

LeGrand lifted his eyebrows. "Is he indeed?"

"Very much so. I hadn't been on this island a week before I learned he was overtaxing the market women and putting the profits into his pocket."

The lawyer shrugged. "A politician's trick."

"He also sold me a mule that he knew might kill someone—and it did."

"He only sold the mule, Mr. Clinton. You bought it."

"Do you honestly think he has got himself involved in this land business simply to help what he calls a constituent?"

"That is what he says."

"Don't you believe it. Dufour wouldn't bend a finger to help his own mother. What he's up to I don't know, but you can be sure he'll profit from it somehow. If he brings it off. Tell me something. Have you met Antoine Constant?"

LeGrand nodded. "This morning."

"Is he actually the complainant in this affair, or is Dufour simply using him?"

"He assured me, Mr. Clinton, that he never signed the land transfer.

That if his signature appears on that transfer it was forged. That he was cheated."

Barry gave up trying to decide whether the man was honest or not. "Well," he said, "we'll see."

They had a queer notion of honesty, these people, he told himself sadly. It was one of the things he would have to work on if he were ever to teach them a better way of life. You weren't dishonest if you cheated a man; you were simply more clever than your unhappy victim. The victim might be your own brother. If he were, he very likely would boast of your cleverness to his friends, thinking it wonderful that he had a relative so smart. It was a philosophy that tainted the entire social structure, from the wealthiest élite in the capital to the poorest barefoot peasant. Be smart. Be shrewd. Take advantage of every opportunity, no matter who suffered. You wouldn't be criticised for it. You'd be admired.

What a way to live. And, of course, he was powerless to change it. But he *had* hoped to be able to show a few of the people on Ile du Vent how foolish it was, and how costly in the long run for all of them. He had hoped to show them how it undermined all their relationships and made each man an island. He had hoped to do that.

IN HALF AN HOUR Dufour returned with Antoine. The latter had evidently not anticipated having to make a business call. He was unwashed and only half dressed. His feet, Barry noticed with a grimace, had not been washed in days.

Barry kept him standing before the desk and questioned him.

"Are you the former owner of the land the church now stands on?"

"*Oui, mon Père*. I still own it."

"Where did you get it?"

"In payment of a debt, *mon Père*."

"When?"

"When I was magistrate here."

"Meaning you caught some poor family in a squeeze and forced them to give it up to you?"

"No, *mon Père*."

"All right, you stole it legally then. But now you say it was stolen from you by *Père* Mitchell."

"*Oui, mon Père*."

"If that's the case, why have you waited so long to make your claim?"

Antoine shrugged. "I didn't need the land before."

"But now you do? Why?"

"I am poor."

"When you decided to get the land back, why didn't you come to me? Why did you go to Dufour?"

"He is the magistrate."

"You did go to him? He didn't come to you?"

"I went to him."

"Who told you to?"

"No one, *mon Père.*"

"It wasn't *M'sieu* Lemke?"

"*M'sieu* Lemke?" Antoine seemed genuinely bewildered.

"Or Pradon Beliard?"

The bewilderment fled. The man gave a start and sent a frightened glance at Dufour.

Touché, Barry thought, and had trouble hiding his triumph. It was Beliard. But Lemke may have directed the operation.

He leaned forward, holding the fellow motionless with his gaze. "If you do get your land back, Constant, how much will you have to pay Beliard?"

Felix Dufour thrust himself forward. "*Mon Père*, this is outrageous! This man knows Beliard, yes, but Beliard has nothing to do with the case!"

"Answer my question, Constant. How much?"

"Nothing."

"Nothing?"

Antoine shook his head.

But you're sweating now, Barry thought. Your mouth is twitching. You're scared.

"You say you never signed the land-transfer papers, Constant. If you didn't, who did?"

"I don't know."

"Are you accusing *Père* Mitchell of forging your name? You are, of course, even if you're not aware of it. Do you know what it means to make such a charge?"

Antoine looked at the magistrate again.

"He knows," Dufour said impatiently. "I have explained everything to him."

"Have you, though?" Barry frowned at the man before him. "Let me tell you what it means, Constant, because I think you were talked into this for someone else's benefit, and you're going to be a much sadder and wiser man if you go through with it. If you accuse *Père*

Mitchell of having forged your name to a legal document, you're going to have to prove it in court, in the capital. You won't have Felix Dufour to speak for you there. You'll have to sit on a witness stand and answer questions on your own. Not the simple questions I'm asking you, either, but hard ones shouted by a shrewd lawyer determined to find out if you're lying. And if you're lying he *will* find out, don't ever doubt it. I'm not a lawyer, Constant. I only think you're lying. But the lawyer hired by the church to defend *Père* Mitchell will be the smartest, cleverest man to be found in all St. Joseph. When he gets through with you there won't be a lie left in you. Do you understand?"

Antoine Constant blinked at him, then turned to frown at the magistrate and LeGrand. He was confused. This was something to think about, *oui*. Had he made a mistake, maybe, in listening to the quick tongue of that dandy, Beliard?

He could taste fear in his mouth. They hadn't warned him it would be like this. There would be nothing to it, they had said. Nothing at all. As easy as catching a *pintard* after the *piti-mi* bait was soaked in *clairin*. The Father would be shaking in his shoes at the very thought of losing his precious church.

Only the Father wasn't shaking. This was something he hadn't foreseen. The Father was threatening *him* when it ought to be the other way round. There was going to be trouble here, *oui*. This man behind the desk was a bad one to tangle with. He had been a fool, maybe, to let Beliard and Dufour talk him into this.

He licked his lips and waited for Barry to speak.

"Well," Barry said, "haven't you anything to say?"

Felix Dufour pushed forward. "What is there to say, *mon Père?* This man, even though he was once the magistrate here, is only a poor peasant. He has been wronged. We ask only that the wrong be righted."

"Dufour, if you interrupt once more I'll throw you out of here."

"But——"

"Be quiet! Now then, Constant, have *you* anything to say? After all, it's *your* future these two are gambling with, not their own. Speak up."

Antoine Constant gnawed at his lower lip. What he would give to be out of this! What an idiot he had been. Felix was right: he was only a peasant, and a stupid one at that. The affairs of clever men were not those of fools. The goats and the sheep spoke different tongues. But it was too late, too late. If he backed down now, after letting the charge be made and causing *M'sieu* LeGrand to come all the way from the capital, the rage of Dufour and Beliard would be unbearable. LeGrand would probably send him to prison.

He sadly shook his head. "I have nothing to say, *mon Père*."

Barry leaned toward him. "Are you *sure?* This is your last chance. Unless you drop this now, you'll have to go through with it to the bitter end."

"I—I have nothing to say."

With a sigh Barry turned to the lawyer. "All right, let's see your evidence."

"Do you have the transfer papers, Mr. Clinton?"

"I have them." Barry unlocked a drawer of the desk and took out a small metal box, one left behind by Leander Mitchell. With a smaller key he unlocked the box.

LeGrand opened the battered briefcase and laid a half-dozen mildewed notebooks on the desk. "These are the records kept by Constant when he was magistrate. With your permission we will compare the signatures."

Barry was not surprised by what he saw. Dufour, after all, had prepared him for the revelation. He looked long and hard at the signature on the transfer papers, then at those in the notebooks. Then he raised his head and frowned at Antoine Constant.

"Come here."

Antoine nervously approached the desk. Barry thrust a pen at him. "Write your name. On this piece of paper here."

With great care Antoine did so.

Barry examined the signature and felt his hands clench on the edge of the desk. It matched those in the notebooks. It was nothing like the one on the transfer papers.

He straightened and looked at his three callers.

"All right, gentlemen. On the evidence you appear to have a case. We'll see now if it will stand up in court. I bid you good day."

When they had gone he sank back onto his chair. He had lost his church and knew it.

The drums were still throbbing.

25

S T. JUSTE WAS CURIOUS AT LUNCH. "What's Dufour up to now,
Mr. Clinton?" he asked. "He looked pretty pleased with himself when he walked out of here."

"There's something I haven't told you, Clement."

"Oh?"

"I thought it was too fantastic to be worth telling. But apparently
it isn't. Those two with Felix were a lawyer from the capital and an
islander named Antoine Constant who claims to own the land the
church stands on."

St. Juste all but choked on a mouthful of chicken. "Mr. Clinton!
Are you serious?"

"I wish I weren't."

"He claims to own the land?"

"It's quite a story." Barry was not reluctant to tell it. The telling
served to clarify the details in his own mind. As he went over it he
was aware that Lucy had stopped moving about the dining room and
was standing quite still with her hands on the back of a chair, gazing
at him with an expression of incredulity. He was, of course, speaking
Creole. It was easier for St. Juste than English.

"So there you have it," he concluded with a shake of his head.
"Somewhere in the act there's a trick, of course. Mr. Mitchell never
forged that man's name. But what the trick is I can't imagine. I do
know why they're doing this. When I tossed the name Pradon
Beliard at Constant he jumped as though I'd jabbed him with a
needle. It's fairly obvious, I think, that Pradon has been my old man
of the sea right along."

"Do you have proof?"

"Depends on what you consider proof. He's working for Lemke,
of that I'm positive. Mrs. Lemke says he sees her husband every day,
and why should he do that unless he's handing in a progress report,
so to speak? It's Lemke who's after me, of course. I know why but
can't tell you. Pradon is simply his hatchet man."

"You think it was Pradon who started that story about Toto's being dead?"

"I think so, yes. I think he also put Dufour up to selling me the mule. Not that Dufour wouldn't have sold me the animal anyway, if he'd thought of it."

"It was Pradon who burned the church?"

Barry reached into his pocket and took out the empty cigarette package he had been carrying around for days. "I told you about the passageway between the grotto and Catus' *hounfor*. The day I walked through it with Micheline I found this."

"American cigarettes!" St. Juste exclaimed.

"Whoever burned the church that night probably used that passageway. I can't think of a soul on the island other than Pradon who might smoke American cigarettes. They're not sold here or in Anse Ange. They *are* sold at the company store in Fond Marie."

St. Juste moved his head slowly up and down. "And he's just the sort to have brought some along when he came here, to show the peasants what a big shot he is." He frowned, handing the package back. "Do you suppose he put Micheline up to accusing you of——"

"No. She herself wanted to hurt me."

"Is he the one who spread the story that Catus let that little girl die? That you'd said so?"

It was Barry's turn to shake his head in bewilderment. "That puzzles me; it really does. Catus did let the child die. She only had malaria; she could have been saved. I told him about it—not accusing him, mind you, but explaining, instructing if you like, in the hope he would co-operate a little better in the future." Barry glanced at Lucy, saw that she was still drinking in every word, and decided it no longer mattered. She was Pradon Beliard's aunt, true, but she had no particular feeling for Pradon. She certainly wouldn't run to him with any tales. "We talked in Catus' house, just the two of us," he went on. "The door was shut. Unless someone was listening outside, I don't see how we could have been overheard. The only other person who knew the truth about the child's death was Mrs. Lemke. I'm positive she didn't discuss it with anyone."

"Someone must have heard you."

"Someone must have."

"Micheline lives in the house next door."

"Yes."

"And, as you say, she wanted to hurt you at that time. If she wanted badly enough to hurt you, she wouldn't care what she did to her brother."

"I prefer to think Pradon is the one responsible, though how he could have known about it I don't know. Getting a rumor started must require a certain sinister skill. He's proved himself an expert."

"And you're convinced that he's behind this fantastic attempt to get the church away from you, Mr. Clinton?"

"You would be too if you'd seen Constant's face when I mentioned his name. Yes, I'm certain. The scheme may have originated with Lemke—it very probably did—but the one who talked Constant into it was Pradon."

"You need a lawyer yourself, Mr. Clinton," St. Juste grumbled. "That Beliard ought to be behind bars."

Barry's smile was a tired one. "What I've told you isn't evidence. It's only what I think."

"What you know."

"But I can't prove it."

Lucy brought sliced cachimans for dessert. Barry noticed that neither he nor St. Juste had a complete fruit and recalled that on entering the dining room he had seen the little dog industriously chewing on some black seeds. He smiled, glad to know that she intended feeding the animal. Most of the peasants left their poor half-starved pets to shift for themselves, considering it practically a major crime to give them food a human might eat.

She said, leaning over him, "*Mon Père.*"

"Yes, Lucy?"

"If this Antoine Constant takes the church away from you, what will he do with it?"

He was startled by the quaver in her voice and turned his head to look up at her. Her whole face was trembling. A film of moisture veiled her eyes.

"Why, I don't know, Lucy. Turn it into a house, I suppose, and live there."

"Can he do that?"

"If he owns it he can."

"But he doesn't own it! A church belongs to God!"

"Yes, a church belongs to God. But if Constant can prove he has a prior claim, he can do what he likes with it."

THE HOURS OF WAITING CREPT BY. In the afternoon Barry was surprised to see his housekeeper, attired in her best white dress, go across the red-earth clearing to the old church and disappear inside. Puzzled, he went as far as the door to see what she was up to. She was kneeling at the rail, gazing at the cross on the plain wooden table that now served as an altar.

Strange. She was a faithful church-goer on Sundays, of course, but he had never thought of her as being especially religious. She had never discussed matters of faith with him. Had the conversation at lunch disturbed her?

He did not intrude. If she wished to pray to the God old Mitchell had taught her to believe in, that was her affair. It was good to know there was one person on the island who did believe, and cared enough to pray. He returned quietly to the rectory. It was almost an hour later when Lucy came out of the church and went back to her kitchen.

All morning the drums had throbbed. The sound continued through the heat of the afternoon and into the evening. After the evening meal St. Juste walked up to the village.

"Waiting," he said on his return. "That's all they're doing: waiting. I'd say there were fifty or so at the *tonnelle*, Mr. Clinton, most of them just standing around watching the drummers and dancers. The rest are in their own yards, waiting."

The drums were beginning to make Barry jumpy. "How long can this sort of thing go on?" he asked.

"Well, there are *vodun* affairs that last a week, I'm told."

A week? If it went on for a week, Barry told himself, he would be starting at every snap of a twig or rustle of a leaf. Not going out of his mind—he still put no stock in such nonsense—but caught like a fish in the net of his own nerves. The drums did something to you. The waiting was worse. Should he go up to the village and try to bring matters to a head? Would it force a showdown if he did? He asked St. Juste's opinion.

The Couronne man said soberly, "Don't go, Mr. Clinton. That would be a very foolish thing to do."

"What do you think might happen?"

"There's just no telling. These drums aren't bothering you much. I've been watching you and I can see it. But Negroes react differently. I'm one and I know. You've seen what happens at a service. I suspect the drums have a good deal more to do with it than all that reciting of prayers and what not. There's something in the sound of the drums that works on a Negro's blood and nervous system, like a drug, and makes him do things a white man would never do. I don't think a white man could ever be possessed, for instance, though I've heard of some who thought they were."

"You don't think I could be possessed?"

"You? No, Mr. Clinton." St. Juste smiled.

"Why?"

"You're too questioning. Even if you wanted to be, and tried to be, you'd be searching your own feelings too much. To be possessed a man has to let himself go. I'm not saying I think all possessions are a fake, mind you. Only that a man can't get into the proper mood while full of doubts and trying to analyze himself."

They were talking under the campêche tree. The sound of the drums rolled over them in the darkness.

"Have you ever been possessed, Clement?" Barry asked.

"No, Mr. Clinton."

"You have been to *vodun* ceremonies, of course."

"Oh yes, I've been to ceremonies. I used to go often. It's a queer business. A lot of it's pure superstitious nonsense, any sensible man knows that, but at the same time some of it's pretty mysterious. At least it is to me."

"I'm sure it would be to anyone. There are mysteries in Christianity too."

"*Vodun's* different, though. In Christianity your mysteries all happened long ago. You only have a record of them. In *vodun* they're likely to happen in front of your eyes."

An interesting point, Barry thought, though perhaps open to debate. What about the innumerable miracles reported by Christians since Bible days? The Catholic shrines where the mysterious was thought to occur every day? The thousands of people who testified to having received miraculous answers to their prayers?

He would have liked to probe the subject more deeply but a glance at St. Juste silenced him. The man was not as calm as a stranger might have thought him. His face twitched. He was nervously scratching a wrist. A battle was going on inside him.

These drums aren't bothering you much, Mr. Clinton, but Negroes react differently.

"Let's go inside," Barry said quietly.

St. Juste swung on him. "Mr. Clinton, why don't you get out of here? It's foolish for you to stay. We can get someone to take us across to Anse Ange!"

"Now? In the dark?"

"Yes, now!"

Barry put a hand on the man's arm. "I've thought about it, Clement. Don't think I haven't. You go if you want to; there's no reason in the world for you to stay. But, you see, I'd only have to come back. And what would I say to the Bishop if I came back and found the mission destroyed?"

St. Juste stood staring toward the village. "Damn them!" he whispered. "Damn their stupid souls to hell!"

It was one of the very few times Barry had heard him swear.

ALL NIGHT THE DRUMS THROBBED. Barry kept the lamp burning on the table beside his bed. Shortly before three, the office door opened and St. Juste's voice reached him through the curtain.

"You awake, Mr. Clinton?"

"I haven't been to sleep, Clement."

"I haven't either. Do you mind if I stretch out on the cot here? I kind of think it might be smart for us to be together."

"Why?"

"Maybe you haven't noticed, but the beat of those drums has changed."

Barry sat up in bed, listening. He could detect no difference in the sound. "Does that mean something, Clement?"

"It could," St. Juste replied from the other room.

At four-thirty Barry could see no point in lying there wide awake any longer. He rose and dressed, drew aside the curtain and stepped into the office. The door was open. St. Juste was not there.

Barry went outside. There was a sudden movement at the corner of the building. St. Juste's low voice came to him through the darkness.

"Is that you, Mr. Clinton?"

"Yes. What's up?"

"Listen."

He listened. The drums were still. After nearly thirty hours of incessant throbbing they were silent. The night seemed to be holding its breath. Barry advanced and found St. Juste peering toward the village.

"They stopped ten minutes ago, Mr. Clinton."

"And now what are we to expect?"

"I don't know. I wish to God I did." The man's voice was unsteady.

Barry put a hand on his shoulder. "Aren't we being a little dramatic? he said. "This isn't the heart of Africa, you know. Or New Guinea. It isn't one of those movies in which the beleaguered explorers crouch in the jungle, surrounded by howling savages. Let's go and make some coffee, Clement."

St. Juste voiced a nervous laugh. They went to the kitchen. When they opened the door the little black and white dog, shut up inside, ducked under the table and began to bark. It was a startling sound in the long-awaited stillness. Barry felt St. Juste stiffen and heard him suck in a breath.

The sound aroused Lucy and she came from her room, tugging at her dress, just as Barry finished lighting the second of two lamps. She, too, was jumpy, he saw. He said quickly, "It's all right, Lucy. We were awake and thought we'd have some coffee."

She stared at the door. "The drums," she whispered.

"Yes. They've stopped."

She turned to look at him. He saw her make an effort to pull herself together. "Shall I—shall I make some breakfast, *mon Père?*" she asked.

"I suppose you might as well."

She took half a dozen eggs from the kerosene refrigerator and broke them one by one into a cup, carefully examining each before transferring it to her mixing bowl. You never knew when a native egg might be bad. Before putting the mixture into the frying pan, she spooned some into a dish and gave it to the dog, smiling at Barry as she did so. St. Juste sat motionless at the table, watching her. When Barry addressed a remark to him a moment later, he had to come out of an apparent trance to answer it. He had been watching the dog.

"Uh—what did you say, Mr. Clinton?"

"I said it seems peaceful after all the racket."

"Yes. Yes, it does."

Lucy finished scrambling the eggs and served them. Before picking up his fork, St. Juste glanced at the dog again.

BARRY WAS IN THE CHURCH when Edith rode into the clearing at nine o'clock. He heard the hoofbeats of her horse and guessed who it was. By the time he reached the church door she had dismounted in front of the rectory and was talking to St. Juste.

She spoke to St. Juste for several minutes, the Couronne man maintaining silence until she had finished. He began to protest then —at least he seemed to be protesting—but she cut him short. He gave her an unhappy look and shrugged his shoulders. Edith turned from him and went into the office.

When Barry entered the office, she was standing with her back to the desk, clutching the edge of it with both hands. Her only greeting was a nod, but she followed him with her eyes. When she spoke it was as though she were reciting a speech carefully rehearsed, so long rehearsed, in fact, that the words could now be delivered without emotion. Barry thought she looked tired. There were shadows under her eyes.

"I've come to say good-by," she said. "I don't feel I ought to stay here after what's happened."

He nodded. "It isn't very pleasant."

"I talked to daddy yesterday on the radio. Warner will take me over to the mainland in the launch and he'll meet me there."

"Did you tell your father why you're leaving?"

"Yes. He wanted to know my reason."

"I see." He wondered what Jeff would think, being told that the Reverend Barry Clinton was accused of fathering a native girl's child. Not that it mattered about Jeff's knowing. He had nothing to hide and would make no effort to hide it. In fact he had already told Peter Ambrose the entire story in his letter.

Edith seemed uncomfortable in his presence. She was fidgeting now. She had taken the pen off his desk and was turning it round and round in her fingers. "If there were any way I could help you by staying," she said, "but there isn't. And the situation at the Lemkes' is simply intolerable. He's drunk all the time now. I'm sure daddy will fire him when he finds out."

He smiled. "I don't think being fired will bother Warner Lemke much."

"He's horrible."

He saw that she wanted very much to go. He held out his hand. "Thank you for coming over to say good-by."

"When shall I—shall I see you again, Barry?"

"I'll be stopping at Fond Marie to say good-by to Peter on my way to the capital. Perhaps then."

"On your way to the capital?"

"I'm certain to be transferred out of St. Joseph." If, he added mentally, there's anything left of me to transfer. "Good-by, Edith." He let her hand go and stepped back. She walked out of the office ahead of him.

When she had mounted, she rode part way across the clearing and looked back as though waiting for something. At the same time St. Juste came from the kitchen with a suitcase. The face of the Couronne man was full of misery. He halted before Barry and put the suitcase down.

"She says I'm to go back with her, Mr. Clinton. I'll have to unless you order me not to."

Barry turned his head slowly to look at the girl on the horse. She quickly looked away, but not before he saw her expression. He felt his hands clench at his sides. What was there in the human heart, he asked himself, that made it hunger to hurt others when it was hurt itself? First Micheline, now Edith.

"You can't very well refuse, Clement."

"She said I was sent here to help with the building, and since there's no work being done I'm not needed. I won't go if you tell me not to. I don't want to leave you at a time like this. But she's Mr. Barnett's daughter and I work for him. I might lose my job."

"You've got to go," Barry said. He gripped the man's hand. "Good-by, Clement."

"Good-by, Mr. Clinton. You take care of yourself."

St. Juste picked up his suitcase. Edith turned her horse toward the path. Barry stood before the rectory and watched them go, the white woman riding, the Negro trudging along after her with his gaze on the ground. Would he see either of them again?

He became aware presently that he was standing in the sun without a covering on his head, and the heat was making him dizzy. He went into the office and sat down.

THERE WAS NOTHING TO DO; that was the worst of it. Being alone was bad enough, but being alone with nothing to do was a kind of living death. He tried to invent things to do. He rearranged his possessions in the stuffy little bedroom that had been Leander Mitchell's. He straightened the bottles and boxes of medicines on the office shelves and emptied the drawers of the desk and sorted out papers. What were the sick people of Ile du Vent doing for treatment? Were they doctoring themselves with roots and leaves as they must have done before his coming? Or were they simply lying in their airless, gloomy little houses and hopelessly suffering? Some of them must be pitifully anxious for this ghastly business to end, so they could seek his help.

If only one person among them would have the courage to appear in the doorway and say "*Mon Père*, I need help." One, just one, to make a crack in the dam and let the stream begin to trickle again.

He sat at his desk and went through his file of record cards, gazing at some of them a long time. Fifine César, his first patient: those enormous, adoring eyes. Tina Nerette: was Lemke sleeping with her again? Was his being "drunk all the time now" only a pathetic attempt to hide from himself the extent of his degradation? And here was Toto Anestor, the lad who had been killed picking up a handkerchief . . .

He clenched his hands on the desk and laid his head on them. If only he had been allowed to come here as Leander Mitchell had come, with a fair chance to make good on his own merits. There were so many things he had wanted to do. The clinic. The gardens. The school. A campaign of education against the hookworm so many of them suffered from. The introduction of cash crops. The sermons he had planned to drain away the useless parts of their *vodun* and substitute an understanding of Love . . ."

Even such little things as a tooth to fill that ugly gap in Catus' mouth. Only a couple of weeks ago he had written to a dentist in the capital, enclosing a sketch and asking that a tooth of the right size and shape be sent by mail. It would have been so easy to fashion a simple bridge . . .

Why? he asked himself. Why? Why? Mitchell had his chance. Other men are given a fair opportunity. Why, when I came here, was there a Lemke at my heels determined to destroy me?

Lifting his head, he saw by the clock that it was time for lunch, a lunch he would have to eat alone. He pushed himself to his feet and went along to the kitchen.

In the doorway he halted. The little black and white dog lay gasping on the floor beside a dish of food. Lucy, on her knees, was staring fixedly into its face. He stepped forward, frowning.

"What's the matter, Lucy?"

She looked up with a start, her own face shapeless with terror. He had never seen such terror before. She tried to speak to him but no sound came. Her lips moved, her whole face moved, but there were no words.

He knelt to look at the dog. Its eyes were strange and there was foam on its teeth. He said angrily, "What have you done to it?" Then suddenly he knew. "This dog's been poisoned! You've been testing the food on it!"

Lucy sank onto a chair, shaking.

He snatched the animal up and carried it to the office. It was warm and twitching in his arms, but when he placed it on the table and bent to examine it, it gave a last convulsive jerk and was still. He stood for a moment gazing down at it. Then he carried it slowly back to the kitchen.

"I'm sorry, Lucy. We'd better bury it." He placed the dog on the floor and took up the dish. "Is this what it ate?"

She nodded.

"What is it?"

"Some meat from a chicken I bought this morning."

"A chicken? But you always buy live ones."

"This one was alive too, *mon Père*."

He frowned. "I don't understand this. Where is the rest of the bird?"

She brought to the table a platter of Creole-fried chunks of chicken, obviously intended for his lunch. He lifted each piece and smelled it, shook his head, then with a knife and fork began carefully to break the meat apart. Lucy watched him. Suddenly she cried out and pointed to a piece of breast in which his probing had exposed a slender black thorn. She removed the thorn and held it between her fingernails, as though afraid it might turn and stab her.

Barry bent forward to examine it. "This was put into the chicken when it was alive?" he asked.

She nodded.

"And made the flesh poisonous without killing the bird?"

"*Oui, mon Père.*"

"How can they do that?"

"I am not sure. I only know some people are able to. Perhaps the cooking makes the poison active."

"What sort of thorn is it?"

"*Mon Père*, I don't know. Perhaps it is not the thorn, but something they put on it."

"Well, take it out and bury it," he ordered. "Bury the chicken too. Then scrub the platter and your cooking things with plenty of soap and hot water. Never mind about lunch."

When she had gone, he looked down at the black and white dog again. So this was the meaning of St. Juste's prediction that something would happen when the drums fell silent.

How long could he last if they were determined to poison him? Not even a devoted Lucy with all her vigilance could protect him for more than a few days.

26

Some time during the afternoon Lucy disappeared. Barry did not see her go, did not know she had gone until he went to the kitchen at four o'clock to tell her he would have something out of a can for supper. Then he was unable to find her.

He wondered whether she too had left him, frightened away by the poison. If she had, there was nothing he could do about it. He returned to the office and sat at his desk. He was trying to put down on paper, for the benefit of his successor, a brief but exact account of all that had happened since his coming to the island.

At five he heard a sound outside and glanced out the open door to see Lucy coming across the clearing. Something in the way she walked made him go to the door to watch her. He saw that she was exhausted. Her dress was torn and stained with red clay. Her hair looked as though she had been dragged by it. He hurried toward her.

"What is it, Lucy? What's wrong?"

She shrugged. "Nothing is wrong, *mon Père*. I had to walk a long way, that's all."

She carried a small basket. A folded banana leaf hid its contents. "What have you been doing?" Barry asked.

She hesitated. "Finding some greens that will be safe for you to eat."

He looked at her in astonishment. He would never understand her. He could think of nothing to say but a simple "Thank you, Lucy", but stood watching her, shaking his head, as she continued on to the kitchen.

Later he went to the kitchen and found a pot bubbling on the charcoal fire, and when Lucy invited him to lift the lid he recognized the greens as terminal shoots of the mirliton vine and realized how far she must have walked. Mirliton was scarce on Ile du Vent. It was one of the few things that had not grown well in his own garden on the ridge.

On the worktable beside the charcoal stove stood two soft-drink bottles, one empty, the other full, and a small pan that contained an inch of liquid in which a handful of leaves floated. He looked at Lucy quizzically. "What's this?"

"A medicine I made, *mon Père*, in case we are taken sick."

"Oh?" He was both amused and curious. "What's in it?"

"Just some leaves I gathered. Good ones for the stomach."

"But why the kola?"

"So it will not taste so bad."

She knew what she was doing, apparently. He watched her pour two inches of the leaf-decoction into the empty kola bottle, holding back the leaves with her thumb. Then she filled the bottle with the sickly soda-pop the islanders were so fond of, and carefully pressed the cap on. When he would have dipped a finger into the pan to taste her "medicine", she thrust his hand aside and shook her head.

"Don't, *mon Père*. It is too strong that way. It will burn your mouth." And before he could protest, she snatched the pan and hurried outside with it.

For supper he had the mirliton greens and salmon from a tin, being careful to save some of each for her. When he volunteered to help with the dishes, for something to do, she pushed him gently toward the door.

He returned to the office. Half an hour later he was startled to see Alma Lemke ride into the clearing.

She had come with a suitcase. When he took it from her and helped her out of the saddle she said calmly, "I've left the plantation for good, Barry. I'll stay here tonight if I may and take a sailboat over to Anse Ange in the morning."

He was not really surprised. "You and Warner are finished?"

"Yes."

He looked after her horse, tethering the animal beside his own at the clearing's edge, then led her into the office. It was not quite dark. He gave her a drink. "Have you had anything to eat?" he asked.

"I'm not hungry."

"If you want to tell me what happened——"

"I think he's out of his mind," she said. "It's more than rum this time, I'm certain." She let her breath out in a long pulsing sigh, as though in his presence a block of ice inside her were just beginning to melt. "The other night he was on the veranda, drinking. I accused him of being the father of the child Micheline is expecting. He laughed at me and I left him. Then I heard him shouting. Not at me, not at anyone . . . Just shouting. He's been acting strangely ever since."

She was at the end of her rope, he saw. There was little left of the good looks she had been so proud of only a few weeks before. Her eyes were dull from want of sleep. Her face was gray. She wore one of the plain white dresses she had used as a uniform when helping him with patients. What a difference, he thought, from the woman at the farewell party who had employed every feminine trick to make herself worth noticing.

He said with a wry smile, "We seem to have reached the end of the road together."

"Yes. Don't we?"

"Did Edith and St. Juste get off as planned?"

She nodded. "That was when I packed up and left—while Warner was taking them over in the launch. I didn't want trouble."

"He'll know where you've gone, of course."

"I suppose so. He thinks I'm in love with you."

"In love with *me*?"

She emptied her glass and looked at him. "Does that surprise you?"

"Well, I——"

"It doesn't matter. He isn't likely to come here after me. He might run into Micheline."

"She's left the island."

"Oh? Where has she gone?"

Barry told her what had happened. It was a relief to be able to tell someone. He talked of the drums, of St. Juste's prediction that something would happen when they stopped, of their stopping, of the poisoned chicken. He paced the floor while telling her. His voice grew louder in the room and he felt himself sweating. When he suddenly stopped pacing, the room was nearly dark. He pressed his hands to his temples.

"I can't think any more," he said. "I'm stupid. I feel as though I *had* been poisoned." He sank onto a chair and put his head in his hands. "I know now how old Mitchell must have felt, exactly how he felt. There just isn't anything to do except wait, and the waiting is murder."

Alma rose and stepped behind his chair. He felt her hands on his shoulders, strong, comforting. The peasants loved her hands. There was magic in them, they said. She could drive away pain with them.

"It's a mess, isn't it?" she said quietly.

He looked up at her. There was just enough light in the room to let him know she was smiling.

"I'm worse off than you are, if that's any consolation," she said.

"I suppose you are."

"For you there'll be a chance to start over somewhere else, if you can make the Bishop see the truth of what's happened here. You may be able to do that. But I'm really finished. I've made a complete mess of things."

"You can divorce Warner."

"Then what?"

"Go back to the States . . . I don't know."

"I don't want to go back to the States."

"What do you want?"

She pressed his shoulders again and then took her hands away. "Forget it," she said. "You have troubles enough without trying to solve mine for me as well. I think I will have something to eat, if Lucy won't mind."

He walked with her to the kitchen. Except for the chirping of the cicadas the clearing was quiet. A few fireflies drifted about. The kitchen was in darkness.

"She must have gone out," Barry said, lighting a lamp. "Here, I want to show you something." He was consciously searching for things to talk about. It seemed important to keep on talking. But when he looked for the bottle of medicine Lucy had made, thinking to amuse her with the story of its preparation, it was not on the worktable. He looked in some of the cupboards. It was not there either.

He told the story anyway, while she ate some crackers and cheese. It amused her less than he had hoped.

"You ought to leave here," she said. "If they want to poison you, they will."

Ever since discovering the thorn in the chicken he had been toying with a half-formed idea. He leaned across the table toward her and said now, soberly, "Suppose I let them think I *have* been poisoned."

Alma looked at him curiously, without comment.

"I could, you know," he went on. "Beliard isn't the only one who can spread false tales. Lucy would help me. Suppose I let it be known that I *ate* that poisoned chicken. That I'm ill. That I've died."

"I don't see what good——"

"There'll be some sort of ceremony to celebrate the event, won't there? I'm sure there will. Catus and the whole gang of them will be there. What if I were to walk in on such an affair, big as life when they think me dead? What do you suppose might happen?"

She thought for a moment, then shook her head. "I don't know. But I don't like it."

"It might be an interesting experiment."

"It might be dangerous."

"I'm in danger just sitting here. I'll be in danger when I eat breakfast tomorrow, and every meal thereafter. In the end, as you've just predicted, they're certain to poison me." He stood up, looking about him. "Where the devil can Lucy have got to? She never goes out at night."

"Can she be asleep somewhere?"

"I'll have a look around."

He took a flashlight and looked in the old storeroom which had been made into a bedroom for St. Juste—the room he would have to occupy tonight, he supposed, with Alma using his. He looked in Lucy's room, then went outside and walked completely around the rectory, calling her name. On an impulse he entered the old church, remembering how often she had gone there lately to pray. But the search was unsuccessful.

Alma had looked too. They met at the office doorway, shaking their heads. "Wherever she is, she won't be away long," Barry predicted. "Suppose we get you placed for the night. Then we can sit and wait for her."

"So you can ask her to spread the rumor you were talking about?"

"So I can ask her what she thinks of the idea, at any rate." He tried to smile, but Lucy's absence had made him anxious. "Where will you sleep? My room would be best, I should think."

"I don't want to put you out," she protested. "I can sleep on the office cot."

"You take my room. I'll use St. Juste's."

"If you don't mind, I'd rather we weren't so far away from each other. This business is giving me the creeps."

"I'll use the office cot then." This time he did manage a smile. "Since the Bishop isn't here to be shocked."

When he had carried her suitcase into his room and found clean sheets for the bed, they sat outside the rectory in the darkness, waiting for Lucy. There was much to talk about and no sound of drums to make the conversation difficult. Barry drew from her a complete account of her husband's recent behavior. At times they did not talk at all, but listened to the small night-sounds in the clearing and watched the fireflies.

Suddenly he was aware that the drums were throbbing again.

He rose abruptly and took a few steps forward, stopped and stood listening with his hands clenched at his sides. The sound came from a different direction this time. From the ridge. He listened a long while to be sure, and knew he could not be mistaken. He began to shake. By God, if they were holding a *vodun* service in the new church . . .

Alma came to his side. "What is it?" she asked. Her voice was low, vibrant with apprehension.

"More of the same. I've had thirty hours of it. I don't believe I can stand much more."

Were they holding a service in the church? He couldn't believe it. They wouldn't dare—not, at least, until they'd got the church away from him. Yet the sound was from that direction, definitely. He felt Alma's fingers on his arm and turned to face her. He was violently trembling.

"Come and sit down," she said.

He let her lead him back to his chair and dropped onto it. The sound of the drums filled the clearing. He had been right in saying he could not stand much more of it. There wasn't so much difference between black men and white after all. He remembered the signs of impending explosion on the face of St. Juste and knew the same signs were on his own. He must stop shaking. He must get hold of himself.

Alma had stepped behind him. He felt her hands on his shoulders again. The tide of tension slowly ebbed.

When he was able to breathe normally again, he looked up at her. She was leaning over him and the movement brought her face close to his. "Thanks," he said. "I don't know what I'll do when you're not here."

Her hands went on putting strength into him, the hands the peasants said were magic. "I don't know what I'll do either," she said.

"I've leaned on you ever since the day you brought in that fellow with the bad leg."

"We *have* worked well together, haven't we?"

"I've been able to talk to you, tell you things. You always seemed to know what I was getting at."

"I learned to know. I didn't at first."

"How do you mean?"

She drew his head back against her body and her hands moved to his temples, defying the drums to touch him. "Before we began to work together I was a—bitch. There, you see? The word comes hard now. It makes me cringe. Before, I'd have used it without thinking.

I *was* a bitch. It isn't all Warner's fault, what's happened to him. I'm partly responsible."

"I don't believe it."

"I was bitter and cynical. I couldn't see good in anyone, not even in you. Worse, I was full of prejudices. Have you any idea how full of prejudices I was? It frightens me."

"I don't think I understand."

"Why was I so angry when I learned that Warner had been having an affair with the girl at Fond Marie? I knew the kind of man he was. I knew there'd been other women before. Yet I was furious for the first time. Can't you see why? This time the girl was black."

"Well?" he said, frowning.

"It shouldn't have mattered, if I'd been making any sense. The color of her skin shouldn't have been the important thing. But it was."

"And now?"

"Something has happened to me, from coming here to the mission and being with you, helping you. I'm beginning to see things straight. I want to be decent."

"You've always been decent."

"I wish that were true," she said. "My God, how I wish that were true."

"It *is* true, so far as I'm concerned. I've never known you when you weren't wonderful."

"You've known me. You just haven't known my thoughts."

"And do I know your thoughts now?"

"Perhaps. I'm not sure. I'm in love with you; you probably know that; you must be blind if you don't. I'd marry you if I could, and if you wanted me. But I'll never have an affair with you. Does that surprise you?"

"No," he said. "It doesn't."

"There was a time when I would have."

He reached up and held her hands. "There was a time when you might have. But I feel the way you do now. It would spoil what's between us. There *is* something between us, of course. I've known it for a long time."

She said quietly, "What is it? Is it love?"

"I think so, if I know what love is. Does that sound strange? Who does know what love is? I thought I was in love with Edith. There may even have been a crazy moment or two when I thought I could love Micheline. I was wrong there in both cases, so wrong in Edith's case that it shocked me. But if love is wanting to understand and be understood, wanting to share, wanting to be with someone, then I'm in love with you deeply. Much too deeply to risk losing you through an affair that would make us both feel guilty."

She nodded. "That's how I feel. I've never felt that way before."

"This way we can go on, in spite of Warner. Anything else would destroy the very thing we want. You'll get a divorce, of course. You can't possibly go back to him."

"Yes, I'll get a divorce."

"It won't mean we can marry. You understand that, don't you? Unless, of course, this tale about my being the father of Micheline's child is believed and I'm asked to leave the ministry. So long as I *am* in the church——"

"I know."

"It's pretty hopeless, isn't it?"

"Hopeless?" she said. "No. A thing doesn't have to be complete to be wonderful. Sometimes it's better when we don't want too much, isn't it? I can be happy for a long time with what we have." She bent over him and put her cheek against his. "I'm glad we got this out of our systems, Barry. I feel much better." Then she straightened. "Do you mind if I go in now? I'd like to lie down and think about it."

He stood up and watched her go. Stood gazing at the rectory doorway long after she had disappeared inside. He felt strangely calm in spite of the drums. Perhaps not all the tension in him had been caused by his troubles with Catus. Perhaps this other turmoil had been churning away at the same time, unrecognized but nonetheless violent. He felt almost relaxed, almost happy. He sat and let the feeling flow over him. The distant pounding of the drums no longer had any effect on him.

She was right: a thing did not have to be complete to be wonderful. At least not all at once. Perhaps one day this would be more than it was now. Who could say what might happen?

Something at the edge of the clearing caught his eye and he pushed himself erect. A shadowy figure glided through the dark toward him. He took in a breath, then saw that it was Lucy. She halted before him.

27

"MON PERE, I have just come from my sister's house," Lucy said gravely. "My nephew, Pradon Beliard, is sick. I said I would ask you to go to him."

"Pradon? Sick?" Barry could not believe it.

She shrugged. "I don't think you should go, *mon Père*. I don't think you should help that man after what he has done."

"What's the matter with him?"

"Who knows? He says he is dying."

"*Is* he sick, Lucy?"

Again she shrugged. "I suppose so. He lies on a couch, groaning. But that man has done you a great wrong, *mon Père*. Besides, he wants to steal God's church. If you help him without making him confess what he has done, you will be making a great mistake."

Barry scowled at her. "What are you trying to tell me, Lucy?"

"Me? Trying to tell *you*, *mon Père*?"

"I see." But he did not. "If Pradon is ill, why hasn't he sent for Catus?"

"He knows very well Catus can't save him. Only you with your medicines."

"Very well, I'll go to him." Barry strode into the rectory and rapped on the wall beside the drawn curtain. "I've got to go out on a call," he said when Alma answered. He told her what had happened. By the time he had finished packing his bag, Alma was in the office.

"I'm going with you," she announced.

"Good. I'd be uneasy leaving you here alone."

"I just hope that little monster is sick enough so I can gloat. Or is that being very unchristian?"

"It's being very honest. I share the feeling. Ready?"

She touched his hand. "When you are, darling."

He had his flashlight, but Lucy asked him not to use it. "It will be better if we are not seen," she said. "Just follow me, *mon Père*." She herself needed no light to find her way over the island paths. Her bare feet knew every stone and root.

They met no people. The route she chose by-passed the village and avoided most of the main paths. Except for the sound of the drums, now loud, now soft but never ceasing, Barry might have thought the island fast asleep. It was a long route, though. They were forty minutes reaching the outskirts of Petit Trou and another ten working their way around that community of dark and silent houses to the abode of Beliard and his mother.

Barry struggled in a whirlpool of emotion. There was something queer about all this, something strange in Lucy's attitude and behavior. Why had she gone to visit her sister tonight without telling him she was going? Why had she gone at all? In all the weeks she had worked for him she had never done so before. And that business of the kola bottle this afternoon—what about that?

Be alert, he told himself. There's something going on here. As Lucy pushed open a gate and hurried toward a doorway outlined in lamplight, he hung back and caught Alma's hand. "I don't like this," he whispered. "Be careful."

"I know." Alma nodded. "She's up to something."

The young man from Couronne lay in pajamas on a couch by the wall, staring wide-eyed at the door. His mother, a timid-seeming woman several years younger than Lucy, stood wringing her hands by a table in the center of the room. It was a more expensively furnished room than most of those Barry had entered as a doctor. Tables, chairs, and lamps had certainly come from mainland shops. There was even a curtain at the single window. But the man on the couch was no longer concerned with putting on a front for his peasant neighbors. He was pure peasant himself, moaning in terror and drenched with sweat. His eyes swelled like inflated balloons as he watched Barry step toward him.

Barry sat on the couch and laid a hand on the sick man's forehead. Alma moved the lamp table closer and stood beside him.

"Stop groaning, please, and open your mouth."

"*Mon Père*, I am dying! I know it!"

"Open your mouth. And don't expect sympathy. If you die, I'll be the last person to mourn you." So much, Barry thought, for the bedside manner. Let the worm squirm. Apparently there was nothing much wrong with him anyway. He had only a slight fever, and the solid pressure of a hand over his appendix produced no evidence of pain.

Pradon's gaze clung to his face as he made his examination. It sought to read his every expression, to discover what he was thinking. It was the gaze of a badly frightened man. Go ahead, Barry thought, be frightened. Be terrified. You've had this coming to you, my friend. You've earned every second of it. He dragged the examination out. Alma, Lucy, and the boy's timid mother watched in silence.

"Are you in pain?"

"*Oui, mon Père! Oui!*"

"Where are you in pain?"

"My stomach! My chest! They are on fire!"

"When did you eat last?"

"At s-supper. About seven o'clock."

"What did you eat?"

"A fish, *mon Père. A poisson nègre.*"

"Fresh?"

"I—I think so. My mother cooked it——"

Barry turned his head to frown at the woman. "Was the fish fresh?"

"*Oui!* I bought it myself on the beach only an hour before he ate it, *mon Père!*"

"Is that all you had for supper, Beliard?"

The sick man stared at Barry's face again. "That and some—some bread."

"You had nothing afterward?"

"Only some rum. Only a little."

"Nothing else?"

"My aunt brought some kola. I drank that."

Barry felt himself start and hoped his face had not given him away. Rising, he glanced at Lucy. She had seated herself. She sat stiffly erect with her hands gripping her knees and her gaze fixed on him. He made a business of lifting his bag to the lamp table and opening it, but looked quickly about the room. The kola bottle, empty, stood on a table by the wall. So far as he could tell from the gaudy label, it was the same bottle. He remembered the herb decoction she had refused to let him taste.

He had to think fast. She had poisoned the kola, of course, but how strong was the poison? Had she meant to kill her nephew or only make him sick enough to require a doctor? He tried to recall what she had said to him in the clearing about making Pradon confess his crimes before helping him. Her exact words eluded him. He was too excited.

He glanced at her again, hoping for a clue. She sat like an ebony image. He took a bottle of pills from his bag and, watching her, said casually, "I think a few of these will make you well again."

Lucy leaned toward him with a convulsive jerk, as though the words had been a hot wire touching a nerve. He saw her long black fingers dig fiercely into the flesh of her legs. With her eyes, her open mouth, with every fiber of her being she was pleading with him. He reached into the bag again and brought out a notebook and pencil.

"But," he said, turning now to look down at the man on the couch, "before I save your worthless life you're going to make it worth saving."

Beliard cringed from him. The room was still as a grave.

"Well?" Barry said.

"I—I don't know what you mean."

"I mean this." He paused to think of what he would say, knowing he must not let the opportunity slip away from him. He had more than himself to think of now. There was Lucy. Good, wonderful, faithful Lucy who had turned on her own flesh and blood for love of him—or for the church; it didn't matter which. And Alma, whose future was now one with his own. He must not let them down.

"Because of you, Beliard, the people of this island hate me. You persuaded Felix Dufour to sell me that mule. You said Toto Anestor was dead when he was not. You burned the church and killed the mule at the altar to make the people think their *vodun* gods were angry." He spoke slowly, letting the words fall on the upturned face like drops of water. He watched the face intently for any slightest indication that he was going too far. He must not go too far. Every accusation must be a true one, a hammer blow the sick man could not dodge. "You told the people I accused Catus of killing the Desinor girl. You put Antoine Constant up to his crooked claim on the church property. Be quiet, Beliard!" This when he saw Pradon's mouth come open and begin to twitch. "I know you did all these things. It won't do you any good to deny them. I *know*. So why should I save your miserable life?"

"But—but you are mistaken, *mon Père!*"

Barry shrugged, tossed the bottle of pills back into his bag and turned away. "All right, if that's the way you want it. I won't waste my time with you."

"*Mon Père*, wait! Please!"

Bag in hand, Barry strode to the door.

"Wait! Wait, *mon Père!* I admit it!"

Barry halted, turned. For a moment he almost felt pity for the man. Never before had he seen such supplication on a human face. Pradon, up on one elbow, stretched a trembling hand toward him. He walked back to the couch.

"Very well, you admit it. That's a start, at least. Now we'll have it in writing. And don't tell me you can't write. I know you can."

"But I didn't do these things for myself, *mon Père!* I had to do them! *M'sieu* Lemke ordered me to!"

"You can put that in writing too." Barry thrust the notebook and pencil at him. "Here you are. Go ahead. Write."

"I—I can only write in Creole, *mon Père,*" Pradon moaned.

"Creole will do nicely. Catus Laroche can read it. Just be brief and very clear. You might begin by saying 'I persuaded Felix Dufour to sell *Père* Clinton the mule. I spread the lie that Toto was dead when Louis and *Père* Clinton took him to the mainland.' Go on from there. Leave anything out and you'll do the whole thing over again."

There were but two sounds in the room while Pradon laboriously wrote: the heavy breathing of the room's occupants and the scratch of his pencil on the notebook pages. Barry heard one more sound, or felt it: the thudding of his own heart. Would it work? Would Catus believe what was on the paper when it was thrust into his hand? He glanced at Alma and saw that she was pale. He knew he was pale himself. He prayed, and tried with all his might to believe the prayer would be heard and answered.

The scratch of the pencil stopped. Pradon was holding the notebook up to him. He took it, read what was written and thrust it back.

"Put down the names of those who saw you write this. Your witnesses. Leave space for their marks or signatures."

The pencil moved again. Barry took Lucy by the arm and led her outside into the yard.

"Tell me," he said when they were well away from the door, "what was in the kola bottle, Lucy. Was it a true poison? Will it kill him?"

She shrugged. "He will think there is a fire inside him for a long time, *mon Père.* But he will not die unless he dies of fright."

"You're a wonderful woman, Lucy."

"*Mon Père,* he would have stolen God's church. I could not let that happen."

He went back inside. When he and Alma had signed the book and Lucy and Pradon's mother had made their marks on it, he shook some pills from a bottle and placed them on the table.

"You are to stay here on the couch and take one of these every hour until daylight. The sickness will go away slowly, not all at once.

You'll be in pain, but you will not die and after a while the pain will disappear. I hope it will make a better man of you before it does." He turned to the timid woman by the table. "Give him a glass of water with each tablet and keep him on the couch. He must not get up. If you let him get up, I won't be responsible for what happens. Do you understand?"

She nodded, gazing wide-eyed at her son.

Barry closed his bag, motioning Alma and Lucy to the door.

28

THE DRUMS WERE STILL THROBBING when they reached the mission. If anything, the sound was louder.

"You know where I'm going, of course," Barry told the two women. "I think I'd better go alone."

Alma shook her head. "I want to be with you."

Lucy, too, insisted on accompanying him. "There is something you don't know, *mon Père*," she said. "I must be there to tell you."

"But it may be dangerous. There's no telling what will happen when I show myself."

They would not be left behind.

The ceremony would be in front of the church, Lucy thought, and at her suggestion they went to the ridge by a path that would bring them out at the rear of the new rectory. Again she asked Barry not to use his flashlight. "You will see why, *mon Père*, when we get there."

It was a difficult climb, part of the way through steep gardens. There was no moon. The night was black but alive, quivering to the rhythm of the drums. The sound became thunder as they climbed toward it.

Lucy was right: Catus Laroche had chosen the open space in front of the church for his service. Light for the festivities was supplied by half a dozen lanterns strung among the pomme-rose trees. At least a hundred islanders stood about, watching the white-robed *hounsis* dance and chant.

Barry saw a number of persons he knew. The lawyer from the capital was an interested spectator. Little Felix Dufour stood out in a white shirt and black bow tie, with his untidy hair curling about his ears. Big Louis César played the *maman* drum. Dauré danced. Sergeant Edma was present in his much-washed khaki uniform, wearing a revolver on his hip. It was an important occasion, obviously . . .

He gave a start when he saw Warner Lemke, and heard Alma take in a breath behind him when she recognized her husband. Lemke stood at the rear of the crowd, a bottle in his hand. Why had he come, Barry wondered. Simply to gloat? Or at the right moment, when passions were high, would he step forward and urge the crowd to carry their *vodun* into the church itself? That would be like him. The ultimate indignity, which to him would be the ultimate triumph.

He saw Catus then. The *houngan*, wearing dark trousers and the familiar red shirt, stood behind the three drummers, his arms folded on his chest, an expression of intense concentration on his face. Hating me, Barry thought. Hating me for sleeping with his sister, which I didn't do. Why wasn't Catus dancing? Why wasn't he calling on his *vodun* gods to bless the service with their presence? Was there still a dim glow of doubt in his mind?

Lucy tugged at Barry's arm. "I think, *mon Père*, you should appear to them from inside the church."

He was puzzled. "From *inside*? What do you mean?"

"It is God's house. And they think you are dead."

"Dead!"

She nodded. "The chicken, *mon Père*. On my way to Pradon's house this evening I said you had eaten it and were sick. Now they think you are dead, and if you walk out of the church and confront them——" She drew him toward the rear of the building. "You can get in through a window without being seen."

Barry looked at Alma and saw that she was as startled as he. Was this strange woman always going to be a step ahead of their thoughts? Could she read their minds? He put a hand to his shirt pocket to be sure the precious notebook was still there. *Should* he try to startle them by appearing from the church?

"I don't like it, Barry." Alma was shaking her head at him. "They may panic and run away."

"No. Catus won't run." He saw suddenly what would happen, what had to happen. "I'm going to do it."

"Darling, be careful!"

He left them with a nod and crept along the side of the church, not afraid of being recognized but aware that any one of the hundred or more at the ceremony might notice a movement there in the darkness and be tempted to investigate. Getting through the aperture was simple enough once he reached it. Inside, he glanced toward the altar and, on an impulse, dropped to one knee for a moment and bowed his head. When he faced the entrance he saw that he would be in full view of the crowd the moment he pushed the doors open and stepped out. A vertical line of light was visible in the crack between them now, from the ceremonial lanterns outside. The steps must be fully illuminated.

He stopped in front of the doors and took in a breath, as though about to plunge into a pool. His heart was thudding. He was soaked with sweat.

He threw the doors wide and stepped out.

There was a gasp from the crowd. Two of the three drums were instantly silent. The third gave out a dribble of beats as though its player's hands were incapable of stopping. He saw Catus Laroche unfold his arms and take a step forward before turning to stone. He saw them all staring at him. Folding his own arms, he waited.

They did not panic. A whisper, a murmur sped through them and for a moment they seemed on the verge of flight, but then they looked at Catus, waiting to see what he would do. Catus turned his head and saw them waiting. He made himself tall. Slowly, step by step, he approached the church. When he reached the foot of the church steps he halted.

Barry could see his hands and face trembling. Could see the beads of sweat, like balls of bright glass, rolling down his black skin.

"I have something for you," Barry said. He took the notebook from his pocket and held it out. "Here."

The *houngan* climbed toward him, his gaze fixed immovably on Barry's face. His hand mechanically reached out. His fingers closed over the notebook but he seemed incapable of lowering his gaze to look at it.

"Read it," Barry said. "Read it carefully."

With an effort Catus looked down at the book. His lips moved as he read. He lifted his head.

"Where did you get this?"

"That should be obvious. From Beliard."

"When?"

"Less than an hour ago. I went there with Lucille and Madame Lemke. Beliard's mother was there. Their names are under his, as witnesses. Every word of what you see there is true and can't be denied." Barry moved down a step and put his hands on the shoulders of the red shirt. "I've told you all along that I was your friend, Catus. Now if you're the man I think you are, you'll turn around and read that statement to your people."

Catus read the statement to himself again. Like a blind man, groping, he turned. When he motioned the crowd toward him, his arm trembled. When he began to speak, his voice was a whisper and they could not hear.

He began again. "The Father has brought a statement from Pradon Beliard. It is true because Pradon has signed it and there were witnesses—his own mother, for one—when he wrote it. I will read it to you." He spoke as though in a trance, and they listened in complete silence, unmoving. "'I, Pradon Beliard, persuaded Felix Dufour to sell *Père* Clinton the mule that killed Toto Anestor. It was I who spread the lie that Toto was dead when Louis and the Father carried him to the mainland. He was not dead then but died later in the hospital as the Father has told you. It was I who burned the Father's church and killed the mule at the altar, to make people think the *mystères* were angry. It was I and Felix Dufour who told Antoine Constant to say he had been cheated out of his land, which is a lie. It was I who spread the lie that *Père* Clinton accused Catus of killing the Desinor child. Most of these things I did because *M'sieu* Lemke paid me to do them. The last I did because Micheline Laroche told me to. Why Micheline wished to hurt *Père* Clinton I do not know. But I know that he is not the father of her child. *M'sieu* Lemke is the child's father. I saw them together many times.'"

Catus stopped reading and let his hand fall. The notebook fluttered from his fingers, sliding down the church steps until it reached the ground. He sat down and stared at it, and Dauré César, at the front of the crowd, came forward and picked it up and held it out to him. But he did not see her. His face was in his hands now. The shoulders under the red shirt rose and fell. He was crying.

The crowd looked at him in silence and began to move backward. In a few minutes there was no one left. The space before the church was empty.

WARNER LEMKE WAS STARTLED when Barry first appeared in the church doorway. He had not expected such a development. He had come to the ceremony because it promised to be amusing and because he was too drunk to go looking for Tina. The unexpected appearance of Barry sobered him a little, and the words Catus read from the notebook sobered him more. But he had been drinking heavily for hours and was still drunk when he slipped out of the crowd and went stumbling down the path from the ridge.

He was also shaking with fury.

That Beliard! That stupid, blundering fool, to write such a statement and sign it! Lemke felt the dark earth heaving under his feet and the trees tumbling to crush him. He was trapped in an earthquake. He was a man fleeing a monstrous black hand that reached out for him.

He was finished. He would have to leave the island now. At once, tonight, he must find a boat and get across to the mainland, before Catus Laroche recovered from the shock of that damned confession and came after him. Even on the mainland he might not be safe. Catus might follow him. Catus *would* follow him. He was sure of it. He would have to run, keep on running, until he was clear of St. Joseph altogether.

He sobbed as he went reeling down the ridge in the dark. But he was shaking with rage too. He would find a boat, yes, but on his way to the shore he would stop at Beliard's house and settle this thing. No sniveling black bastard was going to turn on Warner Lemke and get away with it.

FELIX DUFOUR LEFT THE RIDGE in haste too. Panic made his feet fly. Those words read by Catus sang in his head like wasps, and the sound of their singing made his eyes pop. "It was I and Felix Dufour who told Antoine Constant to say he had been cheated out of his land, which is a lie." God in heaven!

What would happen now? That lawyer from the capital would go to Constant, and Constant in his terror would babble the whole story. The stupid fool wanted an excuse to back out anyway; he was terrified of the Father. And this confession of Beliard's would allow him to renege without fear of punishment. He would claim to be the frightened victim of two shrewd schemers.

Felix moaned as he ran. It was he and Beliard who would be arrested and thrown into jail, not Constant. Arrested! He, a magistrate! But he was no longer magistrate. At this very moment, now, he was a fugitive. Why, why had he listened to that insufferable Beliard? Why? What had he been thinking of?

He stumbled up the steps of his house and got the door open, rushed inside and lit a lamp. For a moment, helpless, he stood in the center of his living room gazing wildly about him. What would he take? What *could* he take? He wanted so many things—the beautiful mahogany furniture for which he had paid so much, the handsome calendars on the walls, especially that lovely one with the snow-topped mountains, his clothes . . . But there was no time, no time!

He rushed into the bedroom and dragged a suitcase from under the bed. Hurry! Hurry! He must be gone before Sergeant Edma returned from the ceremony. That Edma was a man who couldn't be talked out of a thing, couldn't be bribed. He threw things into the suitcase and slammed it shut, scurried back to the living room, looked around, blew out the lamp.

There was a man in Tête Cabrit who would take him across to the mainland if paid enough. But hurry! Edma would be here any minute. Run, run! Good-by, house. Good-by to being magistrate. Good-by to Ile du Vent and being important. Oh God. Good-by to everything.

Bent by the weight of his suitcase, he hurried down the dark village street. As he reached the lower end of it and turned along the path to Tête Cabrit, Sergeant Edma entered the village from above.

EDMA CLIMBED THE STEPS and banged a clenched hand against the magistrate's door. He waited a moment, scowling, then seized the knob and pushed the door open. He strode inside.

"Dufour!" His voice was very stern, very much the voice of authority. He used it again. "Dufour!" He struck a match and bent over the lamp.

The lamp was hot. Dufour was here then, or had been here and was gone. The sergeant finished lighting the lamp and drew his revolver from its holster. He looked around. He strode into the bed-room.

Clothes on the bed. More clothes on the floor. Bureau drawers open. The sergeant rubbed his jaw with the barrel of his gun. How the devil had Dufour got here from the ceremony ahead of him, that short-legged little politician? He himself had walked fast all the way. To be sure, he had not run—for a soldier to go bounding through the dark like a common peasant would be undignified. But he had wasted no time.

He walked through the house. Empty. Well, Dufour was gone. Gone where? Probably to Pradon Beliard's house. They would want to talk things over, those two, before either made a move. The sergeant shrugged. He had to arrest Beliard anyway. He would get them both at once. He returned his weapon to its holster and went out, not forgetting to put out the lamp and close the door behind him.

WARNER LEMKE ARRIVED at Beliard's house five minutes before Sergeant Edma left the house of the magistrate. He thrust open the gate and staggered up the path to the door. He was still very drunk. Some-where along the way from the ridge he had flung away the rum bottle, but he had tipped it to his mouth and emptied it first. His mouth was sticky and burning. He kept licking his lips to keep them from sticking together.

He jerked the door wide and lurched inside. At once he began cursing the man who lay there in pajamas on the couch. Beliard's mother rose from a chair beside the couch and looked at him with wide, frightened eyes.

Lemke staggered forward. "You double-crossing nigger bastard!" he shouted. "I'll teach you! I'll wring your rotten neck! I'll break every bone in your body!" He thrust out his hands.

Beliard's mother recovered from her paralysis. She looked wildly about her and rushed across the room. She seized a broom.

"You get out of here!" she screamed. Her thin hands curled on the broom handle and she brandished her weapon in Lemke's face.

Lemke tried to knock it aside.

She hurled herself at him. The broom crashed against his face and head again and again, like a huge moth against a lamp shade. It was a peasant thing made of twigs. It raked his eyes, and when he threw up his arms to protect his eyes it tore his mouth and neck. He stumbled backward, the woman relentlessly pursuing him. He could not catch the thing and hold it. When he tried, it eluded his grasping hands and found his face.

He turned and fled over the threshold. Beliard's mother slammed the door.

Lemke staggered into the yard and halted. Tears streamed down his cheeks, mingling with the blood drawn by the woman's broom. He was sobbing now. His own tears blinded him. A woman! An old woman with a broom. It was more than he could stand. A miserable old peasant woman with nothing more than a broom had driven him from the house as though he were a dog. He turned away, crying like a child. But he could not find the gate. His dragging feet took him blindly across the yard in the wrong direction.

Sergeant Edma, halting at the gate, saw a shadowy figure moving toward the rear of the yard. He drew his revolver. The police-and-army training manual was quite clear about a situation such as this. He knew exactly what to do.

"Halt!"

The figure did halt for an instant. He thought it turned toward him. But then it moved away again, faster.

"Halt or I shoot!"

The figure broke into a staggering run.

Sergeant Edma raised his gun and took careful aim. It was his duty. He fired twice. The fleeing figure stumbled, fell, and was still.

The sergeant, hurrying forward, wondered which of the criminals he had stopped from escaping, Beliard or Felix Dufour. When he shone his flashlight on the fallen man's face and saw that it was white, he opened his eyes wide and began trembling. After a while, though—after making certain there was nothing he could to do bring his victim back to life—he shrugged his shoulders.

This would take some explaining, yes, but he could hardly be disciplined for it. He had twice ordered the man to halt, hadn't he? The fault was M'*sieu* Lemke's then, not his own.

29

THE REVEREND PETER AMBROSE reached Ile du Vent at eleven o'clock on a Saturday morning, nine days after the affair on the ridge and its island-shaking aftermath. He was a bit wobbly from the sailboat voyage across the channel and allowed himself to be carried from the boat to the beach in the arms of a husky young native who set him down very gently and grinned at him.

"Will you wish a horse from the mission, *mon Père?*" the fellow asked. "I can go up and bring one down for you."

Peter decided to walk. It was not a particularly hot morning, in fact it looked like rain, and he had a good deal to think about. A letter he had received yesterday from Barry was in his pocket: an amazing document, full of really wonderful news.

He climbed the trail slowly, meeting a number of islanders on their way down. Without exception they greeted him politely, the men lifting their hands to their hatbrims. Peter was pleased. A line in Barry's letter about the "essential goodness" of the islanders came back to him. He hadn't questioned Barry's judgment, of course. An outsider might have found it difficult to discover anything essentially good in people who only a few days ago had been bent on murder, but the peasant mind was no riddle to Peter. He smiled at the thought that it would be no riddle to the new Bishop, either. The latter was coming to St. Joseph directly from service in Africa. Moreover, he was a man Peter had known for years and regularly corresponded with. There would be a decided change of atmosphere in St. Joseph when he arrived.

As he neared the mission the old man began to smile. He was not expected. He had sent no message to announce his coming. He had visions of a startled Barry gazing at him in utter astonishment and rushing forward to pump his hand.

He trudged into the clearing and saw a line of people outside the rectory door, and a woman in a white dress in the doorway talking to them. Alma Lemke, he thought, and began to frown.

"And we hope," Barry had written, "that when the talk has died down a bit you will pay us a visit and make us man and wife. We simply can't think of being married by anyone else."

Peter shook his head. He was not enthusiastic about this. Did Barry really think himself in love with that woman?—really believe she was the right wife for him? Of course it was none of his business and he certainly had no intention of interfering, but he had always been just a little wary of her. Edith Barnett, now, would have made any man a good wife. A thoroughly charming girl. Still, there might be a side to Mrs. Lemke that he was unaware of. And Barry was no fool. If they wanted him to marry them, he could hardly refuse.

Alma had seen him. She was running across the red-earth clearing to greet him, calling his name as she came. Peter halted and held out his hand.

"Mr. Ambrose! What a wonderful surprise! Why didn't you tell us you were coming?"

"I thought I'd let it *be* a surprise," he chuckled. "I've some very good news for Barry."

"Good news?" He saw an expression of apprehension wipe away her smile. "You don't mean he's being transferred?"

"No, no, my dear. The very opposite. I mean we're going to have a new Bishop in St. Joseph and there's no longer any danger of his being transferred."

Her reaction was so tremendous that Peter was puzzled. It was as though he had told her she was guaranteed a place in heaven. Her face became radiant. A light filled her eyes. She was a most attractive woman, he suddenly realized, and wondered why he had never noticed it before. A *most* attractive woman. Really beautiful.

"Please," she said, clinging to his hand, "oh, please go up to the ridge and tell him! He's got to know at once! I can't leave. I have all these patients to look after and some of them have been waiting hours. Please go, Mr. Ambrose!"

"He's up there at the new church?" Peter asked.

"He took the morning off to work on the rectory. We didn't expect so many patients today."

"I'll go at once," Peter said, and squeezed her hand before turning away.

He heard the sound of hammering long before he arrived on the ridge. Good, he thought; the boy has been able to find some workers again. When he reached the top of the path and saw how many workers were swarming over the nearly finished rectory, he stopped in astonishment. There were twenty, at least. They were flooring the upstairs veranda. Big Louis César, on the ground below, was handing up planks.

A man on the veranda saw Peter and spoke to Barry, who was on his knees, bare to the waist, wielding a hammer. Barry stood up. A glad shout left his lips. He swung himself over the veranda rail, dropped to the ground, and made for Peter at a dead run.

"Peter! Peter Ambrose!"

It was several minutes before he was calm enough for Peter to tell him about the new Bishop. Another moment passed before Barry was able to answer.

"You mean I'll be allowed to stay here?"

"I'm sure you will," Peter said, smiling. "I know this man well."

"And he won't—he won't insist on my tearing down everything they believe in and leaving them in a vacuum?"

"He may have a few suggestions, my boy. After all, he's had a good deal of experience in situations similar to this. But on the whole I think you'll find him an understanding man. I seem to remember that he admires Albert Schweitzer a good deal and maintains that the important thing in missionary work is to put across Christ's teachings and bring men together in the Lord's brotherhood. He'll expect results, mind you, but I think you'll find him quite liberal as to methods."

"Thank God," Barry said fervently.

"I've just been talking to Mrs. Lemke. She seemed as pleased as you are."

"Of course she is! Alma would be heartbroken if we had to leave here!"

"I had no idea she was so interested in our work," Peter said.

Barry seized him by the hand and drew him toward the rectory. "You've no idea what kind of woman she is, Peter. The finest in the world, that's all. Absolutely the finest. Did you see her working with the natives? How they worship her? Here, look at this house of mine. It's nearly finished." The words came from him in a flood as he pulled Peter into the rectory and led him from room to room. "Kitchen. Dining room. The new clinic, twice as big as the one down below. And a waiting room to boot, so they won't have to sit outside under the trees when the place is jumping. Come upstairs! Watch your feet on these treads, we haven't got them nailed down yet. Look at this. Our room, hers and mine, when you've done your duty by us. I'm using it now. Alma sleeps at the old place. Can you beat that view of the sea and the channel? That breeze? And these other two are guest rooms. One is for you, when you come here on vacation this summer. We'll want you to marry us then, Peter. We'll wait that long for appearance's sake but no longer, I warn you. Peter! Peter! Thank God for the new Bishop!"

Peter, chuckling, patted his face with a handkerchief and leaned against a wall. "Do you mind if I sit down for a minute? I'm out of breath from listening to you."

Barry brought chairs from his own bedroom. They sat in the empty room that would be Peter's and looked at each other and laughed. Presently Peter said, "What about Catus Laroche? Where do you stand with him now?"

"I don't know exactly. The day after Lemke was shot I persuaded him to go to the mainland and try to find his sister. He hasn't returned. We had no chance to talk about anything much before he left."

"When he returns, what *will* you talk about?"

"Well, not about his attempt to poison me, if that's what you mean. I can't hold that against him, Peter. He had his reasons for wanting me dead, or thought he did. The memory of that poisoned chicken disturbs my sleep now and then; I won't deny it. But poison as a weapon doesn't horrify these people as it does us. Leaves, roots, herbs—they're part of a peasant's everyday life."

Peter nodded. "That's the right attitude, I'm sure. If you had him arrested you'd gain nothing. Besides, you'd have to prove him guilty."

"I don't want to prove anyone guilty."

"Did you have many in church last Sunday?"

"The church was full," Barry said. "Which surprised me, because almost no one came to Lemke's funeral." He leaned toward Peter with a frown. "How did they take Lemke's death at Plantation Couronne, Peter? Who will they be sending over to take his place?"

"The fact that he was shot to death gave them a jolt, of course. There were no personal reactions that I could see. As for sending someone else, I'm not sure they will. The price of sisal is still dropping, Jeff tells me. They may simply abandon their acreage over here."

"I hope they do. The land is needed for food crops."

"Well, there'd be a lot of dickering to do. It's their land, you know. You might lease it or something."

"Do you think Jeff would talk to me?"

"Why shouldn't he? Because of Edith, you mean?"

Barry nodded.

"I can't see why Jeff should be angry with you just because you and Edith didn't hit it off," Peter said, shrugging. "But be patient, boy. I know the word 'patience' is Greek to you, but it *is* in the dictionary. Let me sound him out. The world wasn't built in a day."

"I know. Six days." Barry kept a straight face. "It's in the Bible——"

"—If you'll look for it, boy," Peter finished with a grin.

30

CATUS LAROCHE RETURNED to Ile du Vent that afternoon. An hour after setting foot on the island he appeared at the mission. Barry and Alma were discussing their marriage plans with Peter Ambrose.

"*Mon Père*," the *houngan* said, "I found my sister in the capital and brought her back."

"I'm glad to hear it, Catus."

"She is sorry for what she did. She has told me why she did it. I know now that you were in no way to blame."

"We're going to forget all that, Catus. All of us."

Catus glanced at Alma and Peter and seemed to hesitate. "There is something else I would like to discuss with you, *mon Père*," he said. "Can we talk in private?"

Barry led him across the clearing to the old church, closing the door behind them when they were inside. He walked down the aisle and sat on a bench near the front. Catus, following, gazed at the altar table a moment before turning to face him. He remained standing.

"*Mon Père*, my people think you died and came to life again, like this Jesus you believe in."

"I know."

"Is it true?"

Barry smiled. "If I said yes, would you believe me?"

"You have never lied to me."

"No, I've never lied to you. I won't lie to you now, Catus. I *could*, and there'd be no possible way for you to know I was lying unless Lucy told you the truth, which she would never do. I've thought a good deal about this. I've been tempted, don't think I haven't, to let you and your people think a miracle took place. The power such a belief would place in my hands would be tremendous. But I've decided against it. In church tomorrow I'm going to tell the people exactly what happened. I didn't eat your poisoned chicken, Catus. Lucy discovered it in time."

Catus sat on a bench across the aisle and frowned at him. "You will tell the people this? Why?"

"Because I think we've made a start, you and I, toward discovering what we believe in, and magic has no place in it. We've got to be honest with each other, Catus, or we'll wind up as enemies. We've got to be honest with the people too."

"Am I supposed to stop believing in the magic of *vodun?*"

"Unless you feel it is genuine, yes."

"How am I to know whether it is genuine or not?"

"By a simple test that can be applied to any set of beliefs. If a thing is good and helpful, accept it. If it is bad, consider it false. Remember this: no man has ever actually solved the mystery of life, Catus. No man can tell you who you are, or who I am, or why we are here. All religions, yours, mine, all the others, are simply a search for truth. Look for it in darkness and you're going to find only dark and frightening answers. Search in the light and you'll lift yourself up *to* the light."

"Yes."

"That's why I've brought you the teachings of Jesus Christ. They're good for us. No matter who Jesus was—the son of God, God himself, or just a great and good man—he gave us a way of living together that is better than any other way we know. If every man on this island would heed what he said, we'd all be brothers."

"I agree."

"Then help me to teach what he taught. Make a place for Christ in your *vodun*. Talk about his teachings there and let the light in. Give your people a chance to choose love instead of fear, light instead of darkness. Help them to choose what is best for them."

"Love God," Catus murmured, "and love one another. Very well. But how am I to explain this God they must love?"

"The only way he can be explained. As the greatest of all mysteries, the Father of us all, who made us and loves us and will look out for us if we behave ourselves. We don't know who God is, Catus. We'll never know while we're alive. But if we believe in a *good* creator and use that belief to help ourselves and our fellow men, we're at least on the right track. No one can do more."

Catus rose to his feet, his hand extended. "*Mon frère,* I think you are an honest man. I think I have always known it. It will not be hard to teach my people to love you. I love you myself."

He turned and walked down the aisle, opened the church door, and departed without a backward glance. Barry gazed after him, frowning.

Mon frère, Barry thought. *My brother*. A curious phrase for Catus to use, and the first time he had ever used it.

Brothers. A *vodun houngan* and a Christian missionary. A black man and a white.

This was the real beginning.